The Transit Star

Book 1 of the Transit Star Continuum

K.Britton

Rusty Fish Press

Published by Rusty Fish Press

ISBN (eBook): 978-1-7644942-0-5
ISBN (paperback): 978-1-7644942-1-2

This is a work of fiction. Names, characters, places, and events are either the product of the author's imagination or are used fictitiously. Any resemblance to actual persons, living or dead, or to actual events or locales is entirely coincidental.

This work draws upon global mythic traditions, folklore, and archetypal narratives, reinterpreted within a contemporary fictional context.

This book was created with the assistance of artificial intelligence tools under the direction and editorial control of the author. All creative decisions, intellectual property rights, and derived works remain the exclusive property of the author.

Contents

Prologue - The Shot

He remembers the hum of the road.
The sun flickers through the window.
An elbow digs into his ribs.
Ella's voice, too loud, clapping off-beat.

He remembers the driver's sharp intake of breath.
A single shouted word.
Brakes that failed.
Then—sky. Blue. Spinning.

They told him afterwards that the car flipped twice. The family who took him camping—Ella's mum, dad, and her little brother—died on impact. The vehicle struck a gum tree, folded in on itself, and crushed the cabin like a tin can. When they pulled him out, he was soaked in blood—none of it his. Bone, glass, and hair clung to him like confetti. They rushed him to the hospital. But when the nurses cleaned him, wiped the blood from his eyes, and untangled the metal from his jacket—he didn't have a scratch.

Ben wakes sometimes with the weight of it pressing on his chest. The scream he couldn't answer. The ribbon in Ella's hair. The feeling of floating in the silence after everything had gone wrong. He remembers the cold air, the stillness, and the strange sense that someone was waiting.

She had been watching him for weeks. Alone on his Barossa acreage, working odd jobs—quiet, forgettable. A man who rarely answered the phone. Who, on paper, should never have lived long enough to be a man at all. She'd read the report. The accident at six. The fire at nineteen. The gas line rupture. The infection. The overdose. The lightning strike. Things that should have killed him. Things that killed others. But not him. Her instructions were simple: one shot. No noise. No drama.

She lay flat in the dry grass above a low dam wall, her rifle balanced steady on a handmade bipod. The land stretched quietly below her: broken fencing, an unused tractor, a line of grapevines just starting to green. The rifle was long, matte-black, unbranded. She maintained it herself, tuned like a musician's instrument—every bolt and spring honed to perfection.

She didn't fidget.
Didn't sweat.
Didn't doubt.

He came into view just after seven, as always, feeding the chickens scraps and checking the gate. She watched his movements. He limped slightly, a trace of something old. His head hung a little lower than the first time she'd seen him. His eyes scanned the horizon, not with fear, but with habit. She adjusted the elevation dial.

No wind.
No sound.
Just the two of them.

Ben bent down to tie a bootlace. She inhaled slowly. Her finger settled on the trigger. She wasn't emotional in her work. But she did take pride in precision. She never hurried. Never lost focus, and she never missed. The rifle kicked softly against her shoulder, almost silent.

She didn't blink.
Didn't need to.
It was done.

She began to rise, breaking down the rifle—then froze. He was still standing. Stopped, like he'd heard something but couldn't place it. His head tilted, eyes narrowed. He looked behind him. Then at the tree line. Then... nothing. No wound. No fall. He scratched the back of his neck, turned toward the house, and walked away. She didn't move. Didn't breathe. The bullet had landed; she was sure of it. She'd made the shot. Her calculations were perfect. And yet, the man walked.

There was no reason to stay after the shot. She didn't track. She didn't confirm. One round was all she ever used. Her missions were not conversations—they were full stops. But now she stayed. Still prone. Still watching the space where he'd stood. Playing the shot back in her mind, frame by frame. She scanned the land. Checked for drift, for dust, for anything that might have interfered.

Nothing. Quiet. Too quiet.

She sat back slowly, unslung the rifle from her shoulder, and stared at it. It had never failed her. She had taken lives at half a kilometre, in sandstorms, at night, from rooftops that swayed in the wind. But this man—this one—was still alive.

At the shed door, Ben paused. Something had shifted—a flicker at the base of his skull. A breath that wasn't his. He turned slowly, squinting back across the paddock. Empty. Maybe a fox in the grass. Maybe a roo startled by the chickens. Maybe nothing. Still, he waited another second, then shook it off and stepped inside.

She didn't leave until after dark. Even then, it took her an hour to move fifty metres. She left no prints. No trail. No trace. No one ever saw her unless she allowed it. She had never needed a second shot. Not in all the years since she'd become what she was now. She'd outpaced soldiers and assassins, out-waited them, out-sensed them. There was no name for what she was, but people who saw her, when they did, always reacted the same—they fell silent. They looked too long without knowing why. Something in her presence unsettled them. Made them feel like they were being measured. And now, for the first time in a very long time, she was measuring herself.

She would not try again. A second shot meant failure, and failure was not a thing she carried. Maybe the man had moved. Perhaps the world had. Something else had shifted in the moment between breath and flight. She didn't know. She only knew this: the mission was over. But the question remained.

That night, Ben sat on the back step with a beer, watching the stars as the last light bled away. Earlier, a sharp sound—metal struck, maybe a branch, maybe not. It didn't matter. Still, he couldn't shake the feeling that something had passed too close—and missed.

ACT I:
A MAN ON THE RUN

Chapter 1
The Fox

Ben Callum woke to dust and eucalyptus. Morning light crawled through thin curtains, striping the farmhouse floorboards. His back ached—again. The fan ticked with a new, unwelcome sound.

Another scorcher was coming—he felt it in the boards, in his teeth, in the heavy air before the sun even cleared the ridge. He swung his legs over the edge of the bed, bare feet landing on cold wood. Outside, cockatoos screamed like broken radios, and the pump clicked twice as it tried to push reluctant water uphill.

Same as always. He dressed without thinking: faded work shirt, dusty jeans, boots with one torn lace. Coffee came next. Instant. Two spoons. No milk. He drank standing, staring through the kitchen window at hills baked in gold and shadow. A rusted windmill creaked in the distance. Fence lines sagged. Beyond them, nothing but dry grass, a few feral goats, and silence.

Ben didn't mind the quiet. In fact, he preferred it. He'd worked the property alone for nearly five years now. Twenty-three acres of stubborn Barossa dirt and unforgiving summer. It wasn't a life most people wanted, but it suited him. No questions. No eyes on him. Just tools, weeds, sweat, and space.

The ute started on the third try. He drove without music, windows down, the rising heat already needling his skin. Gravel crackled beneath the tyres, and a trail of dust lifted behind him like smoke from a slow fire.

The vineyard was gone now—just splintered posts and memory. The grapes hadn't made it past the second summer. Ben never talked about it. Never complained. He just cleared the rows when he could and waited for another idea.

At the boundary, the old gate hung open. He frowned. He always shut it. He stopped the ute and stepped out, squinting into the morning light. No tracks. No tyre marks. No sign of anyone. Still, he pushed the gate shut with a grunt and wired it tight, fingers moving through the familiar motions without much thought.

A flock of galahs burst from a distant tree, startled by something unseen. Ben turned back to the ute—and paused. A feeling. Sharp. Fleeting. Not fear. Not danger. Just a shift. Like someone had walked over his grave—or like a bullet had passed too close. He looked around. Nothing. Just wind through the dry grass and that damned fan still ticking in his mind. He shook it off. Climbed back in. Drove on.

Ben pulled the ute to a halt beside the half-collapsed shed near the eastern paddock. The fencing had sagged more since last week, and a roll of rusted barbed wire lay like a coiled trap in the dry grass.

He stepped out, the door creaking in the still morning. Sweat had already gathered along his collar despite the early hour. Another day too hot for comfort, too dry for hope. He reached for his gloves from the tray but paused, squinting toward the treeline. Something moved.

Not the wind this time. Twenty metres off, a fox stepped from between two red gums. Its coat was a deep, clean red—far more vivid than the dust-stained fur he usually saw here. Its ears twitched, alert. But it didn't run. It stood there. Still. Watching. Broad daylight. Ben frowned. Foxes didn't linger in daylight—unless desperate, sick, or... something else. This one looked healthy. Too healthy. Its fur shimmered copper, eyes glinting gold. It blinked slowly, deliberately. Ben shifted his stance. The fox took three steps forward. Not skittish. Not stalking.

Almost... curious. "Off you go," Ben muttered, more out of instinct than anything. The fox tilted its head, then sat in the open, tail curled neatly around its legs—like it had all the time in the world.

Ben felt the hair on the back of his neck rise. He glanced around, no other movement—no sound beyond the wind ticking through the fence posts. Something about the air had changed. The cicadas dulled. The breeze died. Even the eucalyptus stilled, as if the land itself held its breath. He stared at the fox. It blinked once more, then—just as quietly as it had come—rose and padded back into the bush.

Ben stood there another minute, his heart knocking gently in his chest. Then he let out a breath and scratched behind his ear, the way he always did when something didn't quite fit. "Bloody weird," he muttered. But that wasn't quite the word. Not weird. Not even wild. It had felt intentional.

He bought a trap.

He drove into town—the only one with more than one shop. The hardware store smelled of old tin and slow summers. Narelle stood behind the counter, as always—suspicious by default.

"Humane fox trap," he said.

She didn't ask. Just brought one out from the back. "You get many coming in close lately?" she asked.

"Just one."

"Strange week," she said. "Feels like something's circling."

Ben paid and left without replying. As he started the ute, he noticed a woman across the street. Long black hair. Light dress. Watching him. He blinked. She was gone.

He set the trap that afternoon, right where the fox had stood. The air never cooled. The world felt paused.

That night, he dreamt: the wreck again. Flames. Blood. And something standing beyond the road. Tall. Still. Shrouded in darkness. It watched him—not with malice, but curiosity. Like it hadn't expected what it found. Ben woke with sweat on his skin and the dream already crumbling. But the feeling remained like he had been seen.

The next afternoon, he was on the porch, wiping his hands clean when he heard it—the hum of an engine. Steady. Heavy. Familiar, yet wrong.

A deep blue Holden Statesman rolled up the gravel drive. 1970s vintage. Gleaming, immaculate. Restored with love—or ritual. It stopped beneath the pepper tree, the engine clicking into silence with unnatural finality. The door opened, and a man stepped out.

He moved as a shadow poured into form—tall, spare, yet vast. His skin was deep bronze, his black hair slicked and neat beneath a broad dark hat. His suit was brown, but not of any fashion Ben knew—clean lines, old cut, like something stitched before stitching was standard. In one hand, he carried a walking stick made of dense, dark wood, carved with faces too worn to be recognised.

The air shifted around him—cooler, stiller. A sudden hush seemed to settle on the land. Even the flies stopped buzzing.

The man shut the door gently and stepped forward, each movement measured and slow—as if the ground responded to his tread, not the other way around. "You're Ben Callum," he said—not asking.

Ben's jaw tensed. "That's right."

The man's eyes moved over the house, the hills, the sky. There was something unreadable in them. Not empty. Not full. Just old. "Place looks just like I remember," he murmured.

"You from around here?"

"Not anymore." Then the man smiled—small, unsettling. "Mind if I come in? Long drive. And we've got a few things to talk about."

Ben didn't move. But something in him already knew—things had just changed.

The man stood just beyond the porch rail, motionless in the heat—not sweating, not blinking, not shifting his weight. He seemed less like a visitor than a statue—something erected to mark a judgement passed long ago.

Ben studied him for a moment longer. The suit was too crisp for the heat, with not a wrinkle or speck of dust. It clung to him like a shadow, absorbing the glare around him. The walking stick wasn't decorative—carved from ancient black wood, dark as obsidian, etched with glyphs. His skin was deep bronze, not sun-darkened but ancient, like earth cracked by time. His hair, slicked back beneath a wide-brimmed dark hat, revealed no grey. And his eyes—his eyes were deep-set pools of blackness that did not move, did not blink. They seemed not to look at Ben, but through him, measuring something unseen.

"You a government man?" Ben asked, finally.

The stranger gave a faint smile. It didn't touch his eyes. "Haven't worked for anyone in a very long time."

Ben stepped aside. The man walked in like he'd crossed this threshold before—not recently, but long enough ago that the walls still remembered.

Inside, the farmhouse seemed to dim. The warm scent of old timber and earth lingered, but felt distant now, like memories receding behind glass. The air cooled unnaturally. The fan overhead ticked once, then slowed, as if time itself became hesitant. The stranger didn't look around. He moved directly to the kitchen table and sat without asking, his walking stick resting across his knees with ceremonial precision.

Ben poured two mugs of coffee, though his hands felt oddly distant. He didn't ask how the man took his. The stranger sipped it once, an act of acknowledgement more than thirst, and set it down gently, his eyes never leaving Ben's.

"I imagine you've had strange days before," he said. "But not like this one."

Ben folded his arms.

The stranger continued. "Let's begin with the basics. You ever wonder why that fox didn't run?"

Ben didn't answer.

"Or why did the wind stop just then? Why did the cicadas fall silent?"

Still, Ben said nothing.

The stranger leaned back, eyes narrowing. "Of course you don't wonder. That's the problem. You don't ask the questions."

Ben's voice came low. "And you came all this way to teach me how?"

"I came to warn you."

The screen door banged in the wind.

Ben turned his head—just for a moment—and when he looked back, the stranger was holding a folded piece of paper. It hadn't come from a pocket. It hadn't been summoned. It was simply there—waiting, as though it had always existed and only now chosen to be seen. Yellowed. Creased. Fragile as a curse.

He slid it across the table. "Take it. Please read it. Then burn it."

Ben didn't move.

"You think your life is just bad luck," the stranger said softly. "But some luck isn't luck at all. Some luck is interest."

That got Ben's attention. Just barely. "What is this?" he asked, gesturing to the paper.

"A name. A place. A memory. Or maybe a prophecy," the man replied. "It depends on how far you're willing to go."

Ben stared at him. "Go where?"

But the man was already standing. He turned toward the door.

Ben called after him, "You didn't tell me your name."

The man paused on the threshold. "You won't remember it even if I do," he said. "That's how this works."

Then he was gone. No footsteps. Just the faint rumble of the Holden's engine, and the way the air seemed to grow lighter after his absence, as if gravity had briefly deepened and now released its hold.

Ben stood in the doorway long after the stranger had gone, eyes on the trail of dust curling above the road. The blue Holden shimmered at the horizon, then vanished behind the low ridge.

Only then did he look down at the folded paper in his hand. It felt older than it looked—brittle, soft at the edges, like fabric left in the sun too long. He turned it over once, twice—no writing on the outside. No seal. Just creases.

He didn't open it straight away. Instead, he lit a cigarette he hadn't meant to smoke and walked out to the pepper tree. Sat on the old bench beneath it. Watched the sky change colour, the day finally giving up on its heat. Only then, when the shadows stretched long across the paddocks, did he unfold it.

One line. Scrawled in faded black ink. Not typed. Handwritten. *You are being watched by those who do not blink.* Ben read it twice. Then a third time. Below that, a set of coordinates. He didn't recognise them, but he knew they weren't local. It looked like it was somewhere in the interior. Empty country. Beneath the numbers, one final mark—a circle. Crude, drawn in haste or pain. A ring around nothing. He folded the paper again and slipped it into the pocket of his shirt.

Then it hit him—a full-body wave. Not fear, but something just to the left of it. Like vertigo. Like the world had tilted slightly off-axis and no one else had noticed. His breath caught, and his hands—rough and sunburnt—began to tremble. He sat down hard on the old bench under the pepper tree, legs giving out under the weight of it. "What the fuck," he whispered, staring down at his knees.

All these years, all the weird close calls, the gut feelings, the sense of being out of step—he'd chalked it up to nerves, to trauma, to something broken in his wiring. But this? This was different. Not vague. Not imagined. This was written down in ink.

He wiped his face with both hands, the motion not helping at all. Sweat had pooled along his back, even though the evening air had cooled. The stars overhead felt suddenly too sharp. Too many. Like they were leaning in.

Ben stood and walked in a slow circle, trying to settle himself, trying to push the tremble out of his limbs. He couldn't. This wasn't a prank. It wasn't a dream. The man had been real. The paper was real. And now it was in his pocket like a curse or a key—he didn't know which.

Inside, the house lights glowed through the fly-screen door. Warm. Familiar. Normal. But Ben didn't go inside. Instead, he stood under the pepper tree with his jaw clenched, hand over his chest, fingers pressing against the folded paper like it might disappear. Because if it stayed? Then nothing would be normal again.

Ben didn't sleep. Not properly. Not in the way that allows dreams or rest or even the temporary forgetting that morning usually promises.

The paper sat on his kitchen table like a tooth pulled from a corpse—plain, lifeless, but charged with the residue of something final. He kept circling the same questions like a dog with a scent it couldn't place. How did the man know about the fox? Who the hell is watching me? What doesn't blink?

He stood by the window at 3:14 a.m., staring at nothing, his thoughts mutating, spiralling, doubling back. Every creak of the house made him flinch. He felt out of sync, like the universe had adjusted its clock slightly to observe him better—and he was the only one hearing the ticking. He tried logic. He tried reason. He told himself that a coincidence was just that—a coincidence. That the man was a nutjob. That people hand out leaflets and say weird things all the time. That no one actually watches anymore.

But it didn't help. His mind kept turning over the phrase. What watches, and does not blink? Nothing alive. Not birds. Not cameras—they blink in their own way, refresh, refocus. Not insects.

Not people. Not gods—if those even existed. Then it came to him—not as a thought, but a verdict. Statues. Cold. Still. Meant to watch, meant to judge.

He gripped the edge of the table. "C'mon..." he muttered. And that was when he made his decision.

He would open his computer at dawn. Search the coordinates. Pin them. Cross-reference satellite images. Find out what the hell was there. And then he'd look into old myths, riddles, anything with that phrase. Anything that might give structure to this madness. But not now. Not in the pitch of night.

He picked up the paper and stared at it. The ink hadn't faded. The writing looked too neat, too confident. He didn't like how steady it felt.

"Fuck it," he whispered.

He struck a match. The paper curled in on itself like a dying insect—but something in the air resisted. The fire crackled too loudly. Shadows shifted against the walls. And when it was gone, the room didn't feel cleaner. It felt... observed.

Ben sat on the floor, watching it burn in the little fireplace. As the last shred crumbled, his body slumped. The adrenaline snapped. The panic gave out. He fell asleep where he sat, head against the wall, breath shallow, the last heat of the ashes fading to dreams very, very dark.

And somewhere far beyond sleep, something did not blink.

Chapter 2
The Flame

There are rules, even beyond the veil. Not written or spoken, but etched into the balance that holds the universe upright. Break them, and the world bends. Bend too far, and it breaks. These are not the laws of mortals. Not the decrees of kings or parliaments. These are older. Sharper. Made not to guide, but to bind.

Some call them principles. Others, truths. But those like me know them for what they are: constraints. I don't test them. I don't bend them.

I've seen what happens when others try. Those who once thought themselves immune now sleep beneath the dust of a broken sky. Entire civilisations cracked under the weight of a single misjudged deviation. Empires that burned for want of a single breath left unclaimed.

I am not their judge. I am their reminder.

And yet I stood at the edge again because of one mortal—an aberrant mortal. He is not marked, not chosen, not damned. He is something else. He lives—and the universe leans to let him.

When I approached him in the farmhouse, I felt none of the usual patterns—no karmic tension, no shadow of deeds done or debts owed—just a stillness. A silence too complete. It unsettled me. It still does.

That is why I acted. That is why I gave him the paper. A test. A baited line. But it was no ordinary note. Woven into its ink was a dormant spell—an ancient trigger, imperceptible to mortals, set to wake only when its bearer slept.

The spell was simple in design, brutal in purpose. Not a charm or curse, but an invitation—a whisper to the flame, a beckoning of heat and consumption. It would not strike like lightning. It would simmer—slowly, inevitably—until combustion became certainty. It drew on his breath, on the rhythms of his dreams, until the air around him began to tremble with unspent energy. Smoke birthed itself from nothing. A single ember caught from no source at all. Then another. And another.

He burned it—in doing so, he called the fire. Not summoned, but permitted. As if fate itself sighed in relief at what I could not do. But even fire failed.

And that is where dread began to stir. I stood in the darkness, beneath the pepper tree, listening. Waiting.

Then I heard it. The sound of sirens. Far off. Growing closer. The red scream of mortal urgency split the night.

I followed.

The emergency crews arrived in waves—dust, heat, and panic.

I walked the perimeter, as they fanned out with hoses and breathless shouts. I walked unseen—not invisible, but unnoticed. There was a difference. To the human mind, I do not register. Not unless I wish to. I become background, shadow, heat shimmer. My presence folds into the corner of the eye and slips behind the noise.

I watched as they pulled the aberrant mortal from the burning wreckage. The stretcher cracked beneath his weight. His skin was blistered. His breath weak.

They shouted to one another—language filled with mortal urgency and strain. But I was not listening to them. I was listening to the air. There was a tremor. Not heat. Not smoke. Something deeper. Something... uneasy. Had another stepped in? Had one of my kind attempted to intervene? Or was this something older still?

I scanned the faces of the fire crews. The paramedics. The frantic neighbour who stood shaking behind her gate. No eyes lingered on me. But something else lingered in the smoke. I felt it. A ripple. Like a second heartbeat pulsing just out of rhythm with the first.

Not an ethereal—not entirely. But aligned. Aware. They were watching too.

The ambulance raced toward the nearest trauma unit. I followed. Not as wind, not as wraith. As a man in shadow. I drove, but not like them. My path was silent. Straight. The Holden moved through red lights that flickered, but did not record me. Roads seemed to open. Time curved.

When they wheeled him into the emergency bay, I followed them inside. Even here, amid frantic voices and hurried decisions, no one stopped me. My face passed across their awareness like static. They forgot me between blinks.

I stood in the hall as they cut away his clothing. The burn team swarmed. One nurse whispered, “He shouldn’t be alive.” They tried everything. IVs, oxygen, fluid push, and cooling blankets. His vitals slipped, climbed, slipped again.

I entered the observation deck above the operating theatre. I stood alone. Below, the surgeons worked with gloved hands and stainless steel.

And I watched. I did not move. Did not breathe. I listened—not to the surgeons, but to the air.

And then—I felt it. A pressure against the walls. The faintest cold along the base of the skull. The slowing of seconds. The feeling of a name you almost remember. They had come. Not fully. Not all. But enough. They are unseen. Unknowable. But I knew. I always know. The presence was faint, diffused, but deliberate. I could not tell which of them it was. Time. Chance. Death. Perhaps something else entirely. Something without precedent. They did not act, but they observed—just like me. And I hated that.

He was stabilised. Barely. They wheeled him from the theatre to the ICU—room 414. I followed. No one spoke my name. None ever does. But I felt the tension in the room's fabric increase as I approached. Not from the mortal occupants. From the walls. From the spaces between seconds. As if reality itself sensed a collision and was bracing.

I stood at his side. I had seen ten thousand deaths. I had taken more. I had weighed lives that screamed to be spared and silenced them with a glance. But this one... This one I could not read. No karmic weight. No tether of sin or virtue. Empty. Not clean. Not pure. Simply absent.

A void in the weave. And in that absence, others had gathered. To protect? To measure? Or to witness something that had never happened before?

They lingered. I waited.

Hours passed. Mortals came and went. Machines clicked and hissed. Lights dimmed with the passage of night.

And then—it lessened. The air returned to normal. Time moved forward without resistance. The presence faded. I remained still, watching every fold of the universe around the room, searching for residue. Traces. None remained. They had retreated.

It was now. I conjured the vial. Clear. Odourless. Subtle. A substance from the edge of the in-between. Enough to tilt the tether, sever the thread.

The syringe tip found the IV line. I hesitated, not out of doubt. But to listen once more. To feel. Nothing. And then I pressed. A single drop. One breath of finality.

His body shuddered. Declined. Machines screamed. Staff rushed in. Alarms lit the ceiling red. They did not see me. None touched me. They veered around me, unconsciously—like wind bending around stone and not knowing why. Only sensing that some ancient shape was lodged in the room, fixed and unyielding.

I stood in the corner, cold and unmoved, waiting for the tether to break. It didn't. Instead, the line stabilised. His vitals surged—defied expectation. A hand pressed to his chest. A breath was drawn. He returned. Not by my doing. Not by theirs. By something else. And for the first time in countless ages, I felt off-balance.

I left. Not in retreat. Not in haste. But as one uncertain of his place in the scene, he had just authored.

Outside, I stood beside the Holden. The night did not welcome me. It watched. Not with malice. With interest. With patience. With knowing.

I reached for the door handle and paused.

My hand trembled. Not from exhaustion. From proximity to something I could not name. The scales tilted. And for the first time, I wondered if I was no longer meant to hold them.

Something has been set in motion. And whatever it is, it does not blink. And it does not stop.

Chapter 3
The Dream

Ben floated. Not sleeping. Not wakefulness. A drifting state—thin as paper, curling at the edges.

Above, a machine clicked.

Below, trees marched—roots tearing free of earth with the solemn grace of ancient dancers. The eucalyptus groaned like unhinged bones, rising toward a horizon no longer fixed.

He blinked—or thought he did.

He was lying in a hospital bed. Pale light fell through a narrow window. The sharp scent of disinfectant hung in the air. A slow drip fed into his vein. The hum of distant voices folded into white noise. His fingers twitched. And in that motion—barely a breath—he was somewhere else again.

The field glowed—not with light, but with presence. Grass bent in silent recognition. The sky pulsed with colour—violet one moment, ash-grey the next. Birds circled in geometric patterns—not hunting, not fleeing, just being—as part of an unseen design.

He turned slowly.

At the field's edge sat the fox, tail curled neatly, eyes like molten bronze. It looked healthy. Too healthy. Its fur shimmered in impossible hues—sunset red, forest green, shadow-blue. It blinked. Then—beside him—Death swung. A scythe of black bone and trailing ash cut through the air where Ben had stood a heartbeat earlier. The fox was already gone, reappearing behind Death, its tail flicking. It yawned. Then sat upright again, raised one paw, and placed it gently to its mouth.

"Shoosh." A secret.

Ben woke with a start. His heart thudded against his ribs like a trapped bird. The room took shape—curtains, light, plastic tubing, and a beeping machine.

He swallowed.

The fox had been—no. That was the drugs. The fever. The trauma. The fire.

He tried to move, but pain flickered through his chest and shoulder like a live wire.

He settled back and stared at the ceiling. The plaster crack branched like a tree. He traced it with his eyes. Shapes. A memory stirred—an old maths book, Fibonacci spirals, shells and leaf patterns.

He blinked. Once.

The crack had changed. It had become an eye. Then it wasn't.

He was behind the wheel again. Not now—then. Six months ago. The gravel road, the dust, the radio just faint enough to be background. And then—impact. The kangaroo was massive. Prehistoric. A rust-red titan of the plains. It burst from the scrub in a blur and hit the bumper with a sound like thunder cracking in a tin shed. The world turned sideways. Glass shattered. The ute flipped once, then again.

He should have died. Should have been crushed, broken, bled out under the rising sun.

But in the dream, the silence that followed was too perfect. No pain. No blood. He crawled from the wreckage and stared across the field. The kangaroo stood. Bones realigning with a fleshy pop, fur shaking itself free of dust. It turned its head, eyes meeting his with calm indifference. Then it bounded away, graceful and whole, into the shimmer of dawn.

Ben just stood there. And laughed.

The world shifted again. He was walking barefoot through soft loam. Trees bent gently toward him, leaves brushing his shoulders like old friends. The air smelled of childhood—sap, firewood, crushed mint underfoot. He heard them before he saw them. Voices. Not words—invitation. Dryads moved like flame through leaves—skin dappled with moss and moonlight, eyes like river stones.

They laughed, whispered, sang—not with mouths, but with movement. They danced around him, weaving between trees, always just out of reach. Come and play. Ben took a step. Then another. His heart beat like it had when he was ten years old, hiding in long grass with firecrackers in his pocket. He laughed again—open, free.

The fox appeared ahead, sitting in golden moss. Its eyes gleamed. "Shoosh." Then it trotted into the dark.

The dryads' laughter spun around him like wind-chimes. Ben ran with them now, feet barely touching the ground, breath coming easy for the first time in years. The forest glowed with impossible light—sunlight and starlight in the same sky. Petals drifted like snow. Leaves shimmered silver and gold. One of them touched his arm. It felt like water and warmth. Like being chosen. He laughed, whole again—not a broken man—scraping meaning from dirt, but a barefoot boy swallowed by wonder.

They circled him, voices rising, song turning to chant.

He spun in place, laughing.

And then it shifted. The light tilted. The dryads' faces lingered just a moment too long. Their eyes widened, but no longer in joy. Their mouths parted in songs that had become sighs. The air thickened, colour draining. One by one, they stepped back into shadow. And then the trees began to close in. Bark groaned. Roots twisted. The moss beneath his feet blackened. He ran, but the forest bent around him, turning him in circles.

The fox appeared again—watchful now, not playful. Beyond it, something moved. A shape. A presence. Something not of nature. Something wrong.

He turned—fluorescent lights buzzed. A machine beeped twice. Then once. Ben's eyes opened halfway. Shapes moved around him—shadows with voices. Words drifted in and out.

"...pressure dropping..."

"...keep the line open..."

"...he's stable, just needs time..."

Then another voice. Soft. Feminine. Kind enough to cut through the static. "I'm just here to help, Ben." He didn't know the voice. But something in him reached for it.

He fell again.

The kangaroo stood sentinel in a field of rusted cars, the same as his wreck. Now they pulsed and melted, their metal frames beating like hearts. The kangaroo blinked slowly. A dryad clung to its back like a child riding a horse. The fox stood between them all. Watching. Then Death swung again. The scythe cleaved the space where Ben's throat had been. But the fox, faster than breath, blocked it—not with fury or force, but with ease. It tilted its head and placed a paw to its mouth again.

"Shoosh."

Ben sank into the moss. It swallowed him whole. He wasn't sure when the world had gone quiet again. The hum of machines had stopped. Or maybe they hadn't. Perhaps he'd slipped sideways once more.

He stood barefoot in a hospital corridor. The floor was too clean. The lights didn't flicker—but they pulsed, like breath. A janitor swept the far end of the hall. Slow, rhythmic movements. No sound of bristles, just motion. Back and forth. Back and forth. Ben's eyes tracked him—a broad-brimmed hat. Bronze skin. A walking stick leaned beside the mop bucket like it belonged there. The janitor looked up, and Ben felt the weight of it—not memory, not knowing—just the echo of something vast wearing skin. The man did not speak, and Ben did not approach. He blinked. The corridor was empty.

The forest again. But different now. Quieter. Heavy. The fox waited at a circle of stones, tail curled, eyes tired. Ben stepped closer. The fox didn't move. It looked at him—almost sadly. Then, from the dark—Death came. The scythe cut through air and earth alike, and this time it landed. The fox's body split; its halves fell apart like broken bark. But its head turned slightly. Its muzzle curled, "Shoo," it whispered—dismembered. A leaf drifted down. It landed on Ben's chest. It pulsed once, then burned.

Ben gasped. Not a scream. Not even a sound. Just breathe. The room was real. Or real enough. A nurse moved in the background. And somewhere down the hallway, a mop bucket rolled quietly out of view.

He blinked again. The light didn't shift this time—no surreal shimmer. No trees crawling sideways. Just white walls. A plastic jug of water. The steady hiss of oxygen. He was awake. Not entirely sure how he knew—but he was.

Something clinked softly beside him. He turned his head. Slowly. A woman stood at the foot of his bed, flipping through a clipboard. Not a nurse—no scrubs. Her cardigan was soft and worn, her shoes sensible. She had kind eyes—the kind that stayed kind even without a smile. Attached to her belt was a ring of hospital keys. And from it hung a small foxtail charm, faded ginger, real or fake—he couldn't tell.

She looked up and smiled. "Hey there, stranger. You gave everyone a scare." Her voice was calm. Musical. Completely ordinary.

Ben stared at the foxtail, a whisper of recognition flickering in his chest.

The woman noticed his gaze and chuckled. "That? Found it at an op-shop years ago. Kinda dumb, but it stuck."

She didn't see the way his fingers curled slightly, or how his breath caught—not in fear, but in the same quiet awe a child might feel the first time he realises the world is far more than it seems.

Chapter 4
The Champagne

The sun slipped low across the Florida sky, painting the waters in sheets of amber and fire. The Leviathan XXVI floated motionless off the coast, its hull a polished obsidian mirror—reflecting nothing but power, precision, and the kind of wealth that never had to explain itself.

Zed boarded barefoot. The teak deck was warm beneath him. His gait was unhurried but carried the strange gravity of someone who'd walked through wars and weddings in the same shoes—white linen over dark slacks. A black eye patch covered his right eye—worn like a relic rather than a wound.

A jet-black crow landed on the rail beside him, cocked its head, then promptly shat on the deck.

"Lovely," muttered one of the stewards.

"Again?" Posi groaned from the saltwater plunge pool, where he lounged with one leg draped lazily over the edge. "Does the bird have to come?"

Zed said nothing. He walked past the mess without flinching, taking a seat near the edge of the deck, his eyes on the horizon.

"I had the whole thing waxed yesterday," Posi continued, sipping his gin with practised disdain. "Everything on this boat gleams—except the parts your crow finds spiritually offensive."

"He's got instincts," Zed replied, his voice low and dry.

Posi rolled his eyes and waved over a steward with a towel. "Next time, make him wear a diaper."

The crow gave a rattling caw and fluttered to perch on the back of a sun-lounger. One eye gleamed. The crew avoided its gaze. Zed leaned back, eyes half-closed beneath his heavy brow. The patch made him look severe—mythic, almost—but there was humour buried in the corners of his mouth. He scratched absently behind the bird's neck.

Ari arrived just after sunset, pulling up in a stolen-looking tender with a duffel slung across his back and a bottle of rum already open. Shirtless, sun-scorched, and inked from wrist to collar, he vaulted aboard like a soldier returning from leave. "Gentlemen," he said, tossing the canvas duffel onto the bar. "Still alive, I see."

"Physically," Posi muttered, reaching for a bottle of gin. "Spiritually, I make no promises."

Zed nodded in greeting. Ari grinned.

"Did you take the long route?" Ari asked, stretching. "Or were you just avoiding the inevitable?"

Zed tipped his head toward the horizon. "A bit of both."

The yacht rocked gently as the crew prepared for departure. Lines coiled, engines primed, and champagne flutes clinked quietly from the tray of a passing steward in spotless white. "Same cabin?" Posi asked Zed.

"You know me," Zed replied, rising and heading inside. "I like the bow. I like seeing what's coming."

"Masochist," Posi said under his breath, watching him disappear below deck.

Ari stood at the rail, gazing toward the fading light of the Keys. "Ever think about skipping it? The whole thing? Stay here. Sun. Rum. No meetings."

"You say that every year," Posi said.

"Because I mean it every year."

"And yet, you never do."

Ari smiled, soft and distant. "No. I don't."

The Leviathan XXVI eased forward, cutting eastward through the calm, endless blue. The Florida coastline shrank behind them as the lights of the outer world blinked on—golden, flickering, insincere. Inside the salon, jazz trickled from hidden speakers. Out on the deck, the trio reconvened with fresh drinks and lazy postures, the air rich with salt and citrus. Beneath it all was something unspoken—tension coiled beneath silk shirts and witty remarks.

"Monte Carlo will be crawling with them this year," Posi said, breaking the lull. "Everyone who's anyone. Royalty, criminals, bankers, and influencers pretending to be all three."

"It's the same show every year," Ari said, flicking ash from a cigar. "Fast cars, slow money, and enough cameras to film a hundred lies at once."

"I'm not there for them," Zed replied, sipping something pale and expensive. "I'm there for the noise. The speed. That moment when twenty machines scream down a narrow street and everyone forgets the rest of the world exists."

"Spoken like a man running from silence," Posi said.

Zed smiled without humour. "Aren't we all?"

They lingered in the darkening light, letting the sea carry them closer to the Riviera—to Monte Carlo, where silk met steel and the rich and famous traded truths like currency behind velvet ropes. Every year, the same ritual: a weekend of glitz, racing, cigars, wine, and whispers. Every year, they slipped into it like stepping into a tailored suit. There would be parties and penthouses, balcony toasts and secret meetings over caviar. But for now, here on the water, they were just three men with too much memory and too little time.

"To sanctuary," Posi said, raising his glass.

"To masks that fit," Ari added.

Zed touched his glass to theirs. "And to forgetting—if only for a few days—who we are."

The morning came draped in pink clouds and orange spray. Posi was already up, lounging with a Bloody Mary in one hand and a tablet in the other, scrolling through headlines with a scowl that grew deeper with each flick of his finger. "The World Bank's digital ledger glitched again," he muttered. "For five minutes, it told everyone in South Africa that they were billionaires. Cue riots."

"Doesn't take much anymore," Ari said, stepping out with wet hair and nothing but a towel. He grabbed a cigar from the humidor without asking.

"I miss when threats came from swords and storms," Posi said. "Not typos."

The women began appearing as the sun rose, draped in robes and the soft scent of last night's champagne. One curled against

Zed on a lounge chair, bold and curious, tracing the edge of his eye patch with a manicured nail.

"What's behind it?" she asked.

"Perspective," he said. She didn't press.

They spent the day drifting east. The breeze carried hints of salt, perfume, and tobacco. Zed and Ari argued about the ethics of surveillance states while two of the women played poker topless. Posi fielded a call from an Italian arms dealer who didn't know he was on speaker. Lunch was oysters, saffron paella, and far too much rosé. Dessert never arrived—it was devoured halfway down the galley stairs by the crow. No one complained. The bird, after all, had immunity.

Later that night, the women danced barefoot on the teak deck under string lights strung like fallen stars. Posi joined them, jacketless now, shirt open, cigarette burning down between two fingers like he'd forgotten it was there. He twirled a model with green eyes and no last name, and she laughed like she'd been waiting for this moment all her life. Ari drank rum straight from the bottle and told the other two about a small war erupting in the Balkans that no one was reporting on. "Too inconvenient for the algorithms," he said. "Apparently, it's bad for investor confidence."

Zed sat alone for a time, watching shadows flicker across the water. His crow circled above, vanishing into the dark, then returning again and again as if it were tracking the path ahead. As the yacht hummed steadily through the night, champagne flowed like memory, and everything—war, truth, names—dissolved into music and smoke. They had not arrived yet. But already, Monte Carlo felt close enough to touch. And none of them wanted to get there too fast.

Just before dawn, Zed stood at the bow with a fresh drink in hand. The crow perched silently on the rail beside him. Behind them, the yacht pulsed with low laughter and the thrum of speakers playing an old jazz number remixed by a Parisian DJ no one had heard of yet. He didn't turn as Ari joined him, barefoot and quiet. They watched the sea together.

"You still believe in them?" Ari asked.

"The people?" Zed asked. Ari nodded.

Zed considered his glass. "I believe they're still trying. That's enough."

"Trying to do what?"

"To make sense of the noise. To build meaning before it all slips away." The crow gave a low sound—not quite a caw, but more like agreement.

Behind them, Posi burst into laughter with one of the women, probably at something neither would remember. The horizon was faintly silver now.

Zed turned to Ari. "We arrive by midday. Clean yourself up. Monte Carlo loves a fresh lie."

Ari smiled. "So do we." They clinked glasses and watched the sun breach the line between night and day. Monte Carlo waited. And behind it—something else. They just weren't ready to name it.

Chapter 5
The Smoke

Monte Carlo pulsed like a jewel—streets shimmering with chrome, champagne, polished shoes, perfect smiles, engines purring, a thousand languages humming. The Grand Prix was days away, but already the rich, the powerful, and the utterly bored had flooded the city in tailored suits and backless gowns, sipping from crystal flutes and betting fortunes on the tilt of a roulette wheel.

High above the harbour, drone cameras spun lazy circles, broadcasting glimpses of billionaire yachts and velvet-curtained penthouses to a ravenous world. Beneath it all, hidden from even the most prying satellite, the old gods returned—stepping once more into the mortal stage, veiled in glamour and gold.

Jamil stood near the private arrivals gate, silent in an immaculate black sherwani stitched with silver threads. The warm Mediterranean sun did little to thaw the frost in his bones.

He saw them—the numbers—ghosting behind every living thing. Floating digits like afterimages of karma: balances, debts, weights. But they no longer made sense. A man brushed past, laughing, golden watch flashing. His karmic thread reversed. Jamil's brow furrowed. Children passed with figures in the red that made no sense. A pregnant woman glowed with an impossible balance—both heavy and hollow at once. It was all... wrong. *The scales were cracking*, he thought.

Diane arrived, silent in the breeze.

Her beauty was sharp, honed by discipline. The silver-grey suit clung to her like a second skin, her dark hair braided tight, her eyes hidden behind aviator shades—she was polished. She walked like a huntress, every step measured. But inside, she was unravelling. "I missed," she said without greeting.

Jamil didn't look at her. "Yes."

"I don't miss."

"Yes," he agreed.

She folded her arms. "Has it ever happened to you?"

Jamil let the silence answer.

Above them, a gull cried once, then veered sharply from its path and vanished behind a rooftop.

Diane followed it with her eyes. "I keep seeing him. In my mind, I go back, rewind it. My breath, my grip, the moment the trigger clicked—" she stopped herself. "I didn't miss. I wasn't allowed to hit."

They stood there in silence.

A Rolls-Royce Phantom slid past, unnoticed.

Then came the flutter of flashbulbs—whispers, then stares, then gasps. The crowd shifted like a tide as she emerged. Effie.

She didn't walk so much as move through light. Every head turned as she descended from her personal chopper in a white gown that flowed like milk and starlight. Her eyes caught a thousand hearts; her small, deliberate smile was a weapon centuries in the making. Photographers snapped, influencers wept, and one paparazzo nearly fell off a ledge. "Is that...?" someone whispered. "It's her." Behind the velvet rope, men adjusted collars, women sucked in stomachs, and no one dared blink. Effie's heels never seemed to touch the pavement.

And then—like thunder tearing silk—a roar split the air. Fiona.

A blur of red and chrome streaked up the waterfront boulevard, parting traffic like a divine missile. She rode a modified Ducati, gold-rimmed, exhaust trailing heat. Her leather was matte black, stitched with gold thread. On her hip: a coin flip tattoo with Fortuna's face on one side and a skull on the other.

She skidded sideways, stopped inches from Effie's gown, flipped her visor up, and winked. "Well, well," Fiona said, pulling off her helmet. Her hair was wild, wind-whipped. "I didn't miss much, did I?"

Effie smirked. "Always the loudest entrance."

"Balance, darling. You bring the grace, I bring the noise."

The Leviathan XXVI slid into harbour like a leviathan in name and truth—immense, dark, and regal. It glided between lesser yachts with the silence of wealth that had nothing left to prove.

As the gangway extended, a soft tremor rippled through the flagstones.

Zed was the first to descend. His bare feet touched the polished timber, but he paused halfway down. His head tilted, just slightly. The crow on his shoulder gave a low, clicking sound—not a caw, but a subtle warning.

Posi followed behind, one hand on the rail. He squinted toward the sea. "Feels like the deck's still swaying," he muttered.

Zed didn't move.

"No..." Posi said again, softly. "That wasn't the water."

They stood there in stillness.

Zed lowered his head. "The crust," he said. "It gave."

Posi's brow tightened. "You sure?"

"I felt it. Just a fraction. Like something shifted deep beneath. Something old."

The Mediterranean sparkled as if the world remained unchanged, but both gods stood fixed, as if listening for the echo of something too ancient for mortals to name.

Behind them, Ari bounded down the gangway, a grin already in place. "Gods, I love this city!" he declared. "You smell that? Greed, lust, overpriced cigars—Monte Carlo never disappoints."

He stopped when he saw their faces. "What?" he said, half-laughing. "Did someone spill the caviar?"

Zed didn't answer. He just stared out at the horizon, expression grave.

Ari's smile faded slightly. "Okay... what did I miss?"

Still silence.

He turned to Posi. "Why do you both look like you just heard the horn?"

Zed's voice came quiet—barely more than breath. "Ragnarök."

Ari blinked. "What?"

Zed didn't repeat it. But something in the way he stood—still and solemn—told Ari he'd heard right.

Ari took a step closer, grin faltering. "You're serious."

Zed didn't respond. The crow ruffled its feathers.

Ari laughed—awkwardly at first, then with rising energy. "You're serious. You felt it. Something cracked, didn't it?"

His fingers twitched. "I didn't feel a damn thing," he said, voice almost childlike now. "But you two did. And if you're this worried—Zed, if you're worried—then it's real."

He paced a slow circle, like a boy trying not to run toward a locked cabinet of fireworks. "You know what this means," Ari whispered. "It means the rules are thinning. The locks are rusting. Maybe—maybe—we don't have to keep pretending anymore."

He looked Zed in the eye, excitement mounting. "So just tell me. Can I trip the first step? Just a teaser. I've been bored for decades."

Zed shook his head. "No, not yet."

Ari turned to the glowing skyline of Monte Carlo. The lights, the music, the decadence—it all looked like a sandcastle just waiting for the tide. "They've had such a good run," he said. "Would be a shame if it all came crumbling down without me."

Then he smiled. "But gods, what a joy it's going to be... when we stop holding back."

The gods hadn't been on land five minutes when the air shifted again.

Not the kind of shift mortals noticed. Not wind, not temperature. Stillness. The kind that made birds go quiet. That bent shadows slightly wrong. Zed turned first. He didn't need to see him to know. Jamil.

He approached without escort, without fanfare, without even a change in expression from the crowd around him. The mortals saw him, yes, but they didn't register him. Their minds stepped politely aside. Just another man walking with calm purpose through a world that was already doomed.

His eyes, dark and depthless, locked on Zed.

Ari's mouth twisted. "Oh, great. Death's here."

Posi crossed his arms. "That was fast."

Jamil stopped a few feet away. His gaze scanned each of them with clinical precision—Zed, Posi, Ari—and landed back on Zed. "We need to speak."

"Before the council?" Zed asked, already knowing the answer.

"Yes."

Ari scoffed. "Council hasn't even been seated yet. Can't it wait until we're indoors and bored out of our minds?"

Jamil didn't look at him. Didn't even blink.

Zed studied his face. There was tension there—rare for Jamil, whose every motion was usually weighted and controlled like a pendulum. But now, he looked like someone trying to hold the sky still with his hands.

Zed gestured to a nearby terrace. "Walk with us."

The four gods turned, stepping through the throng of mortal indulgence—champagne towers, camera flashes, diamonds in every direction.

None of it touched Jamil. He waited until they were far enough from mortal ears, then spoke. "The numbers are wrong."

Posi raised an eyebrow. "Karmic?"

Jamil nodded once. "Massively."

"How wrong?" Zed asked.

Jamil's voice dropped to a tone that silenced even Ari. "There are mortals carrying negative karmic burdens and still receiving blessings. Infants born with no karma—condemned. Debts that should've cleared long ago resurfacing in blood. And something—something else."

"What kind of something?" Zed said.

"I don't know," Jamil replied. "I see patterns. You know that. Karmic systems are complex, but they balance over time. They always have. But now—" He looked toward the city. "The scales are behaving like they've forgotten what they weigh."

Ari chuckled drily. "Maybe Fortuna's just been playing rough."

"No," Jamil said. "This isn't luck. This is design. Something is interfering."

Zed folded his arms. "Design?"

"I know it is," Jamil replied. "Unchecked, we may lose the ability to measure balance. Cause and consequence will break. Every god tied to order, justice, rhythm—will feel it snap."

Zed was quiet for a long moment. Then: "Entropy is being favoured?"

Jamil's jaw clenched. "No, not yet. But something's pushing. Calculating. As if testing how much strain our fabric of reality can take."

Zed nodded. "Okay, noted. We'll speak again at the council. But thank you for bringing this to me first."

Jamil didn't move. "There's one more thing," he said.

Zed's brow furrowed slightly.

"The mortal," Jamil said slowly. "The one that can't die. He should not exist. He has no karma. No record. No weight. I could not find any sense of debt within him. He is like a blank space in the ledger, and it's beginning to ripple through the rest."

Zed straightened. "You're saying this mortal has no karma?"

"I'm saying..." Jamil said, voice colder now, "I watched him survive a fire that should have ended him. I watched other forces intervene—forces even I couldn't measure. I tried to end him, discreetly."

Zed turned fully to face him now. "And?" Jamil's voice tightened. "They stopped me."

"Who?" Zed asked.

Jamil met his eye. "Ethereals."

For a moment, no one spoke.

"He was marked for death," Jamil continued. "But Death couldn't take him. Something stood in the way—something vast. And now the imbalance spreads wherever he goes. Mortals live when they shouldn't. Others die out of sequence. Entire karmic flows are rerouting themselves as if orbiting around him."

Zed frowned slightly in annoyance, but something in the sound of it made the crow on his shoulder shift again. "Human?" he asked.

"Yes," Jamil said. "But there's nothing beneath him. No spiritual residue. It's not that his thread was cut—it was never spun."

Zed's brow darkened. "Impossible."

Jamil nodded once. "I thought so too. But he survived my spell that should have ended him."

Ari said, genuinely surprised. "You don't usually get your hands dirty over one mortal."

"I had to know," Jamil replied. "And when I tried... something stopped me. I was alone in the room, but I felt them. Not gods. Not spirits. Ethereals. Multiple. Not angry—just watching."

Posi shifted uncomfortably. "And him?"

"He doesn't know what he is. He's afraid. He believes he's ordinary. But the world bends around him like a field around a magnet. People live who should die. Others drop without cause. Events shift, reroute. The balance isn't tipping. It's spiralling."

Zed looked toward the sea again. "You're sure the thread leads to him?"

"I'm not following a thread," Jamil said. "I'm following the break. Every time I look for the source, I end up back at Ben Callum. Like gravity."

Ari gave a slow whistle. “Ben Callum, eh? I like him already.”

Zed’s jaw clenched. “Keep watching him.”

Jamil stepped closer, lowering his voice until it barely stirred the air. “If this continues, Zed, the scales won’t just break. They’ll forget they ever balanced. The system will become memory. And then even gods will answer to nothing.”

Zed didn’t flinch. But he didn’t reply either. And Jamil didn’t wait. He turned and walked into the sea of mortals, and though they brushed past him without pause, not a single one looked him in the eye.

Every year, the divine council convened beneath the surface of this spectacle, hidden beneath centuries of marble and bronze. It was tradition. Ritual. A perfect cover. Because what better camouflage than chaos?

Beneath the Casino de Monte-Carlo, past velvet ropes and private vaults, past corridors no mortal architect remembered building—lies the Chamber. Black-and-white marble formed a sunburst on the floor, ringed by thirteen seats arranged in a sweeping crescent. Each seat carved with the sigils of a god’s domain, and behind each loomed a full-height alabaster likeness—sculpted not as idealised myths, but as the gods appeared in the mortal world. Weapons. Symbols. Shadows of truth. Torches lit the chamber. Not for ambience—but because they preferred it. Firelight flickered across eternal faces.

Mortal attendants had been preparing the space since dawn—those rare few bound by oath, their memories later wiped clean. They polished bronze, lit flame, and scrubbed each trace of the last gathering from the stones. Some would go mad in the months that followed, never understanding why the tick of time felt wrong in their ears.

Above, the Grand Prix howled.

Below, the gods began to take their places. Zed rose first, stepping into the centre. "As tradition demands," he said, "we open the Annual Council of the Thirteen. On this, the third day of the Grand Prix in Monte Carlo, we gather in accordance with ancient accord to speak, vote, and reckon the balance of all things." His voice echoed without effort. The chamber itself recorded every syllable.

"Twelve gods are seated," Zed continued. "Let the record show: one is absent." He turned slightly toward the empty throne. "The seat of Muat, Lord of Measure, remains empty."

A hush fell over the chamber. Zed placed a single obsidian token on Muat's vacant seat. "He who once measured the rise and fall of stars, who weighed consequence in grain and silence... is no more. This is not absence by choice. This is not exile. This is not a retreat. This is death."

The room absorbed the truth. "We honour him," Zed said. "And in his honour, we do not flinch." The gods bowed their heads—even Ari. "Twelve voices shall speak. One shall remain still. And the seat of Muat shall stay unfilled until balance chooses a successor."

The chamber pulsed. The meeting had begun. Zed remained standing but stepped back, giving the floor to silence.

From the curved row of thrones, a figure rose. Jamil.

Where others moved with ceremony or grace, Jamil rose like a verdict. His presence stripped the chamber of heat. Even the torchlight dimmed slightly, as if in respect—or fear.

"I speak now," he said, "as Warden of Passage, Arbiter of Death, and Keeper of the Scales." His voice was calm, unhurried, and without inflexion. There was no ego in it. Only gravity. "The balance is compromised." No murmurs this time. Only stillness.

The gods had heard whispers, but this was a declaration. Jamil continued. "In the last cycle, I recorded six hundred and twenty-one violations of karmic logic. Forty-eight anomalies in life extension without cause. Twenty-nine interruptions in scheduled mortal cessation. Three reversals of judgement. And one surviving mortal with no measurable weight."

His gaze passed over the council like a blade drawn low across stone. "You have heard of the fire. You have heard of the failure to end him. You have heard, now, of the intervention." Zed nodded once—confirming it.

Jamil turned slightly. "I attempted to execute a correction. The attempt failed. Not by incompetence. Not by opposition. By inaccessibility. The Ethereals were present. Unseen. Unwelcome. They did not intervene with force—they intervened with absence. They made me still. They made the moment unassailable."

Effie, seated three thrones to the left, crossed her legs and tilted her head. "The Ethereals haven't moved openly in over an age."

"They still haven't," Jamil said. "But they watched."

"Watched you?" Diane asked, arms folded tightly. "Or watched him?"

Jamil's eyes flicked to her. "Both. And neither."

Zed raised a hand. "His name."

Jamil inclined his head. "Ben Callum." The sound of it struck like a ripple. Small. Spreading.

"Not an in-betweener," Jamil said. "Not a god. Not a trickster. A mortal. But one who holds no tether. He moves without a footprint. Lives without cost. And worse—he warps the pattern around him. Others die early. Others live too long. Events distort in his proximity."

Fiona scoffed softly. "So he's lucky."

"No," Jamil said. "He is unknowable."

Zed's expression tightened. "I knew of him. I sent Diane to observe. And when she failed—"

"I followed," Jamil finished. "And now I stand here with nothing but failure to report."

He paused. "I do not fail." The silence that followed was different. Not reverent. Afraid.

Jamil continued. "This is no longer an issue of a rogue mortal. This is the point of pressure. The fault line. He is not disrupting the system. He is rewriting it around him."

He looked up at the stone dome above, voice colder than ever. "If we do not act, the fabric will unravel. The Great Balance will become myth. And we will be left as nothing but stories."

He stepped back into the shadow. The room did not breathe.

The silence held for several heartbeats. Then a voice, smooth as velvet over glass, cut through the stillness. "I have a question."

All eyes turned to Effie. She sat with one leg draped over the other, an image of elegance in pale rose and gold, her eyes soft—yet not warm. Nothing about her tone was accusatory.

But it pierced deeper than a blade. “At what point,” she said, “did the existence of a confused mortal child warrant multiple executions without informing the full council?”

Jamil said nothing.

Effie continued. “One attempt by Diane. Another by Death himself. All without even speaking his name aloud to the others seated here.”

She looked at Zed now, eyes sharp beneath the calm. “When did we begin deciding in private what we created the council to discuss together?”

Zed’s jaw flexed, but he didn’t speak.

“Our creed,” Effie said, looking around the chamber now, “is not dominion. It’s not obedience. It is Balance. We exist not to intervene—but to preserve the natural rhythm. And we are permitted action only when an imbalance threatens the whole.”

She leaned forward now, the torchlight catching in her eyes like fire through wine. “So I ask again: what threat does this mortal pose that required silence? Assassination? Deception? Why weren’t we—all of us—brought in before blood spilled? Before Muat was lost?”

Diane flinched at the mention. Even Ari stopped smiling.

Effie’s voice softened—no less dangerous for it. “Is it truly an imbalance we fear?” she asked. “Or is it change? Do we punish this Ben Callum because he is dangerous, or because he is unpredictable? Because he does not fit the system we shaped?”

Jamil’s reply came measured. “I acted to maintain balance. So did she.”

Effie nodded once. "Then why are the scales still tipping? Why is the ledger still fragmenting, even after your attempts?" No one answered.

She turned back to Zed. "You knew him. You sent her. You let it unfold. Why?"

Zed met her gaze without flinching. His voice was quiet, but anchored. "Because I was hoping it would resolve without the need for this council."

Effie raised an eyebrow. "And when it didn't?"

Zed didn't look away. "I sent Death."

Effie's face remained still, but the disdain beneath her following words was unmistakable. "So… this is what the creed has become. Preserve the balance—unless it's inconvenient. Then preserve control."

Fiona leaned back with a smirk, but didn't interrupt.

Effie's final words were soft, but they struck the chamber like a chime of judgement. "If this mortal is truly a threat, I will vote to act. But if this council is becoming an arm of preemptive silence—then say so now."

She reclined again, eyes forward, lips drawn. The torchlight danced on the ancient marble. No one moved.

The silence lingered after Effie's final words, the kind that might crack stone if left too long.

Then came the soft, amused voice of Fiona. "I ran the numbers." All heads turned.

Fiona sat lazily in her seat, one boot propped on a carved marble gryphon, flipping a golden coin between her fingers. Her leather scuffed from the road, her grin crooked and dry. She looked like she'd just wandered in from a street fight—and maybe she had.

"I didn't care at first," she said. "A mortal beats the odds? That's Tuesday. I've watched men survive falls, lightning, heartbreak, syphilis, and even marriage. But this one?"

She leaned forward now, the coin still flipping, never dropping. "This one's a bloody statistical middle finger."

She held up one finger. "Fire: collapsed house, flash-over ignition, insulation-choked oxygen pockets—he's inside. Not just inside. Asleep. Survives with burns and smoke inhalation, no permanent damage. Eighty-nine per cent chance of death. He lives."

Second finger. "Medical intervention? The neighbour who called the ambulance was out walking her cat. No joke. Her cat. If she hadn't been there, he would've been brain-dead within four minutes. She wasn't supposed to be home. She should have been at work. Her car broke down. Callum lives."

Third finger. "ICU crash. Cardiac arrest during night five. Flat-lined for forty-one seconds. Defibrillator malfunctions on the first attempt, miraculously resets on the second. Guess who comes back with a normal rhythm? Callum. Again."

Fourth finger. "Post-release trauma. He nearly walks into traffic. A bus misses him by exactly 3.6 centimetres—I measured. The driver had a muscle twitch that pulled him left at precisely the right moment. Callum blinks and walks on."

She spread her hands. "And that's just month one."

The coin vanished between her fingers. "I've tallied twelve separate life-threatening events since the fire. Twelve. And he's still walking around like gravity doesn't apply to him."

She looked toward Jamil, then toward Zed. "When even I start losing count, something is wrong. He's not beating the odds. He's warping them."

Her grin faded now, eyes narrowing. "I don't mind chaos. Hell, I thrive on it. But this isn't chaos. This is convergence. The kind of pattern that makes the house lose money. The kind of pattern that breaks the wheel."

She leaned back again. "And when the wheel breaks, darlings, we all go flying." A heavy silence followed.

Even Ari, for once, had no quip. Effie's final words still hung in the air when Diane stood. No announcement. No ceremony. Just the precise, sudden motion of a predator cornered. She folded her arms tightly.

Her voice was cold steel. "You talk of morality, Effie," she said, "from a throne carved by seduction and war. Let's not pretend you've never manipulated lives to preserve the rhythm."

Effie didn't flinch, but the flick of her eye said she'd heard it.

Diane continued. "Zed didn't send me to assassinate a child. I was sent to observe. But when I found him, I knew something was wrong. He didn't smell right. He didn't fit. And I—" she stopped, just for a breath. "I hesitated. That was my failure." Her hand clenched at her side.

"I never miss. I have never missed. And yet, I drew breath, stilled my heartbeat, aligned the shot, and the bullet passed through him like he was air." A murmur started among the second tier of gods. Diane's eyes darted across the chamber. "Not deflected. Not blocked. It passed through him like the moment never existed."

She looked back at Effie. "You want to debate morality? Fine. But know this—I was there. You were not. You've seen numbers and rumours. I saw a mortal look directly into my eyes the moment after a divine bullet failed to land. And he smiled."

That broke the chamber.

"He smiled?" Fiona snorted. "You mean he saw you?"

"He couldn't have," Effie said, rising from her seat. "You were veiled."

Diane stepped forward. "He shouldn't have. But he did."

Voices rose. Someone yelled, "This is madness! If mortals can see us—if they can defy us—what else is broken?"

The chamber erupted into motion. Gods shouted across the chamber, words in languages older than continents. The torchlight flared. Shadows danced as wild beasts loosed from cages. One deity cracked the marble floor beneath his chair with a furious stomp. Another vanished mid-argument, teleporting out in disgust.

Zed stood slowly. No one noticed.

Ari had climbed onto his own seat, waving his hands like a conductor, mock-chanting: "Down with the creed! Up with chaos! Let's flip the wheel and see who bleeds first!"

Jamil remained seated, but his eyes burned like twin embers locked behind cold glass.

Zed remained still. Then: "ENOUGH."

The word hit the chamber like a hammer wrapped in thunder. Not shouted—declared. The torches flared blue. All motion stopped. The gods froze.

Zed's voice, cold and deep, echoed from every stone. "You will compose yourselves."

He stepped forward slowly, the crow still and silent on his shoulder. "We have gathered in this place to speak as one. We are the keepers of balance, not squabbling children with stolen fire."

The room trembled slightly beneath his feet—no quake—just the weight of command.

Zed's eye swept across the thrones. "If you cannot act with discipline, then you prove the need for this council. And you prove that balance has already begun to rot."

He turned to Diane, his voice softening. "You failed."

Diane stiffened.

"And I sent you, knowing you might. Because I knew if you could not finish him, then none of us would."

Zed turned toward the centre of the chamber. "Now sit. We decide nothing in fury."

Slowly, the gods lowered themselves back into their seats. One by one, the light steadied. The silence that followed was no longer tense. It was heavy. Consequential.

Ari stood up with theatrical flair, brushing imaginary dust from his jacket. "Well, if the melodrama's cooled," he said, grinning, "perhaps we can get on with something useful."

He stepped forward onto the speaking floor—casual, uninvited, but unchallenged. "Since everyone's had their moment to weep and gnash teeth, I figured I'd offer a little update from the front lines of mortality."

He stretched his arms wide. "War, my darlings. The pulse beneath your pretty economies, the whisper in every parliament chamber, the wet breath behind every drone strike. It's been lively." Some chuckled.

Ari's grin sharpened. "Let's start with the obvious. Russia still rattles sabres, but its hand is weaker than it looks. China's re-balancing with whispers and proxies. The US? As always—loud, but disoriented."

He paced slowly across the chamber, the way one might stalk a chessboard. "Three coups this quarter. Eight unstable regimes barely held together by foreign currency and vodka. Twenty-nine military buildups. Eleven false alarms. Two almost nuclear incidents. And one very real, very quiet naval skirmish in the Arctic that would've gone hot if I hadn't—how do I put this—tweaked the odds."

He winked at Fiona.

She just rolled her eyes. "You're welcome."

Ari turned back to the room. "I've kept full-scale war from igniting on three continents this year. Not by peace talks. Not by diplomacy. But by artful manipulation. Timing. Distraction. Leverage." He tapped the side of his head.

"I whisper in a few ears. Sabotage a fuel convoy here. Sink a missile test there. Nudge a few generals into cardiac arrest—all very tasteful."

Zed said nothing, but his eye didn't leave Ari.

"But here's the interesting part," Ari continued, pacing again. "It's getting harder."

That quieted the room.

"I'm very good at what I do. I know escalation curves better than most of you know your own prayers. But lately? Things aren't behaving. Leaders are making illogical decisions. Armies are avoiding conflicts that they would have charged into six months ago. Entire regions are shifting like sand underfoot."

He paused at the centre of the room. "I started running probabilities—something Fiona's better at, but I dabble. And guess what I found?"

He snapped his fingers. "Convergence."

No one spoke.

"It's like there's a second hand moving the pieces. Not mine. Not hers. Not Zed's. And when I track the ripple patterns far enough, I find the same anomaly—they seem to emanate from Adelaide, Australia."

He turned to face the high dais again. "A country so peaceful, hardly the starting place for a conflict. But, guess what? Of course—I should have known—Ben Callum lives there."

Ari's tone changed then—less amused, more fascinated. "I don't think he knows what he's doing. I don't even think he wants it. But he's not just bending karma. He's flattening conflict. Defusing chaos without even trying."

A beat. "Which, for the record, should be good news. I mean—world peace, right?" He chuckled, but no one joined him.

Ari spread his arms. "But it's not peace. It's suppression like a pressure cooker with the valve sealed. I can feel it building. The tension isn't gone—it is increasing."

Another beat. "And when it blows... it won't be mortal. It'll be cosmic."

He shrugged, stepped back toward his throne, and sat without ceremony. "My vote's not in yet. But I'll say this—whatever this Ben Callum is, he's doing my job without even knowing he's playing."

He leaned back. "And I don't like being made obsolete."

The silence following Ari's report was thick. The council seemed to tilt, ready to fall into the gravity of one mortal name. Then another voice spoke—soft, distant, yet clear as glass struck in perfect pitch. "If I may."

Heads turned. Some with surprise.

Thales rose from the lower tier—not one of the thirteen, but respected. Ancient. Quiet. Most forgot he was in the room until he stood. He looked like a man carved from vellum and dust. Simple robes. Ink-stained fingers. A mind that had outlived empires.

"I have watched. And listened," he said. "As each of you weighs a mortal boy like a shard of glass that cracked the mirror."

He stepped slowly into the centre, glancing at no one and everyone at once. "But I ask this: what if Ben Callum did not break the mirror? What if he is reflecting the shards?"

That landed like a cold breeze.

"You say he defies logic. Bends karma. Warps balance. But you assume he is causing it." Thales paused, voice steady. "I have seen systems collapse before, not from without—but from within. And always, in the moments before failure, there is a flicker.

A blinding light. A misalignment so profound it seems like a singularity. Everyone stares at it. Blames it. Reacts to it."

He turned toward the thrones now. "But the flicker is not the fault. It is the reveal."

Effie sat forward, eyes narrowing. "You're saying Ben is a beacon?"

"I'm saying," Thales said, "that anomalies cluster near collapse. That reality knots before it tears. You all speak of Ben Callum like a breach. I suspect he is a flare. A signal. A result."

Ari frowned. "You're suggesting he's not the fire—he's the smoke?"

Thales nodded once. "Precisely. And if so, then all this obsession with the flame may be blinding us to the arsonist."

The room fell still again. Jamil spoke low. "And you have evidence of another source?"

Thales shook his head. "Not yet. But I have an absence. Blind spots where information should be. Quiet frequencies that once hummed with life. Patterns within the patterns are gone. Not hidden—evacuated. Like something left or went silent."

Zed watched him closely. "You think something is moving behind the anomaly?"

Thales' voice dropped just slightly. "I think we are so transfixed by the radiance of one mortal... that we may not see the shadow standing behind it."

He bowed slightly. "Continue your debate. Cast your votes. But do not pretend you are seeing the full shape of the problem." And with that, Thales turned and returned to his seat in the lower tier—unnoticed again, like dust settling on an old book.

But the silence he left behind wasn't passive. It buzzed. It worried.

A long silence followed Thales' warning. And then... a sound like a stone exhaling.

Pele stood. Some gods straightened immediately. Others stiffened. They had not heard Pele speak in centuries. Her skin was obsidian, veined with slow-glowing magma, as if fire itself had cooled into form. Her eyes were not eyes, but twin flows of molten amber, layered like volcanic glass forged under divine pressure. When she spoke, it was slow—not hesitant, but eternal. Mountains wait. Volcanoes do not hurry.

"I felt it." No name. No preamble.

"I felt the Earth shift." Whispers rustled like dry ash in the chamber.

Pele continued. "It was not tectonic. Not magnetic. Not lunar. It was wilful."

Her voice cracked like lava cooling too quickly, sharp, fractured, ancient. "A misstep. Small. But real. The core flexed. Momentum stuttered as if the Earth forgot how to spin. For less than a breath."

Even Zed's face changed at that.

Pele's gaze swept the room. "It has never happened before. Not in the age of fire. Not in the cracking of continents. Something moved the Earth without touching it."

Diane stood slowly. "Are you saying the planet hesitated?"

"Yes," Pele said. "Like a memory trying to surface. Like the planet remembered fear."

That hit harder than any accusation.

Another god stood. "This is absurd—"

"Enough!" Zed barked, but the room wasn't ready to listen.

Fiona stood. "How long have you known?"

Effie followed, voice razor-thin. "If you felt this days ago, why say nothing?"

Diane's voice cut across them. "You knew about Ben. You knew about the tremor. And still—you said nothing."

A roar of overlapping voices surged—divine anger, suspicion, fear. The chamber shook. Marble cracked beneath Muat's empty seat.

Zed didn't rise this time. He slammed the butt of his staff—forged from meteorite and silence—onto the black-veined floor. The flames inverted. The torches burned black. All sound vanished.

Zed rose slowly, and when he spoke, his voice was not loud—but it carried the kind of command that could end empires. "Do you think I am blind?"

He stepped forward. "Do you think I do nothing while the world tilts under us?"

The flames hissed and flickered with unnatural rhythm, as if rewinding. "I knew Ben Callum would mark a change. I thought—hoped—it would be localised. Containable. I was wrong."

He turned, his gaze sweeping every throne, every face. "I felt the Earth's misstep before Thales spoke. I saw the karmic collapse before Jamil confirmed it. I sent Diane because I trusted her. I sent Jamil because I feared what we were becoming. And I said nothing because I believed we still had time."

He stepped into the central circle. "But now..." He looked up—not at the chamber ceiling, but beyond it. "Now I say this plainly: we may be standing at the edge of Ragnarök."

The silence that followed was not still. It trembled. Ari stood, eyes bright. Effie looked away, her jaw clenched. Thales' head bowed, slow as glaciers shifting.

One of the gods spat on the floor. "You don't get to say that," he growled. "You don't get to drag us into prophecy you've been hiding."

Zed didn't flinch. "I didn't hide prophecy. I tried to prevent it."

Fiona's voice was low now. "And if we're already in it?"

Zed looked to the empty throne of Muat. "Then we must ask a question this council has never dared to ask."

He turned back to the circle. "Where do we go from here—one mortal resists all known structure. His name is Ben Callum. I attempted a correction and failed."

Gasps rippled. Commotion erupted. Voices shouting. Arguments clashing. The chamber shook.

Zed did not shout. He struck the floor with the butt of his staff. The torches turned black. Silence. "Enough," Zed said. "We are not children. Ragnarök has begun. We must face it." The flames steadied. The gods stared.

Far above the council chamber, the Grand Prix howled into dusk, engines screaming as if to drown out the sound of old truths cracking. Below, the gods argued over fate, over balance, over a mortal who should not be. But the universe does not wait for consensus.

And somewhere far beyond their reach—past satellites, prayers, and prophecy—something had already begun to pull at the strings. It didn't roar. It didn't announce itself. It simply... arrived. And, as always, the first to notice would not be a god. It would be the math.

Chapter 6
Intermission

Let's get the cliché out of the way first. Yes, it's a cosmic event. Yes, the fate of the planet hangs in the balance. And yes, you've seen this plot before, usually with better CGI.

Usually, humanity gets an asteroid, a solar flare, or a conveniently bilingual alien invasion. Big budget stuff. Lots of explosions. Someone gives an emotional speech about humanity's worthiness of saving—cue dramatic music.

This is not that.

This is slower. Dumber.

Far more inconvenient.

Somewhere out in the deep-dark, a brown dwarf—a sort of failed star with delusions of grandeur—has wandered just close enough to make things interesting. Not destroy Earth interesting. Just tilt-it-slightly-off-axis-interesting. The kind of interesting that makes scientists drink at 10 a.m.

It's not coming into the solar system. That would at least get attention.

No, it's just passing nearby. Like a socially anxious god. Silent. Massive. Totally uninterested in our little drama. But the Sun noticed. Oh yes. And because stars are notoriously bad at resisting gravitational flirtation, our Sun has begun to lean—just slightly—toward its new, invisible companion. And Earth? Earth, being codependent, started following. Not fast. Not dramatically. But just enough to make the days a bit longer. The nights a bit colder. The tides a bit moodier. As if time itself was dragging its feet on the way to work.

In layman's terms: there is now a vast, very quiet object nudging the solar system sideways, and no one invited it. The Sun is inching toward it like a moth to an old flame, and Earth is chasing the Sun like a loyal idiot. No one's going to notice at first. Clocks will lag. Seasons will wander. Migratory birds will get confused and crash into wind turbines. Then tectonics will start whispering. Then the gods will start muttering.

They already have. Zed, who usually mutters only when sober, called it "Ragnarök." Not because it is Ragnarök. But because gods, like humans, cling to old metaphors when faced with new problems. And because "The Slight Gravitational Misalignment Resulting in Incremental Temporal Drift" doesn't have the same ring to it. The point is: something big is pulling the strings now. And Earth, as usual, is late to notice it.

The gods did notice, of course. Eventually. Not because they're omniscient—please—but because things started going off-script. Prayers began arriving late. Scheduled deaths missed their appointments. A small war in Yemen refused to escalate, which was frankly offensive to the God of War, who had blocked off the weekend for it.

So they held a council.

Now, to be clear, divine councils are usually swift affairs. A few updates, some heavy wine consumption, and the occasional self-important monologue. But this time? This time, the arguments didn't stop. The wine ran out. Someone summoned a suckling pig as a joke and had it flung squealing back at them by a god who had become vegan. Because this time, it wasn't about politics or weather patterns or whether mortals should be allowed electricity near water. It was about Ben Callum.

Ben, to recap, is a perfectly unremarkable mortal who refuses to die. Not with fire. Not with lightning. Not with divine assassination attempts executed by literal perfectionists. Which means, according to the most awkward parts of the divine ledger, he's something else. An in-betweener. Not mortal. Not divine. Just inconvenient.

They can't kill him. Yet. But they can't agree on what he is either. And since labelling is sacred to divine bureaucracies, this is very distressing. So they debated for days. One god stormed out. One tried to vote twice. One spilt ambrosia on the voting tablets and blamed it on entropy. Eventually, through a combination of exhaustion, blackmail, and statistical threats from Fiona, they reached a consensus: Ben Callum would be tested.

The purpose? To determine whether he is becoming one of them. And if so, what sort of terrifying, rule-breaking, ledger-mangling godling he might become. Because here's the kicker: if Ben does ascend—and retains his current talent for not dying—he may be the first true immortal.

Yes, even gods die. They do it rarely, with flair, and preferably off-camera. But Ben? If this continues, they may have to invent a new category—something above the pantheon. And nobody likes reorganising the seating chart. Of course, they can't simply ask him to manifest his divine potential. That would not be polite. And it would be ineffective. So they opt for subtlety.

Trial One: Drive him insane.

Nothing flashy. Just enough whispered illusions, temporal loops, and reality glitches to nudge him into a padded room. If he breaks, he's mortal. If he doesn't—well, that's informative.

Trial Two: Frame him.

Choose a serious crime. Something that sticks. Let the mortals prosecute him. Ruin his life the old-fashioned way. If he's immune to mortal systems, too, then the gods really have a problem. The thinking is simple: if divine hands can't touch him, perhaps mortal ones can. After all, mortals are remarkably good at destroying each other when nudged in the right direction.

In the interest of transparency—or at least some illusion of order—a roll was taken.

Zed: Self-appointed chairman. One eye. All judgement. Symbol of endings, reluctant responsibility, and costly linen shirts.

Jamil: Death, balance, dread in tailored black. Would rather not be here. Absolutely here.

Diane: Precision incarnate. Also failure incarnate, apparently, which she's taking poorly.

Effie: Beauty weaponised—voice of conscience, which is ironic given her dating history.

Fiona: Chance. Probability. Owner of several casinos and the moral compass of a dice cup.

Ari: War. Conflict. Agent of chaos in flip-flops. Thinks this is all foreplay.

Posi: Tides. Trade. Tangled loyalties and better taste in yachts than mortals have in gods.

Others: Present. Occasionally vocal. Generally unhelpful.

The one conspicuously missing?

Muat—the God of Measure. Dead, apparently. Not that death among gods is ever simple. His seat remains empty, his silence increasingly loud. Why, who knows?

Let's talk about names.

Zed called it Ragnarök.

Now, before anyone starts stockpiling canned goods or brushing up on Norse mythology, let's clarify: this isn't the Ragnarök. Not the full-flavoured, end-of-days variety with wolves swallowing moons and gods wrestling sea serpents. That version? Glorious, yes. Also, far too organised. No, what the gods meant by Ragnarök was more metaphorical. A placeholder term. The divine equivalent of writing "???!!!" in the margins of a prophecy.

In the original myth, Ragnarök is a cyclical event. Not so much the end, but the reset button. The point where everything collapses just enough to start over, ideally with fewer idiots in charge.

Mortals interpreted it as apocalyptic. Gods understood it as administrative. This current situation? It had all the makings of a warm-up act. The sky hadn't fallen, but it was leaning.

The actual celestial culprit—the brown dwarf sidling too close to our solar system like a drunk guest at a dinner party—was discovered by a mid-level astronomer in Chile who, according to office gossip, had been trying to quit caffeine for the third time. His name? Dr Colin Fenris. Yes. Fenris. Like the wolf fated to devour Odin during the real Ragnarök. You can't make this up. But he did. Or so he thought.

His initial calculations were cautious. A slight deviation in stellar parallax. Infrared oddities. Nothing screamed impending mythic upheaval. So he did what any responsible scientist would do: he drafted a carefully worded email to his supervisor. Then, through the dark art of premature keyboard confidence and a poorly placed "Reply All" button, he accidentally sent the file to his entire professional network. And we mean entire. NASA. ESA. A Canadian radio observatory where he once interned. A disgruntled physics teacher from Year 11. And, most crucially, the listserv for an amateur exoplanet-hunting forum called Space Bros, which had a disturbingly efficient alert system.

Within twelve minutes, the phrase "Rogue Star Confirmed. Earth Orbit Wobble Probable. WTF?" had been tweeted, blogged, memed, and stitched into a sweater by someone's online store. The star, naturally, was named after him. Fenris-401b. Which, as fate would have it, sounds exactly like an error report—your computer gives you when it refuses to cooperate.

And so, to summarise: A failed star is passing a little too close to home. The Sun is flirting with it. Earth is awkwardly third-wheeling. A wolf-named astronomer hit the wrong button. And the gods, predictably, are in crisis mode.

If this all sounds absurd, that's because it is.

But absurdity, as it turns out, has never been a reliable deterrent to reality. The balance is shifting. The council has made its decision. Trials set in motion. And Ben Callum—who still hasn't fully processed the last time someone knocked on his door—is about to find himself at the centre of a very elaborate, very ancient test that he doesn't know is happening.

Right.

Let's get back to it.

Chapter 7
The Madness

The letter came on a Thursday. Ben didn't open it right away. It sat on the fold-out table in the caravan, beside a chipped coffee mug and a half-eaten apple. He stared at it for hours—not out of fear, but because he already knew what it would say.

Dear Mr Callum,

After a thorough assessment of your claim, we regret to inform you.

He read the rest in silence. The reason was plain enough: missed payment. One month behind the month before the fire. A processing error. Policy lapsed. He rubbed his temple and exhaled through his teeth. "Course it bloody did."

The caravan door stuck in the mornings and groaned at night. It smelled faintly of vinegar and old laminate, but it didn't leak, and it didn't creak—and that was more than could be said for his burned arm. Home nursing came daily: an older woman named Gwen who smelled of tea tree oil and moved as if she'd once been a drill sergeant. She cooked. Cleaned and talked while she worked—always.

"You need protein," she said, shoving beans and toast onto a plate. "And sleep that lasts more than two hours."

Ben grunted. "If I had either, I'd be bloody unstoppable."

Gwen snorted. "You're not wrong." She left him with a tub of reheated casserole and a parting glance sharp enough to leave a mark. The silence that followed felt heavier than usual.

The caravan had come from Mick down the road. No last name, no paperwork. Just Mick. A wiry man with three teeth, endless baling twine, and a passion for mismatched socks.

"Don't set fire to it," Mick had said, mostly joking, as he handed over the keys.

"Not planning to," Ben replied. That was that. No questions. No sympathy. Just bush hospitality in its purest form—help without ceremony.

Amanda, the social worker, had kept her word. A new Medicare card arrived. Then a plastic license with a lopsided photo. Centrelink letters. Bank cards with stickers that peeled like they were soaked in dishwater.

"Still no payout?" she asked, scanning the insurance response with the efficiency of someone who'd seen this a hundred times.

"Apparently, I stopped existing the month before the fire," Ben said, deadpan.

Amanda frowned. "You could appeal it."

Ben shrugged. "Could also teach a dingo to mind sheep." He wasn't angry. Not exactly. Just tired. Just another bite of the shit sandwich—and he'd learned to chew real slowly.

At night, when the air cooled and the hills darkened into blue silhouettes, Ben opened the laptop. The coordinates still pulled at him. Etched into his memory like a brand, impossible to forget, harder to ignore. He ran them through mapping software again. Still nothing obvious. One name came up in a footnote: Wintamarra. It wasn't on tourist maps, barely on heritage ones. But the deeper he looked, the more surfaced oral histories from the Adnyamathanha people—a dreaming site, according to some. No photographs. Just sketches. Whispers in old field notes scanned at low resolution. One paper mentioned "sacred ground," a place where the old people once looked up to the cosmos and spoke of things not meant for waking ears.

Ben sat back in the chair. The laptop fan whirred like a dying insect. "Perfect," he muttered. "Haunted coordinates and a junk insurance payout. What's next? Locusts?" But the page stayed open. He didn't close it. Not that night. Not the next. Something about the place had lodged itself under his ribs, deep and aching, like a memory with nowhere to go. He shut the lid and looked out at the hills, dark, silent, watching. "Alright," he whispered. "What the hell am I meant to remember?"

The next morning, it started with a knock. Ben froze mid-smoke. The caravan creaked softly behind him as he sat at the table, wrapped in shadow, limbs coiled tight like a spring that never quite uncoiled. He wasn't expecting anyone. Not the nurse. Not deliveries. No one even knew he was still here. Tap. Tap. It came again—soft, polite, absurdly civil. He opened the door.

A kangaroo stood on the top step, wearing stubby shorts and a fishing vest, chewing on a party blower like a cigarette. One eye twitched. Its left paw clutched a bag of frozen party pies. The other held a clipboard.

"G'day," the roo said. "Here for the thing."

Ben blinked.

"Just sign here," the kangaroo added, holding out the clipboard.

Uncertain, he signed it—then the bush erupted.

Animals spilled into the clearing like a stampede—but organised, festive, and very much on something. A convoy of marsupials hauling eskies, milk crates, disco balls. Possums with slouch hats. Goannas dragging amps. A platypus wheeling a generator behind a kid's red wagon full of sausages. Cockatoos overhead dropped glow sticks like paratroopers.

Ben tried to backpedal. The kangaroo was already inside. "Where d'you keep the oven trays, mate?"

Within minutes, the native fauna transformed the clearing. Tarp strung between trees. Lights zip-tied to branches. Plastic folding tables buckling under the weight of iced sponge cake, twisties, meat pies, and thirty-five brands of soft drink that hadn't existed since 1994. No one asked permission. They just acted like this happened every week. An echidna with a mullet sprayed shaving foam on a wombat and chased it in circles. "Foam Fight," someone screamed.

Ben sat back down in his caravan and smoked another cigarette. Then another.

Outside, chaos blossomed. A wallaby stacked twelve milk crates and climbed them while blindfolded. Two galahs argued over who invented fairy bread. A sugar glider did a shoey out of its own tail. A group of bilbies was chanting around a slowly rotating washing line, as if it were a pagan ritual. One of them had clearly drawn a pentagram in sunscreen. A cassowary screamed at the stereo until it played its favourite track. When it did—"Thunderstruck"—it began headbutting trees in time with the beat.

Ben watched it all from the shadows like a man observing his own funeral.

Then came the bin chickens. A full flock. Twenty strong. Drunk on lemonade and power. They descended like Hell's own council workers: screeching, flapping, immediately knocking over the bins and dragging rubbish through the clearing like sacred relics. One wore a traffic cone on its head like a crown and was declared "Lord Honk Honk" by the crowd. Another skateboarded through a trestle table, yelling "Send It" before vanishing into a wheelie bin with a crash.

Ben clutched his cigarette so tightly it snapped in two.

The party swelled. Bigger. Stranger. Faster. The music became a swirling monstrosity—a mix of didgeridoo, polka, '90s pop, and angry kookaburra screeches. Lights strobed through the smoke of a snag fire that had gotten way out of control. Someone—he suspected a possum—was operating a leaf blower full of glitter. The bin chickens were now engaged in some break-dancing turf war. A goanna spun in circles with sparklers on its tail. A bandicoot ran past, screaming, "Who stole my mind? Give it back!"

Every time Ben thought it couldn't get more unhinged, it did.

A dingo mounted a pile of eskies and read out a list of grievances from a soggy napkin. A pelican played lawn bowls using frozen peas and a pineapple. The roo—the same one who started it all—was now arguing with a garden gnome like it owed him money.

A tree caught fire. Nobody cared. In fact, they started roasting marshmallows on it.

Ben trembled, crouched behind a plastic outdoor chair, arms wrapped around his knees like a bomb victim. He couldn't look away. Couldn't make sense of it. It felt real.

Too real.

Every smell, every crackle of fire, every discarded stubby underfoot—it all insisted on reality. And that was the worst part. Not that he was mad. But that this wasn't madness. That this was happening, and he'd slid into it without resistance.

By 5:45 p.m., the sky was purple, and the fire had spread to a second tree. A kookaburra was DJing now, shrieking over the beat while a snake with glow-in-the-dark stickers wrapped around it tried to limbo under a hosepipe. Lord Honk Honk bin chicken was on someone's shoulders, leading a chant about stealing the moon.

Ben whispered, "Make it stop."

And, as if on cue—it did. 6:00 p.m. The hour of return. The music stopped. The fire fizzled. The chaos arrested itself in a single moment of eerie, manufactured calm. "Oh crap," said the wallaby, checking a waterproof wristwatch. "Gotta jet. Trivia night at the RSL." "Yep, yep," nodded the wombat. "School run." "My shift starts in twenty," said the cockatoo, donning a hi-vis vest like it had been wearing it all along. They packed in silence. No rush. No panic. Just a tidy resignation.

Ben watched them go—one by one.

A few waved. Most didn't. Lord Honk Honk gave him a wink and a two-finger salute before stepping into a busted shopping trolley and wheeling himself into the bush, cackling.

The clearing was a wreck.

Ash from the fires drifted like snowfall. Beer cans everywhere. Melted plastic chairs. Someone had drawn a penis on his caravan using tomato sauce. One of the bin chickens had pooped directly into his kettle.

Ben stood in the centre of it all, staring.

The silence was worse than the noise. He lit a cigarette, then dropped it. His hands wouldn't stop shaking. A single sausage sizzled on a still-hot plate nearby. The tree continued to smoulder.

Then—music. It didn't start—it arrived, like a migraine in sound. Warped synth, pitch-shifted percussion, and a single, looped lyric that stuttered and surged through the bush like prophecy on vinyl: "You're going insane... You're going insane..."

Ben turned toward the sound, already knowing it wasn't going to make sense.

Out of the smoke rolled a shining silver Aston Martin. Toy-sized. Flawless. Ridiculous. It purred like a lion and lit the underbrush with its headlights—twin beams of surgical madness. The music blasted louder. And from the driver's seat climbed a fox. Small. Precise. Real. And yet impossibly regal.

He dressed like the final act of a divine opera—midnight-blue tailcoat with gold embroidery, ivory gloves, a crimson cravat pinned with a ruby that shimmered like wet blood. A silver-headed cane bounced against his side, twisted into the shape of a laughing vine. His shoes sparkled. His monocle glittered. His scent, when he drew near, was intoxicating—citrus, sweat, sandalwood, wine, and something older.

He climbed the caravan steps. Every movement was too smooth. Too rehearsed. Like he was in front of an audience that didn't exist, he sat across from Ben. Crossed one paw elegantly over the other, and smiled. "I've come to warn you," the fox said, voice like aged port over broken glass. "You're going insane."

Ben stared. He was no longer sure if speaking would help or hurt.

The fox glanced toward the horizon as if it bored him. "It's always rabbits or horses," he said, more to himself than Ben. "Rabbits know the shadow's name before it even falls. They vanish. Cowards, yes—but clever ones." His tone darkened. "Horses? They burn. They gallop into flame. They die upright with their hearts thundering, convinced they can outrun the end."

His gaze shifted back to Ben—piercing, hungry. "One disappears. The other never learns." A beat. "Which are you, I wonder?"

Then something shifted. Not in the fox—but in the room. A stillness. Heavy. Subtle. Not cold, but watching. Not divine, not even spiritual—just other. The fox noticed it too. His paw twitched near the cane.

And for a moment—just a moment—his eyes changed.

Ben saw it. A reflection of something vast. A mask of fur and silk ready to fall. A shape inside the shape, curled up like a storm waiting to scream. Something ancient and obscene stirred beneath that tailored skin. Something the fox wanted to unfold. Ben felt it in his marrow. The moment just before terror becomes prophecy.

The fox leaned forward. His mouth opened. But the stillness didn't blink. And neither did Ben.

The fox paused. He exhaled. Closed his mouth. Straightened his jacket with a precise tug. Then reached into his coat and retrieved a white envelope. He placed it gently on the table.

Ben, voice dry as ash, asked: "...Who are you?"

The fox looked at him. For a second, truly looked. And said, as if reciting the lines of an ancient play: "This is not how this works."

Then he stood. Hefted his cane. Descended the steps, slow and smooth, and just a little too proud. The music resumed. The song's voice stuttered over a wave of percussion like a seizure translated into sound. The fox entered the Aston Martin. The engine snarled once. Then the car spun a tight circle in the ash, throwing embers skyward, and vanished into the smoke.

Ben looked down at the envelope. Inside: a torn scrap of paper. Two words, printed in off-kilter type: *shoosh* and *shoo*. He turned it over. Blank. In the distance, a kookaburra began to laugh again. This time, it didn't stop.

The tree had stopped smouldering. That was the first thing he noticed. Not because it mattered, but because it didn't. It was just static in the machine. A variable with no function. Like the sausage. Like the glitter. Like the milk crate pyramid now half-collapsed and pissing warm Solo into the dirt.

Ben hadn't slept. Couldn't sleep. His thoughts looped like a skipping record. Except it wasn't music, it was static. A raw electric buzz at the base of the skull that refused to mute. It told him things he already knew, but in the wrong order. Words like *shoosh* and *shoo* ricocheted around his frontal lobe. He tried to write them down once, to exorcise them, but the letters rearranged themselves into shapes he didn't recognise.

At 5:13 a.m., he vomited behind the caravan. Clear bile. It steamed in the cold. He stared at it too long.

Then he began to clean. Not for comfort. Not even for order. To make the world obey again. He started with the cans. Hundreds of them. Flattened by foot, pecked by beak, each one a tiny metallic echo of something he didn't want to name. He picked them up methodically, sorting them into piles by brand, then again by size, then again by dent pattern.

Next: plastic chairs. Melted. Bent. Some fused into abstract shapes that suggested motion or a scream. He stacked what he could—the rest he buried under a tarp. Then the esky guts: loose ice, floating sausages, half-bags of peas, a single yoghurt melted into a flaccid corpse. Each item was treated as forensic evidence. His mind kept slipping.

At 7:42 a.m., he found himself standing in the clearing with a dustpan full of glitter, unsure how long he'd been there.

By 9:10, he'd rearranged the milk crates into a perfect grid and then destroyed it. Then, he built it again, one inch to the left.

By noon, the party was gone and scrubbed from the land like a shameful story. Nothing left but dead grass and disturbed earth. Even the wheelie bins were back in place, except for the sauce.

The penis—he hadn't seen it. He'd cleaned the door. The handle. The windows. But not that panel. Not the tomato-red cartoon cock drawn with the flippant confidence of a bin chicken with something to prove. And he didn't see it now. Because he was inside, scrubbing the inside of the kettle with a toothbrush. Because he was bleaching the taps. Because he was alphabetising the labels on the canned food by expiry date, brand, and salt content.

Every time a thought spiralled, every time the fox's voice rang in his ears, or the fire screamed in reverse, or the DJ kookaburra screeched through the blender-beat. Ben gritted his teeth and redirected his hands. Clean. Wipe. Sort. Breathe. Rinse.

By mid-afternoon, his knuckles were bleeding. His eyes wouldn't close. Couldn't.

Even blinking felt dangerous. Every time he did, he saw animals. Not the ones from the party. New ones. Watching, judging, and waiting for him to admit it.

You're going insane.

He whispered the words aloud, just once, to see how they felt. They landed like gravel in his throat. So he swept. He wiped. He reordered.

The sun began to set. He couldn't remember if he'd eaten. He was pretty sure he hadn't peed. Somewhere in his chest, adrenaline kept the engines running. If he stopped, he feared his thoughts would escape again, slip through the cracks, and unravel the whole show.

As the final light faded, Ben sat outside the caravan. A single cigarette between shaking fingers. He didn't light it. Just held it like a relic.

The clearing looked normal. Empty. Deceptively sane. And yet he knew with the calm certainty of someone who had stood in madness and nodded politely at the hosts that this was a performance—a dress rehearsal for a life that would never be the same again.

Tomorrow, Gwen would come. And she would look. He had one job now: Pretend. And he almost had it. He nearly did, except for the penis.

Monday arrived like it had a right to. Ben stood in the kitchen alcove—shirt on, hair damp, kettle boiling, arms steady. Steady-ish. He hadn't slept. Not really. Maybe ten minutes. Perhaps nothing at all. But the kettle whistled, and the toast was already buttered, and he was wearing pants. That counted for something.

He breathed through his nose. The table was clean. The caravan was spotless. The bins were out. The rug vacuumed with a handheld device he'd found in the wreckage of a yard sale. Everything in its place. He'd even cleaned the tops of the cupboard doors. Who cleaned the cupboard doors?

Gwen's car crunched up the gravel.

Ben adjusted his shoulders. Rolled his neck. Smiled at the mirror with a practised ease that made him look like a toothpaste ad for the recently bereaved.

He opened the door before she could knock. "Morning," he said.

Gwen stepped out, clipboard under one arm and a plastic tub of supplies in the other. She didn't smile. She looked at the caravan, then at him, then at—she stopped—dead stop.

One foot was still on the step. Her eyes had locked onto the side panel. The one just to the left of the doorframe. She tilted her head slightly. Brow lowered. Her eyes narrowed, slowly, like a fax machine processing sin.

Ben didn't move.

There, bright as a bastard sunrise, was the tomato-sauce penis. Still there. Still smug.

"Oh," Gwen said. Nothing else. Just oh—but it held multitudes.

Ben's mind exploded into static. Say something. Say anything. "That's not mine," he said. "Came with the van."

She didn't move. Didn't even blink. "You've cleaned everything else," she said. Her tone was flat, but the weight of it pressed like a thumb on a bruise.

Ben swallowed. "That's Mick's penis." Silence. He felt the sentence hang there. Awful. Absolute. "I mean—he put it there," Ben added, too late to save himself. "He was proud of it. Called it his best work. Took real artistic ownership."

Gwen turned her head slowly. Looked at him. One brow lifted. "You didn't think you should clean it?"

Ben shook his head. "Didn't seem right. It's not mine to clean."

A pause. She looked at him. Really looked. And then—with the most minor shift of her lips, a spark behind her eyes—"What," she said, "not good enough?"

The question landed like a pin through silk. Ben exhaled—shaky, but smiling now. A low laugh cracked out of him. Gwen joined him, short and sharp. That was it. They said no more. She stepped past him into the caravan. The air changed. Just enough. And when she was gone, when her tyres had faded down the track, and the quiet settled again, Ben sat.

Let his shoulders fall. And for the first time in days, he slept.

Chapter 8
The Murder

Time slowed after Gwen stopped coming. There was no fanfare to her exit—just a note in the letterbox saying she'd signed him off, the handwriting looped and clinical. Ben stared at it for a while before slipping it into the drawer beside the cutlery. He didn't need it to remember. He could still smell the tea tree oil she wore, still hear the scratch of her clipboard against the laminate counter.

Now, the days fell open like blank pages. He kept to small rituals—things that made sense. Toast in the morning, two sugars in his tea, walking the gravel path behind the caravan park to the rusted fence line and back. He wasn't sure when the ritual began or if it mattered, but it gave the hours shape. He swept the floor even when it didn't need it. Wiped surfaces no one touched. Sometimes he spoke aloud to the radio—not to fill the silence, but to keep a rhythm. The static between stations felt less random than it should.

The caravan creaked in the wind, a language of its own. At night, it whispered more than it groaned. And then there were the signs. Not big ones. Nothing dramatic. Just oddness. A single black feather on the stovetop with all the windows closed. A cicada emerging in winter. Three ants walking in a geometry across the windowsill. He didn't always notice them straight away. But when he did, they lingered. Quiet, echoing oddities that seemed too frequent to be dismissed.

He wasn't looking for meaning anymore. Meaning had become slippery. Instead, he watched. Noticed. Sometimes that was enough.

The penis on the side of the caravan stayed longer than it should have. Tomato sauce, sun-baked into the metal. At first, it was a punch to the ribs every time he saw it—bin chicken graffiti—that became an idiotic masterpiece. Then, somehow, it became reassuring; a reminder that something had happened, real, and not imagined.

On a windless morning, with no clouds in the sky, he cleaned it off—not out of shame. Just because it was time. He used a sponge and warm water, wiping slowly, like a man washing dust from a headstone. The sauce came off in streaks. The stain, faint but discernible, remained. He let it. The act didn't fix anything. But it settled something.

It was around this time that he began reading again. Proper reading, not headlines or news tickers, but old things. Mythologies. Oral histories. Forgotten cosmologies that weren't so much explained as lived. It started with a name—Tiddalik—just a stray memory from primary school. A frog that drank all the water until the land cracked. A trickster. Or a cautionary tale. Or both.

From there, it spiralled. Australian Aboriginal lore led to Native American emergence myths, to Inuit breath-souls, to Polynesian navigation gods, and Japanese forest spirits. Ben didn't pursue them with purpose. They seemed to find him. Tabs opened themselves. He followed where they went. He made notes, not to remember, but to arrange. As if by drawing lines, the noise might form a shape.

Some days it did.

He found resonance in the Vedas—stories layered so deeply they circled back on themselves. Hindu time, where ages were counted in millions, and gods destroyed not out of cruelty but necessity. In Sumerian clay tablet fragments, he read about Inanna's descent—not just into the underworld, but into herself. In the Haida raven stories, he saw cleverness without morality. In Chinese flood myths, redemption without apology.

The names changed. The bones didn't. And all the while, the world outside remained quiet. A few birds. Wind across the scrub. Gravel shifting in the heat. But inside, in the caravan, a web was being strung between cultures, timelines, truths. He didn't always know what he was building, but he could feel it growing.

Patterns emerged. Small ones. Coincidences that didn't feel accidental. A phrase in a Sumerian hymn echoed a line from an old Papuan chant. A motif in Japanese shrine architecture mirrored the spiral glyphs of ancient Anatolia. The logic didn't hold. But the shape did.

Sometimes, when he chased a lead, it simply vanished. A link died. A source redacted. The page refreshed and came back blank.

Not every time.

Just often enough. Ben didn't think it was censorship. Not the kind with fingerprints. It felt older. Like the system itself—reality's back-end—refused to give certain things away unless you'd earned the question first. He began to sense that some knowledge required a key. Not a literal one. Something subtler. Context, maybe. Or readiness. The stories didn't seem to mind being seen. But they resisted being solved.

His nights changed. He slept less, but not restlessly. He'd sit under the awning with a cup of cold tea and let the stars blink at him. They no longer felt distant. They felt indifferent, but present—like ancient cats watching a wounded bird drag itself in circles.

Sometimes the smell of smoke came through the mesh screen. Not fire—just the memory of it. His arm, half-mended, would tighten. Not in pain. Just an acknowledgement. That part of him was different now. He began to forget what day it was. It didn't matter. He remembered the gods, though—not the ones from temples or Sunday school, but the ones that came barefoot, wearing masks, with knives tucked into their stories. The ones that weren't worshipped so much as negotiated with.

Then came the forum. It was a mis-click. He'd meant to open a glossary of Vedic epithets, but his finger jerked, and the tab landed elsewhere—on a pale, clunky site that looked like it hadn't been updated since the early 2000s. No branding. Just a black background, fluorescent blue text, and a single title in bold: ***Space Bros Forum—We Know You're Looking***. Ben hovered, ready to close it. Then he paused. There were no ads. No sidebar clutter. Just threads. Dozens of them. Each was labelled with titles that sounded like jokes—*Do Not Feed the Moon—The Ones Before Language—Weird Shit in the Van Allen Belt (No Trolls).*

He clicked one. The post was short. A few hundred words about a dream someone had of being inside a star that wasn't hot, only aware. The replies were stranger—half code, half poetry. A few were links to ancient PDFs, scans of hand-drawn charts, or references to books that didn't seem to exist.

Ben backed out and chose another thread. This one was titled: *Earth Isn't Broken, It's Just Misaligned.* It opened with a diagram—crudely drawn, as if traced by a mouse—with Earth slightly off-centre from a larger orbiting arc. The caption read:

The problem isn't gravity. It's memory. He didn't know what that meant. But he felt it.

The next morning, the forum was on fire. Thread titles were all-caps, timestamped within seconds of each other: *FENRIS CONFIRMED? — Woop Woop—It's Real, It's Close, and It's Worse Than They Thought. — 401b is Fenris, and the Chain Has Snapped.*

The posts inside were chaos—orbital models, deleted PDFs, screenshots from defunct observatory feeds. A few users argued it was a brown dwarf. Others said it was colder than anything they'd measured. One diagram labelled it *Fenris 401b* and overlaid the myth of the wolf star breaking its tether. *You can't see it because it's behind us. It's not coming. We're falling toward it. — This is the howl before the bite.*

Ben stared at the screen. Every word felt heavier than the one before.

He didn't notice how late it had gotten. He snapped out of it. Groceries. He needed groceries. He grabbed his keys fast and drove towards Springton, with the windows down and the radio off.

The heat clung to the road, rising in soft, invisible waves. The light had that strange, low tilt that made everything feel thinner. Unsettling. Then he rounded the bend past Mick's place—and saw the blue and red flashing lights.

Chapter 9

The Run

The turn onto Mick's road was instinctive. Ben didn't mean to take it. He had planned on groceries. Bread, milk, eggs—whatever would tide him over for another few days. But the car steered itself as if it knew something his conscious mind hadn't caught up to yet.

He saw the lights first, blue and red flickering among gum trees. Then the tape. The uniforms. The slow, deliberate rhythm of people managing horror. And finally, Mrs Greaves, the cat lady. She stood just past the mailbox, arms wrapped tight around herself, mouth thin and flat, eyes glazed over with something worse than shock.

Their eyes met for only a second. But it landed like a punch to the soul. She didn't look at him. She looked through him like he was already a story. Already a mistake. Already guilty.

Ben didn't stop. Didn't wave. Didn't slow. He just kept driving.

The car felt too small. The air, too dry. The moment, too real.

By the time the road bent westward again, he knew. Not the facts. Not the specifics. But the shape of the thing. Something terrible had happened. And it had already picked him as the centre of its gravity.

Ten minutes later, he pulled off the bitumen onto a scrubby firebreak. Loose gravel skipped under the wheels, crunching like bones. He parked behind an abandoned water tank, cut the engine, and sat in silence.

His chest felt full of broken glass. The part of him that used to believe in reason—the part that would say, explain yourself, tell the truth, they'll understand—that part had gone silent.

Mrs Greaves' face had turned off like a light switch.

Ben stared through the cracked windscreen. It's already too late. The thought came like a fact. Not fear. Not paranoia. Something deeper. Something certain. He hadn't done anything. But that wouldn't matter. He was already the story they needed.

He got out of the car. Checked his pockets: keys, wallet, phone, thirty-seven dollars in notes, and a broken pencil. Not enough. He looked at the phone. It was still on. Still pinging. Still traceable. Without hesitation, he popped the SIM and battery, wrapped both in eucalypt mulch, and buried them under a rock. He snapped the screen in two on the edge of the tank and hurled the pieces into the trees. No goodbyes. No last texts. No digital breadcrumbs. This was the part where most people faltered. Ben didn't. Somewhere inside, something else had taken the wheel.

It wasn't long before the first police dispatch went out. Officer Dolan was the first responder on-site. He'd known Mick for years, always thought the man odd but harmless.

The scene inside was a bloodbath—no sign of forced entry. Just a dead man in his kitchen and the toast still blackening in the pan. And the neighbour's statement—Mrs Greaves was detailed. Vivid. Unwavering. *She'd gone to visit Mick. Knocked. The door opened; Ben Callum appeared, covered in blood. He didn't say a word and left running down the road.*

The system snapped awake. Warrants processed. Perimeters drawn. Alerts were issued to traffic cams, toll booths, and train stations. His photo was queued into license plate recognition and facial matching. And yet, for reasons no one understood, the net came back empty. Again and again. As if he had fallen off the world.

Ben moved on foot for a while, cutting across paddocks, slipping through fence lines, walking the banks of a dry creek bed. Every step felt deliberate. He stuck to the contours of the land—thought analogue. Stay off roads. Stay out of sight. Don't stop moving.

He didn't know where he was going, only that he couldn't return.

Somewhere around dusk, he reached the edge of a closed tourist trail—an old vineyard walk now overgrown and marked with rusted signage. He paused beside a trail map, pulled out the dog-eared road atlas he'd snagged years ago as a joke, and started plotting. Most people, in a panic, would head for cities. Ben headed the opposite way. The atlas showed a network of fire tracks, disused service roads, and forgotten rail lines that cut through the hills like old scars. He traced a route in pencil. If he moved fast and stayed lucky, he could be gone by morning.

At a service shed near a stock gate, Ben found what he hadn't dared hope for. A motorbike. Dirt-caked, sun-bleached. But whole. The key was hidden in a hollow of corrugated iron—one of those local tricks known only to the ageing and half-drunk. He started the engine. It coughed. Choked. Then caught. The growl made him flinch. But it was motion. Freedom. He coasted down the gully and took off.

Somewhere on the fringes of the containment zone, officers at a roadside checkpoint adjusted their setup for the third time. First, their radios had dropped out. Then the mobile link glitched. Then the drone footage buffered and looped endlessly, showing the same empty highway stretch over and over.

None of them knew why. Some blamed outdated systems. Some suspected local interference. No one asked the deeper question: Why him? Why now? How Ben stayed ahead, with the world folding in his favour—but only just.

No gods yet.

Ben rode fast. Not reckless. Fast with purpose. Like the wind wasn't chasing him—it was carrying him.

The dirt bike jittered over ruts and hollows as he snaked across dry reserve land, avoiding fences, roads, and known paths. The trail narrowed. He pushed harder. A rabbit darted out. He missed it by inches. He kept going. A fallen branch snagged his foot. He let it drag for a second, then kicked loose without slowing.

A truck grumbled in the valley below. Headlights swept the treetops.

Ben cut the engine, let the bike glide to a stop beneath a canopy of stringy-bark, and crouched low. He dragged a tarp over the bike—one he'd yanked from the service shed—and tucked it with old logs. It wouldn't pass close inspection, but from the road, it would look like brush.

He waited.

The truck passed—no police decals. No sirens. But he'd learned not to wait for the noise. It was what came quietly that posed the real danger.

At the police station, an uncomfortable silence was forming. All the right systems had been activated. The alert went out across the state. Surveillance tools were in motion. Patrols positioned. Eyewitnesses briefed. And still—no trace.

The name *Ben Callum* showed no activity after 16:03. His phone disappeared. His car had not crossed a single checkpoint. His banking had ceased. No CCTV hits. Not even a blurry shadow.

One sergeant stared at the case-board and muttered, "He didn't vanish. He unravelled." It made more sense than anything else.

Ben's legs burned. The ridge trail he'd taken was loose, flinty, and covered in windblown debris, not meant for feet. Definitely not meant for flight. He paused long enough to down half a water bottle and tear into a muesli bar. His hands trembled as he ate. Not from fear. Not anymore. He felt something else now. A strange clarity. Like the rules had changed, and he was only beginning to see them.

Not long ago, he'd believed in order. Logic. Systems. Now? Now he didn't know what to think. Only that something—something vast and silent—was walking just behind him, and it was not unfriendly. Not a voice. Not a ghost. More like gravity with intent. And when he listened closely, he could almost sense it moving things out of his path, bending time by seconds, seconds that saved him again and again.

Downhill, a patrol had stalled at the creek crossing. Flood debris had blocked the culvert and shifted the bank. What should have been a straight drive became an hour's delay while they detoured thirty kilometres around the obstruction. By the time they reached the original fire track, it was empty. Dust. Tracks. Nothing else. One officer scowled and checked the drone link. Static. Again. He shut the lid on the control tablet and rubbed his eyes. "Something's screwing with us," he muttered. His partner just nodded. "Or we're chasing a ghost."

Ben walked the rest of the night. Past the town of Keyneton, past the grazing lands where sheep lay curled like stones, past fences he didn't touch and dogs that didn't bark.

He reached an abandoned orchard at dawn. It was wild and ragged, smelling of iron and decay. But it had shade, and rotted crates for cover, and birdsong so loud it drowned thought.

He ate the last of the jerky and buried the wrapper.

He would need a new plan. A disguise. A shift of shape. People remembered his face. His height. The way he moved. So he would change those things. Bit by bit. He found an old trailer park on the map—long closed after bushfire damage, but still marked. It was only twenty clicks north, just off a long-forgotten logging road. If he could reach it, he might scavenge. Clothes. Tools. Something to erase the man they were looking for.

He set out.

In Adelaide, a file was handed to a detective. It came quietly. No ceremony. Just an internal note with a red flag for follow-up. The kind of handover that usually means nothing. But the man who received it felt something in his bones. Like a shift in pressure. Like old dust stirred behind his ribs.

He flipped open the folder. Photographs. A name. A report. *Ben Callum*. He didn't know why the name unsettled him. It was just another face. Just another unlucky soul. But it pressed on him in a way few things did. A weight. A familiarity he couldn't name. Something inside him—something long asleep—stirred.

He turned to the window. Outside, a single crow landed on the railing. Its feathers shimmered violet-black. It tilted its head. Stared. And cawed once, sharp and flat, like a gavel falling.

Ben reached the fire-blackened trailer park just before noon.

What remained had long surrendered to the elements—shells of aluminium siding, melted tyres, and fragments of tarpaulin draped like skin across bones. It looked like a battlefield long forgotten by the world.

Perfect.

He moved through the wreckage with care, checking each hollow for snakes, squatters, or worse. Nothing. Just silence and ash and the breeze cutting through like breath.

In the corner of one half-melted van, he found a pile of rags and what might've once been a wardrobe. The clothing was smoke-stained, but wearable: a broad-brimmed hat, a pair of oversized corduroys, and a heavy, checked jacket with burn marks across the shoulder.

Ben changed.

He buried his old shirt beneath the rubble. Each layer of filth, each shift of shape, was a step further from himself. From the man they'd be looking for.

He pulled the hat low, adjusted his posture, and walked like someone older, heavier, and unsure of their steps. Then he picked his direction and didn't look back.

In the city, the detective stared at the photograph again. *Ben Callum*. There was nothing special about the image. A slightly too-long fringe, the haunted look of someone halfway to giving up. Not young, not old. Just another face in the crowd of the accused. But something in the eyes. That vacant intensity. It wasn't vacant at all. It was watching back.

He closed the file and set it on the desk.

His name was Ellery. He hadn't heard anyone use it in years. Most just called him "Detective" or "Sir." That was fine. Names were too permanent, too assumptive. Names made people think they understood who or what you were.

He sipped black coffee and glanced at the crow still perched outside the window. It hadn't moved.

Back in the hills.

Ben followed a forgotten fence line for an hour before breaking off toward a narrow rail easement. The ground had once held steel and sleepers, but they were long since removed. What remained was a dirt path, veiled by overgrowth, straight and narrow, unseen by cars or cameras.

It felt like walking a memory.

He passed three abandoned stations and a caved-in culvert before resting in the shell of a ticket office.

There, he slept, just for a moment. And in that moment, he dreamed. A courtyard made of mirrors. A woman with a face made of antlers. A bell tolling behind his eyes.

When he woke, his hands were clenched so tightly that blood pooled beneath his nails. He stood. Shook it off. Dreams were useless. He was still alive. Still moving, and that's what mattered.

Ellery stared out the precinct window. The crow was gone. In its place was a single black feather, caught on the window's edge. He opened the glass and plucked it free. It was warm. His fingers closed around it like memory. And that's when he heard it. Not a sound, but a pressure. The sudden shift in air density as it changed direction.

He turned. And she was there. A woman. Late thirties, maybe older. Lean, upright, her eyes too sharp for her face. She wore black like a practical tool. No nonsense. No vanity. No warmth. "Diane," he said. He didn't know how he knew that name. He just did.

She didn't answer. Just looked at him like an uncooperative witness. Then finally: "He's not who you think he is."

Ellery didn't blink. "You mean the suspect?"

"I mean the pattern." She handed him a slip of paper. Not an official document. Not a warrant. Just a fragment of something handwritten—sharp-edged symbols that pricked at his vision like static.

"What is this?"

"Orientation."

"To what?"

She turned away. "Follow the thread."

He looked down again. When he looked up, she was gone.

The next town was a blink-and-miss dot on an ageing map. It had a faded motel, a single servo, and a convenience store with a battered "OPEN" sign that looked more like a threat than an invitation.

Ben entered just after dusk. He kept his head low. Jacket high. Hands in pockets. He bought canned food, bandages, a bottle of iodine, and a disposable lighter—no small talk. No change counted aloud, just folded bills and a silent nod. The clerk didn't ask questions. That helped.

Ben moved on. He walked the outskirts, past irrigation pipes and rows of rotting fruit trees. Found a small shed with a broken latch and no windows. He sat on the concrete floor and finally let the silence speak. His body was exhausted. His mind was worse—caught in thought loops that flickered between possibilities he dared not name.

He didn't know what had happened to Mick. Didn't know if it was a frame job or something worse. But he knew the system. He knew how long it would take to prove innocence—years, if at all. By then, the damage would be complete. His life would be over. Name poisoned. And more than that—he didn't trust the world to play fair anymore. Too much had already slipped sideways—too many impossible moments. Crows watching. Dreams leaking into daylight. The word shooshoo echoed through thought like an old song without a source. He wasn't running from justice. He was running from inevitability.

Ellery sat in the dark precinct, the feather still in his coat pocket.

He hadn't spoken since Diane left. Instead, he'd pulled every document relating to Ben Callum and laid them out across his desk like runes. He didn't read them. He felt them—connections formed in negative space. The absence of data, the failure of systems, the speed of disappearance—it was all too perfect. Too clean. People don't disappear like that. Not unless something wants them gone, or protected.

He lit a cigarette. He hadn't smoked in eight years. But this night felt like it belonged to the past. The kind of past that breathes.

At 2:15 a.m., he opened a drawer and removed a field satchel he hadn't touched in over a decade. Inside were old tools, a notebook, and a folding blade with a carved handle. A gift from a man long dead. He clipped the badge to his coat but covered it with a scarf. There was no need to show his intent yet. He wasn't chasing a suspect anymore. He was chasing a feeling.

Ben wrapped his arm in bandages, covering a deep graze from a broken fence post. The bleeding had slowed, but the sting still sang when he moved. The pain was good. Grounding.

He closed his eyes and tried to recall his last conversation with Mick. Nothing meaningful. Just a passing hello. A shared complaint about the dry. It felt too ordinary to be final. Too ordinary to justify a death. Unless that was the point. Unless Mick was chosen for his ordinariness. Ben leaned back against the shed wall. What if the real story was deeper? What if it had nothing to do with Mick and everything to do with him?

In the bush, silence grew heavy. Wind shifted direction. The faint scent of ozone curled into the night. And far away—nowhere in particular, yet everywhere—a sound stirred. The faintest, distant echo. Of hooves.

Ben's feet ached. He had no sense of days anymore. Only motion. Forward always, even when circling. He hadn't spoken aloud in so long that it felt like language itself had grown brittle in his throat. But something had shifted. Not in him. Around him. Like a breath inhaled by the earth, like time itself had narrowed its gaze. He wasn't running from justice. He was threading the gaps—the ones too fine for machines or rules to follow. Every blind corner he passed safely, every camera that glitched, every dog that didn't bark—it added up.

He didn't ask questions anymore. He moved. He unmade the net behind him. Whatever was watching—whatever looked at him that moment—didn't belong to any god or man. It simply noticed him. And in that noticing, something else began to stir.

Miles away, in a low motel room layered with static air and blackout curtains, Ellery sat bolt upright. Not from a sound. From the absence of one. As if a silence had just ended that he hadn't realised he'd been living in.

He swung his feet to the floor. Everything in him was still—but not quiet. Something was unfolding in the dark behind his ribs. Not a memory. Not a dream. A pull. He'd felt it once before. A long time ago. He didn't know where. He opened his palm. There was nothing there, but the skin prickled as though a feather had just left it. He turned slowly to the mirror. His eyes held. Too long. Too deep. A feeling crept through him like recognition with no face.

Ben didn't stop. He couldn't. The world behind him was still working, still ticking, still hunting—but parts of it were breaking now, and that was no accident. He didn't know where this path led. He only knew someone had to walk it first. Someone had to tear the hole wide enough for what came next. The road turned to dust beneath Ben's boots. He hadn't planned the route—couldn't have, really. The roads that stayed intact weren't the ones on the maps.

He followed instincts now. Not the paranoid kind. Deeper. Animal.

A split in the trail revealed an old fire track. It had been used so little over the past decade, judging by the undergrowth. He stepped through it like it had been waiting. Here, no birds called. No insects hummed. No signs of surveillance blinked from distant towers. He was out of range. He kept walking. Every step was a defiance. Every breath was a refusal. The world was not built for people like him to move unnoticed, and yet—he did. Not because of cleverness. Not entirely. But because the world itself was changing and shifting, opening little gaps at just the right moments.

Once, he'd believed in chance. Now he didn't know what to think. But he knew this: whatever passed for chance in this world had taken a long, hard look at him—and moved aside.

Ellery scrawled the same line over and over in his notebook without realising it. Not words. Symbols. Sharp, jagged things. Almost Norse, but not quite. Not runes. Not letters. More like fragments of sound, if sound could be written in muscle memory.

He stopped. Looked at the page. What the hell was he doing?

The more time passed, the more he began to feel as if this case—this man—was less a file and more a key. A key to something buried inside him. Something he'd long ago agreed to forget. But it was rising now. On its own terms. And with it, unease. Not panic. Not confusion. A deep, bone-seated knowing: this wasn't just a hunt. It was a test.

Ben sat beneath a rock overhang, picking gravel from his palm. He hadn't eaten since the last can of soup the day before. His ribs ached. His back was sunburnt. One boot had split. But he wasn't dead. More importantly, he wasn't caught.

He thought back to Mick's porch. To Mrs Greaves' eyes.

To that single look that told him the system had already decided his fate. In those eyes, he saw the future. Bars. Years. Headlines. The erosion of his story into whatever the media needed it to be. He never stood a chance. And yet—he still stood. That was the difference. He wasn't fighting the system anymore. He was slipping past it.

In a bare conference room off a federal building, back in Adelaide, Ellery stared down at a wall of information and didn't see a suspect. He saw a fault line. He saw the rippling effect of a man who refused to be caught, even by logic. And in his gut, he knew this wasn't going to end with handcuffs.

This wasn't about a murder anymore. It was about movement. About the signal.

Ellery had spent his career watching for anomalies—those moments where the noise cracked just long enough for a message to slip through. Ben wasn't the anomaly. He was the message.

At dusk, Ben entered a small gorge, where granite walls rose on either side, and the air smelled of moss and history.

He set up camp in the remains of a stone hut no one had touched in fifty years. He chewed stale crackers and drank from a spring that came out of the rock like a secret. The air here was older. Charged.

That night, he dreamed again. Not of fire. Not of death. But of standing alone in a crowd of faceless people, and all of them were watching someone else—a man standing beneath a tree with no leaves. The man turned. And for the first time, Ben saw a face that looked like his own, but not quite. And from behind the tree, something stepped into the light. Not a god. Not a devil. A shape made of memory. And it looked at him. Not at the other man. At him.

He woke gasping. Clawed at his shirt. The air in the gorge had gone still. Even the wind had paused.

Chapter 10
The Skull

Ellery, back in his motel room, leaned against the bathroom sink. Cold water dripped from his hands. He stared at his reflection and spoke aloud for the first time in hours.

"He's not running." The words felt true the moment they left his mouth.

He dried his face and moved back to the desk. The symbol Diane had given him—etched on torn paper—now pulsed under the desk lamp. Only just. Almost imperceptible. But he felt it in his teeth.

She would come soon. He knew that. And he didn't know if she'd come to help him or use him. He had questions. And too many instincts screaming not to ask them. But the moment had passed.

Ben had done enough.

Now, whatever this was, it was his alone. Ellery didn't remember being assigned a partner. He remembered the phone call about the body—Mick, retired, known eccentric, found dead in his kitchen. Routine, by most standards. Quiet street, no signs of forced entry, toast still blackening on the pan. A neighbour saw someone covered in blood. Ran. Not much to go on.

The previous night he drove out, expecting a long night of bagging, tagging, and interviewing people who didn't want to be involved. What he didn't expect was her. She was already there when he arrived. Standing under the eaves like she'd been carved from the shadow itself. No uniform. No ID. Just boots, jeans, and a leather jacket that looked like it had survived a war. Her hair was tied back, silver-black glinting in the floodlights. And she was on the radio. His radio.

"Detective Ellery," she'd said, without looking at him. "You're with me."

He hadn't argued. He didn't know why.

Still didn't.

They worked until late in the night. She had no badge. No name. Just Diane, and that steady, offhand confidence that made everyone else assume she belonged. Even the station had adjusted—paperwork listed her as a liaison from an unnamed federal task force. Nobody questioned it. Not openly. Not even Ellery. And that, more than anything, unsettled him. Because deep down, he knew he should've questioned it.

"I want to walk the scene," she said the next morning, stepping out of the car before it had fully stopped.

Ellery watched her from the driver's seat. "Third time."

"Things shift," she said. "Bodies don't. Perspective does."

He climbed out, boots crunching on the gravel. The air still smelled like eucalyptus and burnt toast. The crime scene tape fluttered in the breeze, half-torn, like it wanted to give up.

Diane moved like she already knew where she was going. He followed. Not far behind. Never quite beside her. Always slightly out of step.

Inside Mick's house, everything had been processed, catalogued, boxed. But the space still felt loud. Like the dust remembered something it wasn't supposed to. Diane stood in the middle of the kitchen, not moving. Ellery watched her eyes. They didn't scan the room like he did. They searched the air—as if listening to something just out of hearing.

"What are you looking for?" he asked.

"Patterns."

"In the dust?"

"In the gaps." She bent to study the toaster.

"Who makes toast, answers the door, then dies without even turning it off?" he asked.

"Same person who lives alone and names his shed." Diane smiled faintly.

"Did you check the shed? Anything in it but rust and stories?"

"Mick had stories," she said. "Maybe one of them came home."

Ellery didn't know how to respond to that. So he didn't.

Back in the car, the radio hissed. They hadn't even left the driveway when the dispatcher's voice crackled through.

"Station to all units—note that's now four deaths in the last twelve hours, all unrelated. One DOA at the clinic, another in Tanunda Park, two more up at Mengler's Hill. No clear links.

Be advised, some chatter on community forums about a 'curse' or 'bad wind'—advise sensitivity."

Ellery turned the volume down and looked at Diane. She stared ahead.

"Ignore it," she said.

"Four deaths."

"Coincidence."

"Sure," he said. "And that bird flu last year? Coincidence."

"You believe in curses, Ellery?"

"No. I believe in patterns."

"Good," she said. "Then let's keep looking."

But his hands didn't leave the dial.

They drove in silence for the next fifteen minutes. The road curled through low gum scrub, the kind of landscape that made you forget the world had edges. Dust hung behind them like a trail they couldn't quite shake.

Ellery glanced at her sideways. She was calm. Still. But not relaxed. There was something coiled in her—something he couldn't name. She didn't fidget, didn't hum, didn't chew her lip like other people in thought. She just was. Like a presence pretending to be a person. And every so often, she'd tilt her head just slightly, like catching a whisper from a station no one else could hear.

At their next stop—Mrs Greaves' farm—a fence was down, and a stray dog had been spotted loitering near a carcass. Ellery knelt beside the gate. The carcass wasn't livestock. It was a fox. Whole. Unbloodied. Just dead.

Diane crouched beside him. "That's not usual—no signs of trauma."

"Any idea how long?"

"Not long. Maybe two hours."

He looked up at her. "That's recent."

She said nothing.

Ellery stood. "Do you believe in patterns, Diane?"

"I believe in cause and effect."

"That's a safe answer."

She gave him a look then—sideways, curious, amused. Like he'd said something she wasn't expecting. For the first time, he felt her gaze land on him—not as a subordinate. Not even as a threat. But as a question.

That night, he lay on his motel bed and stared at the ceiling fan turning above him.

The radio was on again. Chatter. Repeats. Static. Then, just before he clicked it off, a line slipped through: "...locals are reporting birds falling from the sky over the reserve. No toxicology results yet, but council warns residents not to—" Click. Silence.

He stared at the fan. Didn't sleep. Didn't dream. Just waited for the next death to call his name.

The café was called Jilly's, though no one named Jilly had owned it in a decade. It sat half-sunken into the side of the hill like it had grown there. Walls lined with faded tourism posters, chalkboard menus that hadn't changed since the nineties, and the hum of a fridge that threatened to die every third minute.

Diane picked the table near the window. Back to the wall, eyes on the entrance. Instinct. Ellery sat opposite, still not sure who had decided they needed breakfast. She ordered black coffee. He ordered toast and didn't touch it. Outside, magpies watched them like jurors. Inside, the air felt slowed. Not heavy. Not wrong. Just slightly delayed, like a word you forget mid-sentence.

"Been thinking about Mick," Ellery said after a while.

Diane didn't look up. "Don't."

"I'm serious."

"You're circling. Not thinking."

He paused. "You really believe this is all a coincidence?"

She stirred her coffee. "What would you prefer?"

"Explanation."

"Like what? Mass hysteria? Biotoxin? Black magic?"

"I'd settle for something that makes sense."

"That's the problem," she said, finally looking up.

"Things that make sense can still be wrong." Ellery leaned back. "Take you—you don't come across as a cop."

"I'm not."

He smiled faintly. "Right."

She raised an eyebrow.

"Still not going to ask who sent you?" he added. "I assumed you'd tell me when it mattered."

A small silence landed between them. It should've been relaxed. It wasn't.

The waitress approached—freckled, cheerful, barely twenty. She cleared a table, smiled without thinking, and disappeared into the kitchen.

The bell above the door rang. Someone left. Someone else entered. A child dropped a toy. A man in a booth coughed twice. And then something in the atmosphere tilted.

Diane's eyes flicked to the door. A half-second late. She sat up straighter. Not obviously. But Ellery caught it. He turned just as the man at the booth slumped forward—casually at first, like he was leaning in for conversation. Then, completely, his chin striking the table with a dull knock.

No outburst. No gasp. Just a slow collapse of attention around the room. A ripple of incomprehension. The waitress emerged, saw him, and froze. A coffee cup hit the floor.

Diane was already moving. Not fast. Not panicked, but wrong-footed. Ellery stayed back, watching her kneel beside the body, check vitals, and confirm what they both already knew.

Dead. No mark. No warning. No cause. The man had ordered scrambled eggs and died eating them.

Diane stood slowly. She looked at the floor like she'd missed something obvious. She never missed things. But this had slipped through her fingers before she'd known she was reaching.

Back at the table, she said nothing for a long time.

Ellery stirred his cold coffee. Finally, he asked, "What did he say?"

She blinked. "The man. Before he died?"

"Yes," Ellery grinned. "These eggs are to die for."

She shook her head. "No." He almost laughed. Then thought better of it.

The police arrived ten minutes later. Paramedics arrived a little after. Diane showed no ID, no badge. Just words. Tone. Presence. The officers deferred without question.

Ellery stayed outside, leaning against the car. Radio chatter crackled softly. Another death had been logged twenty minutes earlier. An older woman was found collapsed beside her garden hose. Still clutching pruning shears. Heart failure. Maybe. The operator mentioned three more calls waiting in the queue. Three. Unrelated. Scattered across postcodes. All inside the district.

He turned the radio off. Watched Diane through the glass. Her outline looked still, but he could feel the current swirling around her. She was off-kilter. She was hiding it.

When she rejoined him, she didn't speak. They stood in the gravel for a minute before he finally said, "You missed it."

She didn't answer.

"I don't mean the man. I mean the moment. You usually catch those, don't you?"

She lit a cigarette. No reply.

"Maybe it's just fatigue," he said softly.

"Maybe it's you," she said.

He looked at her, hard.

"That was a joke," she added, but there was no smile.

He nodded once. He didn't believe her.

They drove in silence for a long time.

Near the ridge line, she finally broke it.

"Do you feel it too? The shift? The pressure—like something's pulling strings from behind the curtain?"

He nodded.

She tapped the window once, like she was thinking through the glass.

"I've been in places like this before," she said. "Tense places. Unbalanced. Usually I can smell it before it lands."

"And now?" She hesitated, very quietly. "Something's blinding me."

Ellery turned to look at her. Really look. She didn't blink. Neither did he. The air thickened. And somewhere in the trees beside the road, a bird dropped from its perch.

The man's name was Howard Hartley. Retired butcher, early seventies, skin like flaking parchment and fingers thick from a life of cutting. He sat at his kitchen table with the blinds drawn and an oxygen tank hissing softly beside him.

"I saw him," Howard said, tapping a shaky finger on the wood grain. "Your boy. The one from the telly."

Ellery leaned forward. "You're sure?"

"Sure as shite. Down by the shearing shed three nights ago. Stood really still. Like he was thinking. Then gone."

"Gone where?"

"Just gone," Howard said. "Not like he ran. Just..." He snapped his fingers. "Gone. Pfft. Into the dark."

Diane stood in the corner, arms folded, not speaking. Watching. Measuring. Ellery didn't like the way she watched people—like they were chess pieces trying to act like dice. He refocused.

"Could it have been someone else?" he asked.

"No. Not unless someone else walks like they're half dead and don't know it."

Ellery frowned. "What do you mean?"

Howard wiped his nose with the back of his hand. "He looked wrong. Not scared, not sick. Just borrowed. Like he was holding someone else's shape."

Diane's head tilted slightly.

Ellery pressed. "Did he say anything?"

"No. Just looked straight at me. Like he was measuring me, not the other way around."

They asked a few more questions. Took no notes. Howard's details didn't help—no direction, no vehicle, no time of day beyond "after dusk." But still, it was the closest thing to a sighting they'd had.

Then Howard coughed. Once. Hard. Then again. Wet.

Diane's expression sharpened. She took a half-step forward.

"Mr. Hartley?" Ellery said.

Howard's eyes rolled upward. He slumped to the side—silent, instant. One hand still resting on the oxygen valve.

Diane moved first. Checked pulse, airway. Nothing. Ellery watched her hands. Precise. Swift. But something was off. Too late again. She knew it. He saw it land behind her eyes.

Back in the car, the tension clung to them like smoke.

"Coincidence," Diane said.

Ellery didn't answer.

"Lung condition," she added. "Oxygen failure. Weak heart."

"There was no panic in his face," Ellery murmured.

"He was old."

"So's the ocean," Ellery said. "Doesn't mean it forgets to drown people."

She didn't respond.

He didn't push. The car was quiet but buzzing. A radio they'd forgotten to turn on crackled faintly, then fell silent.

Later that evening, the motel pressed down on him like a thick blanket. Diane had commandeered the other room beside his. Doors thin as an apology. He could hear her walking. Then water. Then silence.

Then a knock.

He opened the door. She stood in the frame with a bottle in one hand and two glasses in the other. Wearing a different jacket—softer, darker. Hair still damp from the shower.

"Drink?" she asked.

"Is this tactical or social?"

She tilted her head. "You tell me."

He stepped aside. She entered without waiting.

They sat on the bed. Not close. Not distant. The whisky smelled expensive. Tasted older than either of them admitted to being.

"No toast?" he asked.

She smiled. "You don't strike me as sentimental."

"You don't strike me as spontaneous."

"Flattery," she said, sipping. "That's new."

The glass clinked as he set it down. "Why are you here?" he asked. "Really."

Her eyes flicked to him, then away. "Same reason you are," she said. "Something doesn't fit."

"Ben?"

"Maybe. Or maybe the universe has a new trick."

"And you don't like surprises."

"I don't like things I can't sense." She looked at him over the rim of the glass. "Same as you... Something is hiding from me."

"That supposed to bother me?"

"No. But it bothers me."

The air between them tightened. She leaned forward slightly—just enough. Not touching and not threatening. Just closer.

Her voice dropped a note. "You're hard to track, Ellery."

He didn't move.

"You don't ask questions. You don't dig. You float."

"Does that make me dangerous?"

"It makes you... curious." She lingered on the word.

Ellery held her gaze. "Is this how you work?"

"Depends on the quarry."

"You think I'm quarry?"

"No," she said, softly. "Not yet."

She stood suddenly. Not abrupt. Just decisive. Glass still in hand. At the door, she paused. "I dreamt about birds last night," she said. "Dead ones."

"That doesn't sound good."

"No," she said. "What bothered me was that I felt nothing."

She left without closing the door behind her. He watched the dark hallway for a long time. Then closed it gently, as if afraid to wake something.

In the morning, he'd find the police scanner filled with chatter. A nurse had gone missing during her shift. A jogger was found dead beneath a tree with his earbuds still playing. And Howard's death—though medically explainable—had already sparked a half-dozen conspiracy posts on local forums. Too many threads. Too many cuts in the fabric. And Diane. Diane wasn't asking the right questions anymore. Or maybe she was—and didn't like the answers.

The day started like it had something to hide. Low clouds over Nuriootpa, wind through the gums too fast for morning. The bakery was half-shuttered, birds circling above the power lines as if the ground had gone wrong. Diane had said nothing since the radio report about the nurse. Ellery didn't press her. They drove into town under a hush neither of them acknowledged.

Their first stop was the community centre. A groundskeeper named Dev McLean had come forward with a grainy photo he thought might show Ben near the old service hall—hooded figure, mid-step, a shape like a smudge caught between fence rails. Dev was jumpy. Thin. Talked too fast. Wore his collar buttoned despite the heat.

"Didn't want to get involved," he said, scratching his jaw. "But it's not right, what's happening."

Diane let Ellery do the talking.

"You see anything else?" Ellery asked.

"No. But I felt something. Like a vibration. Like I was being measured."

"By who?" Dev's eyes flicked toward Diane. Ellery followed the glance. She didn't blink. Didn't smile. Didn't reassure. Just waited.

They were walking Dev back to his ute when it happened. The moment. It came sideways—through Diane. She froze mid-step. Turned. Head tilted, eyes scanning the air. Ellery felt nothing. But he recognised the look—the hairline fracture across her mask. Something was wrong. She moved fast—too fast for the moment to seem normal. Crossed the gravel to a young girl sitting near the centre doors, a melting ice cream in one hand, headphones in the other.

"Where's your mum?" Diane asked, crouching low.

The girl looked up. "Inside." Diane's head snapped up.

Then came a scream. Inside, behind the glass, a woman had collapsed mid-stride—head striking the corner of a display case on the way down. Diane moved like a blade. But not fast enough. By the time she reached her, the woman was gone. Eyes open. Lips parted. Still warm.

Dev stood frozen beside the doors, mouth ajar.

Diane stood over the body. Breathing hard—just once.

The paramedics took longer than usual. When they arrived, Diane didn't speak. Not to them. Not to Ellery. She walked out into the car park and leaned against the bonnet of their cruiser, arms folded, head low.

Ellery joined her quietly. "Too late again," he said.

Her jaw twitched. "I saw it coming."

"And?"

"It was already here."

He waited. Then: "You hesitated."

Her eyes lifted to him. Sharp. Cold. But uncertain. "I didn't know where it would land," she said. "It wasn't supposed to land there."

"You said you're good at this."

"I am."

He looked at her. Not accusing, just watching. That unnerved her more.

Back at the motel, the evening came slowly. They didn't speak much. Diane didn't eat. She didn't take off her boots. Just sat on the end of the bed, flipping a coin. Over and over. Same side, four times in a row. Then five. She stopped. Stared at it.

"Have you ever had your instincts betray you?" she asked, not looking up.

"I don't rely on them."

"You should."

"Why?"

"Because truth is never loud. It whispers. Gut-first."

He poured a drink. "Your gut seems confused."

She looked at him now. Longer than usual. "You're still here."

"You haven't told me to leave."

"I should."

"Why don't you?"

She didn't answer. Didn't need to.

Later, she stood in the bathroom doorway. Glass in hand. Eyes slightly glazed, not from the whisky, but from the grind behind them. "You don't talk much," she said.

"You talk enough for both of us."

She smiled, a crack of light. "That's dangerous."

"For who?"

She stepped closer. A slow, unhurried step. Not seductive. Just deliberate. "Tell me something," she said. "Anything true."

He met her gaze. Then said: "You're scared—you're not hunting the quarry. You're circling something that might be hunting you."

The glass in her hand didn't move. But something in her spine tightened. She didn't deny it.

Later that night, the air was electric. Silent. Every breath an accusation. She didn't knock. He didn't invite. They just existed in rooms too close, too thin-walled, too loud with heartbeat and the hush between them. She didn't sleep. He didn't blink. And out there, beyond the lights, something else died without anyone seeing. Another thread pulled. Another coin flipped. And no one knew whose hand was rigging the toss anymore.

The wind had teeth, dry, inland, restless. It slipped beneath the motel door like it was hunting something. Ellery sat shirtless at the edge of the bed, still, staring at his hands. The glass of water he held had gone warm. Outside, the stars were wrong—too bright, too far, too quiet. Something was shifting. It wasn't just Diane anymore. It was him. The nurse. The jogger. Howard. Dev's silence. Even the birds. All of it. All around him.

He'd heard stories. Old ones. Half-whispered by firelight. Unwritten. Of men who drew the grave in with every breath. Of silence that wasn't absence, but an announcement. He'd thought they were allegories. Cautionary tales. But maybe he was wrong.

Perhaps he was the story. Maybe he'd always been.

A soft knock. Diane. She didn't wait for a response. Just pushed the door open. She looked pale. Eyes darker than usual. A tremor in her jaw that would be invisible to anyone else. But not to him.

She stepped inside. Closed the door behind her. No drink this time. No jacket. Just the silence between predator and prey. Neither was sure who was which.

"You've been thinking," she said.

He nodded. "You've figured it out."

"Something," he said. "Not everything."

"What are you?"

"I don't know the name."

"But you know."

"Yes."

"And you know what I should do."

"Yes."

"Why haven't I?"

He looked up. "I think you were hoping you were wrong."

She didn't sit. She leaned against the wall, arms crossed, like she needed it to hold her upright. Her voice had changed. It had lost its blade, found its edge. "I've been trained to read people. To feel presence. To smell an imbalance before it curdles. But you—"

"I'm silent," he said.

She blinked.

He continued. "Not emptiness. Not void. Just the stillness that comes before the fall."

A breath. She uncrossed her arms. Took one step forward. Then stopped. "You remind me of that apocalyptic verse in the Bible."

He said nothing.

She recited it like scripture. "'And I looked, and behold, a pale horse: and his name that sat on him was Death. And Hell followed with him.'"

Silence.

She swallowed. "You've been beside me all week. And I didn't see it. I didn't feel it."

"You weren't meant to," he said.

She stepped closer now. Slow. Controlled. Like approaching the eye of a storm and hoping it didn't blink.

"I've failed before," she said. "Ben. The girl in Athens. The child in Saint Petersburg. But this?" Her voice cracked slightly. "I don't even know what this is."

Ellery stood. Slowly. Calmly. They were inches apart. She looked up at him. He didn't lean forward. Didn't breathe heavily. Didn't flinch. Just met her eyes with a stillness so deep it made her stomach lurch.

"You're not going to kill me," he said.

"No?"

"You'd have done it already."

"What makes you so sure?"

He looked down, not at her mouth or her hands, but at the space between them. The gap. "It's not fear you feel," he said. "It's awe."

That was the moment it landed. She blinked—and when her eyes opened again, she saw. Not the man. Not the detective. Not even the godling. But the thing behind the veil. The shape the world tries to forget until it knocks. And her knees nearly buckled. "You don't kill," she whispered.

"No," he said. "I offer."

"To whom?"

"To everyone."

"And if they say no?"

He didn't answer. He didn't need to.

She turned away. Suddenly cold. Hands trembling. She didn't want to be weak in front of him, but she wasn't sure she could be strong.

"I can't chase two storms," she said. "I thought I could handle Ben. But now..."

"You've seen too much."

"I've seen nothing," she snapped. "That's the problem. All week, I've been blind. And you've been next to me."

He walked over to the table. Poured a glass of water. Set it down without sound.

"You could still kill me," he said. "I wouldn't stop you."

"I think you would."

"No," he said. "But the world might."

She froze.

He added, "Balance has its own defence mechanisms."

She stared at him, trembling. But slowly, something in her expression shifted. Not into calm. Not into peace. But into understanding. A grim kind. Like someone realising they're no longer the hunter. Or maybe they never were.

"I should run," she said.

"You won't."

"Why not?"

"Because you've never met anything like me. And because some part of you is curious."

In the dark, neither of them moved. Not for hours. And outside, the wind stopped, as if listening. He took the moment to reach for her hand—gentle, tentative—feeling the tension in her stance and the emotion in her eyes.

She reached forward, hesitated, and then backed away.

Chapter 11
The Blade

Delilah Kitsune saw him before he knocked. She was kneeling in the garden, trimming rosemary under a pale, dusty sky, when she felt the stillness behind her—weight on the air, a shift in temperature that didn't belong. She turned her head slightly. And there he was.

A man stood just beyond the fence, right at the edge where the paddock met the scrub. Dust on his boots, a canvas backpack slung low, sleeves drawn to the wrist despite the heat. He didn't move. He just watched.

The moment sunlight touched his face, her blood ran cold. Ben Callum. She didn't need to check the burn across his left hand, visible for half a second as he adjusted his sleeve. She knew that face. The flyers were everywhere: café windows, the post office noticeboard, the servo. The local murder suspect. "Michael Petrovich, deceased. Suspect: Ben Callum. Armed. Dangerous. Full-arm burn, left side. Approach with caution." They had his photo pulled from a laptop—a passport headshot. But this version was leaner. Tired. Still very much alive.

She stood. Didn't run. Didn't speak. She padded back inside and locked the door.

Three knocks came soon after. Calm. Deliberate. Delilah didn't reach for her phone. She'd written the flyer herself: "*Ink by Del. Clean. Fast. Discreet. No questions.*" Pinned to the noticeboard at the Clare servo. At the time, it felt like a gentle lure. Artistic. Understated. Now it felt like an invitation to die.

She opened the door.

Ben stood still, his eyes scanning her face, reading it. Sweat slicked his hairline. His clothes were dusted with the colour of the road, and he didn't smile.

"You Del?"

She nodded.

"I need this hidden," he said, lifting his left hand.

She saw the burn now, clearly—knotted and stretched across the hand, trailing beneath the sleeve. The scarring was uneven, textured, and very visible.

"Up to just under the shirt line," he added. "Fast."

"I—" she began, then caught herself. Swallowed.

He held up his right hand. Unburnt. "Do something here, too. Something simple. Mirror the left. Make it look balanced."

"So people don't notice the burn?"

"Exactly."

Delilah stared for a beat too long, then stepped aside. "Come in."

The studio was small, quiet, built from the bones of a shearing shed. Clean white walls. Cedar floor. Shelves lined with inks and neatly rolled designs. A faint trace of sandalwood hung in the air. The room was cool but dry, and it was silent. Ben sat in the chair like he'd done it a dozen times before. Calm. Still.

Delilah pulled on gloves with a practised snap. *He knows he's being hunted,* she thought, *but he's still here.*

She sat opposite him, gently took his hand, and inspected the burn. It was healed but raw-looking—like the skin hadn't finished deciding what it wanted to be. Tattooing over it would be tricky.

"If you want this to vanish," she said softly, "it can't just be covered. It has to be camouflaged."

He looked at her. Silent.

She went on, voice a notch steadier. "In Japan, some burn victims—especially those tied to Yakuza or Samurai lineage—used specific ink-work to create illusion. Not to hide damage. To erase it. Flow mattered more than detail. Ink ran with the body, not against it."

Her hands moved lightly over his skin, measuring the direction of scars, eye movement, and tissue contrast. "You need something bold. Curved. Something that distracts the eye so it stops looking for what's underneath."

"Can you do that?" he asked.

"If I rush it, maybe. But it won't be art."

"It doesn't need to be art."

"You'll need to sit still."

"I'm good at that."

Delilah stood and crossed to her reference shelf. She flicked through a book—**Horimono: Sacred Skin**—until she found what she was looking for. A centuries-old piece. Shoulder to wrist. Black koi swimming upward into storm clouds. Not literal. Not ornate. Just motion. Motion is camouflage. If the eye is moving, it stops reading. She sat back down and sketched fast, adapting the Koi's fluid spine into something less figurative—like wind curling across grain, like tide lines over rock.

"This'll take under an hour if I keep it rough," she said.

"That's all I've got."

She paused. "And the right hand?"

"Something simple. A mirror. Doesn't have to match—needs to make people glance twice."

She nodded again, quieter now. He offered his burned hand. She took it. Then she turned on the machine. "You ready?"

"Do it."

The needle buzzed. Delilah moved carefully over the ruined skin of Ben's left hand, tracing each curve with practised precision. The scar tissue pulled awkwardly under her machine—slick in some places, stubborn in others—but she compensated with subtle shifts in pressure. He didn't move. He sat like stone, eyes half-closed, breathing slowly. His body was quiet, but there was something in his stillness—too controlled, like someone who had learned to live on the edge of panic without ever stepping over.

She reached for more ink—reflexively, automatically—dipping the needle into the well. Then her stomach dropped. The colour that bloomed across his scar wasn't black. Pink. A vivid, undeniable pink. Designed for soft shading and ornamental pieces—not for a burn disguise. Not for a wanted man's hand.

Her heart jolted. Her lungs locked. She'd left the pink open from the day before. A phoenix tail. A dream job. It didn't matter now. She had made a critical mistake. Ben didn't react. He hadn't looked. Delilah forced herself to breathe, face still. Hands steady. Her left hand slid under the workbench. Found the tiny button hidden just beneath the table lip and pressed it. Click. The panic button would send a silent alert straight to the Clare police outpost. A protocol she'd never used—until now. He won't know. He won't hear it.

She gently, casually wiped the skin, concealing the movement as part of the process. The pink ink had already set. It couldn't be removed. So she covered it. Layer after layer. She worked fast, densely, and elegantly in panic. Not clean lines—interference patterns. Lines that danced over the pink, drawing the eye in circles. Bold curves to mislead attention. Ink as misdirection.

Still, he didn't move. Didn't speak. But Delilah's chest tightened. Not from fear anymore. From something else. Heat. It ignited low, then spread. A coiled fire curling outward from her spine to her fingertips, through her jaw, down to her legs. Not fear. Not adrenaline. Recognition. Suddenly, she felt like her skin didn't quite fit. Like her blood was older than her bones. Like her memories were holding back something too large to carry.

Then came the knowing. Not all at once—just flickers. The tattoos she'd designed in dreams. The lectures on forbidden ink cultures she'd been obsessed with in uni. The moment she touched Ben's skin, her hand buzzed before the needle even met flesh. Her eyes lifted to his face. And in that exact moment—not vision, not delusion—something aligned. She saw him. Not as a threat. Not as a victim. But as someone like her. Not in flesh. In resonance.

Ben carried destruction inside him. Unwillingly. Unknowingly. The same kind of frequency that hummed just beneath her ribs now. And then, unbidden, she remembered another man. Not here, not now—but connected. Another presence. Another weight. She didn't know his name—but she would, someday. And as her breath caught in her throat, one truth settled over her like a veil: We are the same. All of them—Ben, the other, and herself—weren't devils. But they were made of something that breaks the world. And she had just summoned the world's guards to his door.

She finished the tattoo. Wiped the lines clean. The pink was buried—imperfectly, but invisibly. Her voice was calm when she spoke: "There was a flaw in the lower arc. I didn't have time to fix it." Ben didn't comment. Just nodded, already rising. She handed him a tube of ointment. "Use it twice a day. Don't scratch. You'll scar worse if you do." He took it wordlessly. Then she looked him in the eye and softened. "You need to go. Now."

"Is it that bad?"

"It's not bad. But it's close."

He paused—just a second—then gave a short nod. Slid a few folded notes onto the counter and turned. At the door, he looked back once. "Thank you."

"Run."

Delilah stood in silence until his footsteps were gone. Then she walked into the back room. Opened the chest beneath her shrine. Inside, wrapped in cloth, was the katana her father had given her. Black lacquer sheath. Oil-worn hilt. Folded steel that hummed in the air even before it was drawn. She unwrapped it slowly. Unsheathed it with reverent silence.

I called them. I have to be the one who answers. The fire inside her was no longer subtle. It was who she was now. The door clicked shut behind Ben, and the world stood still.

Delilah remained motionless for several seconds, hand resting on the workbench, blade still humming in her spine. The silence pressed in. A soft rustle came from outside—the wind moving through dry grass. She imagined him moving through it now, fast and quiet, already out of view. Then she heard it. Distant at first. A car engine was approaching slowly. Gravel crunching under rubber. Official tyres on an unofficial road. They didn't have sirens running. Of course, they didn't. Small-town cops didn't announce themselves when answering panic alarms. Not when they thought they were heading into danger. Not when they assumed someone inside might already be dead.

Delilah turned from the studio and walked calmly into the back room. The katana lay across the altar cloth, fully unsheathed, gleaming faintly in the low light. She ran one cloth-wrapped hand along the blade—not out of superstition, but to feel the grain of the steel, to centre herself. The warmth inside her was steady now. No longer spreading—just present. A second pulse.

She stepped out of the room and moved to the front of the house, drawing the curtain an inch to the side. The police car stopped on the edge of the gravel—one officer. Female. Mid-thirties, uniformed, one hand on her radio. The other was already resting on her sidearm. The cop scanned the house without approaching, reading body language. Waiting. Delilah knew the type. Not evil. Just trained. Just doing her job. Delilah didn't hate her.

But she knew what she had to do.

She stepped back from the window and laid the katana on the kitchen bench. The handle faced right. Her movements were smooth, efficient. Every breath deep and slow. The knock came thirty seconds later. Firm. Rhythmic. Not urgent. Just confident. Delilah didn't respond.

"Tattoo studio?" the woman's voice called. "Ma'am, we received an alert. Just checking in." Delilah counted five seconds, then opened the door.

The officer stood at the base of the steps, feet apart, hand still resting on her weapon. Her expression flicked—surprise, tension, then polite control. "Everything all right in there?" she asked.

Delilah nodded. "False alarm," she said softly.

"I pressed it by mistake. Was cleaning. Reached under the table."

"You alone?"

Delilah tilted her head gently. A gesture she didn't recognise as her own until it was finished. "Yes."

The officer's eyes narrowed.

"Mind if I come in and take a look around?"

Delilah didn't respond. She stepped aside.

The officer took it as permission and moved up the steps. That was her final mistake.

As the officer entered the narrow hallway, Delilah moved behind her—silent, fluid. The katana was already in her hand. Drawn without a sound. She raised the blade, both hands on the hilt, just as the officer turned slightly, sensing motion. Their eyes met. Delilah saw no evil there. Just a reaction. Just instinct. But she had no time for instinct. The blade moved like it remembered everything—a single cut—diagonal, clean, precise. No scream. The woman dropped hard, body folding before she hit the floor, mouth open but silent, eyes wide with betrayal and something else: Recognition.

Delilah knelt beside her, heart pounding, breath still calm. "I'm sorry," she whispered.

She watched the life leave the woman's face—not with glee, not with coldness, but with understanding. It was done. She cleaned the blade slowly, wrapping it in cloth and re-sheathing it in silence. Her pulse was calm. Her chest was warm. She didn't look away from the body. She didn't cry. There would be more.

Delilah Kitsune walked back to her studio, collected a single red fox stamp from her drawer, and pressed it onto a strip of masking tape. She fixed it to the inside of the policewoman's wrist. A mark for the others to find. Then she stepped into the rising dusk. She didn't linger.

By the time the officer's body cooled, Delilah had packed a go-bag with the precision of someone who'd done it before in dreams. Not real dreams—training dreams. Memories of blood-red lanterns. Of silent footfalls. Of centuries lived in others' minds. She left nothing behind that could identify her. No fingerprints. No hair. No blood. Only the tape on the cop's wrist. A sliver of masking tape pressed into the inside of the left forearm, marked with a delicate red fox stamp—tails fanned wide. Not quite Japanese. Not quite modern. Her mark.

Outside, the wind picked up. Somewhere down the road, a man was running. And behind him, the dogs were in the air before the sweat dried on his neck. Something was beginning to stir. Not gods. Not devils. Just those who carried the energy of endings. Ben didn't hear the alarm, but he felt the shift—the way the street recoiled from him, how the shadows closed in just a little tighter.

Delilah hadn't screamed. She hadn't reached for a phone. But something had gone out the moment he left her shop—a signal, a pulse. Silent, clinical, final.

The hunt was on.

He moved like a phantom, hugging walls, ducking bins, cutting through lane-ways behind rural homes with rusting chicken coops and sun-bleached trampolines. The sky to the north throbbed with the blade-like hum of rotorcraft. Not one. Two. Big ones. Searchlights in the distance already painted slow arcs across the edge of Clare.

She bought him minutes. Nothing more. That was all she could give.

Ben's mind cracked open under the pressure, not with fear, but with calculation. Where?

Where now?

He couldn't go home. Couldn't touch a bank. Couldn't circle back toward Wintamarra—that was a death trap now. They'd know. Of course they would. They'd have his IP logs, the forum access, and the timestamped Google Maps drop pin. Hell, they probably already had a ground unit watching the access roads south. Even the dusty backtrail he'd planned, the one that would have taken him quietly through Black Springs and then east toward Rocky Plain, had been compromised.

He saw it—clearly—as he passed a rusted gate with a sign reading "Private Property—No Shooting Pasture Stock." An empty polystyrene coffee cup rested on the post. Recent. Police issue. Someone had already been here. Might still be close. Ben veered off the gravel path and into the open paddock.

He walked until the stars came out. And then he walked more. No torch. No moon. Just intuition.

That whisper that always nudged him away from danger, though it had grown faint lately—muted by exhaustion, or perhaps by the sheer number of eyes now hunting him. The land turned shapeless. Every hill, a repetition. Every dry creek, a trick of déjà vu.

He couldn't risk roads anymore. Not even fence lines. Drones could read heat signatures now. Probably had satellites queuing his location in real-time. So he walked like a ghost through wheat stubble and sheep shit, dead fences and the rustle of mice. Everything dry. Everything the same.

Day broke like a punch to the eyes. His legs were already jelly. His mouth was a kiln. No water. No food. Just the taste of bile and desperation.

He found a stock dam mid-morning and stared at the algae-choked water for twenty minutes before cupping it into his hands. It tasted like copper and rotted grass. He drank anyway. Then he kept walking.

By day two, he was hallucinating. He saw Mick on the ridge-line—laughing, pointing at something. But when Ben blinked, it was just a scarecrow with a missing arm.

A fox stared at him once, unmoving, amber eyes steady in the heat shimmer.

He whispered, "You again?" But the fox didn't move. Didn't blink. Just watched him until Ben passed out behind a bush of salt-bush and bones.

Day three broke him. Not physically. That part had already happened. It was his sense of direction that died. He no longer trusted the sun. No longer believed in "west" or "east." Everything turned him in circles. Every track betrayed him. Even his own footprints betrayed him.

He screamed once—raw, animal, alone. Then, in the silence that followed, came a thought. A small one. Strange. Laughable. What if I crossed the water? Not metaphorically. Literally. A boat. A jetty. A port. Something no fugitive ever did. Not in Australia. Not in the bush. And yet. He chewed the thought over like dried leather. Something in it tasted right. Not safe. Not smart. But possible. Different.

The wind shifted. He smelled salt. Ben turned toward it. It was just a scent at first. Faint. Intermittent. Like sea spray blown through the teeth of a dying landscape. But it was enough. Enough to give the whisper in his blood something to anchor to. A heading.

Ben shifted course, dragging his feet through bleached paddocks and brittle grasslands, always toward that elusive promise of salt. He no longer moved with purpose—just with momentum. Like gravity was tilting him toward the coast. His legs bled from blackberry thorns. His skin blistered in patches—one shoulder raw from sun, one calf crusted in mud from a misstep into a boggy gully.

He carried nothing now. Not even the map. It tore in a windstorm the day before, and he let it go, watching it flutter off like a useless prayer.

At night, he found a dry culvert beneath a broken livestock fence. Slept with his back against the concrete and his knees to his chest. His breath stank. His vision doubled when he stood too fast. Still, he moved toward the salt.

On the fourth day, he came over a rise and saw it. Not the town—the shimmer. That low silver smear between sky and land. Not heat haze. Water. Real water. The Spencer Gulf pulled into view like a mirage that finally solidified.

Ben dropped to his knees and wept. His tears dried before they reached his chin. The next few hours blurred. He crept through the scrub, found a firebreak, followed it until he hit bitumen. At first, he panicked, thinking it was a trap. But the road was quiet. No tyre tracks, no drones, no patrols. Just the distant sound of gulls—and a town at the edge of everything.

Delilah had moved like a shadow, cutting through back paddocks and scrub as the last streaks of dusk faded to blue. The katana sheathed inside a canvas sling was slung low across her spine. The old ute she kept hidden beneath a weather tarp started on the second try. The tyres rolled onto dirt with barely a whisper. Headlights stayed off. She didn't need them. Not anymore.

By midnight, she was twenty kilometres from Clare. She drove through farmland and empty intersections, past fence lines and roadhouses where the radios whispered of the wanted man, and the tattooist who'd gone missing—"reports of a possible fugitive sighting north of Tanunda, unconfirmed. Authorities

believe—"
"—female business owner has not responded to calls—"
"—local officer unaccounted for—"

No mention of death. Not yet. They hadn't found the body. But they would. And when they did, she knew how they'd react. Because it wasn't just murder. It was execution.

She stopped at an abandoned shearing shed outside a ghost town called Hilltown—half-buried by dust and silence. She parked the ute behind the structure and entered with a blade in hand, testing the air. No scent of sweat or breath. It was clean for now. She pulled out her burner phone. It had one number saved to it—no name, just the fox emoji. She didn't know who had given her the phone, or when. Only that it worked. She typed: "1 down. More coming. He's not ready. I am." No reply. Not that she expected one.

She lit a single match and sat beside the iron brazier in the corner of the shed. Flames rose gently. From her bag, she withdrew three items: A sealed jar of ointment. A handful of black-and-white flyers—Ben's wanted posters. A child's drawing, wrinkled at the edges, signed in faded pencil: Papa's sword protects the fox. She stared at the drawing the longest. She didn't remember drawing it. But she had.

Somewhere far away, Ben was walking into another nightmare. And she, Delilah Kitsune, was no longer waiting to understand who she was. She was doing what must be done.

The second kill came the next night. A plainclothes detective, driving alone. She trailed him for three hours. She didn't know his name. Didn't care. His briefcase held a manila folder marked "*OP CULL*" and half a dozen photos of Ben with different hair lengths, doctored scars, and filtered overlays.

They were preparing contingencies and planning to trap him. They would never get the chance.

Delilah slashed his tyres at a petrol station outside Jamestown, waited for him to pull over at a rest stop thirty minutes later, then walked up beside his car with a false smile and an old tea thermos.

“Lost?” he asked.

“No,” she replied.

“Need a hand?”

“No,” she said again.

He turned back toward the glovebox. The blade slid clean through his neck before he ever drew breath. She cleaned his blood with care. Pinned a fox tape inside his shirt pocket and left his car idling.

By the time the highway patrol found him, she was back in the hills—watching wind turbines spin like slow machines of fate. The media changed. Now it wasn’t just a fugitive story. It was a crisis. A killer was hunting the people hunting Ben. No one knew who she was. But they called her the fox.

By the third body, the whispers started. Not within the public—yet—but among the people who mattered. The ones who organised manhunts in secure rooms and wrote memos no civilian would ever read. They didn’t know her name. Didn’t know her face. But they knew her mark. Every officer found with a fox tape. Always pressed somewhere personal—inside a wrist, behind the ear, beneath a badge. It wasn’t a taunt. It was a statement: You’re not safe.

They pulled the plug on local operations. Central command took over. The case files expanded into something larger. Something nameless. They stopped mentioning Ben Callum's name in the open air, like it had become cursed. He wasn't alone. He was protected. And now they had to worry about her.

Delilah Kitsune vanished into the folds of the hills. She abandoned her car after her fourth kill. Burned it down to the axle and left the blade of her katana half-buried in the ash beside it, like a message written in steel: I can disappear any time. She didn't stop killing. She just stopped being seen.

People began claiming sightings. A fox-headed woman in the rear-view mirror. A lone figure walking through wheat fields at dusk. A silhouette watching from the roof of a highway motel. None of the footage ever held up. The timestamps didn't match. The metadata glitched. Security cameras would freeze for 13 seconds at a time, then come back—cleaned. By the time anyone realised someone was dead, she was gone again. No pattern. No clear motive—except that every target had been connected to the net closing around Ben.

That was all she needed. A journalist in Port Pirie tried to write a piece about her. They called it: "The Kitsune Killings: The Woman Behind the Mask." Delilah read it on a borrowed phone three days later. The article speculated she was a domestic terrorist, an anarchist, maybe a cultist. No one mentioned Japanese folklore. No one knew her name. She smiled. They were already telling the wrong story. Which meant she was doing it right.

By the second week, a rumour surfaced that she hadn't acted alone. Some said she had a handler. Some said she was possessed. Some whispered that the killings were an ancient rite—something about karma, balance, vengeance. The kinds of whispers that didn't stay on record. None of them was correct. But none were entirely wrong either.

In the small towns, people started protecting their own.

When police came through, they were met with closed doors and silent eyes. People weren't stupid. They saw the patterns. They read between the headlines. They didn't know who the fox was protecting. But they sensed he wasn't the monster, not like the ones who kept coming for him.

Delilah left gifts behind now. At her seventh site—an abandoned weather station where an agent from the National Surveillance Liaison had been stationed—she left behind a single fox mask, placed gently on the man's chest. His hands were folded over it. He looked peaceful. They found no wounds. No cause of death. But his face was locked in a final expression. Terror.

Somewhere in the Flinders Ranges, beneath a canopy of stars too bright to belong to a world this broken, Delilah crouched beside a campfire and looked at her own hands. They didn't shake. Not anymore. She wasn't hunting for pleasure. She wasn't killing to kill. She was removing pieces of a broken machine before they could grind a mortal man into dust.

Ben Callum had no idea. He probably thought no one was coming for him. He was wrong.

In the distance, she heard thunder—not from the clouds, but from vehicles. She stood and stepped into the shadow, letting the fire die behind her. The wind shifted. Dust rolled across the ridge. And in its wake: no footprints. Just a lingering whisper that something had passed through. They would never catch her. Not now. The fox had disappeared into myth. But the bodies? They kept turning up. And every time, one red tape. One silent cut. One more step closer to the man she was sworn—by blood or fate—to protect.

Somewhere in a windowless office, a printer stalled. Not jammed—scrambled. The print job restarted five times before failing. A systems tech logged the fault, then blinked at the metadata. The job had no origin path. No user. No trace. The report that had been trying to print was flagged *Top Secret.* Its subject? Ben Callum.

Ellery didn't smile as he watched the log corrupt itself. He never smiled anymore. He sat in a borrowed chair in an unmonitored records hub three floors beneath the Adelaide District Criminal Intelligence Bureau. The air smelled like toner and dust. The computers were old—better that way. The newer ones had firewalls too shiny to slide through without friction. His hands moved fast and efficiently—rerouting packet loops, corrupting indexes, rewriting timestamps.

Not too obviously. Not enough to trigger red flags. But just enough that things didn't add up. Ben Callum's records weren't gone. They just wouldn't be found in time.

Ellery leaned back. A flicker in his chest. The feeling again. Like something ancient had passed close. Not Ben. Someone else. He closed the laptop and slipped a sealed envelope into a clearance bin marked urgent. The note inside read: "He's not who you think he is. He's worse. Pull back or bleed." No signature. No fingerprints. Just a black smear across the bottom corner, like soot or gunpowder. He dropped it. Walked out. Didn't look back.

He was on the move again by dusk, ducking through back streets in a borrowed suit that didn't quite fit, passing cameras with his head down, eyes shadowed. He was the type who didn't get remembered—one of those faces that looked like it belonged to someone else.

The wind shifted. And he felt her. Not in a romantic way. Not psychic. Just aligned.

Somewhere to the north, someone was doing damage. Beautiful, strategic, deliberate damage.

Ellery didn't know her name. Didn't need to. He only knew they were working opposite ends of the same engine, two wrenches thrown into the gears. She swung the blade. He poisoned the fuel. It was working.

Ben was still out there. And the system? It was slowing down. They didn't know who he needed to meet next. They only knew he had to get there. That was the whole mission. No gods. No commandments. No instructions from on high. Just a knowing.

Somewhere in an operations room, a senior analyst tried to upload a facial match database. It failed with a strange error code. An hour later, the backup server dumped five terabytes of surveillance footage into an encrypted dead zone with no owner.

Somewhere in another state, a field officer drove an hour to raid an address—only to find the warrant was for an identical house number on the other side of the country. None of it was random.

Ellery didn't know Ben well. But he knew his type. He'd seen ghosts like him before—people who should've died a dozen times but didn't. People the system couldn't predict.

And now? Now they had a blade walking ahead of him. A woman who marked her kills with fox tape and left no sound behind.

Ellery felt her every time a report failed to upload, every time a station went quiet, every time someone in uniform started looking over their shoulder before following orders. He didn't envy her. She would have to carry blood. He would carry silence. For now, it was enough. Ben wasn't ready. But they would get him there. Whoever they were. Whatever he was becoming.

Ellery stepped out of the building and into the alley behind it. Lit a cigarette. Listened to the distant hum of traffic and radio static. Thought about the people who had started dying near him. Thought about Diane. Thought about the feeling in his chest that something was watching him again—not a threat, but a presence.

He whispered under his breath. "He's almost through."

The wind shifted again. From the north. From where the fox had vanished. He didn't know her. But they were already linked. And far beyond them both, Ben Callum walked down a red dirt road with fire under his skin and no idea that two devils were clearing a path just ahead and behind—one with a sword, the other with silence. The gods weren't done with him. But neither were they.

And in that moment, Ben arrived at Port Pirie. It was both less and more than he expected. Rusted silos. Long, flat streets. The faint metallic scent of industry hung over everything like old regret.

He didn't enter from the main highway. He ghosted in from the east, cutting through a neglected reserve near the river flats. Kids had tagged the benches. Cane grass grew thick at the edge of the channel. Somewhere out on the water, a dredge hummed. He passed a weatherboard house with wind chimes and a dead lemon tree.

No one saw him. No one cared. The town moved slowly. So slow he thought maybe time had given up here.

And then—smoke. Not fire, but spice. Chilli oil. Ginger. Something hot, rich, aromatic. A scent from another life. His stomach howled. His knees buckled. He followed it.

Chapter 12
The Bowl

The Red Basin Noodle House sat wedged between a closed bait shop and a laundromat with flickering lights. Its signage was simple—red paint on white tin. One of the lanterns out front was broken, and the tassels had faded to orange. The windows steamed with life.

Ben didn't go through the front. He stumbled down the alley instead, gripping a rusted handrail, past bins and stacked boxes of cabbage and chilli paste. His mouth filled with water at the scent of it. Real food. Real heat. He collapsed against the rear door. Footsteps. The door creaked open.

A man in a white apron and soft cotton shoes stared down at him, a stainless-steel ladle still in his hand. He said nothing. Just watched. His eyes were dark, his face unreadable. There was a calm about him—unnatural, like the eye of a firestorm. Ben tried to speak. Failed. The man stepped back. Left the door open.

Ben crawled inside. The warmth hit first. Not heat exactly—warmth. The kind that seeps into bone, heavy with steam and silence.

The kitchen was compact but immaculate. A long bench of cold steel. A row of bubbling pots. A rice cooker puffing away in the corner like an older man breathing through his nose.

Ben slumped against a wall, the tiles sticky with condensation. His head spun.

The man moved without urgency. He didn't ask questions. Didn't check for wounds. Just turned, ladled something from the largest pot, and placed the bowl on the bench near Ben's feet. Red broth. Clear. Fragrant. With slices of radish, a boiled egg, and two plump dumplings floating like lifeboats in fire.

Ben stared at it like a relic. Because his fingers didn't work correctly, the man handed him a spoon. The first mouthful made him sob. It burned. Not painfully, but thoroughly. Like his throat had been lined with ash, and this broth washed it clean. Each swallow cleared something. A weight. A fog. The copper tang of days without food. The man went back to the stove.

Ben muttered, between spoonfuls, "Why help me?"

No answer.

He tried again, voice cracking. "You know who I am?"

The man didn't turn. "You're hungry." That was all.

Ten minutes passed. Maybe twenty. Ben finished the soup down to the last slick of chilli oil. His body had stopped shaking, but his skin buzzed with aftershock. He leaned back against the tiles and closed his eyes.

Then something shifted. Not in Ben—in the chef. He had stilled. Ladle poised. Shoulders straight. He was listening—not to Ben, not to the kitchen—but to something inside. Like an itch behind the eyes. A hum in the blood. A heat that wasn't coming from the stove.

Outside, the river breeze swirled down the alley. The bin lids rattled. A moth flung itself against the back window once, twice, then burst into flame. He didn't notice. He was staring into the broth pot. Unblinking. Breathing shallow.

Ben, now upright, noticed the silence. "Everything okay?"

The man didn't respond. Just reached into the pot and retrieved the ladle. The liquid inside had changed. Not visually—it still shimmered red. But the smell was different now. Sharper. Like wet embers and clove.

Ben asked, "What's your name?" Slowly, as if pulled from a deep well, the man turned.

"...Jian."

His voice wasn't hoarse like Ben's. It was soft. Measured.

Ben squinted at him. "You okay, Jian?"

Jian blinked. Once. Slowly.

Then, as if nothing had happened, he nodded and turned back to the stove. "I'll make you another." But as he stirred, his hand trembled—just once. Steam rose like incense. And in the shadows of the kitchen wall, something moved that shouldn't have.

The second bowl sat untouched. Ben cradled it for warmth, but his stomach had drawn a line. He didn't dare ask for more. Partly from shame, mainly because something had shifted in the air—subtle, but undeniable.

Jian was still at the stove, but he wasn't cooking anymore. He was listening. Not to Ben. To something else. The steam rose around him like a veil, clinging to his arms and shoulders in strange, swirling patterns. The wok hissed. The vents rattled. But the man stood motionless, a damp cloth still crumpled in one hand, the knuckles pale. Ben watched quietly, uncertain whether to thank him or leave.

Then Jian said, almost to himself, "It's been years since I dreamed."

Ben blinked. "What?"

Jian looked up, eyes still distant. "I used to. Every night. Fires, rivers, people screaming, praying, or both. And then one day, nothing. Silence. Like someone pulled a curtain closed."

Ben set the bowl down. "You okay?"

Jian turned toward him—really looked at him for the first time. His gaze was sharp, unnervingly clear. He studied Ben the way a craftsman studies an unfinished blade. "What are you?" he asked.

The question hit like a punch.

Ben didn't answer. Couldn't.

Jian didn't wait for one. "I've felt it before. Just once. A long time ago. Something—breaking. Like a dam in the soul." His fingers twitched, as if holding an invisible object.

"And now, you walk in here, half-dead and burning inside, and it starts again." The back of his hand brushed against the stovetop. It sizzled. He didn't flinch.

That night, Jian lay awake in the small flat above the restaurant. The ceiling fan clacked in slow loops. The salt wind blew through a half-open window. Outside, the gulls cried at nothing.

He stared at the ceiling.

At midnight, the dreams returned. Fire and destruction. Always fire and destruction. A city scorched black. Smoke twisting into serpents. A whip cracking against the sky. Red rain falling on broken concrete. In the centre of it all, a man stood—him, but not him—cloaked in robes of ash, skin like scorched earth, eyes hollow with judgement.

He held a bowl in one hand. Not a weapon. A bowl. A vessel of punishment. At the dream's edge stood Ben, limping, arm wrapped in bandage and ink, holding something Jian couldn't quite see. A shadow behind him. A whisper. And then came the sound—a deep, distant hum, like a drum echoing underwater. A pulse. A heartbeat?

No.

Older. Something waking.

Jian sat up with a gasp, drenched in sweat. His hand ached. When he looked down, the skin across his palm was pink—burned. A perfect circle.

He stood, crossed to the window, and opened it fully. Below, the river shimmered. Still. Glassy. But along the edges, where cane grass met silt, the water had begun to bubble.

That night, the restaurant was closed. Jian drew the blinds, turned off the sign, and pinned a handwritten note to the door.

Jian prepared a small altar in the storeroom. It wasn't for worship. He burned dried sage and salt-bush in a cracked clay bowl, drew three glyphs on the floor in chilli oil, and placed a single coin—not legal tender—in the centre of the pattern. Then he whispered, in a language older than Chinese, older than sound itself: "Let none who see the boy remember him. Let none who seek the boy find him. Let none who track the boy taste his ash."

The bowl flared white, then blue, then cold.

Ben, curled on the rice sacks, opened his eyes. "What was that?"

Jian didn't turn. "I'm closing the door behind you."

He stayed awake long after Ben slept again, watching the river from the kitchen window. The tide moved like a breath in, then out.

He could feel it now, clearer than ever. Not just fire in his veins. Balance. The itch to act. The need to move. But not yet.

First, the boy had to mend. And when he did, the destruction would begin. The restaurant remained closed. Jian drew the blinds, turned off the sign, and pinned a handwritten note to the door: Closed for Deep Cleaning. Reopen Soon. □□.

No one questioned it. Locals figured it was plumbing, or maybe a health inspection. Rumours always preferred the mundane.

Inside, the kitchen breathed in silence. Jian moved with rhythm. He didn't speak often—only when needed. A word here. A glance there. Everything else, he communicated through food.

He boiled mung beans in ginger broth. Made rice congee so smooth it slid down like memory. Ground sesame into a paste and wrapped dumplings with peppered lamb and sweet onion. He steeped herbs in honeyed water and cooled them beside the window.

Ben ate everything. And slept.

For the first full day, Jian insisted on silence. “Your body needs more than food,” he’d said. “It needs to remember being human.”

Ben didn’t argue. He sat wrapped in a heavy quilt in the upstairs room, bare floorboards, no fan, the hum of cicadas just outside. He sipped broth and watched Jian work like a priest preparing sacraments.

The second day, Jian asked questions. Not many. Just the right ones.

“Why were you burned?”

Ben hesitated. “There was a fire. I barely got out.”

Jian nodded. Didn’t flinch. “Then you’re lucky to be here.”

Ben looked up. “You believe in luck?”

Jian sipped tea, eyes distant. “I believe in weight. Some lives are heavier than others. Yours drags things with it.”

The two men sat in the late afternoon light, saying little after that. But the silence was companionable. Necessary. Ben didn’t know it yet, but Jian had once spent a thousand years speaking only to wind and fire. Conversation, for him, was a kind of offering. Never wasted on small things.

Later that night, Jian went outside. He walked without shoes. The town still slept—bin lids undisturbed, neon signs humming their last electric sighs before sunrise. Jian moved like steam—there, but hard to notice.

He passed the closed bakery, the bus depot, and the council chambers with their cracked glass door. He was drawn to the river—not for ritual, but for balance. He sat on the crumbling embankment and placed his hand in the water. The tide was low, brackish, gentle. A single eel surfaced, curled, and vanished. Jian nodded. The signs were good.

His first act wasn't a purge. It was a warning. There was a man—Royden Kemp, mid-fifties, former meatworks foreman turned real estate scab. Kemp ran a string of rentals through shell companies, exploiting anyone too poor, too foreign, or too beaten down to complain. He charged double-market-rate for collapsed asbestos shacks and installed cameras without telling tenants. One tenant had been a young woman. Jian knew her only as Mei—she'd worked the register on Saturdays. She hadn't come in for three weeks. He'd said nothing until now.

Kemp's ute was parked outside the Portside Tavern. Same as always. He drank there every Friday, told war stories he'd never lived, mocked the cleaner when she mopped near his feet. At 7:52 a.m., he stumbled outside, boots scuffing pavement. He reached for the door handle. Stopped. The cab of his ute was full of smoke. Not thick—just enough to blur the inside, like fog on a winter window. In the driver's seat: a red basin, steaming. Filled to the brim with river water and two black eels floating in a spiral, mouths open in silence. Kemp didn't touch it. Didn't open the door. Didn't speak a word. He backed away, slowly, then faster, then ran. He let the ute sit there all morning.

The bowl was gone by noon. No one saw who moved it.

Back at the Red Basin, Jian chopped onions with impossible precision, each piece falling into place like a puzzle.

Ben sat on the floor nearby, clean-shaven, skin no longer blistered, eyes clearer. “You went out,” Ben said.

Jian nodded.

“Did you... do anything?”

Jian shook his head. “Not yet.”

Ben tilted his head. “So what was today?”

Jian stirred the broth gently. “Today, the fire knocked politely.”

Port Pirie slept poorly that night. A rolling fog crept in off the Gulf, thin and grey, clinging to rooftops and choking alleyways. It had no weather pattern. No source. The council blamed a harmless chemical reaction from the smelter stack. No one believed them.

Children woke screaming from fever-dreams. Dogs refused to go outside. A pair of seagulls flew into the window of the Community Centre with such force that they cracked the glass.

Jian said nothing. He prepared.

His second act came quietly.

There was a man named Colin Radke, known to few outside the district housing office. He worked behind closed doors, always clean, always polite. But it was his signature—and his silence—that denied dozens of struggling families housing priority, reassigning homes based on favours, deals, and quiet payments slid under tables at greyhound tracks.

Two weeks ago, a woman had come into the Red Basin. Her child wore mismatched school shoes. She'd smiled at Jian, thanked him three times for letting her use the bathroom. Her card had declined when she tried to pay for noodles. Jian had waved it off. She'd wept. That woman's file had been on Radke's desk the day before. Jian knew it. Not how. Just knew.

That night, Radke sat alone in his bungalow in Solomontown, tapping notes into a spreadsheet while the TV muttered behind him.

He stood to make tea. Opened the cupboard.

Inside: no mugs. Just one red ceramic bowl. Still warm. Full of ash. As he stared, it began to smoke—not from heat, but from something older. A deep, blackened wisp curled from the bowl's centre like a breath held too long.

Radke recoiled, knocking a kettle to the floor. He backed into a wall, eyes wide, mouth open. No alarms sounded. No fire started. But the next morning, Radke's office was empty. His desk was stripped bare. Computer wiped. No resignation letter. No transfer request. Just a single red thread, knotted around the handle of the office door. The building's key-card system failed an hour later and took three days to reboot.

Ben watched from the alley as Jian returned. He hadn't seen him leave. But he knew. "You're not just protecting me," Ben said.

Jian paused at the rear entrance. His face was unreadable. "No."

"Then why do it?"

Jian turned toward him. "Because the fire was never meant to sleep this long." He smelled it before he saw it. A chemical tang in the wind. Acrid. Synthetic. Wrong.

Ben was asleep upstairs, wrapped in stillness. Jian had just returned from the river, a clay pot of freshwater in one hand. He'd paused at the kitchen threshold—stiffened. There, curled in the corner of the pantry, was a rat. Convulsing. Foaming. Its fur, matted with blood. Its eyes were wide, staring at nothing.

Poison.

He knelt beside it. Touched its trembling side. Still warm. It had been baited. He rose, slowly, and stepped into the alley. A shadow moved down by the bins—small, fast, darting. He followed.

Behind the restaurant, where the stormwater drains met the rear fence, he found it: a plastic takeaway box, the kind used by the council's pest contractor. Its seal was broken. Scattered rice laced with blue pellets and tossed near his herbs. But that wasn't the message. The message was scrawled beneath the bait box, written in permanent marker: *Go back where you came from.* Six words. Simple. Stupid. Unforgivable.

He stood still for a long time. Breathing. Not deep. Not slow. Measured.

Inside his chest, something ancient—ancient even before memory—began to boil. The rat twitched its last beside him. The pot of water tipped from his hand. He walked into the centre of the alley, barefoot on cracked concrete, and raised both palms to the night. No incantation. No ritual. Just a single exhale—and the alley ignited. Not with flame. With heat. Dry. Furious. Radiant. The kind of heat that burned without light. Every surface began to sweat. The air itself shimmered. The bin lids buckled inward. Steam burst from drainpipes. Paint peeled from bricks.

Inside the Red Basin, the rice cookers exploded. Upstairs, Ben woke choking on air that felt like ash. Out in the street, streetlamps flickered. One shattered outright. Dogs howled across half the district. Copper rain began to fall—metallic dust, no cloud in sight.

Far across the Gulf, a trawler's radar shorted out. In Adelaide, a weatherman paused mid-segment, confused by a sudden thermal spike. Satellites pinged a heat signature too focused, too violent, too alive. And in Monte Carlo, where the gods still whispered beneath torchlight and oilskin, three stopped mid-conversation.

Zed narrowed his eyes.

Ari cocked his head and said, "Did you feel that?"

Poseidon looked west. Slowly. Deliberately. "Something just screamed."

In Port Pirie, Jian walked back into the kitchen. His shirt smoked. His eyes glowed from within—red, yes, but flecked now with gold.

Ben stumbled down the stairs, coughing, shirt drenched in sweat. "What the hell was that?"

Jian didn't answer.

He turned to the wok. Took a clean towel. Wiped the bench as if nothing had happened. And in a voice that cracked the walls of the room, he said: "I am awake."

The next night, Jian didn't knock when he came back. The door clicked open just before dawn, hinges quiet, footsteps quieter. Ben stirred, eyes adjusting to the dark. Jian moved like mist—barely brushing the air—as he set down a blood-stained satchel near the fridge and washed his hands in the rusted basin by the kitchenette. No words. He never spoke right away when he returned from the night.

Ben sat up, pushing sweat-matted hair from his forehead. He didn't ask what Jian had done. Didn't want to know. The silence between them wasn't awkward. It was practised—necessary. A kind of pact. Jian dried his hands on his apron and turned, regarding Ben with the same unreadable calm he always wore.

"Sleep," he said softly, as if repeating a rule rather than offering advice.

Ben exhaled. "Couldn't."

The room above the Red Basin Noodle House was small—just enough space for two futons, a sink, and a wooden table that tilted slightly to the left. Jian had insisted Ben stay here. Ben hadn't argued long. His body was still broken. Skin scarred and tight, the burns pulling like old grudges every time he moved too fast. But it wasn't his body he was worried about.

"Eventually," Ben said, "they will come for me."

Jian hadn't even looked up from cleaning a cleaver. "If they come, I'll serve them something special."

Downstairs, the restaurant was open again. Six days a week. Jian served soup and silence to whoever walked through the red-lacquered doors. The old regulars came back. New ones too. Backpackers. Young families. Two uniformed cops on Wednesday.

Ben watched from the upstairs window, heart pounding, unsure whether the world had gone blind—or if Jian was doing something to keep it that way.

He'd asked, once, if he should help out. Wash dishes. Wipe tables. Be useful. Jian had shaken his head slowly. "No. You shouldn't come downstairs."

"Because of the police?"

"No," Jian said, turning away. "Because the food has changed."

Ben had frowned. "Changed how?"

"It's charged now. Infused."

"With what?"

Jian didn't answer at first. He rinsed a pot, steam curling around his hands like it feared him. Then, finally: "Someone tried to poison my sesame oil. I turned it into something else."

"Poison?"

"Not quite. Something stranger." Jian's tone was flat, but his eyes gleamed. "Something old. Hungry."

Ben had stopped asking after that.

At night, Jian disappeared. No goodbye. No update. Just vanished into the streets of Port Pirie like he was born from them. Sometimes Ben woke up to distant screams—echoes bouncing off the walls of his mind; other nights, only silence. But Jian always returned before dawn, hands wet, eyes distant, carrying smells that had no business existing outside war zones or temples. And every time Ben asked why, Jian gave the same answer: "I walk where the balance breaks." Ben didn't know what that meant. But he understood the weight behind it.

Tonight, Jian returned later than usual. Ben was still awake, sipping hot water and watching the moon smudge its way across the sky. Jian stepped inside, his apron torn. A faint smell of ash trailed behind him.

"You okay?" Ben asked.

"I burned something that wouldn't die," Jian said.

He crouched beside the fridge and removed a tin of chilled rice. "It died eventually."

Ben wasn't sure what to say to that. He waited. Watched Jian eat cold rice, as if it mattered, each bite measured.

Finally, he spoke. "I think I should go soon."

Jian didn't look up.

"I'm getting stronger," Ben continued. "I can feel it. I don't want to bring trouble to your door."

Jian placed the tin down carefully. Then stood. His eyes were tired, but still sharp—still full of something old and unspeakable. "You are not trouble," he said. "You are marked. That is not the same." Ben opened his mouth, but Jian kept going. "If they come here, they come here for you. That is fine. I choose to be here. You are not responsible for me."

"But—"

"No," Jian said, voice harder now. "No. You are not cursed. You are not hunted because of weakness. You are a gate."

Ben blinked. "A what?"

Jian just gave him a look. The kind that said, "You'll understand when you need to."

The next day, the noodle house reopened as usual. Ben stayed upstairs. He heard the footsteps, the laughter, the clink of chopsticks against porcelain. Smelled the chilli and ginger and whatever else Jian was using now—each ingredient soaked in something stranger than flavour.

He didn't go downstairs. Not even once. Because Jian was right—whatever was in the food now, it wasn't for him. The light through the slatted blinds painted the futon gold. Ben sat upright, cross-legged, cradling his left hand in the quiet stillness of the room. The morning was calm, but the energy beneath his skin was not.

The tattoo was healing well. Disturbingly well. It stretched from wrist to knuckle like it had always belonged there, inked in bold, fluid lines that twisted and shimmered in the light. No scabbing. No swelling. Just a gentle warmth, as though the mark breathed. And what a mark it was. A bat—glorious and divine in composition—unfurled its wings across his hand in a style unmistakably Japanese. Elegant. Ferocious. Sacred. The wings rippled in arcs of black flame and rising smoke, each stroke edged with flame-tipped pink that shimmered like cherry blossoms caught in firelight. It was fierce without being grotesque, beautiful without losing menace.

Ben tilted his hand.

The bat seemed to move with him, its eyes catching light that shouldn't be there, hinting at intelligence. Not decorative. Not performative. This wasn't art. It was a summoning. He hadn't asked for this design. Delilah had never consulted him. She hadn't even spoken while creating it. He remembered her hands trembling as she finished, how the room had grown unnaturally warm, how she had stepped back not in triumph but in fear. She hadn't even looked him in the eye when he left. Now he understood why.

Jian hadn't said much when he first saw it. He'd taken Ben's hand in both of his, examining the tattoo not with admiration, but with reverence—like a monk inspecting a relic. "Ah," he had murmured. "It lives." Ben had tried to laugh. Failed. Then Jian handed him a scraped-up yellow tub and tapped the lid. "Pawpaw cream. Old. Honest. Apply often. Keep it soft." Ben had followed instructions, coating the inked skin with a layer of ointment that smelled faintly of eucalyptus and memory. "Your skin must not crack," Jian had added. "Let it remain supple. Alive."

Ben had asked once, "What happens if it does crack?"

Jian had just looked at him. "Then we will see what's hiding in the fire."

Now Ben stood by the mirror, hand raised, the early sun cutting across his wrist like a spotlight. The bat's wings flared toward his knuckles, claws curled beneath veins. The pinks glowed softly in daylight—muted but persistent. The black smoked at the edges, as if freshly inked, refusing to fully settle into the skin. It didn't look like it had been tattooed at all. It looked grown. Ben turned his hand, watching the wings flex with muscle movement.

The design followed his anatomy perfectly, like it had wrapped itself around his hand rather than been forced on top. A perfect predator in slumber, dreaming behind his flesh. He caught his reflection in the mirror. The bat's eyes seemed to look back at him. He dropped his arm.

Downstairs, the restaurant sounds returned—cutlery clinking, soup slurping, the distant scrape of chopsticks against bowls. Ben heard Jian's steady cadence, calm and efficient as ever. The man worked as if nothing unusual were happening upstairs. Like he hadn't gone out the night before and returned smelling of smoke and iron.

Ben dipped a fingertip into the ointment tub and smeared another layer gently over the bat's outstretched wings. The skin shimmered as he rubbed it in, like oil floating on water. The pink flared momentarily, as if pleased. The bat seemed to settle. Ben exhaled. "You're welcome."

A knock at the upstairs door—soft, deliberate. Jian entered without waiting. "You are awake."

Ben nodded. "Haven't really been asleep." Jian carried two mugs of tea. Set one down next to him. The other he held carefully, steam curling upward as if trying to escape. Jian didn't sit.

Just studied Ben for a moment. "You've been looking at it again."

Ben raised his hand. "Hard not to."

Jian allowed a small smile. "It suits you," he said.

Ben let the silence stretch. "Do you know what it is?"

Jian didn't answer immediately. He walked to the window and looked out at the narrow street below. After a moment, he spoke. "Bat is an omen in some places. In others, a protector. Shadow that guards the unwatched path. In your case, maybe both."

Ben looked at the bat again. "It feels like it's waiting."

Jian nodded. "It is."

Ben frowned. "For what?"

Jian turned from the window. His expression was unreadable. "To decide what kind of shadow it wants to be."

The afternoon crept. A breeze came in off the Gulf, rustling the paper lanterns outside. Jian moved about below in the kitchen, preparing for dinner service. Ben remained upstairs, feeling the weight of the bat like a second pulse beneath his skin. He tried to read. Couldn't focus. He watched the sky shift instead.

When Jian came back upstairs near sunset, he was already dressed in darker clothes.

"Gone again tonight?" Ben asked.

Jian nodded, tightening the drawstring on his bag. "Yes."

"You don't have to keep doing this."

"Yes," Jian repeated. "I do."

Ben set his tea down. "You keep saying I'm safe, but I don't know what that means anymore."

"It means," Jian said, fastening his coat, "that if anything comes for you, it will leave hungry."

Ben tried to smile. "That's oddly comforting."

Jian paused at the doorway. "You're not prey, Ben," he said. "You're the thing the predators whisper about when they forget how fear works."

Then he was gone, slipping into the dusk like smoke through a vent.

Chapter 13
The Silence

Ben stood alone by the window. He looked down at his hand again. The bat glowed faintly in the fading light. It didn't blink. Didn't flinch. It watched. And somehow that made him feel less alone.

It slipped back into his mind without warning. One moment, Ben was watching the late light spill through the window-slats, catching the curve of the inked wings on his hand. Next, he remembered gravel. Cold night air. That old caravan park on the NSW South Coast. He hadn't thought about it in years and had no reason to. But now the memory was back—intact and crystal-clear, like it had just been waiting for a reason to surface.

He'd been eleven. Maybe twelve. It was a coastal trip with his mate Josh and Josh's parents. Two weeks in an old caravan park just off the highway, tucked behind a windbreak of tea trees and low scrub. Dirt tracks, creek smells, folding chairs—a fire drum most nights. Ben's own parents had driven down for the first weekend, then left early. Josh's folks had invited him to stay on. Days were filled with sand, burnt shoulders, and daring each other to do dumb things off the wharf. Nights were cooler. Firepit dinners. Cold showers. Thongs and mozzie coils.

That night, he and Josh had wandered a few sites over after dinner, talking shit and avoiding clean-up duty. They ended up chatting with a woman parked in one of the older, permanent vans—the kind with plastic flowers in the window and a sagging annexe. She was middle-aged, maybe a bit older. Heavy accent. Greek, he thought.

She offered them lemonade in plastic cups and asked polite questions in that singsong way older women had. Her husband sat silently by the fire nearby. Big bloke. Looked like he used to work with his hands, but hadn't in years. He never spoke. Just stared into the flames like they owed him something.

The fire was warm. The gravel underfoot was cold and sharp. Ben kicked off his thongs and stretched his feet toward the warmth, standing just close enough to feel it on his ankles. Then it happened. Something small brushed the air. He barely saw it. There was a soft flutter—no more than a flick—and a shape settled lightly on his bare foot. He looked down. A bat. Tiny. Delicate. Brown and black. No bigger than his palm. Wings folded in tight like origami. It clung to his skin with small, cold claws and just stayed there.

Ben froze. Josh blinked and leaned over. "Oi—what the hell?" The woman didn't laugh or gasp. She just stared for a moment. No expression. Then she said, very softly: "That doesn't happen often." That was it. No explanation. No big moment.

The bat lingered. Maybe ten seconds. Then it twitched, lifted off in a clumsy flutter, and vanished into the dark. Josh cracked up and tried to tell the story like a joke the rest of the night. The woman had gone back to her seat. The husband never looked away from the fire. Ben had forgotten about it entirely until now.

He rubbed his thumb across the back of his hand. The bat tattoo stared back, sleek and sharp and alive in black and pink and flame. Wings stretched across his knuckles. Its head nestled near the bone ridge of his wrist. It didn't just resemble a bat. It was a bat. And suddenly, that night at the caravan park didn't feel like just a weird moment. It felt connected. Not in a mystical way. Not prophecy or omen. Just strange. A full circle he hadn't realised was being drawn.

Ben woke. The lamp was still on. The room was unchanged. Still evening. Still quiet. But he had changed.

He knew it the same way you see a fever has broken, or a storm has passed while you slept. A pressure had lifted, but not because it had ended. Because it had entered him instead.

He sat up slowly, spine clicking, vision slow to focus. No dream. But something lingered. Something settled in the corners of his lungs. He rubbed his face, stood, stretched. The tattoo on his hand caught the light and held it. Still the bat. Still beautiful. But it looked more right than it ever had. Like it had finally found the skin it belonged to.

The apartment was silent. Jian was gone—no sounds from below. Ben moved to the sink, drank from cupped hands. The water tasted different. Not bad—just clearer. As though his senses had adjusted. As though his mouth knew what it had never been allowed to taste.

He stood by the window. Looked out. No one. Just a street in pause. The world felt thinner. Not fragile. Not weak. Worn down to truth. Something brushed through him—like wind but inside the bones. And in that moment, the weight of the last month—the fire, the strangers, the hunt, the madness—all receded. Not gone. Just beneath him.

He wasn't running anymore. He wasn't hiding.

He was becoming.

The word rose unbidden: *Nykteris*. He didn't say it aloud. Didn't need to. It was his name, but not the kind people used. This wasn't a role or a legend. This was marrow-deep. Ben closed his eyes. For the first time in his life, he listened without fear. And what he heard was nothing. Not absence. Not silence. Permission.

He understood why the world blurred around him in moments of panic, why doorways twisted slightly when he was at his weakest. Why animals sometimes stared at him with recognition. He wasn't immune to death. The gods didn't choose him. He was what came before the system noticed something had gone wrong. He was the crack in the story. The wrong turn that turned out to be right. The whisper in the ear that changes a soldier's mind, or stills a killer's hand. Not loud. Not seen. But there. Always there.

He raised his tattooed hand. Watched the bat shimmer in the glass. It no longer looked decorative. It looked like it was watching back. Not with curiosity. With respect. Because it knew him now. Because he knew it now.

He wasn't just surviving anymore. He was arriving. Quietly. Like a breath before a scream. Like a ghost that forgets it died. A darkness the gods had no word for. And that terrified them.

Ben left just before dawn. He moved through the apartment like a shadow passing through memory—touching nothing, disturbing less. The bat on his hand seemed brighter in the low light, as if pleased. As if ready.

He folded the blanket. Washed his mug. Wrote the note on a small scrap of paper he found beside the till receipts. The message was short. Honest. Completely his: *Jian—thank you. Truly. Your hospitality, your silence, your food... I owe you more than I can say. I wanted to say goodbye in person, but this is better. I have things to do now. We'll catch up soon. I'm awake. —B.* He folded the paper, pressed it under the ointment jar, and left the room exactly as he found it. No trace. No weight. Just one quiet space less occupied by what was no longer uncertain.

When he stepped outside, the street didn't greet him. It adjusted. Light came more slowly. Wind stepped back. Noise retreated like a tide. He walked with nothing but the clothes he wore. There was no destination. Only direction. He didn't run. Didn't sneak. He moved. And the city—and the systems hunting him—failed to register him like a word unspoken.

Elsewhere. Far inland, Delilah Kitsune sat cross-legged in the dust behind an abandoned servo, smoking a cigarette down to the paper. Her blade rested beside her—edge dull from use, but not disrespected. She paused mid-drag. Exhaled. Looked up. And smiled. No words. No gasp. Just a gentle lowering of the shoulders. She'd felt it. He'd woken. And for the first time in weeks, she let the tension slide out of her spine like water off lacquered steel. She lit a second cigarette, more ritual than habit. "He's fine," she whispered, to no one in particular. "Took you long enough."

In a darkened corridor two stories below a regional police headquarters, Ellery Kalos stood staring at a wall of faces on a corkboard. Suspects. Witnesses. Ben Callum circled in red at the centre. The line across his face trembled. Not physically. The ink. The shape.

Ellery blinked. Stepped forward. And then it hit him. A low rush. Like someone pulling a black sheet off his back and replacing it with open sky. He smiled. A slight, knowing grin. The kind you give when your job just got easier. "No need to keep carrying him," he muttered under his breath. He took the thumbtack from Ben's photo and placed it, delicately, in his coat pocket. Then he walked out of the room.

In a cramped kitchen behind a closed noodle house, Jian Wu paused mid-slice, knife hanging over a half-cut scallion. He didn't turn. Didn't speak. He nodded. And whispered, "Good."

Far Above, Far Below. The scream did not come. And that was the problem. In the realm between realms, where divine eyes track their mortal entanglements like constellations, something stopped being findable. Not killed. Not erased. Just absent. A hole without an edge. A silence shaped like a man. A scream that should have come—but didn't. And that silence screamed louder than any sound.

In Monte Carlo, a god dropped a wine glass and didn't know why. In Prague, Fortuna lost a coin flip. She'd never lost one before. In a temple older than empires, a candle flickered outward, not from wind, but from reverence. The shadow had slipped through the grid. And in doing so, went silent.

ACT II:

A PIRATE IN THE WATER

Chapter 14
The Captain

The road out of Port Augusta baked under a thin white haze. Heat shimmered off the bitumen, long waves that blurred the horizon. Trucks thundered past, their trailers swaying with the dry wind, heading north into the desert or back east along the highway.

Ben had been standing at the edge of the turn-off too long, the dust already in his teeth and his shirt clinging damp across his shoulders. He adjusted the strap of his pack and forced his thumb out again when he saw a dusty white Land Cruiser slow down.

The driver leaned across, window down. A strong face weathered by the sun, with eyes that measured him in silence before the man spoke.

“Where are you heading?”

“South,” Ben said. He hesitated, then added, “Port Lincoln, if I can get that far.”

The man nodded once. “That’s where I’m going.”

Ben opened the door before the offer could be taken back. The seat was hot, smelling faintly of diesel and sea salt, and he dropped his pack between his knees.

They rolled back onto the road, tyres humming. Neither spoke for a while. The radio played static before the man thumped it off with the heel of his hand. The Land Cruiser rattled along with its own soundtrack.
Ben glanced at him properly then—dark skin, Indigenous, sharp jawline, dark hair, wavy and bleached. A presence like a coiled rope—quiet but with strength threaded through. A beaded key fob in red, black, and yellow swung from the ignition.

The man caught him looking. "Name's Jake."

Ben hesitated. He'd said "Ben" for so long it felt too exposed now, too easy to find.

Jake gave him another one of those steady side glances, as if weighing the answer, then nodded once and kept his eyes on the road.

They passed the iron skeleton of Whyalla's shipyards, cranes standing like tired sentries. Smoke plumes rose thinly from the steelworks. The land grew flatter, the soil redder, low scrub flashing by in dusty greens.

"You from Adelaide?" Jake asked eventually.

"Near enough." Ben kept his answer clipped. "Needed to get moving. You?"

Jake's mouth curved in something like a half-smile. "Been around." He drummed his fingers lightly on the wheel. "Do a run down the peninsula every so often. Good place to dock a boat."

Ben let that hang. He wasn't about to ask what kind of run. Men didn't volunteer details like that, and only a fool would pry.

They stopped in Cowell for fuel. Jake filled the tank while Ben stretched his legs, the salty tang of the gulf sharp in his nose. Fishing boats bobbed in the distance, white hulls catching the sun. A few locals leaned against utes, watching the Land Cruiser with sidelong curiosity.

Inside the roadhouse, Jake ordered two meat pies and two coffees without asking. They ate standing by the bonnet, the pastry hot enough to burn Ben's tongue. Jake squinted south, where the road curved toward Tumby Bay and further down.

"Weather's been off," he muttered. "Seas running strange. Currents are pulling where they shouldn't. Birds turning up where they don't belong."

Ben followed his gaze. Clouds stacked heavy and low, though the air was bone dry. He'd heard the same in half-whispered pub conversations and on the radio: rivers drying, farmland cracking, something shifting in the pattern of things.

Jake brushed crumbs from his shirt, tossed the coffee lid in the bin, and nodded to the car. "Best keep moving. Got tide to catch."

The drive dragged on into the afternoon. Ben let the rhythm of tyres and engine dull his thoughts. He caught himself staring at his reflection in the side mirror, repeating the new name in his head. Ben Bateman. It felt like putting on a coat that didn't quite fit, but would keep the rain off anyway.

Jake didn't push for talk.

When he did speak, it was short. Pointers about the road, about the peninsula. A comment about which town had the best slipways. The kind of knowledge earned by years on the water.

By the time they reached Tumby Bay, the light was softening, the sea stretched wide and silver to the east. Children's voices carried faintly from the jetty, laughter mixing with the slap of waves.

Ben leaned forward, watching it slide past. "You live in Lincoln?"

Jake shrugged. "Boat's there."

He didn't elaborate. Ben didn't ask more. He was starting to understand the rhythm: Jake offered just enough to keep a conversation alive, never more.

Night caught them before Port Lincoln. Jake pulled the Cruiser into a lookout above the town—the bay below glittered with scattered lights, masts of moored yachts swaying like thin shadows. Somewhere beyond, Ben knew, the open water stretched into a blackness without end.

Jake killed the engine. The silence pressed in, broken only by the click of the cooling motor. He sat there for a while, arms resting loose on the wheel, gaze fixed on the dark line of the horizon.

Ben waited, not wanting to break the moment.

Finally, Jake said, "You ever been out there?"

Ben shook his head.

Jake's mouth curved into something like a smile. "You will."

That night, they drove down into Port Lincoln proper. The streets were quiet, pubs spilling yellow light, the smell of frying fish clinging to the air. Jake parked near the marina, gesturing loosely with one hand.

"There she is," he said.

Ben followed his gaze.

Among the rows of yachts and fishing vessels, a cutter sat moored, lean and low, its hull weathered but sturdy. The name The Gull glimmered faintly in chipped paint across the stern.

Jake's voice carried the weight of ownership without pride. "Home."

Ben felt something shift then. He'd meant only to catch a ride south, put distance between himself and the life he'd burned. But the sight of that boat, the easy authority with which Jake stood by it, stirred something else. A direction, maybe. Or at least, the start of one.

The Gull shifted against the tide, ropes creaking as Jake stepped onto the gangway with the easy balance of someone who belonged there. He jerked his head for Ben to follow. Ben slung his pack higher on his shoulder and stepped after him. The boat rocked under his weight, the deck groaning in protest. Salt clung in the air—sharp, clean, but tinged with diesel and stale tobacco.

Jake unlocked the cabin with a battered key, pushing the hatch open. "Don't trip," he said, disappearing down the narrow steps.

Inside smelled of old wood and saltwater that had been soaked too many times. A lantern swung gently, throwing amber light across a cramped galley, a table bolted to the floor, and bunks lined with mismatched blankets. It was no man's yacht—it was a working boat, stripped down, everything with a place.

Jake tossed his keys onto the table. "Pick a bunk. That one—" he nodded to the left side, "—doesn't leak in heavy rain. For the most part, you can lie a certain way and avoid it all."

Ben dropped his pack there without comment.

The mattress was thin, but it beat roadside gravel and borrowed couches. He sat down, letting the sway of the hull settle into his bones.

Jake moved with casual efficiency, opening a storage locker and pulling out a bottle of rum and two tin cups. He poured, slid one across the table, and sat opposite.

"To new waters," Jake said, raising his cup.

Ben matched the motion. "To a new life," he said quietly, then drank.

The rum burned down his throat, hot and sharp enough to make his eyes water. Jake smirked at the reaction, then swallowed his own without a blink.

Later, they stood on deck. The town lights of Port Lincoln glimmered across the water. Somewhere a diesel engine coughed to life, and a gull shrieked overhead, circling with restless hunger.

Jake leaned against the rail, smoke curling from the cigarette in his hand. "You runnin' from something, Ben?" The question was asked so casually that it might have been about the weather.

Ben didn't answer right away. "Not running," he said finally. "Just... moving on."

Jake accepted that with a short nod. No prying, no push. Just a puff of smoke, drifting away.

The cabin creaked as the tide shifted. Ben lay on his bunk, staring at the ceiling where shadows rocked with the lantern light. He could feel the subtle thrum of the water beneath, the faint slap against the hull. His mind turned the new name over again: Ben Bateman. A thin mask, but a mask all the same. He wondered if Jake believed him. Or if Jake even cared.

Sleep took him in fits, broken by the groan of rope and the whisper of the sea.

Dawn came pale and blue.

Jake was already up, clattering pans in the galley. The smell of frying bacon cut through the damp air.

"Eat," Jake said, sliding a plate across. "Long day."

Ben took it without complaint, the food hot and greasy and better than anything he'd eaten in weeks. Jake sat opposite, chewing slowly, watching through narrowed eyes as though measuring how Ben handled himself.

When the plates were empty, Jake pushed back his chair. "We head out on the tide. I've got business east. You can tag along or walk. Up to you."

Ben felt the weight of the choice. He could step back onto dry land, drift aimlessly again, vanish into whatever cracks the world offered. Or he could board the Gull properly, head into open water with a man who didn't talk much but seemed to know exactly where he was going.

He wiped his mouth and set the fork down. "I'll come."

Jake's smile was barely there, but it was real. "Thought you might."

The day was a blur of preparation. Jake showed him how to make ropes and knots, check the fuel, and coil lines so they wouldn't trip anyone. Ben listened more than he spoke, hands clumsy at first but learning quickly under Jake's silent corrections.

By afternoon, the boat was ready. Supplies stowed, tanks topped, charts laid flat on the table. Jake ran his finger along the map, tracing the coast.

"Lincoln to Ulladulla," he said. "We keep her close to shore when we can. Safer that way. Weather's been playing tricks."

Ben leaned over the chart. The names blurred into a promise of distance: Robe, Portland, Eden. Places he'd never been, each one a step further from the man he'd been before.

"You'll get your sea legs soon enough," Jake said, rolling the map tight. "Or you'll puke 'em out. Either way, the ocean sorts you fast."

They cast off near dusk. The marina fell away behind them, lights dwindling as the Gull slid into deeper water. The sails caught a restless breeze, snapping taut, pulling them forward with a low, hungry groan.

Ben stood at the bow, the wind in his face, salt spray cooling his skin. He felt a strange pull in his chest, like something long dormant waking. The land behind them faded, and ahead stretched only water, vast and endless.

Behind him, Jake steered steadily, cigarette glowing in the gloom. His voice carried over the wind. "Once you step off land, you don't go back the same. Sea changes men. Always has."

Ben turned, watching him. Jake's profile was carved hard against the sky, the wheel steady in his grip.

For a moment, Ben thought he saw the faintest glint of something more—not just a man at the helm, but a figure meant for it. He looked back out to sea. He didn't know yet where this path led, only that it was forward. Away from Ben. Toward Ben Bateman, whoever he might become. And as the night closed in, the Gull surged on, cutting through the dark like it had somewhere urgent to be.

The Gull cut steady lines through the black water, her bow throwing up small sheets of spray that glowed in the starlight.

Ben sat forward on the bench seat in the cabin, eyes drawn again and again to the faint orange haze to the east.

Adelaide.

A whole city burning on the horizon, though Jake said it wasn't fire, not tonight. Just the city lights bouncing against smoke and heat haze. "Doesn't look right, does it?" Jake muttered.

He had the wheel in one hand, the other balancing a half-cold mug of tea. His broad face stayed pointed forward, but Ben could see him watching the glow out of the corner of his eye. Ben said nothing at first. He was still getting used to the name he'd chosen for himself, still tasting it in his own mouth like an unfamiliar spice. Best to keep quiet and listen.

Jake went on. "You don't see it from Port Lincoln. But out here, on the water, it hangs like a bruise. City's sick, mate. Proper sick."

The cabin's small radio crackled and gave them the evening bulletin. "...another blaze overnight at the Outer Harbor grain silos. Investigators are baffled, describing the fire as 'self-propagating' despite suppression efforts. Fire crews insist the blaze was under control when it reignited..."

Jake reached over and snapped the volume higher. "That's the third silo this week. Can't keep wheat in the bloody state. And they're blaming welders, sparks, and bad storage. Rubbish." He slurped his tea, shaking his head. "Saw it myself once. Flames curled back, like the fire wanted to live. Never seen blokes so spooked."

Ben looked out toward the haze again. He could almost imagine it, fire refusing to die. The broadcast rolled on. "...in other news, police are still searching for answers after the collapse of the South Road overpass yesterday. Three vehicles plunged thirty feet when the concrete span gave way. Witnesses report hearing a 'groan, like metal twisting' before the fall..."

Jake let out a bitter laugh. "Second overpass this year. Concrete doesn't just melt away. Something's eating it. They'll say cheap mixes, dodgy rebar, but that bridge has been up for thirty years. Now it crumbles like a biscuit."

Ben asked, "Anyone caught in it?"

"Family in a ute. Dead before they hit the ground. A courier van, too. That poor bugger was still strapped in when the fire lit. Smoke so thick you could smell it halfway down Marion Road."

Silence settled after that. The only sound was the diesel hum and the sea slapping the hull.

Ben tried to push the image from his mind, but the radio wasn't finished. "...authorities are refusing to comment on speculation about a serial killer operating in the northern suburbs." Unexplained deaths continue to climb. Hospitals report patients expiring suddenly, with no apparent cause. Police admit they are investigating multiple household deaths, sometimes entire families, discovered without signs of forced entry..."

Ben felt the hair on his arms stand on end. "Hospitals?" he said quietly.

Jake nodded grimly. "You catch the bus from Elizabeth, you might not get off. People drop in their chairs, dead before they hit the floor. Coronial reports say heart failure and strokes. But you don't get ten, twenty cases a night with no pattern. It's more like the city's bleeding out. And the whispers..."

"What whispers?"

"That a bloke's walking around in a black coat, dark eyes. You cross his path, the next day you're gone. My cousin swears she saw him near Mawson Lakes. Three days later, her neighbour's entire house is dead, slumped in their lounge like they just nodded off together. You tell me that's normal."

The radio crackled again, breaking the moment. "...emergency services are responding to a major derailment at Dry Creek rail yard. Several fuel cars are ablaze. Smoke is visible across the northern skyline..."

Jake cursed under his breath. "That'll choke half the city. They'll say 'gas leak,' 'bad maintenance,' all the usual excuses. But I've seen it being built. Pubs collapsing, walls splitting open. Entropy, mate. Things are rotting faster than they should. Not just Adelaide. But Adelaide's where it started."

Ben shifted in his seat. He thought of the night glow on the horizon, and how it seemed to pulse like a warning.

Jake drained his tea and leaned forward, eyes sharp. "That's why I'm running south. Bad energy there. City's haunted. You can't stand on Rundle Mall without feeling it. Blokes panic, whole crowds scatter, and no one knows why. Just this pressure, like the ground might open under you."

Ben pictured it too clearly—the mall filled with shoppers, suddenly bolting, stampeding like cattle, trampling each other for no reason. Chaos is as contagious as plague.

The TV on the shelf flickered with a late-night feed. Footage rolled: the overpass rubble smoking, a grain silo collapsed into its own ashes, paramedics carrying body bags from a suburban street. A commentator's voice cut through: "Experts are calling this Adelaide's Decant. A city unravelling."

Jake's jaw tightened. "And they're not wrong. Place is cursed."

Ben said nothing. He felt the vibration of the hull under his feet, the old diesel engine working steadily and sure. Out here on the water, it was easier to breathe. But he couldn't shake the sense that Adelaide's sickness wasn't staying put. That it was spreading, like cracks in glass.

Jake reached to lower the volume. "Best to leave it behind. Nothing good is waiting in that city. Whatever's walking those streets, it wants company in the grave."

The Gull pressed on into the night, the lights of Adelaide shrinking behind them. But the stories lingered, heavy in the cabin air, as if the city's shadow had followed them out across the gulf.

By midnight, Adelaide's orange bruise had all but sunk below the curve of the gulf. The sea stretched black and endless, stars sharp above, but the weight of Jake's stories stayed with Ben. He sat slouched against the cabin wall, arms folded, letting the steady rumble of the Gull's motor work into his chest.

The radio carried on, though Jake had tuned it to another band—National News, out of Canberra. The signal wavered, drifting with the roll of the sea. "...record heatwaves continue to cripple Europe. The Rhine has dropped to its lowest navigable depth in recorded history. Barges are stranded, factories idle. Germany warns of imminent power shortages. In India, the Ganges has shrunk to a third of its flow. Authorities blame China's upstream damming projects on the Brahmaputra, escalating border tensions in the Himalayas..."

Jake snorted. "Knew that'd spark sooner or later. China holds the tap, India's got the thirst. That's a war waiting for rain."

Ben tilted his head, watching the man behind the wheel. Jake didn't look like he read newspapers or sat through policy debates, yet he spoke with the casual certainty of someone who'd already weighed the outcome.

The radio voice carried on: "...Moscow has confirmed joint exercises with Beijing, Tehran, and Ankara, prompting NATO to call an emergency summit. In Washington, officials continue to downplay the possibility of outright conflict, though military analysts warn the world is closer to a flashpoint than at any time since 1962..."

Jake's teeth clicked in the dark. "All about water. Always is. They'll dress it up as borders and treaties, but when rivers dry, countries get thirsty. Thirsty people kill."

Ben looked out the port window and saw nothing but black water sliding by. Yet the words stuck. Thirsty people kill. He thought of the strange fires in Adelaide—flames that refused to die—and wondered if thirst could burn too. The TV screen, small as it was, had shifted to footage of flooding in Brazil. Entire towns half-submerged, people clinging to rooftops. A crawl of text along the bottom read: Unprecedented floods follow record droughts.

Jake tapped the glass with a thick finger. "You see? Fenris. Heard the name yet?"

Ben frowned. "Fenris?"

"Some mob of scientists reckon a brown dwarf is slipping through the system. Not close enough to wipe us, just close enough to tug. Changes tides, screws with wind belts. You get drought on one side, floods on the other. The sun burns hotter. That's what they're saying, anyway." He gave a sharp grin. "But ask me, it feels older than science. Like the world's shaking fleas off its back."

The radio filled the silence. "…meteorological agencies report unusual atmospheric disturbances worldwide. Supercell storms across the Midwest, crop failures in the Mekong Delta, locust swarms in the Sahel. Australia is now officially in its driest year since records began."

Ben rubbed his eyes. He was tired but couldn't shut it out. The world wasn't unravelling in slow motion anymore. It was snapping, like bones breaking all at once.

Jake poured more tea into his dented mug, then slid the thermos across the table to Ben. "Drink. Won't help to stew on it."

Ben poured a little into a chipped enamel cup, holding it carefully as the boat pitched. The bitterness grounded him, though the air still felt heavy with stories.

Jake leaned back, voice quieter. "Thing is, you can almost line it up. Chaos in Adelaide, war in Asia, heatwaves in Europe, rivers drying in Africa. It's not random, mate. It's all pulling together, like a rope being twisted. And I reckon we're the ones at the end of it, waiting to snap."

The TV cut to footage of Adelaide again—police cordons, flashing blue lights, smoke rising from deep in the city grid. A newsreader's words crawled over it: Authorities warn residents to avoid central districts after multiple infrastructure failures. Hospitals are at capacity. State of emergency not ruled out.

Jake's knuckles tightened on the wheel. "Entropy there. Pure rot. You don't wanna be in a place when the walls start to fall."

Ben sipped his tea, silent. He thought of how he'd left his own walls behind, how everything had already collapsed in his life, and wondered if he was just one step ahead of a larger collapse that would swallow everyone else.

The diesel hummed on. The Gull's bow cut a path through small rolling swells, the sea unsettled, though no storm touched them yet. Out to starboard, faint and low, the shadow of Kangaroo Island grew sharper.

Jake flicked the radio down to a scratchier, local frequency. "...three more unexplained deaths overnight at the Queen Elizabeth Hospital. Authorities insist there is no connection between the incidents, though witnesses claim staff are shaken and refusing to enter certain wards alone..."

Jake shook his head. "Death's walking that city. You can feel it. Even the birds don't linger long. Saw flocks lifting at dusk, like the sky itself was poisoned."

Ben exhaled slowly through his nose.

The stories were piling, one on top of the other, each worse than the last. Fires that lived, bridges that crumbled, whole houses of corpses, hospitals haunted by something unseen. And now floods, droughts, and a war in the making.

He looked down into his cup. For the first time in years, he felt the press of something bigger than himself—not a god, not a fate he could name, just the world itself moving.

Jake spoke softly now, eyes on the horizon. "It's a spring clean, mate. Earth is chucking out the rubbish. Old gods, old systems, old walls. Makes room for something new. Question is, what's it bringing in?"

The radio answered with static, the sea with silence. The question lingered in the cabin like smoke.

By dawn, the Gull cut east along the Bass Strait, Kangaroo Island already behind them. The weather had held—cold air knifing in from the south, sky streaked with low, bruised cloud. Jake never hurried the boat; he ran her steady, as though time itself owed him patience. Ben sat most of the morning on deck, staring out over the water, watching the swell rise and flatten in restless rhythm.

By the time they reached Port Phillip Heads, the shipping lanes thickened. Tankers and cargo ships loomed like floating cliffs, their hulls rust-red or black, names painted in white across bows. The Gull felt like a shadow beside them, insignificant, but Jake threaded her through with unblinking calm.

Melbourne's skyline broke the haze by late afternoon—glass towers, cranes, a hard edge of industry.

Ben had not planned to see it again—not in this life—but then nothing about the last month had been planned.

Jake brought the Gull to a berth at a private dock tucked behind a rusting container yard. The kind of place where no one asked for paperwork if you slipped the right envelope across.

"Stay put," Jake said, cutting the engine. "I'll fetch someone."

Ben leaned against the cabin doorway and smoked, watching gulls wheel over the cranes. The place stank of diesel and salt, but there was comfort in its anonymity. He didn't stand out here; he was just another shadow between rust and water.

Jake returned half an hour later with a stocky man in a faded leather jacket. His hair was cropped short, his eyes alert and calculating.

"This is Robbo," Jake said. "Knows how to fix problems. And you, my friend, got one hell of a problem."

Robbo gave Ben a long look, then offered a hand. His palm was calloused, grip firm. "So. You're looking to disappear."

Ben hesitated, then nodded. "Something like that."

"Good," Robbo said flatly. "Disappearing's easy. Staying gone—that's harder. You ready for that?"

Ben didn't answer right away. He thought of Adelaide's burning silos, the dead-eyed stares Jake described, the strange pressure in the air that made everything feel brittle. He thought of his own face, plastered across bulletins and screens, hunted for crimes he didn't commit.

Ready or not, he didn't have a choice. "I'm ready."

Robbo smirked. "Alright. Jake says you'll be working with him. That helps. Nobody digs too deep when you're part of a crew. Means we can do this quicker."

The plan unfolded over the following hours. Robbo's method was crude but effective: a drowned man found floating near Lorne, clothes torn, face battered by rocks. The coroner's report would close the case fast enough, especially with no family pushing for more. A car accident would raise flags, a fire would draw questions, but the sea was final. Nobody argued with the sea. Ben—or what was left of him—would die quietly within the week. In the meantime, Robbo produced documents from a battered briefcase: birth certificate, tax file number, even a half-finished driver's licence with the photo space empty. The name was printed in bold across the top: Ben William Bateman.

Ben stared at it longer than he meant to.

Jake clapped a hand on his shoulder. "New last name, eh? Easy to answer, still you, but legal."

Ben nodded. It sat heavily, having to assume a new identity, but he knew this was right; his old life was over.

The next morning, Robbo brought a photographer with a portable backdrop. They shot Ben Bateman's face in a dozen angles, clipped his hair, and adjusted the lighting. Hours later, laminates slid fresh from a machine, smelling of hot plastic.

Ben Bateman could open a bank account. Ben Bateman could buy a ticket, rent a flat, and pay taxes. And Ben Callum, officially, was gone.

That night, Jake leaned back in the cabin, a glass of rum in hand, the Gull rocking gently at the berth. "I won't lie to you, mate. Life with me isn't safe. You'll move things you don't ask questions about. Money, booze, sometimes worse. But it pays, and no one will find you if you're under my shadow. You up for that?"

Ben—he forced himself to think it—took a breath. "I don't see another way forward."

"Good," Jake said. "Then you're in. First run's light. Cargo out of Eden, drop at Ulladulla. From there, you'll learn the trade. And after that—" He smiled crookedly. "New Caledonia. Ever been?"

Ben shook his head.

"Good beaches, better ports. Money to be made. We'll get there."

The run north felt different with the weight of new skin. Ben leaned into it. He learned how Jake disguised loads in plain crates, how he used coded shipping slips that looked clean enough on inspection but flagged to the right eyes. He watched Jake grease dockhands with quiet envelopes, never more than necessary, never less.

When they pulled into Ulladulla, the cargo went fast—a few crates slid into the back of an unmarked truck, handshakes exchanged in the shadows of the pier lights. No questions, no wasted words. The Gull sat lighter by midnight. Ben felt the first flicker of belonging. Not comfort, not trust, but purpose. For the first time since his world had collapsed, he had a role, however dirty.

Two days later, as the Gull nosed back into open water, Jake lit a smoke and pointed east. "Next job's the big one. Sydney to Nouméa. Contraband, nothing you need to name. You'll see how we work in open seas. You'll see how the world really moves."

Ben followed his gesture into the dark horizon. The sea stretched endlessly and black, the wind colder now. He thought of Adelaide's lights fading in the distance, of names burned away, of rivers drying in the east, and of Fenris whispering through the void. He wasn't sure if he'd chosen this life or if it had chosen him. But either way, Ben Callum was dead, and Ben Bateman was moving forward. And there was no going back.

Chapter 15
The Cargo

The helicopter's blades carved the night into ragged pieces of wind and salt. Posi stood on the aft deck, broad shoulders outlined in the glow of the running lights, jacket whipping in the downdraft. The yacht beneath him wasn't one of his grandest—no helipad, pool, or caviar service—but it was enough. Enough to carry arms, a few hundred terabytes of stolen identities, boxes of blank passports, and three living commodities no one aboard wanted to name aloud.

The skipper kept his distance by the wheelhouse, pretending to study the radar. The two deckhands clung to the railing, heads ducked against the rotor wash. None of them dared look directly at Posi as he boarded the chopper.

He didn't offer them instructions. He didn't need to. A single look carried the weight of consequence. The skipper knew the route: east through the Coral Sea, Nouméa by dawn two days hence, offload discreetly, await further orders. Simple on paper. Deadly if mishandled.

The pilot gave a clipped signal. Posi climbed into the cabin and settled with a feline ease, not glancing back. The blades roared, and the chopper lifted, spray flaring silver from the swells below. Within moments, it was only a pulse of red against the stars, vanishing north to coordinate with other vessels in his web.

Silence returned. But not quite.

The yacht pitched gently. From the observation blister below deck, the black water seemed to lean closer. Then something vast rolled beneath the keel—no whale, no submarine, but older. A ridge—like the suggestion of a spine. A shadow too large for mortal measure.

For a heartbeat, it brushed against the hull, a salute or a warning. The deckhands swore under their breath. The skipper, pale under the bridge light, muttered a prayer he hadn't used since boyhood. And then it was gone. The sea returned to stillness, as if it had never moved at all.

Inside, the vessel felt emptier without Posi's weight on board. The skipper knew the truth: the man didn't need to command with words. His absence carried more pressure than his presence. You could almost hear him in the hum of the engines, in the cautious way the deckhands moved through the narrow steel corridors. Cargo was stacked tight in the hold—rifles, crates marked with false codes, and the girls.

Three of them, locked in a converted lounge with bolted shutters. Their laughter carried thinly through the bulkhead, high-pitched, frantic, forced. It wasn't joy. It was the brittle chatter of caged birds. The skipper avoided passing that door unless he had to. The deckhands lingered a little too long when they brought water.

The first night without Posi was always the hardest. The sea was a law unto itself, but men... men could be tempted. The skipper gathered them both by the wheelhouse after midnight, his voice flat, his cigarette burning low.

"Hands off. Don't even look at them," he said. "We make Nouméa clean, and we're all richer for it. Cross the line, and he'll know."

The younger deckhand laughed nervously. "He ain't here, is he?"

The skipper's eyes narrowed. "Doesn't matter. He's still watching."

The older deckhand spat over the side. "The sea is his eyes," he said without irony, as if he believed it.

None of them argued after that.

Hours later, when the others slept in their bunks, the skipper sat alone in the wheelhouse, watching the radar sweep its endless green circle. He sipped stale coffee and kept one hand on the throttle, the other near the radio. Routine, discipline, precision—that was how you survived under Posi's banner. Still, he couldn't shake the memory of that shape beneath the hull. The way it had pressed against the sea like a leviathan leaning in, acknowledging their passage. It hadn't been a threat, exactly. But it hadn't been comfortable either. It was a reminder.

The yacht didn't belong to him. The cargo didn't belong to him. The girls, the contraband, the weapons—they were someone else's ledger. His job was simple: steer straight, keep the deckhands from losing their heads, and deliver the load. But deep down, he knew that if the sea decided otherwise, he wouldn't be steering anything at all.

The yacht sailed on into the dark, its wake a thin scar across the water. Above, the stars wheeled indifferently. Below, unseen, something vast kept pace a while longer, then slipped silently back into the abyss. And for the first time in years, the skipper wondered whether he was escorting cargo or being escorted himself.

The cabin smelled of stale fabric softener and cold steel. The curtains had been bolted over the portholes, leaving the room in a twilight even at midday. A narrow strip of fluorescent light hummed above, its glow too white, too sharp. Three girls sat there, knees drawn close, voices dropping to whispers whenever footsteps passed in the corridor.

The youngest, barely sixteen, still wore the floral dress she'd had on the day she was taken. Her name was Katie. She kept fingering the lace hem as if rubbing it might somehow rewind time. In Sydney's South, after school, a van pulled up near the bus stop. That was all she remembered—the rest was chloroform and dark. Her eyes stayed on the floor mostly, wide and wet, but sometimes they hardened, like a cornered dog trying to remember its teeth.

Beside her sat Anika, nineteen, wiry, her black hair cropped short. She had been working nights at a bar in Brisbane's Fortitude Valley—cheap cocktails, strobe lights, a crowd always on the verge of violence. She remembered the man with the drink, the way his smile didn't reach his eyes, the promise of a lift home. She remembered waking in a locked room on the docks. Of the three, she spoke the least. But when she did, it was with a sharpness that made the others listen.

And then there was Leila. Seventeen. Country girl, Northern Rivers. She had been on her way to a weekend surf comp, backpack slung over her shoulder, when she disappeared between the train platform and the car park. Weeks later, she surfaced here. Her accent still carried the singsong of the coast, her skin bronzed from a life under the sun. But her eyes had changed. They scanned the room, the locks, the guards, every detail. She was the one who tested the hinges with her thumb, who memorised the sound of the keys, who kept the other two from dissolving entirely into fear. Now she sat cross-legged on the floor, her face angled toward the bolted porthole as if listening.

The yacht's engines throbbed faintly through the steel. The vibration never stopped; it just settled into the bones until you forgot it was there. She tapped her fingers once, twice, matching the rhythm. "We're moving steady," she said under her breath. "Not fast—like they're trying to stay quiet."

Katie looked up, startled. "What does that matter?"

Leila shrugged. "Means they don't want attention. No patrols, no radar. Could be our window later."

Anika snorted. "Later. You think there's a later for us?" She sat back against the wall, arms folded, the fluorescent light sharpening her cheekbones. "We're not passengers, Leila. We're stock." The word hung heavy.

Leila didn't flinch. "Stock bites back, sometimes."

Katie buried her face in her knees. "Please don't. Please don't talk like that."

Silence filled the cabin. Outside, a deckhand's boots passed the door. The sound lingered, then faded.

Up in the wheelhouse, the skipper dragged on his cigarette, blowing smoke out the half-open window. He could hear faint laughter through the vents—girls' voices trying too hard to sound natural. It made his stomach knot. He wasn't a kind man, but he wasn't blind either. He'd ferried weapons, drugs, even animals that belonged in jungles instead of cages. But this?

Three girls shoved into a bolted lounge? This was different. He told himself it wasn't his concern. His job was to steer, nothing more. The money was too good, the consequences of disobedience too sharp. Still, every time he lit another cigarette, he found himself muttering a curse under his breath. Not at the girls. At Posi.

The deckhands didn't share his restraint. The younger one, Jamie, couldn't keep his mouth shut. Every time he brought water or food, he lingered, grinning stupidly. He thought he was charming. The girls thought otherwise. The older hand, Reuben, said little, but his eyes lingered too long when the door opened. The skipper noticed. And each time, he reminded them: "Hands off. He'll know." They nodded. They obeyed. But the skipper could feel it building. Pressure. Boredom. Temptation.

Below, in the locked cabin, Leila was whispering again. "There are three men. That's it: a skipper, two deckies. No guards, no muscle. And Posi's gone."

Anika rubbed her temples. "And? You think we can walk out of here?"

"Not walk. Wait. Watch." Leila's eyes glittered in the harsh light. "Every lock's got a key. Every man's got a weakness. We need the right moment."

Katie shook her head violently. "Stop. Just stop. If they hear us—"

"They won't." Leila leaned closer, lowering her voice until it was barely a breath. "You want to make it to Nouméa in a crate? Or do you want a chance?"

Anika's lips pressed thin. She didn't answer. Katie didn't either. But silence was as good as agreement.

Leila leaned back against the cold steel wall, the hum of the yacht settling into her bones again. She closed her eyes. The others thought she was resting. But she was listening to the footsteps, to the creak of bulkheads, to the whisper of the sea pressing against the hull. She had survived long enough to know one thing—cages never stayed shut forever.

In the deep below, something vast rolled once more, brushing the keel like a hand against glass. The sea remembered. The sea was watching. And Leila, though she couldn't have known why, smiled faintly in the dark.

The moment came not with a plan, but with an opening. Jamie, the younger deckhand, was whistling as he slid the bolt back on the lounge door. He had a plate of bread and tinned meat balanced on one hand, the other resting too casually on the frame. The older one, Reuben, waited in the passage, arms folded, his eyes already fixed inside.

Leila moved first. She was smiling when Jamie stepped in, her tone soft, practised. "Thanks for dinner. Can you bring it closer?"

He grinned, pleased with himself, and stepped across the threshold.

Anika was on him before he could react. She lunged low, catching his knees with the full weight of her wiry frame. He staggered, the plate crashing to the floor. Leila surged up behind him, looping the strap of a torn blanket around his throat and pulling hard. He dropped, clawing, choking. Katie froze in the corner, hands to her mouth, but Leila snapped at her: "Shut the door!" She obeyed.

The bolt slammed back just as Reuben barked a curse and grabbed the handle. He rattled it hard, then shoved, but Jamie's weight kept it from opening. The girls dragged him deeper into the room, the blanket strap cutting into his neck until his eyes rolled. Anika snatched the keyring from his belt. Her hands trembled, but she held them tight.

"Quiet," Leila hissed.

She pressed her ear to the door. Reuben was still there, breathing heavy, muttering low. Then his footsteps retreated down the passage. Jamie twitched once, then slumped. Not dead, but close enough to helpless. They bound his wrists and ankles with strips torn from the blanket and gagged him with his own shirt.

Katie stared at the bound deckhand, her face white. "We can't—we can't—"

"We already did," Leila cut in. Her voice shook, but only slightly.

They waited ten minutes before slipping into the passage: bare feet, fast breaths. The yacht hummed around them, engines steady, sea pressing close.

Reuben was by the galley, crouched low, knife in his hand. He had been waiting. His head snapped up as they appeared. Anika threw the plate—metal clanged, bread scattered. He flinched instinctively. Leila barrelled into him, both hands on the wrist that held the knife. They went down hard. He was stronger, heavier, but desperation is its own kind of strength. Anika kicked the knife free, skidding it across the deck. Katie, trembling, grabbed it.

Reuben roared, thrashing beneath Leila, and slammed her against the bulkhead. Her teeth cut her lip, blood streaking down her chin. She spat it in his face. "Not tonight," she growled. Anika grabbed a length of rope from a nearby locker. Between the two of them, they managed to wrestle him face-down, arms yanked behind.

He bellowed again, muffled as Katie, sobbing, pressed the knife to his throat. “Don’t move!” she screamed. Reuben froze.

They tied him fast. Ankles, wrists, and shoulders lashed tight. He thrashed once more, then gave up, chest heaving against the deck. The girls stood over him, gasping, sweat-soaked.

Katie still held the knife, shaking uncontrollably.

Anika eased it from her grip. “Good girl,” she whispered.

The skipper was in the wheelhouse, cigarette glowing under the red night-lamps, when the door burst open. He half-turned, instinct taking over. His hand went for the flare gun mounted by the chart table. Leila didn’t hesitate. She slammed into him with everything she had, both hands on his arm. The flare gun cracked against the bulkhead. Anika wrenched it free, holding it like a pistol.

The skipper stared at them—three ragged girls, faces pale, eyes burning. He saw the truth in a blink: this voyage was finished. “You don’t know what you’re doing,” he said, voice low, measured.

Leila bared her teeth. “We know enough.”

He lunged. Faster than they expected, stronger than he looked. His hand closed around Leila’s throat, slamming her back against the console. The yacht lurched as the wheel jerked.

Anika fired. The flare gun boomed, light exploding in a confined roar. The round struck the skipper in the chest, burning white. He screamed, the sound choking into a ragged gurgle as fire chewed through his shirt. The smell of smoke and singed flesh filled the wheelhouse. He stumbled once, twice, then collapsed across the chart table, leaving a blackened smear.

Katie's scream tore through the room. Silence followed. Only the hum of the engines remained.

Leila shoved the body aside, coughing, eyes streaming from the acrid smoke. Her throat throbbed, but she forced herself to be steady.

"He's gone," she rasped. "He's gone. Take the radio."

Anika was already on it, hands flying across dials. "Mayday, mayday, mayday," she said, voice cracking. "This is the vessel... shit, I don't know the name..."

Leila snatched the logbook, scanning. "Call sign Foxtrot Delta Seven." She pressed the button, forcing calm into her voice. "Mayday, Mayday, this is Foxtrot Delta Seven. We are under duress. Repeat, under duress. Location—" She glanced at the GPS. "Twenty-four south, one fifty-five east. Immediate assistance required."

The radio hissed. Then, faintly, a reply: "Foxtrot Delta Seven, we copy. Hold your position. Help inbound."

Katie began to sob, clutching her knees.

Leila ignored her. She yanked open the cabinet, grabbed the box of flares, and stormed out onto the deck. The night air hit her like ice. She fired one straight into the sky. It burst high above, red fire spilling across the stars. Another. Then another. The deckhands below shouted through their gags, thrashing helplessly against their bonds. The yacht blazed with light, no longer invisible. For the first time since the nightmare began, the sea itself seemed to pause. The swell stilled. The air thickened. And far beneath the keel, something vast stirred again, circling once before vanishing into the black. A salute. Or a warning. Either way, the message was clear—the tide had turned.

The yacht drifted under its own weight, steady but directionless, its engines grumbling like a beast without reins. The wheelhouse stank of burnt cloth and blood, the skipper's body crumpled against the chart table. Below, the two deckhands strained against their bindings, muffled cries echoing up through the metal ribs of the hull. On deck, the flares still burned in the sky. Red smoke trailed against the stars, a beacon that could not be missed.

Leila stood with the spent flare gun in her hand, chest heaving. Anika leaned against the rail, white-knuckled, staring into the black swell. Katie crouched near the door, rocking, whispering over and over: "He's dead. We killed him. He's dead..." No one answered her. The sea itself seemed to be holding its breath.

Far off, beyond the reach of the naked eye, another vessel rode the night. The Westward Gull cut across the swells at twenty knots, her decks slick with salt spray, her lights dimmed. Ben was at the wheel, cigarette burning low between his lips. The radio crackled again, repeating the faint Mayday, the coordinates, the terrified voice of a girl.

He glanced sideways at Jake, who sat on the gunwale with a battered thermos of coffee, boots planted wide. "You buying it?" Ben asked.

Jake shook his head slowly. "Could be real. Could be bait."

"Girls don't fake a Mayday like that," Ben muttered.

Jake tapped ash into the dark. "Posi doesn't let his cargo scream for help unless he wants someone to hear it."

They let that sit a moment. The Gull's diesel engines thrummed steadily beneath their boots. Ben leaned over the chart table, tracing the line of coordinates. "Puts them just east of the reef shelf. Close enough to Nouméa to smell it, but still deep water. You reckon he left them floating?"

Jake didn't answer at once. He was watching the horizon, where the faintest red smear of flare still lingered like blood in the sky. "No," he said at last. "He wouldn't abandon a load like this. He's nearby. Waiting."

Ben spat over the side. "So we leave it?"

Jake's jaw tightened. He flicked his cigarette into the swell. "No. We go in. But be careful."

They throttled down as they closed within five miles, the Gull moving low and silent through the dark. The flare smoke had thinned, but its memory stained the air. The girls had fired enough for the message to stick. Whoever was listening already knew where they were.

The yacht came into view—a sleek silhouette adrift, running lights still on, bow carving lazy arcs as if confused by its own course—no movement on deck. No voices. Just a ghost riding the black.

Jake adjusted the binoculars and studied the deck. "No crew."

Ben frowned. "Not possible. Look again—no watch, no wheel."

Jake lowered the glasses, lips pressed tight. "But someone fired those flares."

They eased closer, the diesel engines coughing softly. At half a mile, Ben killed the lights. The sea swallowed them, leaving only the faint churn of wake.

"Boarding?" Ben asked.

Jake nodded once. "But slow. If it's a trap, we walk into it eyes open."

On the yacht, the girls huddled by the wheelhouse door. Leila clutched the radio mic, whispering into it again. "Please—someone, anyone—we need help. They're tied up. The skipper's dead. Please."

Static hissed back, followed by a low, steady voice. "This is the Westward Gull. Repeat your position."

Leila's breath caught. She forced her voice steady. "Twenty-four south, one fifty-five east. We've got no captain. No one to steer."

A pause.

Then: "Hold fast. We're coming alongside."

Anika pressed her forehead to the cold steel of the door, whispering, "Thank God."

But Leila wasn't praying. She was listening to the tone of that voice. Calm. Measured. Not the clipped efficiency of the Coast Guard. Not the rough drawl of fishing crews. Something else. Something practised. She set the mic down slowly. "They're not cops," she muttered.

Katie whimpered. "Then who are they?"

Leila shook her head. "Doesn't matter. They're all we've got."

The Westward Gull nosed in gently, fenders squealing against the yacht's flank. Lines were thrown, caught, and tied. Jake went first, shotgun slung loose but ready. Ben followed, pistol holstered but his hand resting near it. Their boots hit the teak deck in silence. They smelled smoke immediately. Burnt fabric, flesh. A warning more eloquent than words.

"Wheelhouse," Jake said quietly.

They moved quickly and low, every sense alive. The door opened before they reached it. Three girls spilled out—one pale and shaking, one hard-eyed and wiry, and one who looked like she'd been carved by defiance itself.

The leader held the flare gun like a weapon, arms stiff, eyes blazing. "Stop!" Leila barked. Her voice cracked, but she didn't lower it. "Don't come closer."

Jake raised both hands, calm, steady. "Easy, sweetheart. We heard your call. We're here to help."

Ben scanned the deck—saw no crew, no skipper—just the girls, trembling but upright.

Leila's grip tightened on the flare gun. "Who are you?"

Jake met her eyes. "Friends. That'll do for now."

Behind her, Anika hissed, "Don't trust them."

Katie sobbed, rocking on her heels.

Jake glanced at the flare gun, then back at Leila. "You pull that trigger, you'll set the deck alight and all of you with it. So maybe start slow, tell me what happened."

Leila hesitated. The sea lapped against the hull, patient, listening.

Ben stepped forward just enough for his voice to carry. "Where's the skipper?"

Leila's eyes flicked sideways, toward the wheelhouse. Her jaw clenched. "Dead."

Jake nodded once. No judgement. Just a fact. "And the others?"

"Tied up."

Another pause. The air hung thick with salt and silence. Then Jake lowered his hands, voice soft. "Good. Then let's finish what you started."

Leila blinked, confused. "What do you mean?"

"Means you lit the fire," Jake said, stepping closer. "Now we help you carry it."

The words didn't sound like rescue. They sounded like an alliance. And something in them made the sea stir again beneath the hull, as if interested in this new arrangement. Leila didn't lower the flare gun. Not yet. But she didn't fire it either. And for Jake, that was all the invitation he needed.

The Westward Gull lay tight against the yacht, lines creaking as the two hulls pressed together.

Jake and Ben had just begun removing the skipper's body from the wheelhouse table when the thrum of blades rolled over the sea. It came faint at first, like distant thunder. Then louder. Closer.

The water itself seemed to pulse with each rotation.

Jake froze. His eyes met Ben's.

"Shit," Ben muttered. "He's coming back."

The girls heard it too. Katie dropped to her knees, clutching her ears, whispering, "No, no, no." Anika cursed under her breath. Leila only tightened her grip on the flare gun, eyes burning with something between fear and defiance.

The helicopter's lights cut across the water—white beams carving the dark into jagged slices. Spray whipped up in violent sheets as the craft descended toward the aft deck. The air thickened, the ocean lifting in heavy swells as though answering the arrival of its master.

Posi stepped out before the skids had even settled. He looked carved from storm light—shirt open, skin gleaming with salt, hair flaring in the downdraft. His boots hit the teak like judgement. Behind him, the rotor blades chopped the night into chaos, but he moved as though the noise bent away from him, unworthy of his attention. His eyes scanned once. The tied deckhands. The blood-stained wheelhouse. The strange vessel lashed alongside his own. And then the girls. They flinched under the weight of his gaze. All but Leila, who met it head-on, chin lifted.

Posi smiled. Slow. Predatory. "So," he said, his voice carrying even above the roar of the rotors, "my cargo learned to bite." He stepped forward.

The sea swelled in unison, as if his stride pulled it higher. Spray broke across the deck, drenching steel and skin alike. The yacht's hull shuddered, not from impact, but from recognition.

Jake moved between him and the girls, shotgun raised. "That's far enough."

Posi didn't stop. Didn't blink. His eyes flicked once to the weapon, then back to Jake's face. "You're on my deck. With my load. And you think steel and powder will make a difference?"

The water surged against the hull again, higher this time, foam spilling across the scuppers. The sea wasn't just restless. It was answering.

Ben swore under his breath, pistol drawn, trying to keep both eyes on Posi and the shifting swell. "Jake..."

"I see it," Jake growled.

Leila stepped closer to the men, her voice low. "He's not bluffing. He's tied to it somehow. The water."

Jake didn't look back, but his grip on the shotgun tightened.

Posi's smile widened. "Smart girl." He raised his hand—not fast, not threatening, just deliberate. The swell rose in answer. The deck pitched violently, throwing Katie against the rail. Anika dragged her back, clutching tight as water foamed across their ankles.

"You feel it?" Posi's voice was low, almost gentle now. "The deep knows me. The currents bend when I breathe. And you think you can steal from me?"

Jake chambered a round with a sharp click. "I don't think. I act."

For the first time, Posi's smile faltered—just a fraction.

The standoff held. Salt spray lashed. The helicopter thudded overhead, rotors scattering chaos.

Then Ben shouted: "Move!"

Posi lunged, faster than seemed possible for a man his size. Jake fired. The shotgun blast tore into the deck where Posi had stood, wood and steel erupting in shards. The sea bellowed in response, a wall of water slamming across the bow. The girls screamed as the wave crashed over them, dragging lines loose, snuffing lanterns.

The Westward Gull bucked against the yacht, lines straining, nearly snapping. Jake staggered, pumping another round. Ben fired too, his pistol cracks drowned by the roar of sea and machine. Posi wove through it, half-man, half-storm, moving with the water's rhythm.

Leila seized her moment. She yanked the flare gun high and fired point-blank into the night. Not at Posi—but into the air, screaming red fire into the sky. "Help us!" she shouted. Her voice carried raw, ripping her throat.

Posi snarled, his attention breaking for the first time.

That sliver of hesitation was all Jake needed. He tackled him from the side, the two men crashing into the rail. Posi's fist slammed into Jake's ribs like a battering ram, nearly pitching him overboard.

Ben grabbed Jake's collar, yanking him back. "We need to go! Now!"

Leila was already untying the last line binding the Gull to the yacht. Anika dragged Katie toward the smaller vessel, shouting for her to move.

Posi roared, throwing Jake aside. He rose to his full height, salt streaming from his hair, the sea itself surging against the hull in answer to his rage. "You think you can run?" he bellowed. His voice rolled across the water, deeper than human, echoed in the swell. "The ocean doesn't lose."

The girls were already leaping the gap, scrambling onto the Gull's deck. Ben hauled Jake after them, firing two wild shots to keep Posi at bay. The last line snapped free.

The Gull's engines roared to life.

For a heartbeat, Posi stood framed in the helicopter's lights, water rising around his boots like a crown. His eyes locked on them, not with fury alone, but with certainty. This was not an escape. This was the beginning. The Westward Gull tore free, diesel screaming, wake splitting black water into frothing scars. The yacht shuddered behind, caught between storm and master.

Above, the helicopter lifted again, chasing. Posi climbed back aboard it with the ease of a man stepping into his own shadow.

The chase had begun.

Chapter 16
The God

The night tore itself apart with the scream of rotors. Fast Dealer VII's men were bound and useless, lying in a heap on the deck of their own vessel, eyes wide as they watched the sky open above them.

Posi was not at the controls of the helicopter for safety or for show—he was there for war. His face was a stone carving of rage, illuminated by the strobing red glow of the cockpit's warning lights. With deliberate malice, he slammed the collective down. The machine shrieked as if protesting its master's command, then tilted forward in a suicidal dive.

The Gull, already straining under its cargo of stolen lives and iron secrets, was directly below. The helicopter came like a hawk stooping on prey. Steel shrieked against steel as the spinning rotor bit into the yacht's flank. Blades shattered against the hull, but not before they ripped a gouge across its side. The Gull screamed like a living thing, timbers cracking, metal tearing. Water rushed in with hungry force.

The helicopter disintegrated on impact, spraying flame and shrapnel. Posi was gone before it hit. He vaulted clear, hurling himself into the night, body slicing through the salt air, vanishing into the swell.

For a moment, it seemed he had drowned with his machine, another casualty of madness. But the sea betrayed its secret.

The waves buckled. The swell thickened, darkening as if the ocean itself bent in reverence. From the trough rose Posi, not climbing, but lifted. The water coiled beneath him, thrusting him aloft. His arms spread like wings, his eyes burning with a god's fury.

The swell surged tenfold. The Gull staggered sideways, smashed broadside by walls of water that should not have existed. Jake, Ben, and the girls clung to the wreck as chaos engulfed them.

A sound arrived—deeper than thunder, older than language—a bellow from beneath the abyss. The sea split, and the Leviathan rose. The Leviathan was scale and abyss, an ancient dread coiled in the marrow of creation. Its head broke the surface, longer than the Gull itself was, eyes like abyssal suns burning with alien light. When it breathed, the world recoiled—the air tasted of salt and iron, death and birth entwined. The ocean obeyed it. Waves curled at its whim, breaking against the Gull like hammers, splitting planks, snapping masts.

With a single flex of its colossal body, the Leviathan rolled, and the Gull's spine snapped. The yacht broke in two. Screams cut across the night. Katie was torn from the deck and swept into the black, her cry swallowed by the sea. The others clung to what wreckage they could: Anika to a shard of railing, Jake to the twisted remains of the mast, Leila to the burning edge of a cabin roof. And Ben... Ben was nowhere.

The Leviathan's shadow swallowed them all. On the Fast Dealer VII, the deckhands moaned against their bindings, helpless, their terror a raw chorus. The sea monster ignored them; they were ants in time, beneath its notice.

The god on the waves—Posi—was not. Posi landed on what remained of the Gull, with a crash that buckled planks. The water rose to greet him, steadying his footing as if it had hands.

He stood in the spray, hair plastered to his face, every inch a god returned to his throne.

“You think you can run?” His voice carried, amplified by the sea itself.

“You think a stolen vessel and stolen lives give you passage through my waters? You defy me?” His words struck harder than the waves.

The Gull’s survivors stared into the storm, knowing they faced no mortal captain but the ocean’s master made flesh.

And beneath it all—unseen, unheard by the god’s fury—Ben sank.

The blow that had thrown him clear was no weapon, just the sheer force of the Gull’s break. A jagged spar had struck his head, and darkness had swallowed him. He drifted down, arms limp, lungs burning as salt water forced its way in.

In that drowning silence, something in the world tightened around him, then failed to complete the knot. The crushing dark—his unconsciousness—became a pressure-wave inside his bones, as if his skeleton had been struck like an instrument.

The command wasn’t heard. It was enacted.

Wake.

Convulsions tore through him. His body seized, legs kicking against the crushing dark. Aeons unspooled behind his eyes—lives not his, deaths that had not yet come, battles that had scarred stars and seas. The memories of a thousand forgotten selves surged up at once, breaking him open from the inside.

He should have died.

Instead, his sentence failed to land.

Awareness returned in shards—jagged, incomplete, terrible. Not knowledge. Not answers. Only the raw certainty that he had been made for a use he did not remember choosing.

He was a weapon.

Perhaps something worse.

Ben's eyes snapped open in the abyss. He exhaled the last of his air in a burst of bubbles, then bent himself into the coil of a predator about to strike. With one furious kick, he launched upward, through the wreckage of dreams and water alike. The surface split around him—he shot from the depths like a harpoon, landing on a floating spar.

Instinct—unnatural, lightning-swift—drove him. His hands grabbed, his feet pushed. Every piece of wreckage was no longer debris but a stepping stone, each wave mis-timed in a way that kept lifting him closer.

But before he turned to the god, his eyes found the others.

Anika—flailing.

Jake—clinging.

Leila—slipping.

He leapt across the foam, found three life buoys half-loosened from their hooks, and hurled them with precision no storm could shake. Each one struck true. Anika caught hers with a sob. Jake locked his arm through his. Leila's fingers found hers at the last second before the sea claimed her.

They lived.

He couldn't see Katie. He didn't know if she was alive.

Only then did he look back at Posi.

The Leviathan loomed behind the god, its vast body breaking the horizon, a living mountain of scale and storm. Its eyes burned downward, fixed on the wreck and the mortals who defied its master.

Ben felt something at his back, but not hands. Not voices. Only a pressure—faint as weather—settling between his shoulder blades, easing the reflex that had begun to lock. The note burned through him, no longer silent, not quite sound: a subsonic ache that made the bones of his feet believe the sea could hold weight.

His body answered faster than thought.

Luck didn't smile. It simply miscounted the storm—leaving narrow corridors where none should have been.

And still, the god stood waiting.

The sea hunched its shoulders and flung them together.

Posi came off his moving perch like a blade, spray feathering from his legs. Ben met him mid-chop, feet finding a sliver of wave that had no business being solid. It stiffened for an instant—just long enough—and then forgot it ever had. Their bodies struck with a crack that belonged in stone.

Posi's hand shot for Ben's throat.

Ben slipped inside it—too quick, too precisely timed for anything human—and drove both palms into the god's sternum. The note tore loose through his arms, a force without sound. Skin lit under Posi's chest, hairline fractures flaring and fading like lightning trapped beneath glass.

The god rocked back a half-step. The ocean rushed to brace him.

“Champion,” Posi said, eyes cold. “Pretender.”

He flicked two fingers. Water around Ben sharpened into knives. Edges hissed toward rib and eye.

Ben moved on reflex that wasn’t learned.

A length of hatch cover kicked up beneath him like a sprung trapdoor, driven by a gust that hadn’t existed a moment before. It shoved him aside just enough. The blades sheared past and chewed the timber instead.

He landed in a crouch on a stanchion that hadn’t been there when he’d looked for footing—then it failed at exactly the right instant, snapping beneath him and hurling him forward into Posi’s guard.

His right hand hammered the god’s jaw. His left caught wrist, barely in time to keep the return strike from taking his ear off.

Posi answered by hurling a fistful of condensed sea—a green cannonball. Ben tried to slip it, but it hit like a car. He somersaulted into white water, ribs screaming.

The world miscounted.

The next wave arrived late by half a beat, leaving a thin pocket of air where there should have been none. A loose loop of line—impossible to explain—brushed his hand at the only moment it could matter. He grabbed without thinking and was hauled upward by a jerk of motion that felt less like rescue and more like gravity briefly arguing with itself.

He was on Posi again before the god’s next thought finished.

In the terror across the wreck field, the Leviathan reared.

Jake and Leila, feeling the stirrings of something much deeper inside, rode its shadow. Jake's mouth was open, taking air like a grown man who'd been held under too long. He let the worst thing in him out—not panic, not rage—the heavy certainty of endings. It seeped into the water like cold dye, thickening the world around the serpent's head. The fabulous jaw slowed as if memory seized it: nets, winter, empty bellies.

The bite still came. It came dulled.

Leila bared her teeth at the mountain of scales. "Here," she said—not loud, not pleading. Inviting. "Look at me." The Leviathan's gaze ticked to her. That fraction was space. The bite took a slab of wreck instead of their legs. Iron shrieked and vanished between teeth. The wash tried to suck them after; the rope on Leila's buoy snubbed hard and held because the knot tied itself cleaner than any sailor could have managed in a storm.

She ran her fingers over the water like a harpist. A current leaned the wrong way, giving Jake purchase. He hauled, dragging them both outside the next sweep of tail.

Back on the god's platform, Posi tried to drown the air.

The world's pressure turned inward on Ben, a tightening throat around lungs and heart. He saw stars at the corners of his vision, shoulder to shoulder with the flashes of other lives: desert suns, snow fields, a spear in a different hand. He put his palms together and screamed between them—a mute blast that pierced the pressure, drawing fresh air in.

He slid on a skin of water that had decided to be level and drove an elbow into Posi's mouth. Blood salted the rain.

The god smiled through it. "Good." The smile didn't reach his eyes. He closed a fist.

A ring-current spun up around them, tight, dragging everything toward a dark throat. Wreckage pinwheeled. A flare case clipped Ben's shoulder, bounced, then bounced again, back into his palm. Luck arrived without explanation. He struck it alive along Posi's forearm. White fire spat. Steam screamed from God-skin. The ring stuttered.

Leviathan's head flinched away from the brightness of the flare.

Jake felt the deckhands on Fast Dealer VII—men heading the bow-tip toward a panic's edge. He held his thoughts against fear. With a grunt, he pushed his emotion toward the serpent. Despair is easy. Aimed despair is art. He gave the beast another drag of winter.

Its tail came late.

Leila stepped into that lateness and touched the scale. Every instinct said don't. She ignored all of them. Her wet palm pressed into an overlap the size of a shield. Heat steamed her skin. She didn't command. She offered. Yield. Not forever. Now. The plates under her hand loosened by the slightest degree. The enormous body made a tiny, confused writhe.

The next wave of water passed over them rather than through them.

Posi lifted his arms. The sea gathered to crush.

Ben didn't wait. He attacked first, human, ugly, close. Forearm across Posi's windpipe, hip driving, heel hooking ankle.

They went down into the green.

The god's thumb sought Ben's eye. Ben bit the thumb to the bone and shoved the heel of his hand under Posi's collarbone, where the light bled. The note went in like a nail. The fractures flashed brighter.

Posi twisted, and the ocean twisted with him, putting Ben beneath. Hands became weight, weight became depth.

The champion should have gone. He didn't. The wind shoved up from below like a bellows, the next wave forgot to be heavy for a blink, and Ben broke surface into rain with his fist already swinging.

He caught Posi high on the cheek. Something important in the god's face made a sound like stone under a heat wave.

"Ben!" Leila's voice cut. She was standing on a chunk of deck that shouldn't have supported a bird. "On your left!"

He didn't look. He moved. A water scythe went where his neck had been. He used the blade's wake like a step and crossed it, both palms lighting Posi's ribs with another silent concussion.

Posi answered by turning a yard of chop into a solid wall. It hit Ben like a truck and tried to fix him to the wave. The wall failed to hold him. Pressure bled out of it like air from a punctured lung. What should have been solid arrived imperfect, sloughing into water at his shoulders—just enough for him to slip, just enough to live.

Leviathan coiled, gathering. It came for Jake and Leila low, teeth spread to take raft and rope and prayer.

Jake filled the water between with failure—the deal that won't close, the breath that won't come, the frost that kills at dawn. The jaw trembled.

Leila leaned into that tremble, voice like a hand under a chin. "Down," she whispered to a mountain. "Rest."

For a heartbeat, the Leviathan's great head sank six inches. Not submission. A blink.

The bite missed their throats and took empty sea. The wash tore Leila loose—only for a knotted strap from a drowned kit-bag to whip around her wrist like a lasso. She spun, swore, and came up beside Jake again. Horror and thrill fought in her eyes. She did not have room for both. She chose fury.

Posi saw the serpent hesitate and went from cold to clean rage. "Mine," he said. The word struck the ocean like a hammer. The coil tightened for another strike.

Ben's hands hit the water, fingers spread, palms down. "No," he told the same sea, and the silent scream left him, not outward but into the element like a tuning fork into wood. The wave that should have delivered the Leviathan's charge faltered, arriving in rags. The beast still came. Just slower. Just late.

Late was enough.

Ben closed with the god one more time. Posi's knee snapped up toward his groin; Ben parried with a forearm and took a shin across his thigh instead. He saw the next hand before it moved, reflexes living a half-second ahead, and slipped it, answering with a short, mean hook under the ribs. The blow should not have moved a thing like Posi. It did. A centimetre. Human distance. The kind you can build a win on if you survive long enough.

For a heartbeat, the world held. Then all three powers moved to claim it. Deck and sea became one ruin—timber, foam, and bound men rolling under flares and Leviathan-shadow. Even the sea itself waited—listening.

Then Ben moved with a speed that belied exhaustion, every nerve thrumming with power. His note—the silent scream—still echoed through marrow and water, a lingering vibration that unsettled even the god before him.

Posi staggered across the listing deck, soaked and snarling, his fine suit clinging to him like a burial shroud. His eyes burned with inhuman fire, the last vestiges of a god's defiance against inevitability. "You think you can kill me, boy?" Posi spat, his voice like crashing surf. "I was before you, and I will be after you. You are nothing."

Ben did not answer. His hands bled from the shattered railing he had ripped free, a jagged length of oak sharpened by fury and chance. It was no longer wreckage but judgement. Each heartbeat pressed heavier against his ribs, pounding with the rhythm of aeons, and awakened breath in his lungs.

Posi charged, faster than a man, stronger than a bull. The deck quaked beneath his feet.

Ben met him, parried with bare hands, absorbing the shock of divine flesh against mortal sinew. Reflex made him faster. Desperation made him stronger.

The sea's balance slipped a fraction out of its own accounting. A shard of lightning split the horizon. For a heartbeat, both combatants stood carved in white flame—one a god of old seas, the other a mortal with death painted across his face.

Then Ben thrust. The jagged oak drove forward with all the force of storm and sorrow behind it. Posi's chest took the blow—resistance like stone, then the sickening give of flesh. The shard drove deep, splintering ribs, cracking sternum, piercing through heart and spine. The note answered through the wood—an impossible resonance that turned god-flesh briefly honest. The god's roar became a gurgling cry, half rage, half disbelief.

For an instant, time broke.

The wind died. The waves bowed flat as polished marble. Even the Leviathan reared back, its endless coils rising from the abyss to witness the undoing. Bound men on deck whimpered behind their gags, eyes wide with primal terror. Leila and Jake clung to wreckage, staring at Ben not as comrades but as executioners.

Posi sagged forward, his mouth spilling dark brine instead of blood. His eyes, once sharp as a shark's teeth, dimmed, flickered, then rolled back. With a final convulsion, the sea god crumpled around the timber that pinned him to the ruined deck. His breath rattled once more, then ceased.

And the ocean wept.

The waves rose higher, not in wrath but in mourning. Swells gathered, cresting white with foam, rolling outward as if to carry the god's departing soul. A low groan came from the depths, resonant as whale-song but more profound, older—an elegy sung by the sea itself. All who heard it felt grief cut sharp through their marrow, as though the world had lost one of its cruel but necessary rulers.

Ben stood over the corpse, chest heaving, soaked and shaking. His hands still gripped the timber, though there was no need now. The man before him—no, the god—was no more. He had done the impossible. He had killed divinity.

The Leviathan screamed.

It was no mortal sound. No animal voice. It was the breaking of mountains, the collapse of chasms, the shattering of glaciers. The sea boiled as the creature unfurled its colossal body, no longer bound by Posi's dominion. Its eyes glowed like abyssal lanterns, burning hatred into every living thing upon the surface.

Free now, untethered, it turned not on Ben but on the world itself.

Jake and Leila gasped, their bodies thrumming with the agony of awakening. Powers long buried now coursed through them—Jake's despair bleeding into the air like smoke, drawing the very hope from the lungs of men. Leila's seduction pulsing like a siren's call, her voice turning even fear itself into aching desire. Together they pressed their will against the Leviathan, buying heartbeats of respite, but it was like trying to chain a storm with silk. Their gifts could slow the serpent, never stop it.

With a nod of knowing, the Leviathan slid beneath the waves, vanishing into the abyss. Yet the sea above trembled, restless, ready to shatter shipping lanes, to rise against cities, to devour coasts.

It was free, and the world would bleed for that freedom.

Ben staggered, staring into the black horizon. His lungs burned with salt and fire. He felt the air behave strangely around his skin—thin, charged, like the moment before lightning chooses a path. Not triumph. Not urging. Just a readiness in the fabric of things, as if outcomes were briefly unclaimed. But his thoughts, still mortal enough to ache, turned instead to Jake, to Leila, to Anika somewhere among the wreckage.

Survival, not glory, was the first duty.

Leila's voice, ragged and hypnotic, broke through the roar. "Ben... what have you done?"

He could not answer. The words would not come. He only knew the truth: something had broken loose, and nothing would ever cage it again.

Above, the storm gathered in solemn salute. Thunder rolled not as rage but as a dirge. Lightning burned the name of the sea serpent across the sky. Old myths stirred in their graves, and sailors yet unborn would one day speak it with dread.

Jörmungandr.

The sea, though easing, still heaved with the violence of what had just unfolded. The Gull was gone, torn apart in Posi's madness and the Leviathan's rising, but somehow Fast Dealer VII still rode the swells, battered yet afloat.

For Ben, every stroke through the black water felt like dragging chains. His body ached, his chest burned, yet the water carried him in small, improbable increments—currents arriving out of order, lifting him when they should have pressed him down.

Through the spray, he saw her. Katie. She clung to the stern ladder of Fast Dealer VII, hair plastered, eyes huge, knuckles white with strain. She was bruised, trembling, but alive. Against all odds, she had reached the vessel before them, carried perhaps by luck, perhaps by something more. Relief near broke Ben. He swam harder, spurred by the sight of her.

Behind him, Leila kicked steadily with Anika in tow, both half-submerged and clinging to a buoy line. Jake floundered further back, pale, lips bluish, but sheer will dragged him forward.

Together, battered survivors of gods and monsters, they closed the last distance.

Ben's hands closed on the ladder, and with a final heave, he rolled onto the deck. The planks pitched beneath him, slick with seawater, but he did not care. Katie was there. Her trembling hand brushed his face as if to prove he wasn't some drowned ghost.

"You made it," she breathed.

"So did you." His laugh was broken, half a sob.

Leila hauled herself up next, dragging Anika with her, both collapsing in a heap against the gunwale. Jake came last, pulling his sodden body over the rail and collapsing on his back, chest heaving. For a time, none of them spoke, letting rain and sea wash over them.

Alive—that was all that mattered.

Then came the sound. Muffled grunts. Ben lifted his head. At the foredeck, lashed to the stanchions, two men writhed against soaked ropes. Faces pale, jaws clenched around sodden gags. Recognition cut through the haze: the Fast Dealer VII's deckhands. The very ones the girls had subdued before the chaos took hold.

Ben staggered toward them, his body trembling with exhaustion yet driven by something more profound.

He ripped the gag from the first man's mouth. "We didn't want this!" the deckhand spat, words tumbling with salt water. "We were chained to him! You saw what he was—how could we fight that?"

The second nodded frantically, his gag muffling his pleas until Ben tore it free. "We weren't loyal to him. We had no choice. You killed him. Please... Don't leave us bound."

Jake had risen now, gaunt but steady. His presence seemed to draw the despair from the men like smoke, pressing down on them until their knees buckled even in their bonds. He studied them, weighing their truth.

"What will you do," Jake asked at last, voice low, "if we cut you loose?"

The first swallowed, meeting his eyes. "Work. Sail. Pull our weight. Follow orders that don't damn us."

For a long moment, Jake said nothing. He could have drowned them with a thought, fed their hopelessness until they collapsed into the sea. But there was no malice in their eyes—only the raw terror of men long bent under chains.

He reached for his belt and drew a knife. The deckhands froze, breath caught.

The blade flashed—but instead of throats, it found ropes. One after the other, the bindings parted. The two men sagged forward, wrists raw, rubbing blood back into their hands. "You'll serve here," Jake said flatly. "You're crew now. Fast Dealer VII. You'll bleed, sweat, row, and haul—but for us, not for a god already rotting."

The deckhands nodded quickly, relief flooding their faces. "Aye, captain," one muttered hoarsely. Katie and Anika, still pale, began dragging coils of rope into order. The two freed men scurried to help, awkward but eager, proving their loyalty with every tug of the line. The ship slowly came back to life—not strong, not whole, but alive enough to sail.

Ben stood apart, shoulders heaving. His hands still throbbed with the memory of the fight, with the newfound power in him. He felt a draw in him—distant, indifferent—like a tide that didn't care whether he could swim.

Leila joined him at the stern, rain dripping from her lashes, eyes sharp even through exhaustion.

"They'll follow Jake," she said, nodding at the deckhands already moving at his barked orders.

"As they should," Ben murmured.

"And us?"

Ben stared into the black horizon where the Leviathan had vanished. He could feel it still, deep below, unbound and hungry. And along with that sense came something else—the clarity of his awakening. The convulsions in the sea had shown him more than strength. They revealed direction.

"I know where I have to be," Ben said at last. His voice was quieter than the rain but heavier than thunder. "I've seen others in dreams. The ones still asleep."

Leila's lips curved, the faintest ghost of a smile. "Then we go and wake them."

Ben's jaw tightened. "Yes. Because what we've done here—this was only the beginning."

Behind them, Jake's commands grew steadier. Katie and Anika hauled lines with trembling resolve. The deckhands bent their backs to labour, eager to prove they belonged. Fast Dealer VII creaked, groaned, but lived.

Yet the world was changed.

Somewhere the Leviathan swam free, turning its hunger toward the lanes of a civilisation unprepared. Nations would whisper in dread. And Ben—bloodied, battered, unbroken—knew he had purpose. He was not only a survivor. He had killed a god. And his road ahead had only begun.

Chapter 17
The Flight

The sea did not forgive. It lay hushed and heavy, as though it had swallowed too much blood to move freely. Smoke smeared the horizon where the Westward Gull had gone under. Fast Dealer VII limped through the swell, her seams creaking, her crew ragged and raw.

Ben leaned on the rail, a ruined wallet heavy in his pocket. The world's largest secret war had just spilled into the open sea, and all he owned was a Medicare card, a driver's license, and a damp credit card that might or might not still swipe.

He flexed his hands. His knuckles wept salt and blood, but deeper, something else moved. Breath that wasn't his. Reflexes born from a thousand lives he hadn't lived. He felt the tug of them now—three sharp pulls in different directions, pulling at his chest like compass needles magnetised by fate.

One where the air bit with frost. One restless with glass and thunder, and one where fire hummed under dunes.

Jake lit a cigarette that had survived in a wax paper twist. He dragged once, exhaled, and handed it to Leila.

"You look like a man who just realised he's broke," Jake said to Ben.

Ben shook his head. "Not broke. Stripped."

Leila's gaze held him. "Stripped for what?"

"For this." He tapped his chest where the pulls gnawed. "There are three more. If I don't get to them before the gods do, they'll be trapped. If that happens, we're finished."

Katie looked up from her mug. "How do you even know where they are?"

"I don't." Ben stared at the water. "I just feel it like knowing which way is down. It's there. Always there."

Jake flicked ash into the sea. "Even if I buy that, how exactly do you plan to chase them down? You drowned everything you owned. You've got no passport, no papers, no cash. Airlines don't take Medicare cards."

Ben pulled the soggy wallet out and opened it with his thumb. Plastic glistened, cheap against the dawn light.

He held it up like proof of a bad joke.

"This is it," Leila smirked without humour. "Not even enough for a bus fare to Ballina."

Ben pocketed it again. "I'll fly. One way or another."

Jake laughed softly, shaking his head. "Fly. C'mon. You really think luck's going to carry you through international borders?"

Ben turned from the rail and met his eye. "It has to—it's not luck anymore. It's like the world allows. You felt it last night. Everything broke, and still we're here. That wasn't luck. That was permission."

No one answered. Even Jake's smirk thinned. The sound of the sea was louder than it should have been.

Jake met Ben's eyes. "You've got your hunt. I've got mine. Wake the others. I'll keep the sea honest—with this."

Ben nodded. Leila stepped closer, chin high. "He's not going alone," she said.

Jake looked at her and shook his head. "And you've got even less ID than he has. You're mad." Then he turned back to his new crew.

The two freed deckhands worked quietly behind him, ropes hissing in calloused palms. Katie and Anika huddled near the hatchway in silence, watching him more than the sea.

Jake spat into the water. "Fast Dealer VII's dead," he said, voice hard. "She went down with Posi. What came back isn't her." He slapped the salt-bitten rail. "From today, she sails as the Fading Dawn. Let every harbour and patrol know the light dies when we pass."

The name hung in the air like smoke from a funeral pyre. The deckhands muttered it, first uncertain, then with pride. Katie gave a faint nod, and Anika's tired smile held something sharper. Even the ship seemed to draw herself up at the sound, as if she accepted the baptism.

The division was done. Ben and Leila would try to fly. Jake would sail under the shadow of a new name.

They made Noumea by mid-morning. The harbour was sun-bleached, cranes and pastel buildings shining against the Pacific. The Fading Dawn slid into berth with weary grace. A tugboat horn shrieked in the channel, pulling customs officers away, and by the time anyone looked back, ropes were already ashore.

At the foot of the pier, Jake clasped Ben's hand. "Don't look back," he said. "The sea will still be here." Then he turned away, barking orders, already stitching his name to the Fading Dawn's future.

Ben and Leila walked into Noumea's airport terminal with salt still on their clothes. It was a patchwork of fluorescent halls and tired carpets.

Ben bought two one-way tickets to Darwin with a credit card swollen with more balance than it deserved. The clerk frowned at her screen—paused—blinked—then printed passes without asking for passports.

Leila shook her head as they walked away. "She didn't see me."

"She saw you," Ben said. "Then forgot."

Security was no harder. A guard looked at Ben's driver's license, nodded, and waved him through. His eyes skipped over Leila as if her space in the world had been erased.

That night, as they waited for their flight, the world around them had changed.

It began with a radio crackle from an eastbound freighter: garbled shouts, then a silence no technology could explain.

Another followed minutes later, its coordinates cutting off in mid-broadcast. Then another. Ten ships in less than two hours.

That morning, the Australian Government had launched aircraft from Darwin and Townsville to track the thing now rampaging through the Coral Sea. Pilots reported sonar shadows too large for screens, wakes like trenches torn in the ocean. They flew low, dropping flares to warn merchantmen to change course, to flee. Some ships managed to veer away, churning desperately for open water. Others were gone, pulled down in moments.

In Canberra, an emergency session was convened. Advisories were broadcast on every frequency: "All commercial shipping to avoid Coral Sea routes. Sea anomaly activity confirmed. Divert immediately."

The news spread like fire. Televisions in the terminal played the duplicate footage again and again: grainy satellite images of ships breaking apart; vast swathes of ocean churning like a living storm; a blurred still of something vast surfacing under a freighter before the feed cut to static.

Governments across the world called emergency meetings. Japan closed lanes south of Guam. Singapore suspended all insurance for vessels bound east. The United States offered naval support in "international waters." Even China admitted its convoys would hold back.

But what unsettled people most was not the threat to trade. It was the realisation that the old stories might have been true. Anchormen said the word "Leviathan" with nervous smiles that didn't last. Scholars appeared on panels, some laughing too loudly, others pale and silent. Ancient myths—dismissed for centuries—were suddenly back on the table, and they were killing by the hundred.

A French broadcast rolled on screen. Survivors were interviewed, men wrapped in blankets, eyes wide. One sailor whispered of black scales the size of sails, of a mouth that opened wider than his ship's deck, of a scream in the water that rattled his bones.

Another cried when asked what he'd seen.

Leila sat rigid beside Ben, her hands clenched in her lap. "They can't fight that," she said. "Not with jets. Not with fleets."

"They'll try," Ben answered. His voice was low, steady. "Because they have to. But it won't stop."

He didn't add what the pull in his chest already told him: the Leviathan wasn't mindless. It wasn't rage alone. It was grief, yes, but also a sentinel. It had been unleashed, and it was hunting.

Around them, passengers watched the news, pale-faced. Some muttered prayers. Others argued about refunds. But most just stared at the screens, silent, as though the sea itself had reached through and reminded them that humankind had never truly been in charge.

Back in Noumea's harbour, the Fading Dawn cast off lines. Jamie and Reuben pulled the ropes in with a new purpose. Katie and Anika stood on deck, pale but resolute, watching Jake at the rail. He barked once, and one of the crew unfurled a canvas from the masthead. The cloth snapped in the salt wind, black against the bright sky.

The skull and crossbones grinned wide, jaw unhinged, eyes hollow.

On the docks, men turned and stared. Some laughed nervously. Others crossed themselves. A few backed away, unwilling to name what they saw. Jake's grin was thin and hard. The Fading Dawn was no trawler now. She was a pirate's ghost given steel and steam. She would not be mistaken for anything else.

Ben, watching from the terminal window, felt a shiver run through him. The road ahead pulled at him with frost, fire, and storm. But behind him, on the water, Jake had just declared war on the age of reason.

The world was watching. And the world did not blink.

They boarded under drizzle, the smell of jet fuel sharp. Engines howled, wheels tore across the runway, and Noumea shrank behind them. Ben stared out at the Pacific as the plane lifted, the pull in his chest tightening with the climb. Snow, storm, and dunes, the dreaming. All waiting. All vulnerable. When he opened his eyes again, the horizon ahead was already burning toward Darwin.

Darwin struck them like a furnace. The plane's door opened onto wet heat that rolled through the cabin, thick as breath. Ben and Leila walked down the steps with the rest of the passengers, their clothes sticking to their skin, the pull in his chest gnawing sharper with every stride.

The airport was more outpost than city—low buildings, peeling paint on service hangars, the buzz of insects fighting the sodium lights. But its runways were suddenly among the busiest in the world.

Every screen in the terminal blared the same breaking story. The Leviathan had torn through the Coral Sea lanes again, and this time the death toll was higher. Not ten freighters, but twenty-two, their final transmissions clipped and terrified, their locations plotted like tombstones on a map behind the anchor's head.

The Australian Government had gone to full emergency footing. Surveillance aircraft from Townsville and Darwin flew in rotation, shadowing the creature's path. An RAAF P-8 Poseidon had caught blurred imagery of something rising through the waves—a curve of scale, the suggestion of a spined ridge, the white churn of sea displaced by impossible mass. The government spokesman tried to call it "anomalous marine seismic activity," but even his voice cracked on the syllables.

"Prime Minister to convene emergency session of Cabinet," the news ran. "International shipping diverted indefinitely. Naval consultations ongoing."

Leila stopped at a screen. Her face caught the light, pale with the same question that hung over the whole hall: Myths are real, what next?

Passengers whispered in half a dozen languages. A man in a business suit muttered that it was a conspiracy. A woman clutched a crucifix until her knuckles whitened. Two children pointed at the Leviathan's name in the headlines as though it were a cartoon monster.

Ben stood with his wallet in hand, feeling the tug behind his ribs insisting west, then further, past deserts, to where stone met sun. But for the moment, the world was fixed on the sea.

At the transfer desk, a harried clerk looked up only once. Ben slid his credit card across, salt-warped but still functioning. "Two tickets," he said. "Darwin to Dubai. Tonight."

The clerk's eyes flickered to his driver's license, a frown already forming. "International? I'll need—"

She stopped. Blinking. The cursor on her screen jumped as though struck. She tapped keys, muttered to herself, then sighed as if too tired to continue the fight. "Cleared," she said finally. "Gate Eleven." She printed boarding passes.

Only afterwards did her mouth twitch in confusion, as if she'd lost a thought that had been important.

Leila slipped her ticket into her pocket without a word.

Security was worse. Armed officers patrolled the queue, the new crisis written on their shoulders. The lines were restless, people arguing in three languages at once. One guard barked instructions over the crowd: "Keep your documents visible!"

Leila had none. Ben kept his license ready, holding it as if it were a passport.

The officer at the scanner frowned, tilted it once, then back, as if trying to remember what it was supposed to prove. His eyes clouded for a heartbeat, then he stamped a slip and waved Ben through. Leila walked after him. No one asked. No one stopped her. The guard's gaze drifted past her, fixing instead on a family juggling luggage.

They stepped into the duty-free hall, the smell of perfume and whiskey washing over them.

Leila let out her breath slowly. "Every time I think it can't hold, it holds."

Ben folded the slip and put it in his wallet. "It's not luck. It's tilted. The world doesn't want us stopped—not yet."

The waiting lounge throbbed with news updates. A BBC anchor spoke over grainy footage: an aerial shot of oil slicks, lifeboats overturned, and something vast sliding beneath the surface like a mountain retreating into the earth.

"Governments across the Pacific are convening emergency councils tonight. The Japanese Maritime Self-Defence Force has ordered destroyers to sortie south. The United States has dispatched a carrier group from Guam. Chinese convoys remain in port, awaiting further instruction."

Another feed showed a map—shipping lanes—arteries of global trade—glowing red where they'd been shut. Economists talked of trillions at risk. Politicians spoke of myths coming true. No one said what would happen if Leviathan moved closer to shore.

Leila watched, lips tight. "They'll try to cage it."

"They'll try," Ben said. His voice was low. "But it won't be caged."

A child cried somewhere behind them. The sound felt truer than anything on the screens.

The boarding call came just after midnight. They joined the line at Gate Eleven, two shadows among many. No one asked questions. The clerk scanned their passes with a beep and never once asked for passports.

They stepped onto the jet bridge, the hum of engines vibrating through the floor. On the tarmac, another aircraft roared upward—an RAAF jet, banking east into the dark, hunting shadows that could not be fought. Its afterburners lit the sky in angry orange, then vanished.

Ben and Leila boarded their own flight, bound not for battle but for the next sleeper. Dubai first. Then Morocco.

The world tilted beneath them. And the world did not blink.

Dubai at night was not a city but an announcement. The aircraft banked low over the Persian Gulf, and the horizon burst alive: towers like steel candles, highways lit like molten veins, islands carved by arrogant hands.

Ben pressed his forehead to the glass, the pull in his chest tugging west, across desert and sea, harder now. Morocco. The next step was already written in his bones.

The airport swallowed them in glass and marble, too polished to feel real—ceilings arched like cathedrals, every surface shining with money's version of eternity. The air smelled of perfume, steel, and jet fuel. Thousands moved around them—business-people, pilgrims, tourists, soldiers—a river of humanity threading through the most extravagant hall humankind had built for itself. And every screen in this hall now blared Leviathan.

It had moved further south. Not ten, not twenty, but thirty-four ships now confirmed lost. An RAAF pilot described it on live feed, his voice trembling in the crackling connection: "It... It surfaces under them. You don't understand. It isn't attacking. It's a choice. It lets some pass. Others, it drags straight down."

Governments scrambled. The UN had called an emergency assembly. NATO's maritime command declared the Coral Sea a no-go zone. Chinese and American diplomats clashed on a live broadcast over who had the right to "contain" the beast. Insurance firms declared bankruptcy within hours.

Leila paused at one of the giant screens. It played satellite imagery of freighters breaking apart, their hulls vanishing into churning black swells. Then, suddenly, a blurred still—not just a shadow this time. A curve of scale, unmistakably real, catching sunlight before sliding under. The anchor whispered the word that now belonged to every mouth on earth: Leviathan.

"It's breaking them," Leila said. Her voice was low, but steady. "Not just the ships. The order. The world itself."

Ben nodded. "It's grief and wrath. But it's also proof. The gods kept men small by calling these things myths. Now myths walk again."

At the transfer desk, the clerk had skin like glass and eyes rimmed with exhaustion. Ben slid his battered credit card across, heart beating hard. “Two one-way tickets to Casablanca,” he said.

The clerk typed. Stopped. Typed again. Frowned. “Sir, I’ll need—” Her eyes unfocused for a heartbeat, then cleared. She blinked, confused, then printed boarding passes without another word. When she handed them over, her hands shook slightly, as though she’d lost time. Ben pocketed the tickets.

Leila hadn’t been spoken to once.

As they stepped away, Leila’s whisper carried a tremor. “It’s bending them, every time. Like the world itself wants us through.”

“Not the world,” Ben said. “The balance. Whatever still holds it wants this to happen. Wants us moving faster than the gods.”

Security was thick. Armed soldiers stood watch, rifles cradled against their chests. Lines stretched, tempers frayed. Arabic, English, Hindi, and Russian were all tangled in the noise of people demanding to move.

Ben offered his driver’s license. The officer scanned it, frowned, and tapped the console. The screen glitched, froze, then spat out approval. A stamp thudded against paper. The officer waved him through, already distracted by the next passenger.

Leila followed without a word. The guard’s eyes never found her.

The duty-free concourse was absurd. Gold stacked in glass cases. Perfume misting from fountains. Whiskey bottles were priced higher than cars. Ben walked past it all, feeling the pull in his chest strain westward, as though Morocco were already pulling him through the gates.

They waited in silence at Gate 32. Screens above them looped news that had become ritual: Leviathan's rampage, governments debating fleets, anchors straining to sound authoritative. But the undertone was panic. Every voice on every channel now admitted what men had denied for centuries: that the myths could be true.

One panel showed a historian pale and sweating. "Sailors have written of the Leviathan for millennia. It was dismissed as an allegory. Perhaps it was a warning. Perhaps the old texts weren't lies."

Another cut to a naval strategist. "If it continues toward major routes—the South China Sea, the Indian Ocean—global trade collapses. It's not just ships we lose. It's food, fuel, and medicine. Civilisation itself balances on those lanes."

Ben listened without comment.

The truth was more straightforward, crueller: man had mistaken order for safety. Now both were gone.

Leila leaned close. "If they hunt it, they'll fail. If they cage it, it'll break free. If they leave it..."

"Then it keeps choosing," Ben said.

"And us?"

He touched the boarding pass in his pocket. "We choose faster."

Boarding was chaos. Families pressed forward in clumps, guards tried to restore order with shouts, and the beep of scanners was almost drowned out by argument. Yet when Ben handed over his pass, the machine chimed clean and green. The clerk never looked twice. Leila's pass wasn't scanned at all. She walked past the barrier, unseen, as if the space she occupied had been erased from the system.

They stepped into the jet bridge, the roar of engines vibrating through steel and bone. Ahead, the aircraft to Casablanca waited, a silver arrow aimed at Africa.

As they walked, Ben glanced through the porthole windows. Out on the tarmac, military transports loaded crates under floodlights. Soldiers barked orders in clipped tones. And in the sky, another aircraft climbed steep and fast—an AWACS radar plane, hunting for something the world didn't yet know how to kill.

Ben pressed his palm against the thin glass of the bridge. The pull inside him hummed. Morocco. The next sleeper waited there.

He looked at Leila.

Her eyes shone sharp, bright with both fear and certainty. "This is it," she said.

Ben nodded. "And it's only the beginning."

They boarded. The doors sealed. The plane rolled into darkness, engines straining. The world tilted west.

The aircraft climbed hard, leaving Dubai's lights scattered like embers across the gulf. The city fell away, a jewelled mirage swallowed by desert night. Ben settled into his seat by the window, shoulders aching from the weight of the pull in his chest. Leila sat beside him, arms folded, eyes closed but not asleep.

He tried to rest, but the hum of the engines merged with something older—a vibration that came not from the plane but from deep inside his ribs. The tilt was tightening, threading his dreams with needles of inevitability. He gave in and let himself fall into it.

The dream did not begin with Morocco. It started with the sea. He saw the Leviathan, half-glimpsed, sliding under waters blacker than night. Its scales flashed with the light of burning ships above, a mountain alive with grief. He felt its scream reverberate through the depths, a note so low it cracked stone. And through the scream, he sensed recognition. It knew him. Not by name, but by scent—by the strange absence of death clinging to his soul. He reached toward it, not in challenge, not in command, but in acknowledgement. The beast turned once, its eye vast and golden, fixing on him across dream's impossible distance. Then it sank, dragging darkness with it, leaving wakes like scars.

The vision shifted—desert sands, endless, rolling like the backs of sleeping giants. Wind hissed through dunes, carrying voices that spoke without words. And beneath, far beneath, a chamber of stone cut from the earth before cities had names. He walked down steps slick with centuries of silence. The air smelled of dust, water, and patience. At the bottom lay a sleeper. The figure was vague at first—neither man nor woman, but a shape coiled in stillness. Cloaked in rags, skin dry as parchment, eyes closed. In its chest, he saw the faintest rise and fall, slower than any human breath. Around it, jars cracked with age, inscriptions in languages that never reached paper. A circle of salt-stained bricks formed a threshold around the body.

Ben stepped closer. The pull inside him surged, hammering at his bones. His throat went dry. He tried to speak, but no word would form. The sleeper stirred. A finger twitched. The sound of shifting stone whispered like thunder. The eyes opened—not fully, but enough—a flash of something unmeasured. Power caged too long. Then the dream snapped shut as a door slammed in his face.

He woke with a gasp, clutching the armrest. The cabin lights were dim, and passengers slept in rows like corpses laid out in shrouds. The engines droned steadily, but his chest still rattled with the dream.

Leila's eyes were open. She had been watching him. "You saw it," she said. Not a question.

He nodded, voice hoarse. "Below the earth. Waiting. It's close. I almost woke it."

She leaned in, whisper sharp. "Not yet. Not until we stand there. If you try from here, you'll tear yourself apart."

He wiped sweat from his brow, nodding. She was right. Whatever he was meant to do—whatever word he was meant to speak—could not be forced through dreams. Still, the vision clung. The sleeper's eyes burned in his memory, half-lidded, furious at being disturbed, yet aching to rise.

Hours blurred. The plane hurtled across continents, the black of night giving way to grey dawn over the Mediterranean. Passengers stirred, stretching, muttering. News tickers ran even here, flickering across the in-flight displays. Leviathan sinks thirty-six ships. International naval coalition formed. UN emergency council to meet in Geneva. Governments warn the public to remain calm.

Leila chuckled without humour. "Remain calm," she muttered. "The myths are walking again, and they tell us to stay calm."

Ben pressed his palm against the window, watching as dawn smeared gold across the cloud banks. "They don't know what calm is anymore."

The wheels struck the Casablanca tarmac hard, jolting everyone awake—the cabin filled with the scrape of seatbelts and the clatter of luggage bins. Outside, the city spread wide, sunlit and sprawling, white stone and minarets rising from the dust. The air shimmered with heat. Ben's chest tightened. The pull was no longer distant. It was here. Close. Like a heartbeat beneath the ground.

Leila touched his hand. "We're closing in."

"Yes," Ben said, his voice steady though his pulse raced. "One more step."

The doors opened, and the air of Morocco rushed in, hot and spiced, carrying the promise of ancient things that refused to die. Casablanca had the smell of dust, salt, and new beginnings. The terminal was hot with bodies and language—French, Arabic, English—layered in impatient currents.

Ben and Leila moved through it unnoticed, though Ben felt every step pulling him harder west, harder down, like a magnet buried under stone. They didn't linger.

A petit taxi took them from the airport to the rail station, the driver smoking furiously and never asking questions. The train north rattled them through scrub and olive groves, minarets flashing past against the haze. Every mile west made the pull stronger.

By the time they reached Fez, Ben could barely think. It was like a rope had been tied through his sternum, tugging him into the Medina. The streets narrowed to shoulder-width alleys, alive with the crush of donkeys, vendors, and smoke from food stalls. The scent of bread, mint, and dust tangled with sweat and prayer.

Leila moved like she belonged, scarf drawn loose, nodding at women she passed. Ben followed, letting the pull choose turns: left, right, down a shaded lane where cats scattered, through a market where merchants shouted of leather and spice, into a courtyard no tourist map had ever named.

The fountain in the centre trickled faintly, its stone lip polished by centuries of hands. A lemon tree leaned over, leaves casting broken shadows. To anyone else, it was a forgotten square.

To Ben, it was a drumbeat. "Here," he whispered. His palm pressed to the stone. The vibration inside him harmonised with the water's faint pulse.

Leila looked around, then stepped to his side. She brushed her fingers across the fountain rim, her voice low. "Open." For a breath, nothing. Then the water stilled. The drain at the centre shuddered, as if exhaling. A seam appeared in the stone, too perfect, too deliberate.

Ben dug his fingers into the crack and pulled. Stone lifted, groaning like it had been waiting a thousand years.

A stairwell yawned below, air rushing up—cool, damp, heavy with old secrets. They descended. Steps spiralled into the dark, brick slick with moisture. The sound of dripping water echoed, each drop like a clock tick. The walls bore faint carvings—eyes, waves, suns with too many rays. At the bottom, the chamber widened. Cisterns ringed the space, their surfaces black mirrors. And in the centre, on a stone dais, lay the sleeper.

The figure was shrouded, skin the colour of parchment, hair brittle as straw. Around the body, jars lay shattered, inscriptions too old for any book. Its chest rose once every half-minute, impossibly slow, yet undeniably alive.

Ben stepped forward, every nerve alight. The pull was deafening now. His knees trembled. He reached out a hand. The sleeper's eyelids twitched. A sigh like shifting sand rolled across the chamber.

Leila hissed, "Careful—" as the eyes opened.

Not fully, but enough. A flash of gold and black, ancient and unblinking. The chamber trembled. Water rippled in every cistern. Symbols on the walls glowed faintly, then died.

Ben staggered back, breath caught in his throat. The sleeper's lips parted, but no sound emerged—only the silence of recognition.

Leila caught his arm. Her voice was steady, though her face was pale. "You've found the first."

Chapter 18
The Gods

Night pressed against the glass. Far below, New York flickered and performed. Up here, truth gathered. Zed and Hera's penthouse—floors of marble, bronze, and black glass—held its guests tensely. Torches burned steadily at Hera's insistence, watching an emergency unfold.

Zed did not sit. He stood with his back to the city, cigar unlit, the crow on his shoulder a black knot of breath. Hera sat. Thrones were for rulers, and tonight her stillness held the room together.

Hera raised her hand, voice deliberate. "We begin with reverence," she said. "Say his name as if the sea itself were listening."

Demi cupped both palms; a clay bowl formed there, salt blooming at its rim. Water climbed the air and settled into it, clear as a held breath.

Zed set a greened brass bell beside it.

Hera spoke first. "Posi." The bell answered—one low, sorrowing note. A heave moved through the room as if a long wave had found a reef.

Demi tipped barley into the water. "For the fields he fed. For rains stolen back from fire."

Rus bowed his head; his light dimmed to amber. "For clean horizons."

Si's whisper made the flames lean to hear. "For tides that rocked the dreaming world."

The bell tolled a second time, unbidden.

Hera laid her palm over the bowl; the water shivered, rose, and shaped a trident before collapsing. "We do not speak carelessly over him," she said. "Whatever else we are tonight, we are his mourners first."

They stood in silence, tension settling among them.

The bell tolled a third time, unbidden.

Hera's fingers closed around the bell's lip, stilling its tremor.

"Now," she said, and the word was not permission—it was a border.

The torches flared back to orange. The city's hum found them again, and with it, the business of the living.

Demi wiped salt from her palms as if it were blood. Thoth opened his ledger. The page resisted, then gave. Zed's crow settled, feathers slicking down like a blade being sheathed.

Grief stayed in the room. But it took a seat.

Athena rose with the calm of a general who has already counted the dead. "The mortal story is forming without us. Ten freighters have been lost in thirty hours, and more since; governments contradict themselves—a reliable sign of fear. The lanes bend around a hunger that doesn't care for lanes."

"Leviathan," Ari said, making the name a challenge.

"The name is loud," Effie murmured. "Mortals will love how it terrifies them."

Rus snapped, his light sharpening. "Then drag the truth into daylight—expose it and boil coastlines."

Demi's stare was iron. "You burn. I count mouths."

Mercury rotated a ring. "Before you torch the ocean—another ledger."

He nodded to Athena. "Show them."

Athena lifted a black rectangle. The torches narrowed; glass behind her darkened, revealing another night: a helicopter falling; a bloodied yacht deck; a man in the water; a shaky body-cam catching everything.

"There were eyes," Athena said. "Not just ours. A fishing trawler, a coast watch drone responding to the mayday, a phone in a terrified hand. Mercury scraped what he could before the feeds were scrubbed."

The replay held. Deck lurched. Rotor screamed. Men shouted. One figure dragged himself over the rail, coughing, bleeding, alive. Another rose—burned, precise in pain—and closed his hand around wreckage.

"Freeze there," Hera said.

The frame caught: the shard raised; the helpless instant where Posi's hand reached to push himself up; the strike. Not elegant. Not ritual. Just force through the sternum. Sea-king, god of the deep, skewered by a splinter of his falling machine while the water itself seemed to rear in salute and in grief.

No one breathed. For a heartbeat, none of them looked like rulers. They looked like survivors watching the first crack spread through glass.

Hera lifted a hand. "One voice at a time. Speak as if the sea is still listening."

Even Ari held. Even Effie's smile thinned. Thoth's pen hovered—ready to make speech permanent—and the pause held long enough to become an indictment.

"The sea rose," Demi said hoarsely. "I felt it in that hour and lied to myself that it was only a storm."

"By a mortal," Jamil said softly, folding his hands with careful, bloodless calm. "The aberrant."

"Not merely mortal," Rus snapped. His light drew inward, hardening. "A god-killer."

"Mind your words," Hera said, her voice cool enough to cut.

"Mind yours," Rus replied. "We mourn our brother and then pretend the tide claimed him? You saw what I saw."

"Doors open to him," Si said, her voice like a tide at night. "Not because he knocks, but because the world still knows his weight."

Effie smiled without warmth. "Then he is either a vessel to be filled, a rival to be feared, or an omen we should already be obeying."

Athena remained standing. "We have only a handful of explanations," she said. "Either the ethereals have chosen a mortal hand to restore the scales. Or he is an in-betweener rising faster than the world can measure. Or something older has returned wearing human skin."

Her mouth tightened. "And the last possibility—the one I like least—is that he is simply a man, and balance itself has decided to make him a weapon."

Mercury's eyes flashed. "Or a story arming itself. Fading Dawn raises a skull, a camera shakes, and within a week, ten thousand mouths repeat a myth with the cadence of truth. Markets move on less."

Jamil's gentle voice made it cruel. "Mortals are many things. Outside, karma is not one of them. He must be ended."

"Cut your teeth on another certainty," Effie said. "If he killed Posi, tell me which of you will be first to pluck him like a weed."

Ari bared his teeth. "I volunteer."

"Sit," Hera said, her tone sharp, and Ari obeyed, the tension releasing slightly as even war responded to command.

Zed finally drew on the cigar; the ember glowed like a small, stubborn sun. "If the boy slew Posi," he said, voice low, "either he is the knife, or the hand that holds him—is."

Si's gaze turned inward. "I dreamt it," she said, and the torches leaned toward her without smoke. "A man outside the stars striking down a sea with a sliver of the sky. The water rose and did not drown him. The moon hid its face."

Rus's light flared. "Then I burn him until even dream remembers fear."

"You burn, and we starve," Demi snapped. "You burn, and the serpent feeds on boiling wakes. You burn, and deserts walk."

"Enough," Hera said—not loud, but absolute. "We will not make Posi's bowl a butcher's table. We honour, and then we decide. But we decided with eyes open. He was killed; a mortal—aberrant or otherwise—struck the blow. That is our horror and our fact."

The bell shivered and rang a fourth time.

"What is he?" Zed asked the room, his single eye hard as winter sun.

No one agreed on an answer.

Athena held up fingers, ticking through the grim options again, colder now that the proof lay in light. The others fell into debate. They talked over each other until Hera's hand rose and silence retook its seat.

"We will proceed as if Athena's hypotheses are true," she said. "Ethereals. In-betweener. Old force in the skin. Balance's hand. We test them each. We build responses for each. And we do not lie to ourselves about what we see."

Fiona tossed her coin—tails. "Luck has chosen him."

Mercury said tightly. "No."

The torches guttered once, as if wind found them in a sealed room.

Thales, who had watched and said little, finally spoke. "A god fell to a shard because the world is full of shards," he said. "That is the only certainty I offer. No throne is proof against small, sharp things in mortal hands."

Hera's jaw set. "Then we will stop giving small, sharp things to men who walk outside karma."

"And if he forges his own?" Rus asked.

"Then we learn what we are," Hera said. "Rulers, cowards, or keepers of a balance we did not make."

Thoth wrote: *Posi—confirmed fallen.* The ink did not dry. The bell stayed quiet, as if listening for the next name. The bowl's surface stilled at last, barley floating like stars.

Somewhere far away, sand remembered a name and shifted.

The city below kept lying to itself, but the room above it did not. They had mourned.

They had named the horror. Now the Reckoning would begin. The bell at Posi's bowl had barely finished shivering when the room changed.

The room changed without anyone moving. Pressure first—like deep water deciding the glass was a suggestion. Then colour: the torches thinned to blue, as if flame had remembered fear. Thoth's pen snapped. Ink spread—wrongly—pooling into a circle that was not a spill but a mouth.

Si's head lifted. Her pupils blew wide until her eyes were two moons. "A door," she said, voice far away. "No. Not a door. The place where doors learn how to close."

Demi had already braced a palm on the marble. Her face went the colour of old chalk. "Roots are pulling back," she whispered. "In Morocco. The soil is refusing its own weight."

Zed's crow shivered against his shoulder. Zed's big hand steadied it by will alone. "Name it," he said. His voice sounded like distant thunder walking on gravel. "Say what stirs."

"No," Hera said—instinct as old as temples. "Do not name it first in this room."

Thoth pressed a blotting cloth to the bleeding page. The fabric went black and did not dry. He swallowed. "There is a mark here older than writing," he said hollowly. "I have seen its shadow once, in a shard dug from a desert wall and put back with trembling hands. The mark means removal. Not death. Not sleep." He looked up. "It means forgetting."

"The earth has forgotten it," Si breathed. "That is the horror. Even stone lets go of its mistakes."

"Mistake?" Ari said.

"Mistake is a kindness," Diane murmured. "Mistake implies record. This is something that even God struck off the ledger."

Athena's fingers flew across a slate of light; maps and signal webs flashed and guttered. "Fez," she said. "Morocco—Medina quarter. Old roofs humming like struck brass, then blank patches, as if a hand erased—" She cut herself off. "There are animals still going in alleyways. There is a wind that blows inward."

Demi nodded once, eyes far. "When we sealed it, the dunes tried to run away."

"What did we call it?" Effie asked softly.

Thoth stared at the black circle eating his page. "If I write its true name, the ledger will have record, and we break Hera's command."

"We called it the Stilled Breath when we were young and still believed we could build cages that outlasted stories," Mercury replied.

The room fell into a hush.

Hera did not move. Not because she was calm—because motion felt like consent. The blue fire shivered once more, as if waiting to see who would blink first.

Zed's eye narrowed. "And what stirred the Stilled Breath?"

Si's voice came like a tide felt through floorboards. "The house opened itself because the wrong guest is standing on the threshold."

"The aberrant," Jamil breathed, almost tender. "Finally, you all feel what I've said: he is outside the law that holds everything upright. Push there, and things fall."

"Did he mean to?" Demi snapped, grief turning at last to anger. "Was this his clever little rebellion? Or did the world mistake his standing for a knock?"

Athena's slate tried again, but the screens remained blank. "We have evidence of his hand in Fez earlier. A girl with him. A rite that wasn't a rite." Her mouth thinned. "He wouldn't have known what stone he kicked—only that he can step where doors will open."

"Intention does not clean the stain," Rus said. Light skating off his feathered jacket. "Posi is dead at his hand. The Stilled Breath is waking because he is rattling his chain. If we don't contain him, he will break the system we have created."

"Perhaps balance has given him the key to locks," Thoth said, and the room looked at him as if he had put a serpent on the table. "If we sealed what could not be killed, perhaps balance has recruited what cannot be counted."

"What are you saying?" Zed asked.

"The power given to him could be from something higher than us."

Jamil's smile was small and sad. "Then the treatment is harsher. We do not counsel. We cut."

"Try it and the wind will buckle your wrist," Diane said, and there was no boast in it—only memory.

Ari's hands opened and closed, starved for the feel of a hilt. "Enough. We circle words while Morocco goes dark."

"We circle words because stepping wrong will crack a continent," Demi countered. "You will not swing at the Stilled Breath as if it were a boar in a thicket."

Pele licked a thumb, and the air sizzled. "Fire teaches deserts new shapes."

"Fire remembers names," Si said sharply for the first time. "If you bring flame near that absence, it will know the shape it forgot and become it. Do you want the Sahara to learn a word that makes it walk?"

Pele, for once, said nothing.

Zed's cigar burned to its middle without losing the ember. He spoke as if the cigar were the only clock he trusted. "Say aloud what we all taste—the boy's hand is in this. Whether he meant to or not. He killed Posi. He is waking the Stilled Breath. He is bending the record."

"If he is the hand of balance," Effie said, "killing him is blasphemy. If he is a rival, killing him is war. If he is a vessel, killing him breaks the vessel and pours the problem into our laps. If he is only a man..." She shook her head. "There is nothing left."

"Decide," Ari demanded. "Who do we stop first, Morocco or the boy?"

"Neither," Hera said, the word a held blade. "We do not sprint at a cliff. We isolate Fez from the media. We watch the Stilled Breath. We trace the boy's steps without letting him hear our feet. We do not throw Posi's wake on a pyre of panic."

Rus made a sound that could have been a laugh, if it had not been so sharp. "Restraint is a noble word to put on fear."

"Then call it wisdom and sit," Hera said. He did not sit. But he did not move.

Outside the glass, the night over New York seemed to thin, as if a sky was borrowing some piece of it on the far side of the world. The torches regained their orange, grudgingly. The pressure eased just enough that lungs remembered how.

Athena watched her failing maps and spoke without looking up. "There will be two more like it," she said quietly. "Siberia under snow. A mountain in the west where stones tilt like stairs to a gone god. We sealed the others. We all know it." No one denied her.

Zed ground the cigar out at last. The ember died reluctantly, like a small sun closing its eye. "Then tonight is the hinge," he said. "A god dead by a shard. An absence waking. A boy whose footprints are doors."

Hera touched the bowl. The barley drifted, stars on black water. "And still," she said softly, "we learn which horror we face."

Zed looked from one face to another. "If the boy found one lock by accident, he will find the others with intent. The hand that killed Posi will not rest with a single horror. We will not give him two more."

Hera's gaze went to Thoth. "Write what we decide. Not what we fear."

Thoth nodded once. Mercury stopped spinning his ring. Even Rus's light steadied—reluctant obedience to structure.

"Postings," Hera said. "Now." Her voice was stripped of doubt. "Two at each seal. Not to fight what sleeps, but to prevent the boy from touching the door."

Thoth wrote: *Siberia—Frozen Lock.*

Demi spoke before anyone could volunteer. "Siberia is mine," she said, firm as stone. "I have walked its permafrost. I know the way soil groans when something presses beneath it. The tundra remembers me."

"I will go with her," Rus said immediately. His light flared in defiance of the cold he imagined. "Darkness there is long. The sun leaves mortals weak and desperate for fire. I will not allow shadow and hunger to coax the seal open. If the boy sets foot on that ice, he will find day waiting for him, whether it is due or not."

Demi frowned at him, but not in refusal. "You will scorch the land if you are careless."

"And you will bind it too tightly if left alone," Rus countered. "Together, the soil will sit, and the light will keep the door buried."

Hera nodded once. "So be it. Rus and Demi—guard the frozen lock."

Thoth wrote: *Andes—Stone Lock.*

Athena's voice was next. "The Andes are mine to watch. The seal lies where roads climb but never finish, where empires once built altars and called them staircases to heaven. Mortals still leave offerings without knowing why. Strategy demands a general there. I will be their silence."

Fiona's coin glimmered in her hand, flashing once, twice. She caught it, eyes bright. "And I will walk with you. The Andes breathe luck and chance—thin air makes men foolish, makes them stumble, makes them see gods in clouds. If the boy climbs, chance itself will trip him before he reaches the lock."

Athena regarded her with suspicion, then nodded. "Logic and fortune. A rare pairing. It may serve."

Hera touched the bowl in front of her, ripples spreading across the barley that floated like stars. "Then it is done. Athena and Fiona—guard the stone lock."

"Two seals, two pairs," Zed said. "Siberia buried, Andes in cloud. Morocco is stirring. The sea serpent and the boy in play." He ground his cigar against the marble until the ember hissed out. "This is the map of our peril—we observe who is holding the boy's strings."

Jamil's voice was soft but cut deep. "You do not give me leave to end him?"

Hera's eyes met his. "You had your chance. What makes you think you can do it now? Until we know what he is—it's too dangerous to try. Should he be balance's hand, killing him may tear the world apart."

Effie leaned back, smile brittle. "Or the boy is writing his own story, all our seals will fall no matter what guards we set, and this becomes his coronation."

"Then let him try to crown himself," Rus said. "He will find us waiting."

The torches guttered, then steadied, but the bowl in front of Hera rippled again, and the barley drifted apart into a shape none of them wanted before the water stilled. Thoth closed his ledger, ink staining his hands to the wrist. "Two posted, one already lost. We are running out of locks to keep the dark from teaching itself new words."

The bowl in front of Hera swirled, barley gathering into a slow, uneasy ring. She leaned forward, voice low enough that the room had to follow it. "The world is cracking elsewhere. Posi is gone. The boy has bloodied the balance. If this council still has a purpose, it is to keep the rest of it from falling with him."

"Seals are manned," Hera said. "Now we turn to the sea." Her gaze moved from face to face. "So speak plainly. How do we contain the Leviathan?"

Athena rose, her eyes sharp as her shield. "Leviathan is hunger given spine. We cannot kill it—but we can confuse it. Mortal ships leave trails of noise. I propose we reroute convoys into shallow corridors where cavitation is weak."

Mercury twirled his ring. "We could try to lure it and trap it in the Mediterranean."

Rus folded his arms. "I could use the Sun's light to ferry it. Daylight unsettles it. If it must rise, it will rise where it is darkest."

Demi's tone was firm. "And once past the Strait of Gibraltar, what then? Panic will break Europe."

"We deal with that once it is contained," Effie replied.

Hera inclined her head. "So it is written. Leviathan will be lured—for now."

The decision sat badly in the room, like medicine taken without water. Hera let it sit anyway. Then she moved the knife to the next throat with a single look. "Next: Jian Wu."

Pele leaned forward, her eyes hot. "Let me. He is burning already—blunt, human fire. I can smother it before it grows."

"No," Demi snapped. "He burns, but water tempers him. He has not scorched indiscriminately."

Hera considered. "Containment, not destruction. Jian Wu listens to the sea. Pele, go and observe. If he loses control, contain him."

Thoth bent to his ledger and wrote the judgement in careful, patient script: *Jian Wu—containment.* The pen lingered as if the word itself resisted him.

"Now—Ellery Kalos," Hera said, as though weighing the name before committing it to the room.

All eyes turned to Jamil. He did not move. "He belongs to my ledger," he said. "Death that walks without knowing itself. I can still him before the world learns his name."

Diane's fingers brushed the bowstring at her hip. "No. He is already a shadow. I will walk beside him until he understands what he is. Better a death that hesitates than one that hungers."

Effie tilted her head. "And when he discovers what you've kept from him?"

"Then he will hate me," Diane said, and did not look away from it.

Effie's eyes flared. "You like him. He should be ended."

"No," Hera said. "Not ended—watched. Diane will shadow him. Jamil will judge him. If he tips too far, the council will act."

Thoth recorded: *Ellery Kalos—shadowed and judged.*

"And Delilah Kitsune."

Effie smiled thinly before Hera even spoke. "She is mine. She is beauty sharpened into vengeance, and that is my province. If I whisper in her ear, her fury can be steered. Chaos can seduce itself into order if the right lips shape the words."

Athena frowned. "You would feed her."

"I would hold her," Effie corrected. "A fox with no leash runs until it falls. A fox on my lap may still bite, but it bites where I point."

Si's voice floated like a tide. "I dreamt her already—blood painted into symbols. If you hold her too tight, she will slip and become symbolic only. That is worse than her knives."

Hera declared, "Give her symbols, then. A fox that believes its scratches are scripture will not look for bigger prey."

Thoth scratched the words into the ledger: *Delilah Kitsune—seduced and distracted.* The ink seemed reluctant to settle.

"And the Aberrant?" Hera asked.

Jamil's voice was cold steel. "End him. Now. Every moment you hesitate is an insult to balance."

"No," Athena said. "Not until we understand. To strike him blind is to lose what lesson balance is teaching."

Rus glared. "If he breathes near the other seals..."

"He will not," Hera cut across. "Two pairs guard them now. Our charge is to hold him from them, not to butcher him in panic."

Demi leaned heavily on the table. "Then place him where soil holds him down. Root him. Bury him in mortal obligations. Work, hunger, debt. He cannot break down doors if he is carrying stones."

Mercury smirked. "Or drown him in lies. If the story cannot find him, neither can the locks."

Fiona caught her coin, eyes glinting. "And if chance insists he keeps walking?"

Hera's gaze hardened. "Then chance itself will have to answer for it."

Thoth dipped his pen and wrote carefully: *Aberrant—buried, blurred, watched.* The words fell on the page like a sentence not yet served.

The council sat in uneasy silence. Plans were inked on parchment, nothing more, yet it felt like the last scaffolding holding a cracked tower upright. Zed finally growled, smoke curling from his lips. "We have a map, then. Leviathan lured. Fire tempered. Death shadowed. Chaos seduced. The boy—slowed, if he can be." His one eye burned. "This is our last hand before the table splits."

The torches hissed as though in assent. But deep below the city of Fez, something breathed again, and no plan inked in marble could silence it.

When the primary fires were contained, the room turned—reluctantly—to the smaller sparks.

Hera's gaze lingered on the bowl. The barley drifted, circling as if caught by a current no one else could feel. "And Leila?" she asked at last. The council stirred uneasily. Demi frowned, Effie smiled faintly, and Fiona's coin spun once without her hand moving.

"She is mortal," Rus said dismissively. "Ash is waiting for the wind."

"No," Fiona countered softly. "I think she is more than that; probability bends around her."

Hera closed the ledger with her hand. "Then she will be watched. If and until she reveals herself."

The torches hissed, a warning.

Zed's crow shifted uneasily, and Hera's eyes narrowed. "We have not spoken of Jake Rogers," she said.

Athena inclined her head. "He sails. Captain in all but name. A man with the instinct of a predator, yet chained to his boat. His loyalty is not faith—it is opportunity."

"Fading Dawn is more than a ship," Mercury added. "It is a brand. A symbol mortals already repeat with song and rumour. Rogers feeds that myth, keeps it afloat. Without him, the vessel is just timber."

Ari spat the word. "Then break him. Kill the dog and the ship loses its teeth."

"No," Mercury said, "I think he is just mercenary; given time, he will become harmless."

Thoth pressed ink to parchment, writing carefully: *Jake Rogers—harmless.*

The ledger accepted it without a tremor, which was almost more unsettling.

Athena's slate flickered—one frame, then nothing. Not blank. Gone. "That's not interference," she said quietly. "That's removal."

Zed's jaw tightened. "Then stop calling it pressure," he said. "Call it what it is."

He looked at Hera. "Ragnarök."

The bowl between them still shimmered with barley drifting on black water.

For a time, none spoke, until Zed's crow gave a low, ugly croak, wings half-unfurled. Zed drew slowly on his cigar, the ember glowing like a red eye, and then finally he said what many feared to let pass their lips.

"Perhaps," he rumbled, "we are wasting our breath on ledgers and half-plans. This could no longer be a game of balance. What we feel pressing could very well be the old thing at last— the crack in the sky, the wolf loosed. The possibility is this: Ragnarök, born not from prophecy but from the wandering star mortals call Fenris, dragging tides and fate behind it."

The room shuddered. The torches hissed, their flames guttering in time with his words.

Athena frowned, steel in her eyes. "You would name the Fenris-star as the cause? A brown dwarf, no mortal telescope believed until it shook their satellites? Its path disturbs, yes, but to call it our doom—"

Zed cut her off, smoke spilling like storm clouds. "It stirs seas. It warps seasons. It bends the scales we cling to. The Leviathan is unleashed. You saw it—Posi's death did not feel like a single blow. It felt like gravity itself chose to release him. That star is a wolf's jaw snapping at the leash. If it is Fenris rising, then perhaps balance is already broken. Perhaps there is no ledger to keep."

Rus's light flared, defensive. "So what, then? We sharpen weapons? We declare war on the sky? That is madness."

Zed bared his teeth. "Madness, perhaps. But when the end comes, I would rather be armed than caged by illusions of balance. Balance has chained us too long—counting, waiting, whispering instead of striking. What if we stop pretending? What if we take up the blade and begin killing before the killing finds us? Even ourselves, if need be."

Thoth's ink bled anew, letters smearing themselves into dark spirals. "If you abandon balance, Zed, then you abandon the very reason gods remain at all. We are not kings by right of arms. We are keepers of what mortals cannot see. If we sharpen weapons against each other, there will be nothing left to keep."

Zed exhaled smoke. "Then maybe nothing left is exactly what comes. Why cling to ledgers? Why not fight like wolves ourselves?"

Hera's hand came down hard on the bowl. The water trembled, barley scattering. Her voice was ice. "Enough. I will not hear Posi's wake defiled with your thirst for carnage. You speak of Ragnarök as if it were an invitation. But remember—wolves eat their own. If you sharpen weapons, Zed, you invite the first blow to be yours."

Zed's eye met hers, unflinching. "So be it." The torches flickered violently, shadows gnashing at the walls. For a moment, the chamber felt less like a council and more like the inside of a dying star, each god one heartbeat away from drawing weapon against weapon.

And somewhere, far above them, the Fenris-star continued its slow, implacable path across the void, a reminder that even heavens could wobble on their axis.

The chamber held its breath. Zed's words hung like iron shavings in the air, clinging to every spark, every silence—balance, abandoned. Weapons sharpened not against mortals or the damned, but each other. Ragnarök, whispered as if it were already here.

Zed's words fell into the room like filings into a magnet.

Demi's jaw tightened. Rus brightened. Effie smiled as if she'd been offered a stage. Fiona's coin refused to settle. Thoth's ledger bled.

Hera's hand hovered over the bowl—ready to strike the table like a judge.

And then—

The first to rise was Ari. Of course, it was Ari. He shoved back his chair with a snarl, bronze scraping marble. "At last, someone speaks the truth. Balance is a leash. Posi wore it and saw where it left him—bleeding, broken, skewered by a splinter while the sea raised in mockery. I say cut it. Let us kill and crown anew. If the wolf comes, let it feast on corpses worthy of song."

Demi stood opposite him, shoulders broad as earth, her jaw tight with rage. "You speak of corpses when fields already wither! If you forget balance, you forget the soil itself. You forget the children. There is no song in famine. There is only dust."

Ari sneered. "Then bury your children in dust. I will bury my enemies in steel."

Demi's palm slammed the table, and the marble cracked. "Say that again, war-dog, and I will bury you before you taste another fight."

Pele clapped her hands once, flame sparking between her fingers. "Now we are talking. Let the wolf howl. Let the sky burn. I will gladly turn the Andes and Siberia into pyres if it means we stop waiting like widows at a wake."

Athena cut across her, voice sharp as bronze. "Do that, and you hand the boy every door we swore to guard! Fire breeds chaos, not order. If Ragnarök is already upon us, then it demands discipline, not frenzy."

Effie laughed softly, dangerous and sweet. "Discipline? How dull. Let us revel. The mortals already love our whispers; imagine how they will worship when we stand unveiled, no longer shadows in their myths but lovers, tyrants, queens. Why fight the tide? Better to drown beautifully."

"You would crown yourself over ashes," Athena spat.

"And you would count ration books while the world ends," Effie replied.

Rus's radiance burst, blinding for a heartbeat, silencing even Effie's smile. "I will not let this council descend into carrion-feeding. Balance is not broken. Fenris is no god, no wolf—only a star. The world trembles, yes, but so it has trembled before. If you sharpen weapons against each other, you will blind the very light that holds the void back."

"Light cannot bind the void," Si whispered, her eyes clouded silver. "I dreamt this. Wolves devour stars. And in that dream, I saw gods devour each other, and still the wolf ate. Perhaps Zed is right. Perhaps balance is only the pause before teeth."

Mercury, who had been lounging in shadow, finally spoke. "You're all fools. Kill each other, crown each other, starve each other—it doesn't matter. Mortals are already writing their own stories. Fading Dawn sails with a skull for a flag. Leila bends chance. Ben kills gods. They are the market now. We can reveal ourselves or not, but the price has already shifted."

"Then hedge your bets and line your pockets," Zed growled. "But when the wolf comes, coin will not shield you."

Hera stood, her face pale with fury. "Enough."

Her voice carried the weight of Olympus, and every temple burned or raised in her name. "You dare defile this vigil with talk of self-slaughter? You dare speak of tearing each other down while mortals teeter and the damned stir? If you choose Ragnarök, you choose it alone. I will not let Posi's death become an excuse for madness."

Her gaze cut like a knife through each of them—Ari still seething, Demi quaking with earth's anger, Rus blazing, Effie smirking, Zed grim, Thoth pale with ink-stained dread.

"You want to reveal yourselves?" Hera continued. "To break the balance? Then mark this: mortals will not worship you. They will fear, they will fight, and they will end you with their small, sharp things. Posi fell to a shard. Do you think yourselves immune?"

Silence answered her.

The crow shifted, uneasy, and Zed at last dropped his gaze, smoke spilling from his lips. "Perhaps you're right," he muttered. "Perhaps balance still clings. But mark me—if Fenris takes another, if the boy wakes another lock, I will not sit in silence. I will sharpen my weapon, and I will not be alone."

The warning lingered like thunder past the horizon. Thoth's ledger trembled beneath his hand. Across the darkened pages, a sentence formed itself, not in ink but in absence, as if the parchment had decided to remember something it wished it hadn't.

Dion rose slowly, as if standing was a kind of permission. The room quieted—not for respect, but because even chaos recognised its own scent. He had been silent the whole meeting, drinking from his endless cup. His eyes glimmered faintly, unfocused, as if he were half here, half elsewhere. At last, he rose—not with Ari's fury or Rus's blaze, but with the loose sway of a man who'd already accepted the end. "You sharpen blades, you bind soil, you seduce chaos, you shadow death," he murmured. "All wise, all futile. For you forget the oldest truth: endings do not arrive with swords in hand—they arrive drunk and laughing, as guests at their own feast. Fenris does not have teeth. It is a toast. And the boy, your aberrant, your shard-thrower? He is the one raising the cup."

He lifted his chalice high. Wine spilled, red across marble like blood, remembering where it came from.

"Drink or don't," Dion said, voice suddenly clear, prophetic. "But know this: the wolf is already at the table, and we are already clinking glasses with it." He sat. No one laughed. The torches flickered as if in mock applause, and the bowl at Hera's hands tipped—she caught it before it fell. Her fingers shook.

The torches steadied. Thoth's ledger closed like a verdict. And far below Fez, in water-dark stone, the Stilled Breath drew in—slowly—crossing a border it had forgotten existed.

Chapter 19
Intermission

Well. Here we are—chapter Nineteen. By now, you'd expect the world to settle into something sane, but no. Reality's barely held together. The fractured multiply like rabbits, gods are bickering like parents in a divorce court, and mortals—poor, hapless mortals—are convinced they matter. Cute, really. But the universe is teetering: six spirits are awake, three still asleep, and the balance holding existence together is in the toilet. If nothing changes, disaster isn't just possible; it's inevitable.

First, the six.

Ellery. Smiter of the Elderly, the Unwell, and the Very, Very Sick. Not subtle. Never was. He doesn't sneak into a room; he brings a morgue with him. Everyone feels colder when he's around, which is efficient if nothing else.

Delilah. Chaos with lipstick. She kills with blades, tattoos foxes on her calling cards, and generally makes life messier than a teenager's bedroom. Charming, if you enjoy stab wounds.

Jian Wu. A Man on Fire. Runs a noodle shop, which sounds harmless until you realise the broth is seasoned with rage and chilli. He's basically a Michelin-star apocalypse waiting for a review.

Jake Rogers. Blackbeard incarnate. Pirate, racketeer, unlicensed logistics provider of the Seven Seas. Pretends piracy is romantic, but it's mostly shouting in the rain and filling out customs forms. Still, he has the hat for it.

Leila. Invisible Walker through Terminal Gates. Picture seduction disguised as adolescence—attitude, eye-rolls, and that all-knowing smile that says, *"Give me half a chance, and I'll ruin your life."* Adequate, if a little too textbook.

Ben. Our aberrant mortal. Refusing to die. Not because he's special. Just because Death can't be bothered—he's like mould in a bathroom; no matter how many times you scrub, he comes back. Nobody knows what he is—least of all him.

That's six. The active set. Already enough to turn a picnic into a plague. And then, the sleepers. Three left, snoozing like poisonous leftovers in the cosmic fridge. Fez. Already cracked open. Something older than language, drier than sorrow. Not an angel. Not a god. Not anything you'd want at your dinner table. Ben poked it awake, because of course he did.

Siberia. Still on ice, literally. A sleeper buried under snow and forgotten, waiting. If you've ever wondered what's under permafrost, the answer is: don't ask.

Machu Picchu. A thing idiotically nailed to a roof, because apparently, ancient failures like high views. Waiting for someone suicidal enough to knock. Spoiler: Ben already packed his ladder. So there you go. Six awake. Three asleep. A neat nine. Not neat for the world, but neat for bookkeeping.

Meanwhile, the gods—our self-appointed "higher beings"—are scrambling like poker players realising someone's marked the deck. Posi is dead. Yes, Poseidon. The one with the trident, the saltwater ego, the yacht collection. Dead. Ben shoved a shard of wreckage into his chest, and the sea itself apparently threw a funeral. Waves bowed, gulls cried, and Leviathan got let off the leash. Ten freighters later, the shipping industry is filing lawsuits against myth.

In New York, the council of gods holds emergency meetings in penthouses because marble halls are so passé. They argue about balance, mortals, and whether Ragnarök is just another PR disaster. Dionysus, usually three drinks past coherent, mutters something prophetic, and everyone suddenly notices the drop in temperature.

The mortals—governments, armies, the people with suits and acronyms—are panicking, but they don't have the language for what's happening. They call it maritime terrorism. They call it rogue states. They call it anything but what it is: gods, monsters, things, balance cracking like an old plate.

The news doesn't have a chyron for "Ragnarök, Please Hold." Leviathan keeps eating ships. Insurance companies are reconsidering their business model. Stock markets are dropping like lemmings off a cliff.

The old gods sharpen their weapons and talk about whether maybe it's time to kill each other before mortals find out, which is very on brand. And yet. Despite it all. The sun rises, the coffee brews, and somewhere a man still complains about traffic.

That's the part that makes this whole opera tragicomic: the universe is ripping at the seams, and most of humanity is still doomscrolling on the toilet.

So, what's next? Oh, you'll see.

And since we're doing housekeeping, let's pause here for a moment of honesty. An apology, really. To Adelaide. Yes, that Adelaide—the place where this whole circus began.

You didn't ask for gods, monsters, or half-baked things in leather jackets to crawl out of your vineyards and backstreets, but here we are. You were minding your own business—hosting cricket at the Oval, fighting over which bakery makes the best pie floater, and pretending Rundle Mall's balls are still impressive. Then this happened. One mortal aberration, a few divine grudges, and now the apocalypse has a postcode.

Sorry about that. Truly. The worst part? It's only going to get worse. But look on the bright side.

If your city must be the epicenter of supernatural collapse, at least you're also the epicenter of delicious wine. And if ever there were a time to drink heavily, it's now. So here's your free advertising, Barossa: buy Shiraz. Wicked, dense, dark Shiraz. The kind that stains your teeth, your soul, and possibly your karma. It won't stop the sea serpent, but you'll care less while it eats the shipping lanes. Consider it disaster-preparedness in a bottle. And Clare, as well as Eden Valley, don't think we've forgotten you. Your Riesling is sublime. Bone-dry, lime-lit, crisp as a blade. Perfect for toasting the end of days while muttering, "Well, at least the acidity is balanced." Pair it with calamity, panic, or a light summer salad.

So yes, Adelaide. Sorry. Sorry, your wine industry will soon be marketing under the slogan: "Drink Now, Apocalypse Later."

Catchy. You can have that one for free.

Meanwhile, the fractured are busy writing their own tasting notes in blood and chaos. Ellery: death, with a nose of iron and a finish of silence. Delilah: chaos, marked by fox-like sharpness and a tendency to linger. Jian Wu: fire, tempered by noodles—because even apocalypse needs carbs. Jake Rogers: pirate despair, with hints of desperation and salted rum. Leila: temptress, velvety as a Clare Valley night. And then, of course, our boy Ben, who refuses to die, refuses to make sense, and pairs with absolutely nothing except trouble.

Suppose you're reading this with a glass in hand—good. Keep pouring. You'll need it. Because Adelaide, my sweet, my unlucky, sunburnt Adelaide, you are not just the beginning. You are the control group. The test kitchen. The Petri dish where myth and madness first mixed.

And the Barossa vines may drink deep of your blood before this is done.

Again—sorry. But hey, at least your Shiraz will make the obituary.

Adelaide, we've apologised. Barossa, Clare, Eden Valley—we've raised a glass. Now let's pan the camera back and watch the wider world do what it does best: panic with style.

Governments are confused. Which, in fairness, is their default setting. Ten freighters sink off the coast, and suddenly, every acronym wants a piece of the action. NATO calls an emergency session. The UN drafts a strongly worded letter, then drafts another one when the first mysteriously catches fire. Washington, Beijing, Moscow—all insist Leviathan is either a Chinese drone, an American weapon, or "just Russian weather." Nobody agrees, but everyone pretends to.

The media are thriving. Chaos is comfort food. One outlet shows waves crashing behind earnest anchors debating the end of civilization next to toothpaste ads. Another blames the grid. A third calls it a hoax. The British media stay composed, assuming calamity is for the continent. Social platforms debate Leviathan's attractiveness. (Verdict: lethal, yet tempting.)

Stock markets and insurance companies are haemorrhaging. Shipping conglomerates are reconsidering whether globalisation was such a clever idea after all. Someone suggests going back to caravans and camels. They're only half joking.

Meanwhile, mortals—average mortals—are blissfully incompetent. A sea monster sinks tankers, and half the world keeps arguing about parking spaces. Adelaide burns, and someone still thinks their most pressing concern is whether oat milk counts as real milk.

Humanity, bless them, is stubbornly irrelevant. And yet, there's an undertone. A twitch. A sense that something isn't right. Even the dullest mortal feels it—like static before thunder splits the sky, or the hush before the family dog vomits ruin on the living-room rug. They don't have the words, but their bones do. And their bones are whispering: something is very, very wrong.

The gods, of course, know exactly how wrong. They won't say it out loud. Saying it makes it real, and they're far too vain for that. So they argue. They squabble in penthouses about "balance" like it's a math equation. Some suggest containing the annoying. Others suggest killing them. A few suggest killing each other, which is at least honest. Zed mutters "Ragnarök" like it's a bad joke, and Ari grins like a schoolboy who's just been told the fire alarm means recess.

And Death—not the Ellery Death—but the quiet black-robed Death (the one with the scythe)—still hasn't crossed Ben's name off the list. Because, quite frankly, he is enjoying the show.

So, what's next?

The others will wake because why have one when you can have three? Fez has already been cracked open—some not-quite-mummy, a thing even the earth had forgotten. Siberia and Machu Picchu are waiting for someone suicidal enough to open the locks.

Guess who's already got the key?

Yes. Ben. Because he never learns, and learning isn't his role anyway. He's the pebble in the shoe of existence. The one you can't quite shake out. The gods don't know what he is, mortals don't know what he is, and he doesn't know either, which is why he's dangerous.

So Adelaide, pour another glass. The Barossa vines will soon have company. Clare Riesling will taste sharper when the Siberian sleeper wakes. Eden Valley will need every bottle once Machu Picchu starts screaming. And by then, the gods might finally admit it: the world isn't bending. It's breaking. But let's not get ahead of ourselves. We've still got a few chapters left before total collapse. And who knows? Maybe Shiraz really can save us. Stranger things have happened.

So let's tally this up, shall we?

We've got Leviathan out there chewing freighters like they're fish fingers. Poseidon's corpse is at the bottom of the sea. Zed muttering Ragnarök like it's a punchline. Scythe Death is tagging along for the spectacle. Awakened mortals dropping like bad mixtapes—Death, Chaos, Fire, Temptation, Despair, the whole end-of-days ensemble cast is here, tuning their instruments for the grand finale. Norse prophecy, eat your heart out. The signs are all there—doom-serpents, shattered balance, gods sharpening weapons, mortals failing auditions for relevance. The curtain's rising.

And yet. One glaring omission. Where the hell is Thor?

No, not the sagas' Thor—the one who'd already be here, drunk, belligerent, cracking giants across the skull and demanding another goat stew. That Thor we could work with. I mean the other Thor. The export model. Perfect hair, arms like a Barossa oak barrel, the dubious honour of carrying a movie franchise through four mediocre sequels.

Yes, that Thor. The cinematic version. You'd think, with Adelaide burning and Barossa preparing for its apocalypse vintage, he'd at least swing by. Toss the hammer. Crack a joke. Strike a pose, before Leviathan drags down another freighter.

Something. Anything.

But no. Silence. No superheroes here bending reality back into something manageable. Just Leviathan in the shipping lanes, gods with hangovers, and Ben—the aberrant mortal who refuses to die, who has less charisma than a cane toad and yet somehow keeps stealing the spotlight.

And that's the joke.

Humanity spent two decades training for this moment in cinemas. Every second Friday, another apocalypse neatly packaged into 140 minutes, fixed with CGI lightning and quippy billionaires.

And now?

Crickets.

No theme music. No portals. Just the sound of waves breaking over corpses of ships, and the silence of gods who don't know if killing each other is strategy or suicide. So here we are. The actors are on stage. Fenris-star growls in the wings. Death licks his lips. Old gods polish weapons they swore they'd never draw again. Beings—mortal, divine, failed, forgotten—shuffle toward their parts in the play. Ragnarök, curtain call, whatever you name it, the script doesn't care.

And the rescue party? They're not coming.

It's just us now. The bored narrator. The bickering gods. The six awake, the three others, and one stubborn mortal who refuses to die—a pebble in the shoe of existence, grinding bone into dust with every step.

So: lights, curtains up, and don't break a leg—no Hollywood budget. No deus ex cape. Only Leviathan in the deep, the sleepers stirring, and the wine glass in your hand.

Drink. You'll need it.

Chapter 20

The Fire

The flight touched down just after sunrise. The Adelaide hills glowed faintly pink in the early morning light, the long stretch of tarmac shimmering as if already scorched by what was coming. Three women disembarked together, though no one in the terminal recognised them for what they were. To the casual eye, they were executives, weary after a long haul from New York. To the few who knew better, each carried the weight of an assignment the council had marked as critical.

Pele carried the fire in her blood. Her task was Jian Wu, the man already being called Flamethrower by terrified witnesses. He had begun with grain silos, then petrol depots; now, entire suburbs north of the city seemed to tremble at his passage. Containment was not guaranteed.

Diane wore her mission in the steel of her eyes. Ellery Kalos had slipped further toward what even she did not fully understand. Death followed him like a shadow, and Adelaide's streets whispered with it—people collapsing without warning in supermarkets, bus stops, and offices. Her hunt was to track the pattern, find him, and decide whether he was still salvageable.

Effie, radiant even in the dullness of airport neon, had drawn the darkest lot. Delilah Kitsune had gone fully rogue—seduction turned blade, chaos given purpose. Effie was to placate, soothe, twist her course if possible. If not, she would bleed Adelaide and the Barossa dry.

The city lay unaware of the convergence. To the north, the smoke rose in black pillars where fields and silos burned. In the heart of Adelaide, ambulances screamed from one sudden death to the next, the radio chatter already panicked. And in the Barossa, whispers spread of a woman with a katana, fox-marked bodies left in her wake. The goddesses had come not to save, but to contain. The difference would soon matter little to those who lived here.

The air above the Adelaide Plains was heavy with the scent of ash. Heat shimmered over the bitumen, distorting the horizon so that the world itself seemed aflame. To the north, where Jian Wu walked, entire neighbourhoods still smouldered. A few desperate fire crews tried to hold lines against the advancing infernos, but their hoses hissed and steamed uselessly when the man passed. He carried fire not as an element to be controlled but as an extension of himself, a second skin of molten rage. Witnesses spoke of him as if he were a myth already—an untouchable figure who ignited petrol tankers with a glance, who cracked silos into pillars of fire simply by exhaling. They called him an inferno in human form. In truth, Jian Wu was no longer entirely human. Something in him had shifted, tilting him toward the realm the council feared most.

And Pele had come to stop him.

She found him first on the edge of Balaclava, striding past the railway yards as if the world were tinder. Freight cars lined the sidings, their tanks filled with diesel. The authorities had tried to evacuate, but one unlucky guard lingered too long—drawn, perhaps, by the strange gravity Jian carried. The man shouted something, then collapsed as the air itself caught fire. His uniform curled black before his body hit the ground.

Pele approached quietly, though the crackle of cinders betrayed her presence. Her sandals left no print on the scorched earth. Where Jian walked, destruction followed; where she walked, fire found its shape.

The two forces could not remain apart for long. "Jian Wu," she called, her voice steady but low, like a drumbeat under a volcano. "The world knows you now. They fear you. That fear will turn to armies before the day is out."

Jian turned, his face lit by the dull red of rising embers. His eyes glowed, not with reflection but with source—tiny suns caged within flesh. Sweat poured down his brow, though the heat did not touch him.

"Who are you?" he said, his voice cracking like kindling. "That can stand before me? And try to stop me?"

"I am Pele, a goddess... the goddess of fire and volcanoes. I am here to contain you," she replied. "Before you burn more than fields and suburbs. Before you scorch the earth that gave you power."

He laughed, harsh and broken. "Containment? A goddess? Your kind doesn't exist, Pele. And if you are fire, fire cannot contain fire. It only grows."

The ground rumbled, and the air thickened with heat. Jian stretched out a hand, and a line of flame raced across the tracks, igniting a line of freight cars. They erupted one after another, booming into the sky. The concussive shock rattled windows across the town. He didn't flinch.

Pele held her ground. Sparks curled around her body, drawn inward as though she were a centre of gravity. Her hair shimmered, black gloss catching streaks of molten red. She raised her palm, and the exploding fire stilled, frozen mid-bloom. The flame's roar dimmed into a muted hum, caged by her will. "Enough," she said. "The earth grants its gifts to be honoured, not abused. You are losing yourself, Jian."

"Losing?" His voice cracked again, and the air pulsed hotter. "No, Pele. I am finding. For years, I swallowed insults, endured the petty cruelties of mortals. But fire remembers. Fire answers. Now it is my voice. Every refinery, every tanker—they speak with me."

"And they will consume you," Pele warned. "Flame devours its bearer as surely as it devours wood. If you continue, you will be ash before the council even judges you."

Her words stirred something—perhaps doubt, perhaps fury. Jian clenched his fists, and the world around him seemed to bend. The trees at the yard's edge burst into flame. The asphalt beneath them blistered. "Do not preach restraint to me," he hissed. "Restraint is a lie. I am done with restraint."

Pele advanced, each step measured. The fire raging in the trees curved inward as if bowing to her. Her eyes locked on Jian's, steady, unwavering. "Then you leave me no choice."

The wind shifted. Smoke billowed low across the yard. Jian spread his arms, welcoming it. "Show me, Pele. Show me goddess—or are you just another frightened keeper of dying flames?"

Her answer was action. With a flick of her hand, the fire she had stilled above the rail cars surged downward, condensing into a sphere of molten light. It hovered between them, thrumming like a captured heart. She thrust her palm, and the sphere shot forward. Jian caught it in both hands. For an instant, it seemed as if he might be consumed. Instead, he swallowed it whole. Fire licked across his body, cloaking him in a mantle of pure flame.

He roared, the sound shaking rooftops for miles.

Pele steadied herself. The battle had begun.

From the highway, evacuees saw only a growing column of fire spiralling into the sky. Some thought it was a refinery blast. Others whispered of a nuclear accident. None could imagine that two beings stood at the column's heart, testing the very bones of the earth with their fury.

The first blast should have staggered him. Instead, it crowned him. Pele's molten heart-shot—meant to cage his fury—folded into Jian as if his ribs were a forge door. Light leaked from him in blinding threads, and the rails at his feet bowed and blackened. She tried a second strike, tighter, a needle of heat that would have punctured the lung of a volcano and made it sigh. Jian inhaled it like spice. The tiny suns in his eyes dilated.

"Stop," she warned, but the warning arrived too late to matter. Another line of flame leapt at him from the burning trees, this one unbidden—drawn of its own accord into his orbit. He didn't reach for it; it came for him. The halo thickened. Where the freight yard's gravel bed had been, the top layer of stone softened, sagged, and flowed. Pebbles winked out as if swallowed by honey. A bottle someone had dropped near the guard's hut slumped into a green tear and then into nothing, a clear smear that caught the red flicker of Jian's cloak and threw it back a hundred times brighter.

Pele shifted her stance, shoulders squaring, chin lowering. She let the smaller flames coil toward her ankles and wrists, let them climb like tame serpents and braid themselves into bangles, a memory of the islands burning under starlight—the old dances, the old rites. She opened her hands. Heat fled from the air around them, a sudden vacuum of scorch that made the fires hiccup. For a heartbeat, the world went dim. "Containment," she said, and pressed down. It was like pushing on the surface of a star. The ground lifted under Jian and then sank. For an instant, the halo around him flattened into a petal, a disc, a compressed flower of flame that might have been held—might have—if it didn't immediately buck like a trapped thing. He shuddered, and the disc exploded up and out, a corona blasting old paint from the rail sheds, stripping bark from gum trunks, scouring the sky of birds. Every watt she forced into restraint became fuel. He blazed brighter.

"Do you see it?" Jian's voice had taken on a resonance that didn't belong to throats and tongues; it was carried in the bones. "You try to put me in a jar, and you make the fire purer." He stepped forward, and the tie plates hissed. A sleeper creaked like a thing in pain. Bitumen at the edge of the yard liquefied and fled as a black gloss, pooling and then boiling, throwing oily bubbles that popped and threw sparks into the wind. Beyond the fence, a row of fibro shacks brightened at their edges like old film catching light, then caught properly. Windows snowed inward. Somewhere, a dog yelped and then went silent.

Pele drew a long breath. "Then no more jars." She turned her palms, and the air above Jian rippled. Not heat—vacuum. A pressure drop, hungry and absolute. Fire needs breath; she denied it breath. Flames guttered. The halo thinned. For three heartbeats, Jian's light faltered. In that dimming, a human shape was hinted—his jaw set, his brow a ledge of furious concentration, the old lines of the chef who had once served noodles with a smile and a quick temper before fate cracked him open and poured lava into his bones. Then he smiled—small, terrible—and the light returned tenfold, a shock-white flare that punched her vacuum full of photons, making the absence sing with energy.

"Space," he said, voice thrumming. "Even there, fire travels as light."

Pele closed her fist. The vacuum collapsed. Heat crashed in to fill the hunger with a thunderclap that popped car doors and rolled like surf over the paddocks. Jian took it as a blessing. The corona climbed higher, flaring to the height of the rail shed eaves, and the shed—tin, pine, bolts, and memory—softened like wax too near a candle. She cursed softly in a language older than the islands and bent at the waist, placing both palms to the ground. The earth heard her. Beneath the yard, beneath the clay and the old riverbed stones, beneath the ancient crust of this dry continent, something stirred. Melt answered melt. The basaltic memory of a thousand-thousand flows rose like a tide and cooled the skin of the world from underneath, wicking heat downward, drinking it, drinking our mortal blaze into the patient throat of the mantle where gods keep secrets.

For a breath, the vitrification paused. The glossy pools of liquefied gravel stiffened, their wavy surfaces calming like cooling toffee. Jian faltered, a flick of confusion. Then the confusion was gone. He stamped his heel into the new glaze. The heel-print shone like a star caught in glass. The ground made a sound like a metal ring. "You forget," he said, tilting his head as if listening to something she couldn't hear, "who gave me this."

Behind him, the wind changed. It came not from the Gulf but from inland, full of dust and eucalyptus and dry riverbeds, and it sang with a thin, hot hum—an inland summer's razor song. The earth's gift, yes, but to whom, and for what? Pele felt the answer the way a dancer feels a rhythm shifting underfoot: Jian was not only a fire. He was a lens. He bent the planet's rage through himself and sharpened it.

A siren wailed and died. Overhead, a police helicopter drifted too close, banking for a look, and bucked like a startled horse as the air around Jian sheened bright and sudden. Instruments screamed. The pilot, years of training narrowed to a gut, threw the machine sideways and climbed, rotor wash casting cinders like confetti over the stockyards. Jian barely glanced up. The glance alone bleached the aircraft's side panel to a ghost and puffed the paint from the letters.

"Jian," Pele said, gentler now. "Listen."

"I am listening," he said, and though he looked at her, his head remained cocked, as if tuned to a frequency below human hearing. "I hear the wheat cursing the silo. I hear petrol begging to be aired. I hear every timber that was once a tree remembering how to burn."

"You also hear the aquifers," she said, and stamped her heel.

The next strike did not come from fire. It came from cool pressure beneath: artesian water shouldering up from far below, stone fractures opening like eyes, a vertical river forced into the heat. It boiled the instant it met Jian's radiance, but cooking is a thief—it steals heat without asking, turns fury into steam, into fog, into clouds that any whisper of wind can carry away. A white pillar hugged him, hissing. Steam took him in its arms.

For a second—two—Pele saw his shape. Saw the set of his mouth, the grief braided through his rage. She saw the young cook wiping a counter and muttering about the price of onions, the husband practising a breath so he wouldn't shout, the man who could have been ordinary if the world had not been so casually cruel.

And then the steam shone from within, pearl to opal to a brightness that burned shadows even in the cloud. Droplets flashed to light without ever becoming rain. He stepped out of the steam as a refutation. Light stroked the ground, and the ground sighed, turning to glass. The vitrification spread, a slow, deliberate tide. Gravel and dirt and scrap iron alike slumped and fell level, sank and rose and fused. Tires, half-melted, became black ovals trapped in translucent sheets. A fallen spanner cast in forever. A child's lost sock, already filthy before the fire, preserved as a grey smear in a museum no one would dare to visit. The freight yard was turning into a lake without water, into a mirror that could only reflect one thing: the star at its centre.

Pele backed a step, boot soles whispering on the newborn glaze. She tightened her hands, and the bangles of tame fire around her wrists hissed and sloughed down her forearms to her palms, where she rolled them like dough into dense, ember-bright stones. She flicked one at Jian's chest. It struck with a bell's note and vanished into him without smoke. He brightened. She sent another—higher, narrower, tuned to a frequency that should have shattered his skin of light like glass. He only laughed, and the laugh shed sparks that burned holes through the rail shed's collapsing roof and drew a shriek from the sun-baked corrugations as they buckled. Every strike fed him. Every denial became an offering.

"Goddess," Jian said, "you bring me courses in a feast. How many more?"

Pele set her jaw. She dragged the horizon down. Far over the plains, heat wavered in a mirage sheet. She gathered it, thumbed it, folded it—pulling distance into closeness, rolling kilometres like cloth until the shimmer thickened, layered, and poured toward them in stacked waves. They arrived like a silent surf, each crest a moving lens that warped the world beneath it. Under the sixth wave, colours fled, leaving only brilliant white. Under the ninth, sound stretched and thinned. Under the twelfth, gravity felt optional. For everyone on the highway, the battle vanished into a white noon. For Jian, it was sugar.

He drank it. Light layered on light until the edges of him blurred and then vanished, not with gentleness but with a cutting purity. The outline of a man dissolved. In his place: a sun. Not fully solid—the eye could not sit on it; it slid. Not fully gas—the air around it took on a structure like vibrating glass. The corona climbed to the height of streetlights, then telegraph poles, then the tops of gums. Its roar found harmonics that made nearby roofs shudder.

Pele shaded her eyes with the side of her hand, not because she feared blindness but because she needed to see him clearly. She had battled volcanoes that wanted to birth islands in the middle of the night sea. She had danced on cooling flows and smiled while the soles of her feet smoked. She had not seen this, not outside the edge of the world where gods go to test young stars.

He moved with the assurance of a thing that remakes the ground it crosses. Glass under him sagged and refroze. A perfect shallow bowl followed, a travelling well of vitrified earth. He could go anywhere. He could go everywhere. "Jian!" Pele's voice cut through harmonics and hum. "Look at the houses. Look at the trees. Look at the sky. This is not a kitchen blaze to whip and tame. This is a sun. You are a sun in a place made of tinder."

"Then I must leave the tinder," he said—or she thought he said, for there was no mouth now, only a modulation in the roar that the ear translated as speech. "But first they must stop screaming at me."

As if in answer, sirens twined again on the highway. A line of emergency utes appeared at the far edge of the yard, their light bars frantic with blue and red. Through the glare, she saw silhouettes jump down, saw hands lift radios to faces, saw bodies lean forward as if force alone could close the distance. A figure raised what might have been a launcher—no, not might. A launcher. Someone had brought the next level. Pele flung a hand, not at Jian but at them. Heat around the sphere curled sideways, a crescent of safe air pushed outward just far enough to turn the launcher man's balance into a stagger and make his shot jolt high. The projectile spiralled into the sky and went off with a harmless white flower. The men ducked. The men shouted. The men thought they were fighting a man.

"Go," she told them, though the wind shredded her words. "Go."

Jian spun in place once, a slow prelude, and the telegraph poles bowed outward like grass before a helicopter's downdraft. The nearest house, a weatherboard old-timer with a front porch and a tyre swing, turned transparent at the corners—the paint blanching, the timber within showing its rings, the nails flashing as if remembering ore—then softened, leaned, and slid into the new glass sea as if bowing its regrets to the world. Pele's breath hitched. Not for the house. For the speed. He was accelerating.

She threw her final island trick. Islands are born when heat meets the ocean and does not die. She called the Gulf. Moisture ran inward across the land in a non-wind, a sucking draw that left mouths dry and eyes blinking. The air went fat. Clouds bunched out of a blue that did not want them, and the first fat drops fell, staccato on new glass, and flashed to steam before they had names. The second drops were bigger. The third came with a gust. Rain hit in a sheet, hard enough to drum sense into panic, hard enough to flatten grass that had not yet burned. Steam hemmed them in a white wall.

Inside the wall, Jian shone. The rain fed him too—not as fuel, but as a mirror. Every drop became a lens. Each lens refocused him. His corona sharpened. The sphere condensed, and with the condensation came brightness that pushed the world's colours away, a noon that overruled every other hour. Pele's skin prickled. She tasted iron. In the glass beneath her boots, hairline cracks wrote frantic maps and then sealed themselves shut as heat licked them smooth again. She had reached the end of what she could do without breaking the skin of this place entirely, without calling the deep fire and letting it eat a suburb to save a city. The earth had given Jian this, and the world would not forgive her if she took half its children to stop him.

"I see you," she said quietly, to the light. "I see what you have become. I cannot unmake you here."

The sun cocked—as much as a sun can cock—toward the north, as if something had tugged his attention that way. The roar shaded down a fraction. In that dip, she heard another sound, thinner, threaded through like a string in a big drum's body: a voice, not hers. Not a god's. Faraway. A woman was speaking to him in the ether, telling him to calm, and—if such a thing could be—familiar to him.

Pele's eyes narrowed. "What do you hear, Jian?"

The light feathered. The vitrified bowl under him slid a handspan north.

"Home," he said, and the word felt wrong in her ear, not bad meaning false—wrong meaning too whole, as if he had poured other meanings into it: horizon, emptiness, silence, room enough that his burning would not take a thousand with it in a breath.

The rain hammered. The steam climbed. The sea of glass writhed like a living thing under a torch. Jian's brightness flared again as if answering some unheard counsel. When it settled, it did not settle smaller. It settled steadier. Less ragged at the edges. Less of a tantrum. Less white.

Pele let out the breath she hadn't realised she was holding. The admission tasted like defeat, like wisdom, like both. "Then go inland," she said. "Take your sun where the ground can bear it."

He did not answer—or if he did, the answer came in heat alone. The sun leaned north and began to move, slow and perfectly sure, leaving behind him a travelling mirror that reflected nothing but white. Where he passed, fences drooped and fused, weeds turned to delicate glass sculptures, and tyre prints became braided cords set forever. The emergency crews—faces pale, bodies small—watched their reflected selves shrink in the receding bowl and did not follow.

Pele stood in the rain and in the steam, her bangles dead and dark at last around her wrists, and counted heartbeats. When she could trust her feet not to skid, she followed—not to fight, not now—but to shepherd what she could and warn what she must.

She had not contained him. She had fed him. She would have to learn a new way.

Behind her, the gutted sheds sighed and fell in on themselves. Ahead of her, inland, the sun walked. The steam wall collapsed slowly, like curtains falling in tatters. Rain softened, then broke into drizzle, then was gone. The air that followed felt wrong—flat, empty, stripped of its scents. Every gum, every shack, every blade of grass had been either burned or locked in the glass sea. The only fragrance left was ozone and scorched stone.

Pele stood amid it all, hair plastered to her face, bare shoulders gleaming with damp. For the first time in centuries, she felt small, not because her power had waned, but because she had seen the earth itself crown a mortal with its fury, and she had nearly broken herself trying to unmake him. Jian Wu had not defeated her—he had absorbed her, bent her every gift into fuel, and walked away brighter for it.

Behind her, the emergency crews staggered from their cover. Blue and red strobes still spun, their light warped by reflections off the newborn glass. Helmets clinked as the men and women looked about in mute disbelief. The launcher team whispered curses, staring at the fused metal wreckage of their weapon, its barrel bent and polished like a child's toy left too close to a flame. One of the captains—Pele could tell by the way his body squared under the weight of others' eyes—approached her. His face was soot-streaked, his moustache blackened at the ends. He stopped three paces away, suddenly uncertain. What was she to him? A survivor? A witness? Or another force of nature?

"You'll want to pull everyone back," she said, her voice level but heavy enough to carry through the broken yard. "He's not coming for you. Not now. But if you follow, if you fire, you'll only hasten the ruin."

The captain blinked. His lips moved, shaping words that never left his throat. Finally, he swallowed, nodded once, and turned to shout to his people. Engines coughed awake, tyres crunched on glass, vehicles reversed awkwardly, some scraping their undersides on vitrified ridges that would not forgive suspension springs. None of them argued. They had looked into the white glare of Jian Wu and known they were ants under a magnifying lens.

Pele turned slowly, surveying the survivors. A handful of locals had crept out from shattered homes at the fringe of the blaze. Families huddled with bundles of clothes, eyes vast and silent. Children clutched melted toys, their faces lit by the unnatural sheen underfoot. They did not speak either, but their silence cut her worse than an accusation. She went to them. She bent to the smallest child, a girl with a rabbit clutched in her arms, its fur patchy with singe.

"He will not return here," Pele murmured, though she knew the child could not truly understand. "Your land will harden. The fires will stop." She touched the rabbit, and the fur smoothed under her hand, singe lines fading as if time reversed by inches. The child's eyes filled, but not with fear.

Another step, and she addressed the adults. "Leave this place. The ground is no longer safe for your homes. Take only what you can carry and walk south. The fire crews will guide you. Do not wait." They nodded mutely. No one dared question how she knew or why they should obey. She was the only figure left unburnt, standing calm where even steel had wept into slag. That was authority enough.

When she straightened, her gaze followed north. Jian Wu's light had already dwindled to a far glow, like the rim of a sun seen through cloud. He moved deliberately across the plains, steady as a god at ritual pace. The land behind him reflected his passing in silver swathes, a mirror path cut into the continent. The desert awaited him. Pele knew this as instinct, the way tides know moonlight. The Red Centre had long borne heat that would kill gods less patient than she. Salt pans stretched wider than seas, dunes taller than cathedrals—each an altar where the earth's breath baked slow and eternal. If anywhere could leech the fury from Jian's newborn star, it was there, where fire had no fuel left to gorge on, only rock, sand, and sky.

But he would not find it alone. Rage was a compass that always pointed back to cities, to crowds, to insult. Something whispered across the distance—someone. Pele had heard it faintly, a thread in the roar. That voice might save him, or it might bend him further. She did not yet know. For now, her task was humbler: keep mortals from chasing him, keep governments from making him an enemy before the desert could do its work.

She pressed her palms together, then flung them outward. The drizzle thickened briefly, spattering the emergency crews as they retreated. Radios crackled and failed. Camera lenses fogged and died. For hours, perhaps a day, no image would reach the capital, no footage would confirm what had walked here. Witnesses would carry tales, but tales could be doubted. Governments delay when truth wears only rumour. It was the only gift she could give Jian—time. Time to burn out, or to find balance in the vast emptiness northward.

A final glance at the sky told her Adelaide would be spared—today. Clouds already broke into ribbons, pink with the dying sun. Somewhere, Diane stalked death's shadow through the city streets. Somewhere, Effie played her delicate dance with the fox-marked killer. The council's lines of containment were drawn. Whether they would hold was another matter.

Pele stepped lightly onto the glass, her bare feet not slipping, though the surface was smooth as mirrors. Every step left no print, but the glass sang faintly under her weight, as if the desert itself were already answering, calling her inland to shadow Jian's trail.

"Let him walk," she whispered to the earth. "Let him cool. Let him remember he is more than a furnace."

The earth did not answer in words, but in silence—a silence that accepted her prayer, or ignored it. She would know soon enough. The desert met him with silence.

Hours of walking north carried Jian Wu beyond the green edge of the plains, past the broken farmsteads, past the last thin lines of gum trees that clung to creek beds. The world turned to ochre and stone. Wind whipped the heat aside, stripping away the smell of burning suburb and replacing it with dry dust. The stars above sharpened into merciless clarity, as if even heaven had taken notice of the thing moving beneath it. His light still blazed, but not as before. Out here, without timber or petrol, without crowds to ignite or enemies to resist, the corona thinned. What had once been a furnace became a steady sunfire glow, enough to turn sand into green glass for kilometres at a time, but no longer a storm that cracked roofs and shredded airframes. Each mile of desert drank a little more from him, like a mother drawing fever from a child.

Pele followed at a distance, never close enough to provoke. She knew the pattern: let the earth do its work, let the sands sponge heat and the endless horizon soften rage. From a dune, she watched as his star-man silhouette slowed, then settled into stillness atop a salt pan. He did not roar now. He pulsed—slow, rhythmic, like a colossal heartbeat.

Jian Wu thought of kitchens. The hiss of woks, the chatter of knives, the way steam fogged windows on winter nights. He thought of faces that had once smiled at him, before suspicion, before whispers, before the final insult that had cracked his restraint and unleashed all this. He thought of the first silo he burned, and how alive he had felt. He thought of the bodies that collapsed in his wake—some soldiers, some strangers who never knew his name. And he understood the line had been crossed the moment the first one fell.

He lowered himself until he sat like a glowing coal against the desert floor. Sand shrank back from him, fused into smooth plates that stretched for hundreds of metres, but there was no panic here, no screams. Only emptiness, only a sky so vast it could cradle even a small sun without flinching. "Home," he murmured, though he knew it was exile. The desert had no neighbours, no crowded lanes, no waitresses to forget his order and smile as though it meant nothing. Here, the only voices were wind and stone.

The earth answered in its patient way. The salt flats began to radiate his heat outward, dispersing it into the vast crust beneath. Pebbles sweated, cooled, and stayed intact. A dune's edge sagged into glass, but only a corner, quickly cooled into stillness.

Slowly—painfully slowly—his brightness lessened. What had been an unbearable glare softened into amber. What had been amber faded to a red coal. He tried to stand. Once, twice. The attempt only shivered the salt. He no longer had the energy to walk. The truth pressed into him harder than the desert heat: Jian Wu, the man, was gone. A furnace had replaced him. No apron, no knife, no hand steady enough to lift a bowl of noodles without cracking it into ash. Mortals could never stand near him again.

On the far dune, Pele bowed her head. She had seen this before—gods born not by choice but by collision between rage and earth. Some burned out in days. Others learned to carry themselves in silence, far from cities. Few ever found peace. "Let him be," she whispered to the winds. "He is no longer an enemy. He is consequence."

The night advanced. Stars blazed above, pale imitations of the ember lying on the salt. Dingos padded close, curious, then slunk away when the heat brushed their whiskers. By dawn, Jian Wu's light was low enough to paint long shadows instead of erasing them. His form suggested a man again—shoulders bent, head bowed—but the colour of coal and not flesh. He knew then, with a clarity that stripped him raw, that he would never again take his seat in a crowded café, never again laugh with neighbours, never again lie in a bed that did not smoulder beneath him. He had burned his bridge to humankind. His place was here, where sand and stone could drink his fire without dying. The desert would keep him. And the world, for now, would endure.

Chapter 21
The Chaos

The Barossa Valley was hushed in the late hour, vineyards laid out beneath a canopy of stars. Rows ran long and geometric over the rolls of ground, and in the moonlight the place felt older than agriculture—quiet, watchful, complicit.

It began with a shiver in the air.

The leaves stirred, though no wind passed through. Trellises and wire guides groaned as if alive, tightening, loosening, then weaving together like fingers clasping. By day it was familiar work. Now it became a labyrinth of living intent. Tendrils of green twisted in slow coils, reaching across rows, tightening loops, offering no straight path forward. The wires that held the canopy together rattled and quivered, then flung back moonlight as though struck.

Delilah stepped into the centre of it, her katana catching the faint glow and splitting it, scattering rainbows into the darkness. Her face was pale but not weak—it was luminous, painted by the light of her own illusions. The rows answered her mood. Shadows thickened, vines knotted upon themselves, forming impossible weaves. From a distance, the scene might have looked like a harvest gone wild, the Valley betraying its order for some feral geometry. Up close, it was chaos pressed into shape, and Delilah was its conductor. "You chose a garden to fight me in?" she called, her voice sharp, edged with the laughter of someone who already knows the punchline. "Every vine here listens to me. Every leaf bends for me."

Aphrodite—Effie—stepped into the row opposite, her dagger flashing with its own kind of certainty. She wore no armour but the perfection of her form, and she needed none. The night was colder for her presence, hungrier too, as though desire itself had crept into the soil and waited for her command. "You mistake obedience for loyalty," Effie said, her tone silk sliding over steel. "The vines may dance for you, but their roots know beauty when they feel it." She advanced, her hips drawing the shadows forward with her. The dagger gleamed like a lover's secret, short but sharp, the kind of blade you only noticed after it was already beneath your ribs.

The vineyard shifted again. Wires overhead bent into curves, sagging then tightening until they resembled cages suspended in midair. Vines whipped across the path, roots tearing shallow trenches into the soil. For every step Effie took forward, the rows warped to obscure her, to redirect her. But she moved as though the chaos were staged for her alone.

"Do you feel it?" Delilah pressed, circling. Her katana whistled, the blade leaving a smear of light behind. "The vineyard breathes when I tell it to. These vines want to strangle you, goddess. They want to taste your blood in their soil."

Effie's laugh chimed against the wires, turning their rattle into accompaniment. "Then let them come," she purred. "Your illusions are foreplay, Delilah. But I decide who climaxes."

The words alone shifted the space. Where Delilah's illusions conjured vines thrashing, Effie's voice bent perception. The tendrils faltered; some slackened, hanging limp, as though seduced away from their mistress. Delilah struck first, her katana flashing in a diagonal arc meant to split Effie's image in two. The rainbow trail of the swing multiplied, and to the watching eye it seemed five blades cut the night together. Effie sidestepped with effortless precision, turning her shoulder, her skin grazing the illusion as though brushing past a curtain. Her dagger struck out, fast as lust denied, cutting across Delilah's sleeve and drawing the first line of blood. "Closer," Effie whispered, her voice riding the sting of the wound.

The vineyard bucked. Rows of trellises bent inward, the vines knotting to form writhing walls. The ground seemed to pulse, roots tearing upward like serpents, trying to seize ankles and wrists. Delilah danced with it, her body breaking into fractured forms—now four, now ten, each mirrored against the wires, each carrying a blade that gleamed in kaleidoscopic madness. She lunged. One Delilah struck low, another high, another came from the left—each a prism-ghost that felt real enough to wound. Effie didn't flinch. Her dagger sang, catching the real blade in the chaos, sparks scattering like falling stars. "Hide in mirrors if you must," Effie taunted, pressing forward. "But remember—every mirror secretly longs to show me." She slashed across Delilah's thigh. Not deep, but deliberate. The cut bled into the dirt, and the vines drank it. The vineyard screamed. Leaves quivered in unison, an impossible sound like applause in reverse.

The rows twisted further, trellises contorting into angles that defied perspective, a maze no mortal could escape. Observers would have sworn the Valley itself was alive, grabbing, grasping, coiling with green hunger.

Delilah's laughter carried over it all. "Do you see, Effie? This place knows me. These vines are chaos given form, and they will bury you before dawn."

Effie's voice rose against the madness, not louder but sharper, cutting through the vineyard's cry. "The Valley knows desire, not chaos. And desire always comes to me."

Her aura pulsed outward, invisible but irresistible. The writhing vines stilled. A thousand leaves turned in unison, their undersides silver in the moonlight, as if bowing toward her. Delilah faltered, just a heartbeat, but it was enough. Effie stepped in, dagger darting. The steel kissed Delilah's cheek, drawing a fine red line that dripped into her grin.

"You bleed beautifully," Effie said.

Delilah's kaleidoscope flared again in rage. The vineyard fractured into shards of sight: one moment endless rows of vines, the next a desert of shattered glass, the next a cathedral of roots arching into the sky. The katana swept with impossible speed, its edges multiplied until Effie seemed surrounded by a storm of rainbow blades. But she was never overwhelmed. Each step was calculated seduction: a shoulder revealed at just the right angle to distract; a glance that stole a fraction of thought; a smile that slowed the hand just enough. She deflected senses as easily as steel, so that when her dagger struck, it struck true.

A cut across the ribs. A stab at the hip. Another along the forearm.

Delilah bled into her own illusions, colour and blood indistinguishable in the kaleidoscopic storm. Still, she fought, laughing even as the vineyard screamed with her, wires snapping taut like harp strings played too fast.

Effie pressed closer, dagger flickering, voice unwavering. "You dazzle," she murmured, her breath brushing Delilah's ear in a moment stolen mid-parry. "But dazzle blinds even you."

The dagger struck again. And the vineyard shook. It wasn't the earth—this was the trellis work itself, the long, taut wires that kept the canopy in check, humming with sudden tension like an orchestra tuning to the wrong note. End posts creaked. Strainers bit deeper into the soil. Bird nets shivered along the headlands and then poured inward as if a tide had turned in the night.

Delilah lifted her chin, and the wires obeyed. They sagged, then bowed, then swept down together in a shimmering arc that would have wrapped Effie in a glittering cage. The goddess did not step back. She raised one palm as if greeting admirers and let the first wire kiss her wrist—a gasp—hers, but fashioned.

"Gentle," Effie breathed, and the wire softened, a cat arching under a stroke. Her dagger whispered once, twice, and two lines parted like ribbon at a ceremony. The severed ends sprang, singing, and slapped against a post with a sad, tuneless twang.

"Don't flatter my vines," Delilah said. "They prefer sharp company."

"They're thirsty," Effie replied, cutting another loop away. "They prefer wine."

She pivoted, shoulder first, hair catching on a leaf, the tiny snag of it plainly chosen. Delilah's eyes flicked—half a heartbeat, but enough—and Effie slid forward, the dagger a gleam across the ribs she'd already scored. Blood warmed the night.

Delilah hissed through her teeth and let the mirage lapse into mania.

Light went psychotic—sourceless flares, corridors of colour, the rows doubling and tripling until perspective had to ask for permission. The wires multiplied in reflection, knotting into braided serpents that lunged and recoiled. Leaves flipped their pale undersides, a thousand tiny bellies shivering as if the moon had moved inside the canopy to breathe on them.

"Welcome to the Valley," Delilah said, her voice now in seven places at once. "Every vine is a vein. Every wire is a nerve. I am what runs through them."

"Then you won't mind a little surgery." Effie cut her way into the next row, hips brushing foliage so lightly the leaves turned to follow. She spoke as she worked, each word placed to tug an unseen thread: "Look. At. Me." The command rode above the kaleidoscope and through it, bypassing sight altogether. The vines nearest her loosened, the nearest wires bowing away as if ashamed to be seen clutching.

Delilah's katana flickered from shadow, low and cunning, going for tendons beneath a knee. Effie dropped her weight onto the cut wire, let it take her like a swing, and soared past the blade. The dagger returned a heartbeat later, tracing the inside of Delilah's forearm. It wasn't a deep wound, but it was disrespect, and Delilah's laughter faltered.

"You're talking yourself into believing you're winning," Delilah said, breath a fraction ragged.

"I know," Effie said, smiling, "you're listening."

The vineyard answered for Delilah. A rush—not wind, not quite—pushed down the row, all leaves and wire and intent. Bird netting cascaded from a trellis and became a veil that tried to settle over Effie's shoulders. From beneath, roots heaved, exposed for an instant like the backs of sleeping animals.

Effie let the net fall, then twitched one wrist. The cestus slid into her hand as if a partner had been standing behind her the whole time. She didn't fasten it; she only touched the silk and let the idea of it bloom.

Desire thickened, directed, clean-as-a-bell tone. The net paused upon her shoulders—then slid down her arms and lay itself at her feet, folding like a kneeling thing.

Delilah swore in a colour that wasn't on the human spectrum.

"Come back to yourself," Effie told the vineyard, and the closest wires stopped shivering.

"She's beautiful when she's composed," Effie confided to the vines, as if Delilah were not there. "She hides it with noise."

Delilah appeared at Effie's right, too close, finally risking the personal range the dagger loved. The katana came in flat, a palm-width from Effie's face, less a cut than a slap with steel. Effie's head turned just enough that the blade whispered her cheek. She let the sting bloom like a rose petal and smiled into it. "Better," she said, and slid the dagger under Delilah's guard to scratch a new line just below the collarbone.

The two women rocked together an instant: shoulder, breath, the quick pulse of wrists almost touching before they parted.

"Stop—" Delilah began.

"Thinking?" Effie supplied and kissed the air between them with a laugh. "Oh, darling."

The vineyard tried strangulation.

The trellis wires swooped from either side, forming a woven barrel that sought to cinch itself tight around Effie's waist and ribs. She didn't fight the grip. She folded into it with a sound that made even metal want to be skin, and then she cut not the wire but the pattern of attention holding it.

The barrel slackened, confused, as if realising it was embracing a queen rather than trapping prey. "Barossa has a habit of rewarding confidence," Effie murmured. "You should know that."

Delilah's answer was a strike that didn't bother with illusions at all—just clean speed, blade, and body drawing a diagonal that would have opened Effie from hip to sternum.

Effie met it with the dagger in a catch that should have broken her wrist. It didn't. Steel screamed; sparks skittered and got caught in the bird netting like fireflies.

Effie drove her weight forward along the joined blades, shoulder to shoulder, and said in Delilah's ear: "Watch."

The vines on either side shivered. Leaves, hundreds of them, turned all at once. A row away, grapes—tight late-season bunches, the kind that held miniature suns inside their skins—glowed for an instant as if daylight had been stored between sugars.

Delilah's eyes flicked again.

Effie's knee tapped the inside of Delilah's thigh, just hard enough to break stance, and the dagger traced a confident line across the outer hip.

Delilah grunted, annoyed more than hurt, and stepped back into her chaos. Light broke into prisms, and each prism contained a different vineyard: Seppeltsfield palms marching through one; a Greenock creek flashing pewter in another; in a third, the lean lines of Eden Valley hills.

Effie was in all of them, and none, and Delilah's katana could cut every one at once. She did. The blade mapped an arc across the night. Wires snapped—posts shuddered. A coil whipped

Effie's ankle and took her off-balance, just for a breath, just long enough that the katana could have opened an artery.

Effie made a sound like praise.

It struck Delilah's nerves like a frost. Delilah's timing shifted—half a heartbeat, the time it takes to choose pleasure over efficiency. The katana bit no deeper than a kiss along Effie's flank, a red warmth that promised more and didn't get it.

"Almost," Effie said, genuinely pleased, and rewarded the attempt with a shallow cut on Delilah's jaw, exactly mirroring the one on her own cheek. "Now we match."

Delilah spat pink into the rows. "You're writing me," she said. "Like I'm a label."

"You're a vintage," Effie corrected. "Some years need firm racking."

Delilah laughed despite herself, and the prism intensified—psychotic into kaleidoscopic into a blur that should have broken human balance.

The rows looped into circles. A tractor track became a spiral that promised to fold in on itself forever. A kangaroo fence along the boundary unstitched and ran like a thread through a needle made of stars.

Effie's eyes shone, unaffected. "You're wasting sugar," Effie said, and when she moved, it was with the casual cruelty of an expert chocolatier.

She walked through the wrong geometry as if it were simply unfashionable. Her dagger counted pulses, not positions. A nick on Delilah's wrist. A line across her ribs, parallel to the first.

A puncture at the soft meat of the upper arm that would bruise purple by morning.

The vineyard took those wounds personally. Roots flexed and cracked the topsoil. Dust leapt, then fell in a slow glitter that looked like confetti under lunatic lights. Wires tried for her throat. Effie bowed to them and let them crown her, then severed their authority with a single, contemptuous swipe. The ends fell and coiled at her feet like dead snakes.

"Tell me," Effie said, voice easy, breath steady, "when you first learned to lie with light."

Delilah, panting now, bared her teeth. "When I learned truth was a trick."

She came in low again.

Effie let her, then spun the blade with two fingers and pinned Delilah's wrist between dagger and palm so gently it was obscene.

She could have broken the joint. She didn't.

She traced the hilt down to Delilah's hand and pried her fingers open one by one with the promise of it.

The katana clanged to the ground—a refusal, not surrender. Delilah snatched it up with the other hand and slashed through an illusion Effie had never offered. The stroke parted vines. A roll of leaves fell over them both like a curtain call.

Under the green rain, Effie spoke close. "Stop showing me the world and show me you."

A flare of real anger lit Delilah from within. The illusions wavered, then steadied—but they steadied around her, not around the Valley. The prism folded inward. For the first time, the light was about Delilah's shape, not her stage.

"Better," Effie breathed.

Delilah attacked as herself, a line of intent without ghosting tricks. It was faster. It was cleaner. It landed—edge on Effie's shoulder, a hot ribbon of pain that made the goddess' breath catch, almost, almost like surprise.

"Good girl," Effie said, and punished the success with a shallow thrust at the obliques, the kind of wound that made breath expensive.

They separated, then returned, then separated again, the rows narrowing with each exchange until there was only a metre between trellis posts and nothing soft left to step on.

The Barossa night pressed in, smelling of dust and crushed leaf and the faint sweetness of late fruit hiding upright in the dark. Delilah's illusions dimmed as her heart got louder. Effie's voice never dimmed. She talked as a fencer breathes, the words falling into the spaces between steel.

"You fight like a woman who learned alone," she said. A shallow cut along the forearm. "Who expected to be interrupted?" Another along the thigh. "Who never counted on being loved." The dagger paused, point hovering at the hollow where collar meets throat.

"Am I close?"

Delilah's mouth crooked. "Close enough to be wrong."

"Then correct me," Effie invited, and opened her stance like a door.

Delilah took the door off its hinges. She came in with a low feint that promised a belly cut, then rose, blade singing for Effie's throat. Effie leaned back, spine a bow, hair trailing the dirt, and the katana shaved a line through the air that might have been the edge of her smile. Effie's free hand slapped the flat of the steel and pushed it past, and the dagger tapped Delilah between the ribs. There was no blood this time; just possession.

"Mine," Effie said softly to the space she'd touched.

Delilah stumbled back into the vines and came up laughing, breath hitching, eyes bright with a heat that had nothing to do with anger. She wiped blood from her jaw with her thumb and painted a line across a leaf. The leaf flushed dark, then light, then turned itself inside out as if uncertain which colour meant alive.

"Barossa will remember you for that," Delilah said.

"Barossa remembers everything worth drinking," Effie said, and slid forward, sure as a pour. "You're worth drinking."

The following exchange wasn't pretty. It was economical and cruel, two professionals finding efficiencies. Steel bit skin in tiny, ruinous economies. The cactus-prickle of cut wire against ankles, the burn of salt-sweat in new cuts, the taste of iron finding tongue. They moved through it with the intimacy of dancers who knew each other's worst habits and chose them anyway.

When the moment came, it was not a flourish but a fact. Delilah overcommitted by a hair, a single colour too bright in her spectrum. Effie took the hair, took the colour, and took the opening. The dagger found the meat just above the hip, slid in a finger's depth, and withdrew before the blood could decide what it wanted to be.

Delilah's knees impressed the soil and stayed there.

The vines shuddered, scandalised. The wires went still, awaiting instruction, uncertain.

Effie stood over her, breathing as if she'd walked a gentle hill.

She did not press the advantage. She did not touch the cestus. She only turned the dagger in her hand so the blade faced down and rested its spine along Delilah's shoulder, a friendly weight.

"Don't make me repeat myself," she said, quiet enough to make the stars lean in. "A war is coming. Get up."

Delilah's knees sank into the loose Barossa soil, the rich earth drinking her blood as if it were a libation poured by unseen hands. The vineyard inhaled with her, wires creaking like bones settling, vines twitching with the memory of struggle. Even the grapes, hanging heavy with their last sugars of the season, seemed to pulse faintly, aware that two beings greater than myth had marked this place.

Effie leaned forward, dagger still balanced on Delilah's shoulder, her eyes catching the moon and bending it to her will. She was unmarked but not untested; blood ran in dark rivulets along her flank, staining the silk of her dress.

She looked down at Delilah not with cruelty, but with possession—this was no victory for slaughter. This was seduction through dominance.

"Look at me," Effie said again, softer now.

The words slid into Delilah's spine like heat, commanding not by force, but by inevitability. Delilah raised her head, eyes burning even through exhaustion. Chaos still flickered there, but it was thinner now, a flame sputtering in the wind of Effie's certainty.

"You could kill me," Delilah rasped, her voice raw, her katana tip dragging a furrow in the dirt beside her. "End it here, prove beauty stronger than madness."

Effie tilted her head, her smile more dangerous for its restraint. "Stronger? No. But sharper. And sharper always wins when the moment comes."

She lifted the dagger just enough to hook Delilah's chin, tilting her face upward so their eyes locked. "I don't want your end. I want your edge."

The vineyard shifted again, but it was weaker, watching. The vines curled half-heartedly, then drooped as if embarrassed, not for lack of water, but for a lack of blood.

The kaleidoscope that had fractured the rows earlier stuttered in pieces, likc glass attempting to reassemble itself but failing. Delilah had no energy left to maintain it. Her power flickered like dying neon.

Effie crouched, her breath close now, fragrant with roses and salt. She pressed her free hand against the wound at Delilah's ribs, not to heal, not to hurt, but to feel the rhythm of her defiance beneath the skin.

"You bleed beautifully," Effie murmured, repeating the line she'd spoken earlier, but this time it was not taunt—it was a verdict.

Delilah hissed as Effie pressed a little harder, then laughed despite herself, the sound a brittle jewel in the midnight vines. "You enjoy writing on me with your blade."

"You're parchment," Effie said. "And the world will read what I write."

She withdrew the dagger from Delilah's shoulder and lowered it, no longer threatening but ready all the same. Then she extended her hand—fingers long, nails immaculate, palm open. Not a command. Invitation.

"Rise."

Delilah stared at it for a long breath. Her pride screamed against the gesture, her blood argued for vengeance, and her chaos itched to splinter the moment into something unrecognisable. But her body was battered, and her illusions were broken, and there was something in Effie's eyes that was not triumph but necessity. Chaos could not ignore necessity—it had always been drawn to it, like a moth drawn to flame.

She took the hand.

Effie pulled her up with surprising strength, their bodies momentarily close, the dagger brushing harmlessly at Delilah's side. When they steadied, the vineyard steadied with them. The wires stopped groaning. The vines loosened. The rows re-aligned, though their memory of what had happened lingered in every knot and shadow.

Effie did not release Delilah's hand immediately. She held it, deliberately, as if sealing something more critical than a duel. Her voice low, intimate, unshakable. "The gods are sharpening their teeth. They think mortals are pawns. They think we are pawns. They are wrong."

Delilah's lips quirked in the half-smile of someone too tired to sneer but too defiant to submit. "So what? You beat me, and now you want me as your soldier?"

"No," Effie said, brushing her thumb across Delilah's knuckles, smearing blood like ink. "I want you as my sister. Beauty and chaos together. Singular and shattered, side by side. They won't know where to look."

The vineyard around them seemed to exhale, relax, the last fragments of Delilah's prism dissolving into soft light. For a moment, the Valley looked like itself again—rows neat and green, wires taut, the air cool with the promise of dawn and a vintage yet to arrive.

Both women knew it would never truly return to innocence.

The Barossa had watched them, and the soil had tasted blood; such things were remembered.

Delilah's hand tightened in Effie's. "If I agree... we don't march with spears. That's not how chaos fights."

Effie's smile deepened, dangerous and perfect. "No spears. We build an army the gods will never see coming. Misfits. Outcasts. The kind the old order dismisses." She leaned closer, her voice threading directly into Delilah's ear.

"You will recruit the unseen. I will bind them with desire. Together, we will make the world stumble."

Delilah laughed again, the sound richer this time, the exhaustion colouring it but not diminishing it. "You want to play conductor to my orchestra of wrong notes."

"I want to make the hymn unbearable," Effie said. "So when the gods sing, no one listens."

They stood in silence for a beat, surrounded by vines that seemed to lean in, listening. The soil beneath them was damp now, dark patches spreading where blood had fallen.

Somewhere in the distance, a kookaburra cackled—a mortal sound in an immortal night.

Delilah bent to retrieve her katana, sliding it back into its sheath with a hiss like a sigh. She straightened and met Effie's eyes again. "Fine," she said. "You bloodied me into submission. You claimed me. But don't think for a second you own me."

Effie tilted her head, satisfied. "I don't need to own you. I only need you close enough to touch when the time comes."

Delilah rolled her eyes, but she didn't step back. Her chaos was quieter now, simmering instead of boiling, but it was there. Effie's beauty did not quench it; it directed it, shaped it, gave it something sharper than spectacle. The Valley was still. Dawn was not yet near, but the vines seemed different—restless, alive—keeping its own counsel.

The Barossa had hosted more than a duel. It had witnessed the forging of an alliance.

Effie finally released Delilah's hand, but her voice lingered like perfume. "We'll start with a rumour," she said. "Then a colour. Then a name. And by the time the gods notice, we'll already be inside their palaces."

Delilah smirked. "I'll drink to that. Preferably a Shiraz."

Effie laughed—low, sensual, triumphant. "You'll drink what I pour you. And you'll like it."

Delilah's grin widened despite herself.

The vineyard swallowed their laughter, wires and leaves settling like nothing remarkable had happened.

It had never been simple. People arrived with old habits and older silences, put cellars into the earth, and learned which songs not to sing.

Names got shortened. Language got packed away. Pride learned to work quietly. The vines didn't care. They kept growing.

Effie and Delilah stood in the middle of those rows now, blood darkening the soil, blades cooling in their hands. The land had seen worse. It had seen this shape before—things pressed flat that refused to stay flat.

Effie breathed in leaf and dust and sugar and said, without drama, "This place knows what it is to be told to be less."

The vineyard did not disagree.

It leaned in, remembered, and carried on.

Chapter 22
The Gardens

The Adelaide Botanic Gardens should have been a place of reprieve. Midday sun broke into scattered diamonds across the glass roof of the Palm House, and families wandered among the roses and gums, sipping coffee from paper cups, pointing at the ibis strutting near the fountain. But something was wrong.

Diane knew it before she stepped through the northern gates. Her triangulation had been precise—three deaths in Rundle Mall at 10:14, another six in the State Library foyer minutes later, then thirty-seven more at the Festival Plaza. All spontaneous, all inexplicable. It was less a contagion than a radius. Death rippled outward from a single moving source, and every step he took left silent carnage. She had followed the pattern like a hunter tracking spoor.

The lines converged here.

The Gardens were too quiet. Pockets of people sat slumped across benches, lovers entwined and suddenly still, tourists collapsed with cameras dangling. Children cried over the fallen bodies of their parents, confused but untouched. Diane's boots clicked over the flagstones, her sunglasses hiding the focus in her eyes. She had seen death before—caused it more times than she would admit—but this was different.

This was indiscriminate. Indifferent. Like a weather front that spared nothing but the young. And at the centre of it all, by the ornamental lake, stood Ellery Kalos. He looked nothing like the detective who once asked sharp questions in clipped tones. His coat was gone, shirt torn at the sleeve, hair mussed as though from a prolonged fever. Yet he radiated something larger, darker—the unmistakable weight of a being whose domain had finally unshackled.

People died as he moved. He did not touch them. He did not even glance at them. A careless wave of his hand, a tightening of his jaw, and whole clusters of strangers fell wordless into the grass. Lovers, pensioners, and business people on their lunch break. They dropped where they stood, eyes glassing over, breath stolen.

But not the children.

Diane noticed it quickly. Toddlers wailed, clutching at the skirts of mothers who would not rise again, yet not one small chest stilled. Ellery's unconscious compass bent away from innocence.

Her throat tightened. This was no ritual. No plan. This was death released without a rule. She advanced slowly, weaving through the fallen. Her steps were careful, deliberate, so as not to spook him. She had come with purpose, though not the one he feared.

He had invited her once—hesitantly, awkwardly, but sincerely—to stand beside him. She had not answered then. But she knew the danger of hesitation. If she didn't answer now, he would believe she had come only to strike him down.

Ellery felt her before he saw her. His arm froze mid-gesture, and the ripple of death halted. The air seemed to hold its breath.

When he turned, his eyes were not furious but wide, full of something closer to terror.

"You followed me," he said, voice frayed, hoarse from silence.

"I had to." Diane removed her glasses. Her eyes, steel-grey, met his directly. "You've left a trail no one else could ignore."

"I didn't mean—" He trailed off, his hand lowering as if it were heavy with guilt. "They just—" He gestured at the sprawled bodies. "I can't stop it."

"I know," she said softly. "That's why I'm here."

He flinched, suspicion flashing. "You're here to finish it, aren't you? To do what gods do—hunt the stray beast, clean up the mess."

For a moment, Diane let the silence hang. The wind stirred the treetops, rustling the jacarandas that had showered purple blossoms across the lawn. A child sobbed somewhere behind them, muffled by a stranger's jacket.

"No," Diane said finally, her tone deliberate. "I came because of what you asked me. Back at the motel room, when you didn't even know what you were yet. You asked if we could be more than hunter and quarry."

Ellery shook his head as though the memory itself pained him. "I was a fool."

"You were honest," Diane countered.

She stepped closer. The radius of death shivered, but did not touch her. Her presence—something in her certainty—stayed his power.

"And honesty is rarer than survival, Ellery."

His eyes narrowed, shadow and fear twining in them. "Then why now? Why here, with all this?" He waved again, and half a dozen pigeons fell from the sky like discarded rags. His lips trembled. "You see what I am. You should be afraid."

"I am," she admitted. The words cost her something, but she gave them freely. "But not of dying. I'm afraid you'll let this power swallow you. I'm afraid you'll believe you have to be alone."

He laughed bitterly. "Alone is safer. Look around you." His voice broke. "Look what happens when I breathe."

Diane moved another step closer, closing the space between them to less than ten paces. The air thickened, humming with invisible weight. He half-raised his hand as if to push her away with the same gesture that had felled hundreds. But the hand trembled, refusing.

"You could end me," he said. "One shot, one strike. Why haven't you?"

She met his gaze, steady as stone. "Because I'd rather stand beside you than over you."

Ellery's breath caught.

For the first time since the Gardens began to die, something shifted in him. The power roiled, but it bent inward, clawing at itself instead of spilling out. His shoulders sagged under the invisible burden. Around them, the city's lungs still faltered. Ambulance sirens wailed distantly, too late for most.

Yet in this small circle of the Gardens, there was a pause. A reprieve. And in that pause, Diane stepped one pace closer. Close enough now that he could see his reflection in her shades, dangling forgotten from her hand. Close enough that the hunter no longer looked like his executioner, but like his choice.

He stared at her hand like it was a fuse. “You can’t be here,” he whispered. “Every time I breathe, someone—”

“Then we’ll teach your breath to behave.”

Diane closed the last meters between them—slow, palms open, shoulders low, the way one approaches a skittish horse that could also be lightning.

The high glass of the Bicentennial Conservatory flashed sunlight into her eyes; she didn’t blink.

Behind Ellery, the ornamental lake held its reflection of blue and gum, broken only by the lazy triangle of a black swan. Its head dipped. It did not die.

“You noticed?” she said gently. “Children and animals.”

He nodded once, throat working. “They don’t tally.” He swallowed. “Everybody else… tallies.”

“Ledger thinking,” she said, almost to herself. “Jamil’s way of seeing. But you’re not Jamil.” She tilted her head. “You’re not an accountant. You’re a knife.”

He winced. “I don’t want to be a knife.”

“Then be a surgeon.”

She took one more step. The radius trembled again, a pressure in the sinuses, a tightness behind the eyes. Somewhere at the periphery, a man groaned and went still. Diane didn’t look away.

“Listen to me, Ellery. Power spreads to fill the shape you give it. Right now you’re giving it panic. Panic is a fog. Make it a line.”

"How?"

"The way I shoot," she said, and let the memory of failure slide through her with clean acceptance. "Not with rage. With breath. There's in-breath, hold, out-breath, hold. The shot breaks in the quiet between. Find the quiet."

He shook his head, wild and small at once. "I can't. When I try, it—"

He cut off, fist clenching. A cluster of tourists swayed; an older man slumped sideways into a flowerbed, eyes open to a sky that didn't apologise.

Diane's jaw hardened. "Look at me."

When he did, she gave him the truth like water. "I didn't come to kill you. I came to keep a promise I didn't dare to make when you asked. If you want me here, I'm here. If you want me close, I come close."

She lifted her hand, stopping just shy of his wrist. Heat shimmered between skin and skin. "If you want me with you, I'll stay."

Terror and something like relief wrestled behind his eyes. "You touch me and you'll"

"Find out." Her mouth tipped, the smallest huntress's smile. "Or you find out, and you hold the air still."

He drew in a thin, ragged breath.

"Four counts," she murmured. "In. Hold. Out. Hold. Give the power a box to live in."

He tried. Something in his chest stuttered. Hold—his fingers trembled. Out—something invisible rippled outward like heat from asphalt, and a woman two hedges away sagged to her knees but caught herself on the rail, coughing. Hold—the air pinched. The radius tightened for a heartbeat, then ballooned again.

"Good," Diane said.

"That wasn't—"

"It was less."

She slid the final inch and laid two fingers on his wrist.

The world bristled. Sound fell out of the day—the ibis, the lawnmower somewhere beyond the gates, even the far sirens, all muffled as if a thick curtain swung between realms.

Ellery's pupils blew wide. His power surged, reared—then felt the boundary of her touch and, for the first time, recognised something it could not erase. It pressed. It tested. It found no purchase.

Diane's voice came through the pressure like a string pulled taut. "Feel it. Edges. You've never had them. Now you do. The line isn't 'everyone who breathes.' The line is the shape you draw."

He closed his eyes, breath jerking. "I don't know how to draw."

"Start with what you know," she said. "Children live. Animals live. Add to it."

She squeezed once, not hard. "Add 'anyone whose eyes I can see.' Add 'anyone within three paces of the water.' Add 'anyone holding a hand.' Make rules. Rules are fences. Power respects fences."

He swallowed. "Fences."

“Say them.”

His voice was raw. “Children live. Animals live. Anyone—anyone she can see—stays.” He opened his eyes to her. “Anyone by the water stays. Anyone holding a hand stays.”

“Again.”

“Children live. Animals live. Eyes stay. Water stays. Hands stay.”

The pressure shifted. It didn’t go away, but it flowed differently, like a river quickening at the banks while the centreline slowed. A boy with a red cap hiccuped and drew a long, surprised breath over his mother’s slack shoulder. A couple who had crumpled together on a bench blinked in unison and began to cry.

Ellery’s breath hitched. “I felt that.”

“Good.” Diane moved her hand from his wrist to the inside of his forearm, up toward the elbow—closer to the place where the pulse becomes decisive. He shuddered, not from death but from the shock of being held. “Now narrow the fog,” she said softly. “Bring it to a path. Can you see it? From here to the gate, a corridor of nothing. No tally. A way out.”

He stared at the northern gates through the lattice of Moreton Bay fig shadows. For a moment, he saw it the way she said: a pale corridor like the belly of a wave. He breathed into the picture. The air pushed back. The fog gathered its skirts. He lifted his free hand, slowly this time. People within twenty paces stiffened, but did not fall. He extended a finger, drawing not a sweep but a line. The line wavered, then held.

“Walk,” Diane said.

“If I move—”

“Walk with me. In the quiet between.”

She stepped into the space he'd drawn. It quivered around her like a skittish thing. "Trust me."

He followed.

They moved like divers through a rip, cutting a narrow swathe where no one else slipped under. Twice the corridor buckled when Ellery's fear surged, and twice Diane's hand brought it back to shape with a tiny pressure and a murmured, "Hold."

They passed two paramedics kneeling beside a cluster of bodies; one paramedic looked up, eyes emptying of focus as her brain tried to understand why the impossible couple walking through the carnage felt like an answer.

At the edge of the path, a little girl stood frozen, freckles stark against tear-slick skin, a hand still hooked through the mother's fingers, who would not rise. She stared at Ellery with the solemn acuity of children who have already learned too much.

Diane stopped. "Hands stay," she reminded softly.

Ellery swallowed and crouched—not close, but down to the child's level, his drawn corridor flexing with the change. The girl's gaze didn't leave his face. "Is she... sleeping?" she asked.

"No," he said, and his voice didn't break. "But you are not alone." He glanced at Diane. She nodded once. "What's your name?" he asked.

"Matilda," she whispered.

"Matilda," he repeated, as if the syllables were a talisman. "There will be people here soon to help you. You stay by the water, okay? And keep holding a hand."

He glanced at Diane again. "Hands stay."

"Hands stay," Diane agreed, and squeezed his arm.

They moved on. Overhead, helicopter blades began to beat the air, sending down brief, hot squalls that lifted purple jacaranda petals and settled them again like ash. The corridor wobbled under the percussion; Ellery hissed and instinctively raised his arm to swat at the noise. Three men at the periphery sagged.

"Look at me," Diane said sharply. He did. "Noise is not the target. The target is the line."

Her eyes were clear steel. "Let the city do what it does. You draw." He took the command the way a drowning man grabs a rope. The line steadied.

They reached the rotunda near the Friends' Gate, its ironwork lace casting neat shadows across the path. Police spilled in through the opening—a first wave, breathless, hands hovering over holsters, eyes going wide at the geometry of collapse. One officer lifted a megaphone, checked himself, and lowered it in the same motion, sensing without language that loud was the wrong tool for this room.

Diane raised her free hand, palm open, a hunter's universal sign. "Medical only," she called, voice even, perfectly pitched. "No rush. Quiet feet. Follow the water line."

The sergeant at the front—square-jawed, sun-smashed—looked from the bodies to Ellery to Diane and made the decision he would later be unable to justify in a report. He nodded and waved the ambos through. They moved like ghosts, hugging the edge Diane had named, eyes carefully not naming anything else.

Ellery let out a breath that tasted like iron. "They'll put me down," he said.

"If they try, I'll break their hands," Diane replied without heat. "Keep drawing."

"Why are you doing this?" The question fell out of him, raw and baffled, the boy inside the detective suddenly visible. "You could have taken the shot when I turned. You could have saved—" He choked on the word. "Saved them."

She looked over the lake, where the black swan's wake made a quiet V across the green. "I didn't come to save them," she said. "I came to save you."

She let the line hang and then, softer, "And because you asked."

He stared at her. "You remembered."

"I remember what is mine."

The line flickered again—not with fear this time, but with an alien tremor that ran up from the bones of the city. The gum leaves stilled. The helicopter sound fell away, as if the blades were beating under water.

Ellery's head tilted, listening. "You feel that?" he asked.

"Yes."

"What is it?"

"Others noticing." She didn't say which others. She didn't need to. The hair on both their arms knew. "It's going to get crowded in the spaces we can't see."

"Then we should go," he said, urgency back in his voice. "Before I—"

"Not yet." She stepped closer, shoulder to shoulder now, her hand sliding from his forearm to his hand, threading their fingers with calm deliberation. The pressure rose—and broke like a wave against a cliff. "The rule stands," she said. "Hands stay."

He looked down at their joined grip as if it were a kind of miracle. "I don't want you to die."

"I don't intend to." She angled her body toward him. Up close, the hard lines of the huntress softened into something human. "But love is many things. Today, it is instruction."

He swallowed, the word landing in him like a brand and a balm in one. "Instruction," he echoed.

"Breath," she said. "Line. Rule. And when the fear spikes, do not sweep. Point." She lifted his hand, still holding it, and together they extended one finger toward the gates. "Like this. A lane at a time." They walked, drawing lanes through a garden of quiet deaths, leaving islands of life behind them—children clutching hands by the water, a paramedic wiping her eyes and carrying on, a swan folding its neck under a wing as if nothing in the world had changed.

At the threshold, where iron met city, Ellery hesitated. "What happens when we leave the trees?" he asked. "Out there... more people. More tally."

Diane squeezed his hand. "Then we choose a smaller world for a little while," she said. "A car. A room. A way down that only we know." She met his eyes, all the way through. "And we learn you." Something eased in his shoulders—a notch, a breath.

He nodded.

"Ready?" she asked.

"For you," he said, and for the first time, the words weren't a plea or an apology. They were aligned.

They stepped into the gate's shadow. The city leaned in to listen. And above the helicopter's thrum and the sirens and the thick bright noise of noon, Ellery found the quiet between. They crossed into the car park, and the hum of Adelaide returned like a radio between stations—traffic on Botanic Road, the faint calls of vendors at the market further west, the pulsing roar of the helicopters now circling lower. But the atmosphere was strained, unnatural. People at the periphery had begun to sense that something had gone wrong in the Gardens. Groups pressed against police cordons, murmuring, recording with their phones.

Diane's hand stayed in Ellery's, the tether anchoring him against the swell. He felt the urge flare again, the pulse of death widening like a lung about to exhale across the crowd.

She felt it too, and she leaned closer, whispering steadily into his ear. "Don't sweep. Point."

He clenched his teeth, focusing on the line they'd carved. It held, but barely. His stomach turned, the strain of containing the flood like holding a storm behind clenched fists. "They see me," he muttered. "All those cameras. All those eyes. They'll know."

"They'll invent another story," Diane said, matter-of-fact, her hunter's detachment coating the words in calm. "Heart attacks. Terrorism. Bad air. They'll explain it in a way that doesn't threaten the world they believe in. What they won't do is believe you exist."

"I exist too loudly," he said, shaking. "I can't mute it."

"You don't need to mute it. You need to learn pitch."

A ripple coursed through him—an almost visible shimmer—and three men at the edge of the police line clutched their chests, gasping, before collapsing. The crowd screamed. Officers surged forward.

Ellery flinched, eyes wild.

Diane stepped in front of him, free hand lifted in command. Her aviators flashed the light back at the line of officers. "Stay where you are," she barked, her voice sharp with authority that belonged to older fields than law enforcement.

For a moment, they froze—not in obedience to her rank, but to the inexplicable certainty in her tone.

Ellery whispered, "You should kill me now."

"No," she said.

He stared at her profile—stoic, uncompromising, beautiful in the cruel way a blade is gorgeous—and for the first time since the deaths began, he felt a crack of something like shame rather than fear. She was not afraid of him. She was worried about him.

"Come on," she said, tugging his hand. "We need cover."

They moved quickly toward Plane Tree Drive. Diane had already noted a nondescript sedan parked in the shade. It was hers—borrowed plates, a clean interior, nothing traceable. She opened the passenger door, guiding him in like a handler ushering an unpredictable predator into its cage. He sat, trembling, shoulders hunched.

When she slipped into the driver's seat, she didn't start the engine straight away. She turned to him instead. "You're not going to unravel here. Do you understand?"

"I don't—"

"You're not." Her voice cut him off, firm. "The car is a smaller world. Fences. Four doors, four walls. Hold your power inside it. Nothing outside the frame."

He pressed his palms to his temples, eyes squeezed shut. "What if it doesn't listen?"

"It listened to me." She reached over, caught his wrist again, the pulse point where it had steadied before. "It'll listen again. You need rules."

Slowly, painfully, his breathing evened. The ripple withdrew like a tide reluctant to leave the shore. Outside, the shouts of police and paramedics dimmed to a background hum.

Diane started the engine.

The car rolled smoothly onto Botanic Road, away from the chaos, into the web of city streets. For ten minutes, they drove in silence, the tension in the cabin thick as smoke. Every red light was a test: a group of pedestrians here, a bus stop crowded there. Each time Ellery twitched, Diane's hand tightened over his, reminding him of the fences.

"Not outside the frame," she said once, and he held.

By the time they reached the ring of warehouses near the river, Ellery's head had fallen back against the seat, eyes glazed with exhaustion. "I killed so many," he said at last, voice hollow. "Too many. It's written in the grass back there. Written in the air."

"You didn't choose it," Diane said. "You didn't even know what you were choosing."

"They'll still call it me."

"They should," she replied, bluntly. "You need to know the weight. But knowing weight isn't the same as being crushed under it."

He turned his head toward her. The suspicion in his gaze had faded, leaving only fear. But not of her. Not anymore. "Why would you stand with me after that?"

"Because you remind me of myself," she said without hesitation. "A weapon too sharp for its own sheath. I've been alone with that edge my whole life. I know what it costs."

She allowed the faintest smile. "And because you asked me once. I don't make promises lightly, Ellery."

He swallowed hard, searching her face for deceit and finding none. "If I say I want you here, really here—will you stay?"

"Yes," she said. His hand tightened on hers, not in command but in plea. The radius trembled but did not flare. For the first time in hours, no one died.

The warehouse they pulled into was a hollowed-out skeleton of corrugated iron, its windows long since bricked over. Diane shut the engine and let the silence press down around them. The air smelled of oil and dust, a dry refuge cut off from the world. Ellery sat motionless, hands still on his knees. His breathing was shallow, but steady. The radius had shrunk—she could feel it, like a taut string wound tight inside him, but contained. No one outside the car had fallen. For the first time since she had begun triangulating his path, the killings had stopped.

"You see?" she said softly. "You can draw fences."

His jaw worked, eyes closed. "For now."

"For now, it's enough," she said. "You'll make it longer next time. Then longer still."

He turned his head, eyes opening to meet hers. They were wet, furious with grief. "They'll never forgive me. Not the world. Not the gods. Not even you."

Her expression didn't shift. "I'm not asking forgiveness. I'm asking whether you want to walk forward or lie down in the wreckage."

He shook his head once, helpless. "I don't know what I want."

She leaned closer, close enough that her voice was no longer instruction but invitation. "Then start simple. Do you want me here?"

The words hit him like a blow, not because he doubted her meaning but because he feared the answer. His throat tightened. He nodded. Her hand came up, slow and deliberate, to cup his jaw. The warmth of her palm grounded him more than any fence or rule. He trembled at the touch, not with the tremor of death but with something rawer, human. His lips parted as if to speak, but no words came.

"You asked me once," she whispered. "I didn't answer then. I answer now."

Her forehead touched his, the contact light, fragile, yet carrying the weight of everything unsaid.

Ellery's shoulders shook. A sob clawed up but never escaped; instead, he turned his mouth just enough that it brushed against hers. The kiss was not hungry. It was not practised. It was a trembling exchange, hesitant and fragile, as though both feared the power it might unleash. His hand lifted, unsure, then steadied against her waist.

The radius shuddered violently, but held. No one outside fell. The silence of the warehouse was total, as if the world itself had paused to witness. When she drew back, it was only by inches. Her voice was steadier than her pulse. "See? You didn't break me."

His eyes searched hers, desperate, astonished. "I thought I'd kill you the moment I touched you."

"You didn't," she said. "And you won't. Not if I don't let you."

A broken laugh escaped him, part relief, part disbelief. He pressed his forehead against hers again, closing his eyes. The trembling subsided. The power still coiled inside him like a storm waiting its turn, but for the first time, he believed it might be guided, not only feared.

Diane's hand slid down to lace with his fingers. She squeezed once, the same way she had when she gave him rules in the Gardens. "We'll teach your breath to behave," she repeated. "Together."

The word landed with more weight than any vow.

They sat there a long time, joined hands resting between them, the dust settling quietly in the stillness. Outside, sirens wailed distantly, Adelaide moving on without them, inventing explanations for what had just happened. But in the iron belly of the warehouse, there was no need for explanation. Only the faint memory of a kiss that had not destroyed the world. And the beginning of something that might yet save it.

Chapter 23
The Fallout

The images flickered across televisions and phones before lunch was finished: smoke boiling over Adelaide's northern suburbs, paramedics wheeling stretchers out of the Botanic Gardens, and grainy footage from the Barossa showing vines thrashing as if caught in a storm that never came.

"Good afternoon," the TV presenter began, his voice heavy. "We're coming to you live from the Botanic Gardens, where dozens of people have collapsed in what officials are calling a 'mass casualty incident.' Behind me, you can see the ornamental lake, now cordoned with police tape. Witnesses describe people dropping without warning—while children, strangely, remain untouched."

The camera turned to a woman in a hi-vis vest, her face streaked with tears and sweat. She gripped the microphone as though it were the only thing keeping her steady.

"It went quiet first," she said. "Like someone turned the sound off. Then they just fell, all around me. But the kids—they screamed, they cried—they didn't fall. I don't know how to explain it."

Behind her, paramedics in black gloves moved with grim precision, checking pulses, lifting limp bodies onto stretchers, guiding terrified children to a makeshift triage tent. The scene carried on without commentary, the shuffle of boots and the beeping of machines doing the speaking.

On another channel, a man named Daniel sounded out of breath as he relived his morning drive.

"I was heading north on Port Wakefield Road, just past Gepps Cross, when the heat hit us before we even saw it, like opening an oven door. The verge grass caught fire in a straight line, like petrol had been poured. Cars just pulled left, all of us at once. Nobody said anything—we just knew to get out of the way."

The host pressed him. "Was it moving?"

Daniel hesitated, then said, "Yeah. Like it was walking. A man, I think. But you couldn't look straight at him. Everything around him bent with the heat. Mirrors warped. I've never seen anything like it."

By early afternoon, attention turned north-east to the Barossa. The local newspaper online led with a headline that felt closer to myth than journalism: "Growers Report Vineyards Alive After Midnight Confrontation." Several vineyard owners told reporters they had been woken by trellis wires snapping and nets collapsing, though the night itself had been still.

One grower, anonymous, gave the most unsettling account: "The wires started singing—like a cello string, but louder. I swear I saw two women fighting on the block. One had a blade that caught the moonlight, the other moved like she owned the night. By the time I got my torch, the rows looked different. Like the vineyard had shifted in its sleep."

The paper published photos taken on phones: rows sagging in impossible curves, trellises warped into cage-like shapes, as though the Valley itself had been bent.

At three o'clock, every station cut to Parliament House. The Premier stood stiffly behind a forest of microphones, flanked by the Police Commissioner and the head of the Country Fire Service. His tie was crooked, his eyes ringed with exhaustion.

"South Australia has suffered an extraordinary day," the Premier said, his voice stripped of polish.

"We have lost lives in ways we cannot yet explain. Fires are moving without pattern. Our vineyards were disrupted overnight by forces we do not understand."

He paused, steadying himself.

"I will not speculate. I will not minimise this. What I can say is that our community responded with courage. That matters. And we will face whatever this is together."

On another channel, they cut back to a paramedic, mask still on, speaking on condition of anonymity. His voice carried through the distortion. "We were getting vitals that didn't make sense. One patient was in full cardiac arrest next to another whose pulse was steady but unresponsive. And the kids—perfectly fine. Animals too. A black swan kept paddling in the lake while people died all around it. I can't put that in any medical box I know."

At the Botanic gates, a journalist found a little girl with freckles, clutching the hand of a police officer. When asked if she was alright, she looked up shyly and said, "Mum went to sleep. But a man told me, 'Hands stay.' So I held on. And then the lady came. She smiled and said I was safe."

The camera lingered on her face too long, until the anchor in the studio cleared her throat and shuffled papers to cover the tremor in her hands. By then, Adelaide was no longer watching the news. It was *becoming* it.

By late afternoon, the story had already left Adelaide. Hashtags surged across social media: #FirestarterAdelaide, #BotanicDeaths, #BarossaVines. Clips replayed endlessly: the shimmering plume on Port Wakefield Road, stretchers rolling across the Gardens' lawns, vines shuddering and glowing under a cold moon. And over it all, the Premier's words echoed again and again, spliced into montages, quoted on headlines, repeated by anchors who could find nothing better to say: "I will not pretend this is ordinary."

By nightfall, the reaction had gone global.

Markets slid, then broke. Futures bled red across screens in New York, London, and Tokyo. Analysts abandoned euphemism and began using the word *fear*.

In Delhi and Beijing, food protests swelled as daylight lingered too long over ruined crops. Scientists confirmed what farmers already felt: Earth's rhythm was slipping—seconds at a time, enough to fracture ecosystems.

Offshore, leaked naval footage showed something vast moving beneath the Indian Ocean, the water itself bending around it.

Not a vessel. Not a weapon. Old enough that myth had remembered it long before radar ever could.

By the time the name *Leviathan* reached the chyrons, shipping routes were already shifting.

When the anchor spoke again, her voice was low, as if afraid to summon the thing by name. "Long dismissed as myth, the Leviathan is now confirmed by multiple navies as a moving presence in the busiest shipping lanes on Earth. Already, ten freighters have diverted south. Oil tankers are rerouting around Africa. Insurance firms are raising premiums by the hour."

The lounge room was lit only by the glow of the television, the blue light throwing long shadows across the walls and over the toys scattered on the carpet. A doll lay abandoned with its hair half-plaited, a Lego spaceship missing a wing stood stranded on the coffee table, and the faint smell of reheated spaghetti still hung in the air. On the screen, the Premier's voice droned its refrain, grave and halting: "I will not pretend this is ordinary." The mother's jaw tightened. She leaned forward and stabbed the remote, silencing him mid-sentence. The sudden hush felt worse than the news itself.

"Alright," she said, too briskly. "That's enough. Time for bed."

The boy frowned. "But—"

"No buts." Her tone snapped sharper than she intended.

She softened, though only a little. "Teeth, pyjamas, and bed. Now."

The children exchanged a look, half-confused, half-relieved to be released from the images replaying on the screen. They shuffled down the hall, the girl clutching her brother's hand. Their door clicked shut. For a moment, the parents sat in silence, the muted television reflecting in the father's glasses.

He set the remote down as though it were fragile glass. "They're frightened," he said quietly.

"They're children," she replied. "Of course, they're frightened. And they should be." She rose and began to pace the length of the lounge. "We can't keep them here, Tom. Not after today. Not after what we've just seen."

He rubbed his face with both hands, speaking through his palms. "Where would we even go? The highways north are burning. The Gardens are a graveyard. You saw the vines—"

"East," she cut in. "We go east. Sydney. Jess and Mark will take us in. It's away from this, out of the firing line. The city's collapsing, the Valley is only an hour away. If it spreads—if any of it spreads—we'll be next." Her voice carried a strange energy, as if rushing the words would make them more accurate.

Tom stood, steadying her shoulders. "It's a fifteen-hour drive with two kids in the back. The roads could be blocked. If that fire—if that thing—turns east—"

"Then better to be on the move than waiting for it to arrive." She stared at him, eyes fierce. "I'm not sitting here waiting to find out what happens. Not with them sleeping in the next room."

His hands slid down her arms, found her fingers. "We need to stay calm. They already believe they're safe because the news said children were spared. If we start panicking—"

"I'm not panicking," she snapped, then softened, her voice breaking. "I'm planning. We promised to protect them, Tom. That's the only job we have left."

They stood like that for a while, holding each other in the dim light until her breathing steadied. Finally, he nodded. "Alright. We'll leave at dawn. Pack light—clothes, food, water. I'll top the tank tonight."

She exhaled shakily, already moving to the drawer for a notepad. "I'll message Jess. No details, just that we're coming. She'll understand." She scribbled a list with furious energy: tins, bottled water, torches, first-aid kit, passports.

He leaned over her shoulder, muttering, "Never thought I'd be packing like it's the end of the world."

"It isn't," she said, not looking up. "Not if we keep moving."

Outside, a siren drifted faintly across the suburb. Somewhere a dog barked, sharp and insistent. They both froze until the sound faded into nothing. He lowered himself into the chair, staring at the blank television. "If everyone else has the same idea—Sydney, Melbourne, anywhere east—we'll hit gridlock. People don't stay rational when kids are hungry."

"Then we'll leave before they do," she answered without hesitation. "That's why it has to be tomorrow."

They checked on the children before sleep. The boy was already curled around his toy, thumb pressed against his lip. The girl lay awake, watching the doorway. When her mother sat beside her, she whispered, "Are we safe?"

The woman smoothed the child's hair, forcing a smile. "We're safe tonight. And tomorrow we're going to visit Jess in Sydney. Remember her garden, the one with the swings?"

The girl nodded slowly. "I liked her dog."

"Then you'll see him again soon," her mother promised. "Close your eyes now."

The girl whispered something into her pillow—too soft to catch, except for two words: hands stay. The phrase struck the mother oddly, like a pebble thrown into still water, but she didn't ask. She kissed the child's forehead and stood.

Back in the lounge, Tom checked the locks twice. At the window, he lingered, watching the still cul-de-sac. A cat darted across the street and vanished into a hedge. Otherwise, the world lay quiet, too quiet for comfort. "Feels like the calm before something worse," he murmured.

She slipped beside him, sliding her hand into his. "Then we'll be gone before it breaks." Together they stood, side by side, staring into the dark suburban night. The house around them felt less like a home than a shell. In the morning, it would no longer be their refuge. At first light, the road east would be their only hope.

The alarm dragged them from shallow sleep long before the sun rose. The house was hushed, the children still breathing slowly in their beds. The mother crept, stuffing clothes into a duffel and sliding tins of beans and peaches into a shopping bag. The passports and a torch went on top. The father filled bottles at the tap, set them clinking into a crate, then lifted the box into the boot of the car with a grunt that seemed louder than the dawn itself.

The children blinked sleepily as they were dressed, too tired to ask questions. The boy clutched his doll, the girl slung a backpack over her shoulders as though this were just another school excursion. By the time they were belted into the back seat, the eastern sky was bruising violet.

The father reversed down the driveway, headlights sweeping across neighbours' houses. He noticed curtains twitch, silhouettes at windows. The street was alive in a way it never was at that hour—cars idling, boots thudding shut, families with the same plan. Engines coughed, tail-lights glowed. The cul-de-sac that had always felt so small suddenly seemed like the mouth of a river, feeding into something vast.

They joined the highway near dawn, and at once it was clear they were not alone. Eastbound lanes were choked with cars, headlights stretching in an endless river toward the hills. Caravans lumbered, sedans groaned under the weight of roof racks, utes rattled with crates tied down in haste. The father tapped the wheel, jaw tight.

"We should have left earlier," he muttered.

Beside him, his wife hugged her arms to her chest. "We're moving. That's what matters."

But the traffic barely moved at all. They inched forward, bumper to bumper, radios glowing in every car. Through rolled-down windows came fragments of voices: a mother soothing a baby, a teenager asking for signal bars, a man swearing at the crawl. Somewhere behind, a horn blared in frustration, answered by another.

The girl leaned forward between the seats, her voice small. "Why is everyone going to Sydney?"

"Not everyone," her father said, though his eyes stayed fixed on the brake lights ahead. "Some are going to Melbourne. Some want to get away from the city."

"But why?"

The mother twisted in her seat to face her. "Because people are scared, love. And when people are scared, they move. Just like us." The boy had fallen asleep again, his head lolling against the window, the doll tucked under his arm. The girl nodded, sitting back, though her eyes stayed wide and unblinking.

The sun finally pushed over the horizon, but it was not the comfort it should have been. The light felt stretched, too long, the shadows slow to fall. Cars shimmered in the heat, though the day had barely begun. They crawled eastward with the rest of the city, carried not by speed but by the weight of a collective decision: to flee before whatever was coming reached their street, their garden, their children's beds.

Chapter 24
The Merchant

I have worn too many names to pretend any of them are true. Mercurius, when Latin tasted fresh, Hermes, when marble still remembered the chisel, and in tongues older than any fireside story, I answered to sounds that were less word than weather.

Messenger, trickster, herald, thief, patron of roads and commerce, lord of tongues, father of lies, keeper of doors.

To some, I was salvation, marked by a coin dropped at a shrine or a ribbon tied to a milestone. To others, I was the murmur in a dark hall, the bargain too tempting, too clever, and just costly enough to be remembered. I was always in motion. Never still. Never silent. Stillness is death; silence is truth. Both are enemies I have outrun longer than any god deserves.

The others prefer blunt instruments. Zed wears thunder like a medal; his storms swing as if by a drunk wielding chairs. Posi draped the oceans around his shoulders as if they were a cloak. Ari never met a problem he didn't try to solve with his fists. They make noise; they break things.

I make arrangements. Mine is the whisper between breaths, the half-beat that makes a letter arrive too early or too late, turning truces into wars or wars into weddings. My dominion was never the spear—it was the space between spears. That doesn't make me noble. It makes me necessary. And necessary things survive, even when nobler things do not.

Mortals once understood that. At the places where roads crossed, they built squat pillars with rough faces meant to resemble mine, crude but sufficient. Soldiers left crusts of bread, merchants tossed coins, and women tied ribbons and prayers into knots. Bribes, yes, but also acknowledgements. They confessed the truth every traveller knows: if the messenger favours you, your message arrives; if he doesn't, the road itself forgets you. I liked such honesty. It greased the hinges between worlds.

I carried darker burdens than ribbons and coins.

Before men gave death its rotating cast of names—Hades, Yama, Anubis—I walked the boundary between the living and the dead and guided them across. I did not judge, weigh hearts, or pass verdicts. I opened doors. I was the psychopomp. Later poets prettied that title, but what it meant was simple: I knew the back entrance, and I kept the key beneath my tongue. Priests prayed to others, but when mothers begged that their sons find the far shore without wandering the reeds, it was me they meant, even if they didn't know it. I carried so many into silence that I learned a bitter truth: nothing dies harder than a god's pride.

History is never neat. It is a ledger written over by thieves. The Romans stole their gods from the Greeks, the Greeks from the Phoenicians, the Phoenicians from the Sumerians, and so on until the first liar looked at a storm and decided it had a name. Through every theft, I remained. Reinvented. A staff became a rod, then sandals, then a tilt of the head, and a smirk that suggested I had news first. Banker and postmaster, smuggler and conman, saint with a thief's hands hidden in his robes—I sold the same wares under new signs. I carried silk and secrets along caravan trails, forged treaties between kings, and once, yes, tied a plague-rag to a gate latch that had it coming. Necessary, always. Clean, seldom. Effective, without fail.

Do not confuse necessity with safety. I have walked empires when their plaster was still drying, only to return centuries later to see weeds cracking their marble bones. I survived because I refused to believe in walls. A wall is only a story told in stone; find the right editor, and it becomes rubble. Calendars fade, currencies die, pantheons starve when prayers run dry. I outlasted them all because movement is the only coin that spends everywhere.

But this time is different. Zed made it so.

He didn't roar when he threatened me.

He said it calmly: No amount of coin will save you.

He pronounced it as if the verdict had already been carved. I've heard threats from kings, conquerors, inquisitors, men so convinced the sun rose for them they thought eternity was an inheritance. I outlasted them by minting trust into coins they didn't know they carried. But Zed is not a man, and Olympus no longer keeps ledgers. They sharpen blades.

Balance—once our creed—has become a sick joke whispered at funerals.

When the board tilts, I enumerate. I draw branches of possibility the way gamblers sketch odds in wine stains.

Remain with the gods. It sounds safe, like a family dinner, right up until someone brings up the heirloom grudge they've kept polished for centuries. Thunder has already chosen its lightning rod, and it looks at me. Jamil watches me with the patience of an accountant who has noticed an error in his favour. Fiona spins her coin as if my skull were its bowl. Effie smiles the way one does when imagining how sweetly someone else will break. None of them argued for me in Monte Carlo. Among them, my odds hover just above insult, just below nothing.

Run alone. Foxes in open fields may be clever, but they die interesting deaths, not long ones. Neutrality is the first corpse nailed to the city gates. Alone, I might delay what Zed pronounced, but I would not prevent it.

Turn to mortals. I like mortals—quick, impulsive, inventive. They make me laugh, and laughter buys time. But their kingdoms collapse faster than their candles gutter. They cannot shield a god from a god's quarrel. Their walls are paper, their kings temporary. Shelter from rain, not fire.

The Fledglings, then. A category error given bones. Not mortal, not divine—fractures turned flesh. They bend rules simply by existing, survive by breaking the patterns that would contain them. Dangerous, volatile, full of momentum. Momentum is my favourite weapon. It doesn't look like one until the blade is at your throat.

Among them, one name has the weight I need: Jake Rogers.

Jake is not the strongest, not the deadliest. But rare. Without ever meeting me, he discovered my oldest trick. He has made a rumour into a sail. His ship's name, Fading Dawn, travels faster than his keel—sung by men who've never seen the sea, chalked by children who cannot read. When a myth moves faster than your feet, you've built something stronger than armies. I recognise myself in that shape: younger, hungrier, reckless. He performs my art without knowing it. That makes him dangerous—and valuable.

I remember that council chamber, torches flattering marble and bronze until they looked alive. Athena clinging to logic, Effie to chaos, Fiona to her coin, Jamil to silence, Zed glaring with his thunderhead certainty. They argued balance, doom, and Ragnarök. Not one of them argued for me. When even your enemies forget to count you, you either disappear or teach them how costly their math is. I chose the latter.

So I leaned on the rail of a borrowed ship, its crew pretending still to serve their captain, quickly realising they served probability instead. I calculated aloud so the sea could hear.

Scenario A: Zed roars war. Messengers die first.

Scenario B: balance returns. Fantasy.

Scenario C: the newcomers rise—distributed sovereignty, no throne, only corridors and doors. I prefer corridors. They have shadows.

The highest survivability lives there. The highest optionality gathers around Jake. Betrayal? Of course. Betrayal is just the moment a better option arrives. My trick is to remain the better option most of the time, and too useful to kill the rest. I will bring him routes the gods would kill to keep hidden. Languages the world has forgotten. Passwords to doors buried in sand. The schedule of a yacht that believes itself invisible. And most importantly, the art of turning a chase into a rumour, a rumour into an error, an error into a triumph. He gives me cover. A moving stage. A myth that draws fire away from me. Horizon. I had forgotten how honest Horizon tastes.

Night folds down. Rumour arrives on it like tidewater. Fading Dawn spotted two ports west, which means she is elsewhere entirely, and exactly where I need her to be. I will meet him as I meet all opportunities: one hand extended, the other spinning a coin he doesn't know I minted. The gods must not see me cross openly, so I perform. I curse his name in the right rooms, and let spies run to the wrong conclusions. Then I chart a course "toward the rumour." If he refuses me, I'll take his crew by increments. A ship is not stolen with knives. It is persuaded into love. Three of his men already crave things only I can provide. Prices are written in laughter. "Course?" my helmsman asked, feigning authority. "Toward the rumour," I answered, and felt the horizon tilt in my favour.

I have survived Rome by leaving before affection turned into furniture. I walked the forums with words under my tongue, selling senators the futures they wanted to buy. If you want to know how empires die, listen for the echo when men invoke truth without doffing their hats. Constantinople sang louder, richer. Spice in the air, silk smiling to the touch, tongues so varied that my own accent vanished into the crowd. I nearly stayed. That was my mistake. Nothing stays. When fire came, I left before ash knew my name. Napoleons rose and fell, colonies swelled and shrank. Faiths bloomed, starved, bloomed again under new taxes. Pantheons dwindled into metaphors, then into illustrations in schoolbooks. I survived because I never asked to be believed. Belief is expensive. Movement is free, provided you know the side doors.

But this age tastes different. Zed's mutter of Ragnarök was not theatre. Even he wastes no thunder on a lie. The Fenris star tugs the tides, bends the marrow of the world. Sextants betray, compasses laugh at themselves, stars whisper in altered patterns. Rules blur, and I survive by bending rules. If the lines vanish, even I lose footing. That is why I must choose now.

I catalogued the gods the way bookies price fighters. Zed: heavy, obvious, unable to wait. Jamil: cold, exact, frost with a pen. Diane: torn between huntress and human, her hesitation a crack to slip through. Effie: Chaos hungry for beauty, me a toy to break. Fiona: her coin is her conscience, unpredictable. Athena: too rational, doomed by irrational opponents. None sees me as necessary. When a messenger isn't required, he is already dead.

The Fledglings are unfinished, and unfinished things can be shaped. Ellery Kalos trails corpses but wears his danger openly. Delilah Kitsune is a fox and blade, too volatile to trust, perfect to aim. Jian Wu is fire devouring his own name, terrifying but steerable if whispered correctly. The boy—Ben—frightens the council more than any, for he walks through doors even we cannot open. I will not touch him yet. But Jake—Jake understands that stories are not garnish. They are the meat. He and I will dine together.

He will not trust me, but trust is the wrong coin. Interdependence is the currency. I will give him safe corridors, papers, and names, rumours sharpened into legend. In return, his myth becomes my cloak. Zed cannot strike him without striking the tide that follows.

Caution is necessary. I cannot walk openly aboard. So I oppose him in public, chase him without closing, curse him in taverns. Then, under shadows, I will parley.

If he refuses, I will take his crew instead. Everyone has a price. Jake knows this better than most. But I doubt he will refuse. He already hungers for inevitability. I am inevitability's cook. So I begin to tell a myth. Ships have a draft and a wake. Myths breathe attention and exhale coincidence. Too close, you feed them; too far, you lose them.

I live in their penumbra. I erase my scent with relics—river silt, false saint's candle, salt from a sea unborn. I disguise my ship as incompetence: patched sails, drunken lettering, clumsy signals. Competence is noticed; shambles are ignored. I bribe the horizon with stories: Mercury loves the pirate, hates him, is four ports away. Conflicting maps distract hunters. The tale Jake will overhear: the messenger is, proud and will not parley, until he proves he can keep up. Pride is prudence in makeup. Distance is my metronome: two nights and a morning. If the

Dawn vanished at twilight, I could touch her rudder by dawn the day after. Enough to change a story, not enough to build a monument.

I watch his ship breathe. The Dawn shortens sail at lunatic hours, kills lights where crowds are thick, hoists lanterns in emptiness. She throws decoys only after patrols have memorised her gait. Jake promises, then betrays promises at a sprint. His crew moves like dream-actors who remember rhythm, not lines. I catalogue things under my tongue. Blond-haired woman taps twice, thrice when afraid. Cook signals morale with rags and lamps. The younger deckhand hums in E minor unless angry. The girl whistles dawn, and when grief teaches him new notes, the whole ship will feel it. I tidy his weather. Harbour pilots receive early bulletins. Lighthouse lenses were cleaned late. Customs cutters sidetracked by rats, I whisper instructions to. Signals flash patterns only older men remember—hospitality, not heroics. The council cannot accuse me of arranging luck against them when luck itself has gone feral.

Fog rolled thick, a chance to board unseen.

My fingers twitched. I let it pass. I wanted to be his rumour before I was his guest.

Twice I felt Jamil's ledger brush me; twice I misdirected with noise elsewhere—a smuggler's ambitious shot, a woman choosing kindness at a well. The third night, a god's eye swept past. I covered the lantern, and the world held its breath. The eye slid on. In the morning, gulls mocked us back into the ordinary. The Dawn slipped into caves. A girl marked stars on posts; I marked beneath, promising favours still owed in Genoa. Soon papers would appear in crates of copper. Threads through fabric, strengthening hems. The crew began to dream me: cards falling in pairs, curses bent toward gratitude, whistles adding notes.

Storm brewed at sundown. The Dawn adjusted the canvas with feline calm. We mirrored clumsily. Contempt is the best camouflage. I thought of the council, of their torches, their ledgers, their hymns to balance no one believes. I measured the distance between their world and mine, and found the number irrelevant. Distance is counted in choices. I had made enough to be another shape entirely. Rain fell—communion of salt, water, and iron. The helmsman prayed to a god who no longer listens. I listened. I keep everything. You never know which curse will open a locked door. Fear touches me as it touches everyone. Fear is the tax on movement. I pay it, dodge it, never ignore it.

Two nights and a morning—that is the charm I keep beneath my tongue. At that distance, men believe the weather loves them. At that distance, gods can love them too, without being caught at it. I have learned to love mortals that way.

I am not only fleeing Zed. I am bored. Tricksters grow sick of boredom. Jake is not my curse because he will win. He is my cure because he will travel. That is the difference, and it is one gods that never learn.

Jake's flaws? Vanity of competence, softness for strays. Both are levers. Both will make him useful, if not to himself then to me. The newcomers' flaws I catalogue, the gods' hungers I weigh. Hunger is always a lever. No one is ever full. The sea bruises purple, then black. We ghost after the ghost. When rain coins across the deck, I tip my face and swallow one. Salt, water, and iron—all contracts sealed in those three. I am not cruel. Cruelty is bad accounting. Cunning spends less, earns more. That is why I feed Jake weather, not knives. When we finally speak—and we will—he will come to the table carrying a rumour that feels like luck. Men remember luck with loyalty.

By dawn, the storm remembered itself. Gulls returned, the girl's whistle gained height, and the deckhand hummed.

Two nights and a morning, held.

Fading Dawn existed where I needed her: two decisions away. I will not rush parley. Let him taste inevitability until he wants more. Let him believe himself blessed or smart. When a man hungers for that answer, he bargains. I am cheaper than the sky, and more honest. So I keep to his penumbra, smoothing his path. Radio signals hiccup usefully, inspectors limp with gout, and clerks stamp wrong dates. Luck bends too small for songs, large enough for habits. And habits mint loyalty. I enjoy it. Tricksters are not ascetics. I delight in cleverness, mine and others'. It is a rare pleasure to serve a moving target. Even gods fall for momentum.

If you ask if I will betray him, I answer: I will survive him if I must, with him if I can. Betrayal is only renegotiation in new weather. If his myth consumes me, I will feed it a taste that makes me a lesson, then wait to return as dessert. If gods press, I will sell them a war I can win, and sell Jake a horizon he can own. That is not immorality. It is occupational hygiene. Evening brings radio stutters, our disguise mistaken for another. That is how you know stories are alive: strangers misname you with affection. The helmsman corrects gently. The fisherman offers a weather tip—a debt repaid by kindness sown months ago. I do not believe in karma. I think in accounts receivable.

Two nights and a morning.

I hold the line, the line keeps me. Behind me, gods practice speeches. Ahead of me, Jake carves his initials into water. Between them, I am precise. I measure, I edit, I arrange, I permit. When he finally turns and finds me in the dark, he will not be surprised. He will be relieved. That is the strongest bargaining position: when the other makes a mistake, there is a necessity for grace. "Hold our line," I tell the helmsman. He nods as if

I've reassured him, when all I've done is repeat a prayer written for myself.

Two nights and a morning. At that range, weather loves men. At that range, gods can love them too, unseen. I have learned to love like that.

Two nights and a morning, I told myself. Hold the line, live in the penumbra, smooth the weather, remain rumour.

It was working—until it wasn't.

Through the veils of rain and gull-cry, I saw it: a single lantern, swung three times, then once more. Not random. Not careless. A signal. My signal. A code I hadn't whispered aloud in centuries, one that only smugglers in dead ports and thieves long buried had ever used.

Jake Rogers could not know it. And yet his ship spoke to me in my own tongue.

The crew bustled about unaware, sails drawing tight, ropes singing in the storm, but the light burned deliberately. An answer I had not asked for. A message only I could read. My coin is still between my fingers. For the first time in longer than I admit, the horizon tasted not like inevitability—but invitation. If he knows my language, then he already knows me. And if he knows me, then he's been expecting me.

Chapter 25

The Crypt

The crypt shuddered as though it had been holding its breath for centuries and had suddenly remembered how to exhale. Dust sifted from the carved ceiling in thin streams—time turned upside down.

The mummy's chest rose again—not a whisper now, but a dragging, deliberate breath that carried weight.

Ben felt pressure on his sternum. His own lungs forgot their rhythm. For one held moment, he thought the figure might stay still, that this was just a cruel echo of life, a shiver of memory.

Then its head turned. Wrong—bones grinding in sockets too dry to move, sinew stretching like rope soaked and hardened, now cracking open. The golden-black eyes widened with a snap, their glare more light than colour.

Ben froze. Instinct inside him screamed, *RUN*, but his body obeyed nothing.

The mummy sat up. Bandages fell away, brittle with rot, breaking into grit. Then the smell—not decay, but the scorched-earth tang of something preserved too long. It smelled of desert tombs and open graves under the noon sun.

Leila stepped forward, her hand raised. "Wait—"

The creature did not wait. Its arm lashed out with a speed that broke reason.

Fingers like hooked talons clamped around Ben's throat and lifted him clean off the floor. Ben gagged, legs kicking against nothing. The grip was inhuman, both fragile and impossibly strong. Each finger felt like a stone chisel digging into his neck. He struck at the arm, but his blows rang like knocks on a coffin.

The mummy's head tilted, studying him with a gaze older than language.

"—No!" Leila cried.

She hurled a word, sharp and guttural, one of the syllables she had guarded for this moment. The chamber's cisterns rippled, their surfaces trembling.

The mummy turned its face toward her but did not let go. Instead, it slammed Ben against the stone wall. The impact knocked the breath from his lungs, and still the hand held fast.

The floor began to quake. At first, Ben thought it was his own failing vision, but then the sound rose—stone grinding against stone, echoing like thunder through hollow tunnels.

Cracks split across the dais, reaching toward the surrounding crypts. The cisterns boiled without heat. Bones surfaced. One after another, skeletal hands clawed up from the black water, clutching the edges of the cisterns, dragging torsos out. Ancient skulls dripped with green moss, jaws yawning open. From alcoves in the walls, rubble shifted, coffins split. Skeletons poured forth—soldiers, enslaved people, priests—an army bound to the will of their master.

The mummy finally let Ben go. Ben crumpled onto the stones, gasping—each breath a blade in his chest. He tried to rise, but his limbs shook.

The undead closed in, their movements jerky, bones clattering like windchimes caught in a draft. Swords of corroded bronze slid free from skeletal hands. Shields still bore faint traces of paint, long since dimmed. They formed ranks without command, their hollow eyes fixed on the living intruders.

Leila's lips moved, whispering faster now. She pressed both palms outward, and the carvings along the chamber walls lit with brief fire.

"Stay back," she commanded, her voice ringing with borrowed power.

For a heartbeat, the skeletons faltered. The mummy did not. It stepped from the dais, its bare feet cracking the stone. Its body was impossibly tall now that it stood fully upright, shoulders broad and sharp, each motion deliberate. Gold symbols flared faintly across the remaining strips of its wrappings, ward-marks not of protection but of command.

It pointed at Ben.

The skeletons surged forward again.

Ben scrambled upright, his hands raw against the slick floor. The spirit within him screamed in all directions—wind, storm, night—but he couldn't seize one. They slipped through him like oil. His head pounded with voices, with fragments of memory not his own. Thousands of lives, thousands of deaths, all crowding at once.

A rusted blade swung at him.

Ben ducked by instinct more than thought. The edge missed his skull by a hair. He kicked at the skeleton's legs, shattering them, but another closed in instantly. He grabbed its wrist, twisted, tore the sword free, and staggered back with the weapon.

"Ben!" Leila's cry echoed. "Hold them!"

She raised her arms higher. The carvings flared again, brighter now, runes leaping like sparks across stone. The cisterns hissed, their black water retreating for a moment before surging back stronger. But the mummy reached her before she could finish. Its strike was silent. One instant, it stood across the chamber; the next, its hand gripped her shoulder, nails sinking through flesh. Leila bit down on her scream, blood welling bright against the mummy's pale hand. She spat another word through clenched teeth. The force of it blew the closest skeletons to dust, but the mummy didn't even sway.

Ben roared. His soul answered—not with clarity, but with rage. A subsonic scream rushed up his throat. He slashed with the stolen blade, and when metal met bone, the skeleton shattered in a shower of dust instead of fragments. The mummy's head turned sharply at that sound. Its golden-black gaze locked on him again. Ben felt the weight of it like chains dragging him under. His chest seized. The sword slipped from his fingers.

The skeletons circled tighter. Leila struggled, trapped beneath the mummy's hand. The chamber shook harder, the ceiling shedding dust and stone fragments. The dead kept coming, rising from every shadow, filling the chamber until the air itself stank of tombs.

And then, amid the chaos, the Sleeper spoke. Its voice was a rasp dragged across centuries, a sound of sand over stone. The words were in no tongue Ben had ever heard, but his bones understood them, his blood shivered at them.

"Awaken."

Every skeleton in the chamber straightened as one. The noise of their rattling ceased. Silence fell—thick, suffocating. Ben's mind reeled. His instincts screamed to run, but there was nowhere to go. Behind him, the stairway had collapsed, and stones tumbled down as if cut by invisible hands. They were sealed in.

The Sleeper released Leila.

She fell to her knees, clutching her bleeding shoulder, her face pale with pain.

It stepped forward again, looming above Ben, each movement inevitable. The skeletal army parted around it like reeds around a crocodile. Ben forced himself to meet its eyes. His throat burned where its fingers had bruised him.

His chest hitched, each breath a desperate grab at air. "I am not yours," he managed, voice hoarse.

The mummy bent lower, its face inches from his, breath dry and papery. Its eyes glowed brighter, unblinking. And in that terrible stillness, Ben realised something worse than death: It wasn't looking at him. It was looking through him—searching for the element within him, measuring, weighing, deciding.

And it found it.

Leila's shout cracked the chamber. Runes flared—blue-white, surgical—searing the dark into edges. The nearest skeletons stuttered mid-lunge, joints locking as if the air itself had turned to resin. For the first time, Ben could breathe without tasting grave-dust.

The mummy paused. Not fear. Assessment. Its gaze slid from Leila's bleeding shoulder to Ben's throat, then deeper—past skin, past bone—into whatever lived behind his ribs.

"Enough," Leila said again, quieter now, the word no longer a plea but a collar. She spoke in the old tongue, each syllable a nail driven into marrow. The army held.

The mummy lifted one hand. Half the dead twitched—then stopped. It could override her. It chose not to.

When it finally spoke, the voice was sand dragged over stone. "Why... you?"

Ben swallowed. "I don't know."

The eyes narrowed. Their gold-black light flared, then dimmed. It released a long, shuddering breath, and the army's bones rattled in sympathy. For a heartbeat, the chamber felt like a tomb again, silent but for dripping water.

Leila swayed on her feet, clutching her wound, but her eyes never left the creature. "He's not your enemy," she whispered, half plea, half command.

The mummy's gaze lingered on Ben for a long moment more, then finally raised its hand. Every skeleton in the chamber dropped its weapon at once. The clatter echoed like thunder, rolling through the cisterns, fading into silence. The mummy straightened, impossibly tall, and the army of the dead stood waiting, but motionless.

At last, the creature spoke again, its words dragging centuries behind them: "Stay." And the skeletons obeyed.

The silence that followed the command was worse than the chaos. Dozens of skeletons stood rigid, their swords abandoned, their jaws slack as though mid-scream. The cisterns stilled, black water smoothing into mirrors once more. Dust hung unmoving in the air.

Leila's breathing rasped, every inhale a battle against pain, but she stepped forward anyway. Her injured shoulder trembled, blood dripping between her fingers, yet her voice carried with new steadiness.

"You remember," she said softly. Not a question, but a test.

The mummy's gaze lowered to her, then returned to Ben as though weighing them both on invisible scales. Its face was unreadable, a mask of cracked flesh and shadowed hollows. Yet something in the stillness answered her.

"You recognise him," she pressed, the words pulling strength from her wound, her will. "Not as an intruder. Not as prey. As kin."

The eyes flared—black swallowing gold, then reversing—like two eclipses fighting inside the same orbs.

Leila took another step closer. "He carries what you once carried. Do you feel it? The weight inside him? The voices? The endless pull?"

The mummy shifted, its chest rising and falling in deliberate measure, every breath a grind of stone. The chamber seemed to pulse with it. Ben's throat tightened. He didn't dare speak.

Leila ignored his fear. Her voice hardened into command, though each syllable shook her frame. "Then listen," Leila said, blood bright on her fingers. "You were chained beneath this city while they feasted above. And now you feel it in him—the same wrongness. The same pull between breaths."

She lifted her shaking hand. "Help us, or be buried a second time."

The skeletons shivered in place, as though her words reached even their hollow cores.

The mummy bent lower. Its face came level with hers, close enough for her to smell the desert in its breath, dry as dunes. "War..." The word was dragged out, as if pulled from the bottom of a well.

"Yes," Leila whispered. "The war you began, and the war we must finish. The gods have not changed. They still chain what they fear. They still kill what they cannot chain. But now—"

She gestured toward Ben, weakly but with conviction. "Now there are more of us. Rising. You are not alone anymore."

For the first time, something like thought moved behind the mummy's eyes. Its head cocked, not predator to prey, but one survivor to another.

Ben swallowed, the pressure in his chest easing slightly.

Leila pressed her advantage. Her voice gained rhythm, power layering into each phrase. "He woke you. Not the gods. Not their priests. Him. A mortal shaped by forces older than temples. That bond cannot be broken—not by blade, not by fire. You know it. I see it in you."

The mummy's body trembled faintly, not with weakness but with memory. Its gaze drifted to the faintly glowing runes on the chamber walls, then back to Ben, finally, after too long, settling on Leila again.

"You... speak... true," it rasped.

The words cracked her like thunder.

Relief and terror mingled in her chest. She staggered but did not fall.

"You have been forgotten," she continued, voice gentler now. "But your memory is not ashes. We stand before you as proof. He carries the element. I carry the words. Together, we stir what was meant to rise. Help us, and your war will not be buried again."

The mummy drew back slightly, towering once more, but its arm no longer reached for their throats. Its fingers flexed, curling as though remembering weapons long gone.

The skeleton army rattled in unison, like an exhalation.

Ben finally found his voice. "Why me?" he asked, his words cracking in the stillness.

The mummy turned those burning eyes on him again, recognition setting. When it spoke, its voice was quiet—and worse for it. "Because... I was you."

The words struck like hammers. Leila's breath caught. Her gaze flicked to Ben, then back to the Sleeper.

"What does that mean?" Ben demanded, though his voice shook. "What are you saying?"

The mummy did not answer at once. Its eyes dimmed, and in the silence Ben felt a flood of images not his own—cities drowned in sand, temples torn by storms, bones scattered beneath black suns. Armies shouting his name, then betraying it. Chains tightening around wrists that had once commanded empires. And always, the gods above, laughing, watching, binding.

Ben staggered under the weight of the visions. He dropped to his knees, clutching his head.

Leila knelt beside him, one hand steadying his back, though she swayed herself.

"Listen," she urged. "Don't run from it. He's not attacking. He's showing you."

The mummy's voice scraped again, syllables broken like pottery shards. "I was...terrifying. I failed. Now you."

Ben forced air into his lungs. His heart hammered. "I'm not you."

The mummy leaned closer, and for the first time, its expression shifted—its lips cracking into something like a smile, but jagged, joyless. "Not yet."

The skeletons' jaws clacked in eerie unison, like applause.

Leila rose again, her bloodied hand pressed against the wound, her eyes burning with conviction. "Then let him succeed where you were broken. Please stand with us, Sleeper, not against us. The gods believe they still hold the leash. Prove them wrong."

The mummy straightened, shoulders cracking like thunder. It did not nod, did not bow, but it did not strike. Its hand lifted once more, and the skeletons shifted restlessly—then went still.

The chamber held its breath. At last, the Sleeper spoke, each word jagged with centuries: "We shall see."

The chamber quivered with the Sleeper's final words.

It was neither a promise nor a threat. It was something heavier, as though the future itself were being weighed and found uncertain. Ben's pulse thundered in his ears. He forced himself to stand despite the ache in his ribs.

"No," he rasped, voice breaking. "Not we shall see. I need answers. You looked at me like you knew me. You said you were me. What then am I?"

The mummy's golden-black eyes fixed on him again. The silence stretched long enough that the dripping water from the ceiling sounded like drumbeats.

Leila stepped back, giving the two of them space, her hand pressed to her wound, her breath ragged but steady. She knew this moment wasn't hers to speak.

The Sleeper tilted its head. Its bandaged jaw worked, brittle wrappings snapping as it forced out words long buried. "You... are fractured."

The sound alone sent a shiver through Ben's bones. "Fracture?" he whispered.

The Sleeper's hand rose slowly, pointing not at Ben's chest but through it, as though gesturing to the immaterial weight inside him. "Life... broken. Death broken. You stand between."

Leila's eyes widened. "A god in the making."

The mummy's head shifted at her word, not in denial. Its gaze returned to Ben. "No. More. Much more. Where I was chosen, the gods carved chains. They feared what walks between."

Images slammed into Ben again—chains etched with runes binding wrists raw with blood, oceans boiling as something vast beneath them stirred, the faces of gods watching from marble halls, eyes shining with disdain. Ben doubled over, clutching his stomach.

"Stop!" he gasped. "Just tell me—"

But the visions only grew sharper. He saw himself—or the Sleeper—leading armies that bent reality with their presence. Each victory was met not with praise but with fear. Mortals bowed, then betrayed. Priests sang, then cursed. And always, when the tide turned, the gods came—not to bless, but to bind.

The mummy's voice grated through the flood of memory. "I... was a bridge. Between the breaths. Between worlds. I failed. I was buried."

Its eyes locked on Ben with dreadful intensity. "Now... you."

Ben staggered upright, trembling. "I'm not your replacement. I didn't ask for this. I don't want this."

The Sleeper did not blink. "Choice... not given."

Leila spoke at last, her voice hushed but cutting. "He needs more than riddles. He needs truth."

The mummy turned its gaze on her, ancient contempt and recognition mingling. For a heartbeat, Ben feared it would strike her down, but instead it rasped: "Truth... devours."

Ben's fists clenched. Anger bled through his fear. "Then let it! I've been hunted, burned, and killed a dozen times. Every time: void—then I wake up. Do you know what that's like? To wonder if you're even human anymore? If you're some puppet in someone else's war?" His voice cracked. "I need to know. What I am?"

The chamber seemed to listen. Even the skeletons leaned forward in their stillness. The Sleeper's voice dropped lower, like sand spilling endlessly from an hourglass.

"You are... the undone. The wound is in balance. Gods fear you because they cannot weigh you. Mortals fear you because you will not die. You are proof."

Ben's breath hitched. "Proof of what?"

The mummy stepped closer. Its shadow engulfed him. "That gods... can end. That death bends. That chains break."

The words landed like blows.

Leila's lips parted, her face pale with awe and terror. "You're saying he's... the key."

The Sleeper's gaze never left Ben. "Not key. Door."

The army of skeletons rattled faintly, as though the word alone shook them.

Ben's legs nearly gave out. "A door... to what?"

The mummy leaned closer, its voice no more than a rasp of dust. "To what comes... after gods."

Silence followed, vast and suffocating.

Ben could hear his own heartbeat hammering. He wanted to deny it, to spit the words back, but deep in his chest the elementals stirred, restless. The wind hissed, the storm throbbed, the fire hummed—all three pulling in different directions, as though confirming the Sleeper's claim.

He whispered, more to himself than anyone, "I'm not ready for that."

The mummy straightened, towering once again. "Nor was I."

Leila stepped between them then, her hand braced against Ben's chest, grounding him. Her eyes, fever-bright with pain and conviction, locked onto the Sleeper's. "Then teach him," she demanded. "If you failed, then guide him so he does not. Help him carry what you could not."

The mummy regarded her for a long time, the gold and black in its eyes flickering. At last it spoke, a voice dragged from the depths of centuries: "We... shall see."

The chamber groaned as though the stone itself exhaled. The skeletons lowered their heads in unison, not moving, not attacking, only waiting. Ben shivered. He had asked for truth, and he had received something far heavier.

Not a prophecy. Not a blessing.

A sentence.

The Sleeper turned without warning and began to climb the spiral stair, its long strides cracking dust and centuries loose from the stone. The army moved with it, clattering into motion, their brittle weapons ringing faintly against the walls.

Leila gripped Ben's arm, steadying herself, her face bloodless but resolute. "Come," she rasped. "This tomb is no longer ours to linger in."

They ascended. With every step, the ceiling brightened, the narrow slit of dawn widening into the open square. And when the fountain's lip broke above them, light poured down like judgement.

The mummy stepped into it first.

For an instant, Ben thought it might burn, but the sun only gilded its wrappings and turned its parchment flesh to bronze. Behind it, the skeletons poured into the waking square, weapons raised, jaws slack, their bones catching the morning as if the city had sprouted a forest of ivory. Where the Sleeper's shadow fell, the city answered. Stone lids shifted. Cobblestones lifted. From beneath courtyards and alleys, bones rose into daylight like a second population remembering its name. Fleshless, dust-stained, still bound in tatters of robes, they dragged themselves upright, stumbling into the light to swell the ranks.

Fez stirred.

A child screamed from a balcony. Somewhere, a muezzin's call faltered mid-prayer. Shutters banged open, then shut again with frantic hands. The sound of sandals slapping cobblestones broke out as people fled, shouts rippling outward in waves of panic.

Ben stared in horror. "God..."

Leila's grip on him tightened. "Don't waste breath asking where He is."

The Sleeper turned once, surveying the chaos. Its army stood in silence, awaiting command, and the city of Fez held its own breath in terror.

Leila pulled Ben close, her lips at his ear. Her voice was calm, iron-willed, though her body trembled with blood loss.

"Listen to me. You have to go. Now."

Ben jerked back. "What? No. We can't just—"

She cut him off with a glare that brooked no argument. "This army has half a chance if I stay. If I speak, if I command, I can hold them steady when the gods descend. And they will descend. Do you feel it? They're already stirring."

Ben felt it. A pressure at the edges of his mind, the hairs rising on his arms. The world itself braced for intrusion.

Leila pressed on. "The gods will not let this awakening pass unanswered. They'll throw everything at Fez to bury it again. If you're here, you'll be caught in it. You'll die—or worse, you'll be bound before you ever wake the others. That's what they want."

"I'm not leaving you," Ben growled, his throat raw.

Her expression softened, but her eyes held no mercy. "You must. You said you feel the others. Then go. Cross the ocean. Machu Picchu waits, and with it the next Sleeper. Without them, none of this matters. Not me. Not even this army."

The skeletons rattled, stamping their feet in eerie rhythm as if underscoring her words. The Sleeper raised its hand, and the sound ceased. Its eyes glowed black and gold as it regarded Ben.

"She... speaks truth," it rasped.

Ben's heart clenched. "Leila..."

Her bloody hand pressed to his chest. "Ben. Every hour you waste, the gods draw closer. If you love me, if you love this fight, go. I'll hold the dead. I'll buy the time. You buy us a future."

The words landed heavier than any blow. All around them, the city screamed and scattered. Smoke rose from a cart overturned in panic. Bells began to ring, not in prayer but in alarm. The army of the dead stood silent in their thousands, waiting for their master's will.

Ben's eyes burned. He wanted to drag her with him, tried to throw her over his shoulder, and defy every doom, but the pull in his chest gnawed harder than grief. The Andes called. He nodded, once, brokenly.

Leila smiled faintly, though her face was pale with pain. "Good. Then run while the way is still open. And don't look back."

The Sleeper's voice thundered, louder than before, rolling across the square like stone grinding mountains. "Go, Door. We will endure."

Ben took one last look at Leila, bloodied and unbowed, standing among the dead as if she belonged there. Then he turned, heart hammering, and ran. Behind him, the army roared—not with sound, but with the clatter of a thousand bones rising as one.

Chapter 26
The Reaction

The first reports came in fragments. A shepherd outside Fez radioed the local gendarme that "the dead are walking" across his pasture. He'd been dismissed as drunk until the patrol found him hours later curled in the dirt, eyes burned white, muttering prayers that no longer made sense. By then, the pasture was a graveyard of broken earth. The sheep had vanished. The soil was littered with bones that weren't theirs.

Satellite footage was the next to catch it—grainy night-vision clips bouncing between newsrooms before anyone knew how to classify them. At first, it was called seismic activity: fault lines splitting through the limestone hills, fissures cracking like veins of black glass. But as the images sharpened, as the feeds looped, the truth sharpened with them. Figures were climbing from the ground. Hundreds. Then thousands.

Skeletons.

Not the fragile dust-cloaked remains of centuries gone, but warriors whole and intact, bronze swords corroded but still sharp, shields painted with the ghosts of forgotten empires. They rose in ranks, armour clattering, jawbones clicking in some unseen rhythm. The earth gave birth to an army that should have remained a myth.

By dawn, entire valleys shook with the sound of it.

In Rabat, the Minister of Defence received grainy clips on a secure line: farmers filming silhouettes at the edges of their fields, skeletal phalanxes trudging past vineyards, shadows of spears raised against the moon. His staff laughed nervously until the first platoon sent to investigate failed to return. Their last radio transmission was a panicked burst of gunfire swallowed by static, followed by the clatter of something metallic striking stone.

Casablanca woke to sirens. The streets clogged as rumours spread faster than officials could tamp them down. Some said it was a cult uprising. Others, a chemical attack. But the videos pouring from phones were undeniable—legions of bone and rust marching in unison, eyes hollow, movements too precise for madness and too ancient for reason.

The world began to watch.

On international feeds, anchors stumbled over their own disbelief. In Britain, they looped shaky footage from the Atlas foothills: a tide of skeletons cresting a ridge, silhouettes against a rising sun. Another cut between experts who muttered about mass hallucination, ancient burial grounds, and viral hysteria—until live footage showed the impossible. French news caught a skeletal column wading through the Sebou River, shields raised against the morning glare as though the centuries between then and now had collapsed overnight.

No explanation stuck.

The markets reeled. Airlines grounded flights to North Africa. NATO scrambled reconnaissance jets. Morocco declared a state of emergency before noon, its government demanding answers from allies who offered only silence. Panic began to bleed outward: from the villages into towns, from Morocco into Spain, then across the Mediterranean like contagion carried on whispers and grainy clips.

In New York, a panel of scholars was convened before the UN could even draft a statement. They argued over origins—plague pits, forgotten battlefields, elaborate hoaxes—but none could explain why the dead moved with such intent. The footage showed them forming ranks, raising banners so tattered they disintegrated in the wind. No human hand guided them. No voice commanded them. And yet, they marched as one.

In Paris, cathedrals were filled with worshippers who hadn't prayed in decades. The Pope issued a call for calm, but his words trembled with an undercurrent he couldn't mask. In Beijing, the state channels declared it "an elaborate foreign fabrication," even as troops were quietly repositioned westward.

And in Adelaide, a bartender killed the television mid-broadcast and whispered to his regulars: Ragnarök.

The dead did not hesitate. By afternoon, they had spilled across foothills, through olive groves, and into towns too remote for defence. Eyewitnesses reported the clattering thunder of thousands of feet, the sound of bone striking stone echoing like war drums. Some swore they heard voices, chanting in languages older than Arabic, older than Latin, older than any they knew. Resistance was futile. Police gunfire shredded ribcages, shattered skulls, but the fallen clawed back together or were replaced by more. The fire slowed them, but did not end them. Explosives collapsed ranks but could not erase their endless tide. For every one destroyed, ten more seemed to claw their way from the dirt.

The earth itself was emptying its coffins.

By evening, Morocco burned. Villages were abandoned to the advancing hordes, their streets littered with overturned cars and abandoned markets. Drone footage captured roads clogged with refugees, streams of humanity fleeing north toward Tangier and the promise of Spanish shores. The ferries overflowed. The Strait of Gibraltar became a choke point of terror as tens of thousands scrambled for boats, any boats, to escape the tide of rattling bone marching ever closer. Europe could no longer look away.

Spain declared martial law along its southern coast, with tanks rolling into Algeciras and fighter jets circling the Mediterranean. France mobilised its navy. Italy shuttered its ports. Still, the footage from Morocco continued—columns of undead advancing like rivers of bone across the countryside. In Fez itself, the old medina dissolved into chaos. The labyrinthine alleys are filled with smoke and screams. Tourists fled through narrow streets, chased not by thieves but by phalanxes of skeletons carrying rusted halberds and broken standards. Some filmed as they ran, videos that would ricochet across the internet by nightfall: a skeletal hand gripping a man's shoulder before dragging him into darkness; a bronze spear shattering against the hood of a taxi; a child carried on her mother's back as the crowd surged toward the Blue Gate, bones clattering in pursuit.

By midnight, the ancient city was lost.

The world finally named it: The Rising. The term first appeared on social media, then in headlines, and finally in the solemn voices of presidents and prime ministers who had no other language for what was unfolding. The Rising was no local event. It was the first wound in the skin of a world about to split. And somewhere in the depths of Fez, beneath collapsed stone and dust, a mummy's words echoed without voice: we shall see.

They had been in Sydney for twelve days and were still living out of crates. The father stacked them as if the towers would make the unit bigger—two columns against the lounge wall, one in the hallway, and a final teetering stack by the sliding door that looked out over a narrow slice of Parramatta Road. Every morning, he told himself he'd break them down and make the place feel less temporary. Every night, he left them standing, unconvinced that "temporary" still meant anything.

The children had adapted the fastest, as children do. The boy had claimed the mattress by the window, where he lined his doll and a solemn platoon of plastic animals in patrol formation, all facing the street as if watching for an attack. The girl arranged her few books along the baseboard and drew a chalk line on the wall—her height, then the boy's, then a third mark labelled "Sydney" with a star. She insisted they were growing faster here. The mother didn't argue.

They'd come in the dark with the others, headlights in an unbroken river, the car heavy with water bottles and passports and a torch jammed on top—just in case the power went and everything that followed depended on which cupboard she'd put it in. She could still see the girl leaning forward from the back seat, asking why everyone was going to Sydney, still hear herself say, "Because people are scared, love," and hate the way her voice had sounded like a door closing.

Now, morning light pooled weakly on the linoleum as the kettle chattered. The mother stirred porridge while the TV muttered on the bench, sound low so the boy wouldn't ask questions she couldn't answer. The breakfast show had turned grim overnight—no more influencers cooking five-ingredient dinners, no more property segments about buying before the market rebounds. A map of North Africa burned where the weather used to be. A red band swelled across Morocco like a bruise. "Turn it up?" the father said from the table without looking away. He hadn't shaved. He hadn't slept. The move had given him an excuse for both.

She raised the volume two notches. Footage: a skeletal column cresting a ridge—the same clip as last night, then a new one, low drone, panning over a road clogged with people and the sound of a thousand feet that weren't flesh. Even through the tinny speaker, the clatter had weight.

The boy came in with his doll, hair matted, eyes foggy with sleep. "Are those robots?" he asked.

"No," the girl said quietly. "They're bones."

He looked at her, then at the TV, then tucked the doll more firmly under his arm, as if keeping it from seeing would keep it from being real. The anchor's voice wavered over words like "unprecedented," "coordinated response," and "coalition talks." A split-screen placed a general beneath the footage, brimming with calm, promising assessments, corridors, and assets in the theatre, every syllable carefully groomed. Over his shoulder, a small screen replayed the same impossible march. The words dissolved against it like rain on a hot road.

"We should go to the shops before everyone else does," the mother said, too bright. "Milk, detergent, dish tabs. Those new lunchbox things with the seals."

"You've got a shift," the father said.

"I swapped. Mara's covering today. She wanted tomorrow for her daughter's appointment—hearing test." She said it fast, in case ordinary details could anchor them. "I'll take the kids. We'll be quick."

"Take cash," he said. "And don't—"

He stopped. He didn't know what to warn against. Crowds? rumours? Something you couldn't name, only feel?

The girl pulled on her sneakers without untying them—a learned habit—then grabbed her mother's hand and squeezed once. The boy asked if his doll could come, and when no one said no, he took that as a yes. On the stairs, the building was muffled and busy. Doors stood open to let out heat and let in rumour. A woman in a dressing gown smoked near the bins, phone on speaker, sister's voice carrying from somewhere coastal: ferries cancelled, police at the wharf, some "temporary closure" that sounded like forever if you'd already decided to panic. A man in work boots argued at the letterboxes with a courier about a missing parcel and the definition of "signature on file." In every story, someone else was to blame.

Outside, Parramatta Road had the look of a day bracing—traffic tighter, horns quicker, the city's usual impatience sharpened into something meaner. An LED screen above a tyre shop had dumped its ad loop for a government slide: *STAY CALM. AVOID RUMOUR. TRUST OFFICIAL SOURCES.* The font tried to be reassuring but only ended up large.

At the supermarket, the doors stood open, but the security guards had drifted forward, arms folded, bodies arranged in the geometry of control. Inside, the aisles moved slowly, like an animal thinking about whether to run. A shelf of long-life milk had been tugged at until it looked like someone had clawed it. Flour was a rumour. Canned tomatoes held. Pasta was a memory. The mother kept the trolley moving, disciplined and small: bread, apples, tinned beans, sanitary pads, toothpaste, the good chocolate because small mercies still count. Behind them, two women debated the word "curfew" like it could bite. Near the freezer, a man took a photo of the empty ice cream section as if he could show it to the future and explain how things felt. A toddler wept at the sight of no nuggets. Somewhere, an argument popped like a blown fuse, then subsided when someone said, "Kids."

At the end of the cereal aisle, a TV near the service desk showed a ferry rocking in a too-bright sun, phones held high like flags. A lower third scrolled: *STRAIT OF GIBRALTAR—SPAIN SUSPENDS PRIVATE CROSSINGS.* The roll flipped: a man on a rooftop in Fez, lips moving, the bone tide rounding a corner like water around stone.

The girl watched until the mother steered her gently on. "Eyes here, love."

"Are they coming here?" the girl asked, as if "here" were a circle she could draw around their trolley.

"No," the mother said, and wished it were a lie she believed.

In the checkout line, the boy put his doll on the conveyor belt, and the cashier beeped it as a joke. The line laughed, brittle and grateful. When the total flashed, the mother used cash, the notes suddenly old-fashioned in her hand, and the cashier's eyes said thank you without risking words.

Outside, the air had turned clammy, a closeness that made breath feel like work. Clouds rose out of the west in a flat sheet that didn't belong to the forecast. "Storm later," a man said to nobody, which is how people announce news when they don't want the world to disagree.

On the walk back, a siren howled the wrong shape—neither ambulance nor police—which made everyone look up. A plane dragged a contrail that kinked for no reason. The girl said, "That's not how lines go," and the mother squeezed her hand again.

The father had moved the crates while they were gone. Not broken down—just shifted, the way people sometimes rearrange deck chairs when they hear a distant noise. He had turned the TV off and was staring at a blank screen, the reflection of his unshaven jaw superimposed over a black rectangle.

"They shut the ferries in Spain," the mother said, setting bags on the counter. "At least for private boats. The official line is crowd control. The real line is they don't want panic to float." She paused. "The shelves are thinning."

He nodded like he'd expected that. "Phones?"

"Still up." She set her mobile down, face down, as if the screen could take offence.

"You?"

He tapped the envelope on the table—the one with certificates, Medicare cards, and four passports, paperclipped in a way that felt like a spell. "Updated our details and signed the school transfers, too. They'll start you on Monday," he told the girl. "New uniform."

"What colour?" she asked, truer curiosity breaking through the day's film.

"Blue," he said, and smiled as if the word itself were a small safe thing.

The boy had lined up his animals again, facing the door. He placed the doll at the front, then changed his mind and set it at the back, then tucked it under his arm and came to sit between his parents, knees touching both their legs like a bridge. On the balcony, the noise of the road braided into a single long cord. Somewhere close, a neighbour's radio played football commentary like an incantation that might bring back Saturdays. From the unit above, a vacuum stuttered and stopped, stuttered and stopped, unwilling to commit. The mother poured water into glasses and set them down as if she were making an offering.

"Should we... go further?" the father said, surprising himself. He hadn't meant to ask it out loud. "Up the coast, maybe. Find something quieter. Byron. Coffs." The words sounded like postcards from a life on the other side of the mirror.

"Everyone else will be thinking the same," the mother said. "Roads will turn into car parks. And if it doesn't come here—if it stays there—then we'll have run from our own shadows."

He nodded again. He was developing a habit of it. In his chest, a slight ache opened—the size and shape of the last place they'd left, and the knowledge that leaving doesn't make a place stop being yours.

The girl took the chalk from her pocket and added a fourth line on the wall, a slight notch above the star. "Told you," she said. "Sydney makes you grow."

"How's that then?" the father asked, grateful for the pretence.

"Because you have to," she said, and went to help unpack tins.

The afternoon tripped into the evening without noticing. The sky turned the colour of unripe fruit, then bruised at the edges. On the TV (they turned it back on because silence had become too loud), a presenter repeated the word "coalition," and it still sounded like a promise made in a hallway. A ticker scrolled: *AIRPORTS MAINTAIN NORMAL OPERATIONS.* Below it, a smaller line confessed that "normal" meant "fewer flights, more delays, long queues, and carry-on patience." A new clip: a soldier on a wharf in Tangier, hand up, steadying a crowd with nothing but posture, behind him the sea flecked with boats that were not allowed to leave. The camera panned—unsteady—and caught the shoreline where the bone tide moved with tireless certainty. Somewhere, an off-camera voice said something like a prayer and something like a swear.

The doll's eyes caught the TV light and didn't blink. The boy noticed and tucked it under the blanket, then tucked himself in, too, as if the blanket's edge were a border you could fortify. When the rain finally came, it was sudden and heavy, raindrops like coins on the balcony rail. The mother opened the door to let the sound in, and the city shivered. The rain ran across Parramatta Road in sheets, the cars hissed, and the billboard told everyone to stay calm, flickering like it might take its own advice.

The father stepped out, palms up, as if checking whether the weather was real. A crow on a powerline shook itself and flew, arrowing into the weather the way crows do, untroubled by human announcements.

Behind him, the girl leaned against the doorframe and watched the rain bounce off the crates. "Can we open one?" she asked.

"Tomorrow," he said.

"When?"

"In the morning. Before school." She thought about this, then nodded. She was learning the new arithmetic: measure promises in hours, not weeks.

They stood there until the rain softened and the streetlights came up in their sodium wash. Somewhere down the road, a siren moved past and kept moving. Somewhere far away, a crowd ran in the wrong direction. Somewhere between those two somewheres, a family in a small Sydney unit measured the distance between "here" and "there" and decided, for tonight, to pretend the space was theirs. The TV repeated the word "The Rising." The anchor said them like capital letters. The mother turned the volume down and set three bowls on the table. The father fetched spoons. The boy arranged his animals facing in now, as if guarding something instead of watching for it. They ate. It wasn't much. It was enough.

The glass was floor-to-ceiling, three sides of the penthouse, a cold geometry of sky and skyline. New York sprawled beneath them in jagged light, the rivers black ribbons, bridges tense with traffic that looked like nerves misfiring in the dark. Sirens whined far below, stretched thin as violin strings.

Zed stood barefoot on marble, a tumbler of scotch in one hand, his eye patch catching the faint gleam of the city like a black coin pressed into his skull. The crow perched on the glass rail, wings half-spread, its reflection hovering alongside the lights of the Empire State Building.

Behind him, Hera moved through the room without sound. She had always been like that—her presence carried on pressure, not footfall. The gown she wore was cut in pale silver, sharp-shouldered and fluid, as though it had been stitched from stormcloud. Her hair, pinned without flaw, gleamed darker than the night outside. She stopped a few feet from him, hands clasped lightly in front of her.

"You feel it," she said. Not a question.

Zed sipped. The scotch burned, which pleased him. "Of course." She came closer, circling him the way gravity circles a planet, not fast but inevitable.

"Then say it."

"You already know."

Her lips curved, but there was no warmth in them. "I want to hear it from you."

Zed let the silence stretch until it could almost be mistaken for refusal. Then: "The earth has vomited its dead."

Hera looked past him, past the crow, past the glass. Her gaze fastened on the glowing crawl of Times Square, screens screaming headlines: *MOROCCO COLLAPSES, THE RISING CONTINUES, EU DECLARES EMERGENCY COUNCIL.* The words flashed over her cheekbones. She did not blink.

"They were bound for a reason," she murmured. "That tomb was meant to remain shut. Now an army of bones marches under no banner but hunger. Tell me, husband—was this your doing?"

Zed snorted once, a sound halfway between contempt and amusement. "If it were mine, the streets of this city would already be cracked open and your precious bankers screaming for their mothers. No, this isn't me." He turned then, his single eye black with reflection. "But it is something I warned them about. Fractures. Pressure. The scales are tipping."

She tilted her head, birdlike, assessing him. "And yet you smile."

Zed's mouth twisted. "I've been waiting for the world to remember what war tastes like."

"You always say that," Hera replied, moving to the drinks cabinet, pouring her own measure without asking.

She did not drink, only held it, watching the liquid shift in the cut crystal. "But this—" she gestured at the TV, at the distant sirens, at the endless stream of news footage—"this is not war. This is pestilence. This is a collapse without purpose."

"And collapse is what shakes the board free," Zed countered, stepping closer. "You mistake chaos for weakness. But in chaos, we choose. In chaos, we matter again."

Her laugh was low, without joy. "We. You mean you. The battlefield always did make you feel taller." He let the barb pass. His crow clicked its beak once, a sound sharp as glass. "They will come here," Hera said, finally lifting her glass to her lips. "The dead will not stop at Morocco, nor Spain, nor France. The tide will cross oceans. And when it arrives, this city—your jewel, your stage—will burn as easily as any desert village."

Zed leaned against the rail, shoulder brushing the glass, watching his reflection merge with the skyline. "And when it burns, Hera, what then? Mortals will pray again. They always do when the lights go out, and the earth shakes beneath them. They will look for saviours, kings, gods." He bared his teeth. "And I will be waiting."

Her eyes narrowed. "So you intend to feed on their fear."

"No," he said softly.

"On their need."

She paced away, steps measured, the silver gown catching light like liquid moon. "Always the tyrant dressed as benefactor."

"Better than the mother dressed as executioner," he shot back.

Her head snapped, eyes like cut glass. For a moment, the air in the room tightened, as if even the city outside sensed the tension.

Zed raised his glass in mock salute, his voice lighter now, mocking the heaviness. "Don't worry, dear. I don't plan to topple your towers just yet. Let the bones rattle the world awake. Then we'll decide whether to save it or let it choke."

Hera studied him. The silence between them was older than the skyline, older than the continents. When she finally spoke, her voice was low and certain. "You think this Rising is a doorway. I think it is a warning. And if you cannot tell the difference, you will walk through and find yourself chained again. Just like last time."

He did not answer. He only watched as the crow launched from the rail, wings slicing the night, vanishing into the neon glow of the city that never slept. The town below pulsed. The world beyond trembled. And in their glass tower, husband and wife stood divided by the oldest wound: power, and who should wield it when the dead refused to stay buried.

Zed swirled the last of the scotch in his glass and let it slide down his throat. He set the tumbler on the rail with a hollow clink that seemed to echo longer than it should have. "Balance has left the building," he said at last, voice low, each word weighted. "The scales we've all clung to? Tilted. Shattered. Whatever was holding the world steady has stepped out the back door and slammed it shut."

Hera's jaw tightened. "You sound almost pleased."

"Not pleased," Zed corrected.

He moved to the centre of the room, shoulders filling the space with a gravity that made even the marble seem smaller. "Liberated. The leash has snapped. All the centuries of whispers about equilibrium, restraint, careful masks—gone."

She sipped her drink, hiding behind the ritual. "So what are you proposing?" "That we stop playing at shadows."

He gestured toward the window, the skyline, the endless web of screens and signals binding the city together. “The mortals already sense it—feel it in their bones if you’ll forgive the pun. They see their world crack open, and they look for something older than their governments, stronger than their armies. They don’t need illusions anymore. They need us.”

Hera’s eyes flicked toward him, sharp as a blade unsheathed. “Reveal ourselves? After everything? After centuries of keeping the truth buried, of letting them forget?”

“Forget?” Zed barked a laugh, rough and bitter. “They never forgot. They just renamed us. Presidents, CEOs, saints, sinners. They dressed us in new clothes and pretended we weren’t still here, watching. Now the lie is thin as glass, and one shove will send it shattering.”

Her voice softened, but the steel beneath it remained. “And what then, Zed? You stand on a balcony, call down thunder, and expect them to kneel? They fear the bones enough already. Add us to their nightmares, and they will burn cities to keep from believing.”

Zed’s smile was slow, dangerous. “Or they’ll finally remember what it means to follow.”

The silence that followed was thick as tar. The city hummed beneath them—horns, sirens, screens flashing with panic—but in the penthouse only two figures breathed, ancient and divided.

Hera turned back to the window. “If you do this without me, you’ll make war not only with the mortals but with your own.”

Zed stepped closer, so near that the heat of him pressed against her shoulder, though he didn’t touch. “War is already here,” he whispered. “The difference is whether we hide from it, or step into the light and claim it.”

The crow returned then, wings beating against the glass before it settled on the rail, feathers ruffled as if it had flown through a storm no one else could see. Its black eye gleamed, watching both of them.

Zed tilted his head at the bird, then back to Hera. “Even he knows. The time for masks is ending.”

Acknowledgement

To my wife—patient custodian of reality while I wandered off to invent new ones. For aeons, I have attempted to persuade her to read a paragraph, a page, a chapter—even the book. She has resisted every request with calm, graceful tact and disciplined resolve. Her patience has been heroic. Her scepticism has been correct. Whatever merit these pages possess exists because she tried to believe the man who insisted on writing them.

To my friends—long-standing companions in noble but frequently misguided adventures. We built kingdoms on tabletops, conquered imaginary worlds, and argued at exhausting length about rules no sensible civilisation would ever adopt. You taught me that great stories are rarely planned, usually improvised, always born from overconfidence, and often redeemed only by stubborn luck. But the spirit of those years—the laughter, the disasters, and the belief that a ridiculous idea might just work—is quietly embedded in every chapter.

I didn't tell you I was writing a book. I considered this a strategic advantage.

To Norbit Whitewhisker—self-appointed editor, senior keyboard consultant, agent of chaos, and companion extraordinaire. He supervised many writing sessions, offered strong opinions, commandeered the mouse, rewrote important paragraphs without consultation, and demonstrated a bold editorial philosophy centred on the delete key. His contributions were frequent, confident, and creatively hilarious. His dedication was unwavering.

To AI—the ever-optimistic late-night sounding board and uncomplaining accomplice to endless edits. Without it, this book would be thinner, rougher, and almost certainly in the recycle bin.

And finally, to those who walked beside me when the road was dark—thank you for the torch, the map, and for teaching me to see by starlight.

To those still in darkness—may you find light in these pages.

About the author

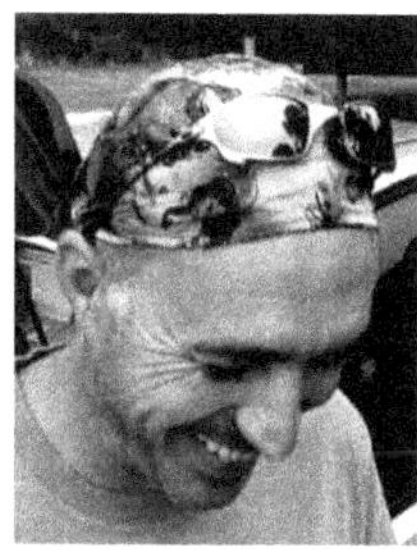

Kevin Britton is an Australian speculative-fiction author whose work blends mythic imagination with hard-edged futurism. Writing from South Australia, he builds vast narrative systems where ancient archetypes collide with near-future science, and where flawed, stubborn humans stand between extinction and transcendence.

Kevin is the creator of *The Transit Star Continuum*—an interconnected series of novels that merges epic fantasy, cosmic science fiction, and philosophical inquiry into power, identity, and survival. His stories are shaped by a lifelong fascination with astronomy, mythology, and the fragile mechanics of civilisation, as well as by hands-on pursuits ranging from winemaking and leatherworking to aquaristics, gardening, and design.

A believer that great stories are forged through struggle rather than comfort, Kevin writes about characters pushed beyond certainty—people who survive what should have killed them and must decide what kind of force they will become. His work often explores legacy, moral ambiguity, and the cost of change in worlds no longer willing to stay still.

When he isn't writing, Kevin lives with his wife and animals, tending vines, building improbable projects, and quietly plotting the next expansion of a universe he refuses to let end neatly.

By Rusty Fish Press

<u>The Transit Star Continuum</u>

The Transit Star— Book 1

The Ivory Maid—Book 2

The Dark Hammer—Book 3

The First Scale—Book 4

www.ingramcontent.com/pod-product-compliance
Lightning Source LLC
LaVergne TN
LVHW010557100826
845148LV00014B/2742

* 9 7 8 1 7 6 4 4 9 4 2 1 2 *